Additional Acclaim for *Homework*

"Riveting. . . . The dark legacy of unfulfilled longing and blighted innocence is illuminated with elegance and insight."

—Carol Verderese, *The New York Times Book Review*

"Immensely compelling and intelligent, profoundly chilling, *Homework* echoes Henry James's *Turn of the Screw*—it's that eerie, beautifully crafted, and brave in its willingness to illuminate the dark side of childhood."

—Francine Prose, author of *Blue Angel*

"Original and compelling . . . sly and haunting."

—*Newsday*

"It has been a long while since I read a book in one sitting . . . but a few pages into *Homework* I knew I was in for an extended sabbatical on the couch. . . . A finely crafted work."

—*St. Louis Post-Dispatch*

"Livesey has written a fine thriller about the dark side of childhood."

—*Dallas Morning News*

"The taut narrative succeeds by making us question both the child and the adult. Subtle, creepy."

—*Detroit Free Press*

"A sinister . . . well-conceived tale, fraught with terror . . . Livesey's spare prose skillfully highlights nuances, augmenting that terror. . . . Highly recommended."

—*Library Journal*

"A terrifying tale of our times—a psychological thriller of love and denial."

—Mary Morris, author of *Acts of God*

HOMEWORK

A NOVEL

Margot Livesey

Picador USA
Henry Holt and Company
New York

www.picadorusa.com

Picador® is a U.S. registered trademark and is used by Henry Holt and Company under license from Pan Books Limited.

For information on Picador USA Reading Group Guides, as well as ordering, please contact the Trade Marketing department at St. Martin's Press.
Phone: 1-800-221-7945 extension 763
Fax: 212-677-7456
E-mail: trademarketing@stmartins.com

Grateful acknowledgment is made for permission to reprint an excerpt from *Pitch Dark* by Renata Alder. Copyright © 1983 by Renata Alder. Reprinted by permission of Alfred A. Knopf, Inc.

The quotation on page 305 is from *Sleep* by Ian Oswald, Penguin Books, London, 1970.

Library of Congress Cataloging-in-Publication Data

Livesey, Margot.
    Homework/Margot Livesey
        p. cm.
    ISBN 0-312-42044-7
    I. Title.
PR9199.3.L563H66 1991
813'.54—dc20   90-20945

First published in the United States by Viking Penguin, a division of Penguin Books USA Inc.

10 9 8 7 6 5 4 3 2

For Callanish.

And for the Roses,
and for Janet and Richard,
and Rich and Chris,
with love.

. . . it is children really, perhaps
because so much is forbidden to
them, who understand from within
the nature of crime.

Renata Adler, *Pitch Dark*

ACKNOWLEDGEMENTS

I would like to thank the National Endowment for the Arts, the Corporation of Yaddo, the Massachusetts Artists Foundation, and Carnegie Mellon University for support while writing this novel.

The quotation on p. 305 is taken from Ian Oswald's *Sleep* (Penguin, 1970).

PART I

CHAPTER 1

It was the Saturday before Easter and all day the weather had
been seesawing between winter and spring. As I approached
the zoo the sun came out again. There was no sign of Stephen
and Jenny among the queue of people waiting to gain admis-
sion, and I sat down on the wooden bench beside the entrance. In the shelter of the high wall, it was warm enough to
unbutton my jacket. I closed my eyes and turned my face to
the sun, feeling the brightness on my eyelids. I could smell the
rising smells of spring—damp earth, growth, decay—as if
these odours, kept prisoner all winter long, were now released. In our garden the daffodils would soon be in bloom.
From within the zoo, barely audible above the noise of traffic
and the cries of children, came a strange honking sound and
then, from another quarter, a muffled roar.

The light dimmed. I opened my eyes. A stand of dark
clouds had covered the sun, and a chilly wind forced me to my
feet. When I glanced up from buttoning my jacket, I saw
Stephen walking along the pavement on the far side of the
road; he had not noticed me. He was looking down, talking
to Jenny. She was holding his hand and smiling up at him. For
a few seconds I stared at them, as if they were strangers, and
then, like one's own reflection glimpsed surprisingly in a
public place, they swam into recognition. I was suddenly
aware of the astonishing fact that this small girl was Stephen's
daughter. The relationship between them was as inevitable as
the force that lengthened the days; whatever happened, she

was connected to him in a more profound way than I could ever be.

While they waited for a pause in the traffic, Stephen caught sight of me and waved. He said something to Jenny. They were hidden by a silver-grey tourist bus. Then they crossed the street, and the three of us came together.

Stephen bent and kissed me on the mouth. "Are we late?" he asked, pressing my hand.

"No, I was early. I didn't know how long the bus would take." I turned to greet Jenny, and found her gaze fixed upon me. "Hello, Jenny," I said. "How are you?"

"I'm fine, thank you, Celia." She smiled, briefly, and I thought how adult she was in her politeness.

We joined the queue for tickets. Immediately in front of us, a man wearing a sheepskin jacket was discussing feeding times with a woman in a green anorak; they both had ruddy complexions of the kind I had come to regard, since I moved to Edinburgh, as peculiarly Scottish. Next to them four sandy-haired boys were arguing, pushing each other back and forth and saying, "I did," "You didn't." Jenny eyed them curiously; her stillness was in marked contrast to their noisy jostling.

Before I first met Jenny, the photographs Stephen kept balanced on the mantelpiece had made me familiar with her appearance. She was unusually small for her age. She had pale skin, the colour of paper, which, framed by her dark, utterly straight hair, looked even paler. In one photograph her mouth seemed slightly crooked, in another not, and this imperfection, if such it was, had the effect of making me, whenever I met her, look and look again in an effort to determine her expression.

"Did you find what you wanted in the shops?" Stephen asked. Jenny was standing on his other side, and I moved slightly forward to include her in the conversation. While I explained how I had walked along Princes Street, trying on shoes, and had then given up and bought a shirt instead, she continued to stare at the boys. "I went into Habitat," I said. "They have some quite nice rugs."

"Maybe we could go and look on Monday. I was saying to Jenny that by next weekend we ought to be sufficiently organised for her to come over to the house."

As soon as Stephen began to speak, Jenny slid away, squeezing between the man in sheepskin and one of the boys. Over their shoulders I saw her weaseling past the rest of the queue. When we reached the ticket booth she had stationed herself in the doorway and was examining each family in turn. "Two adults and a child, please," said Stephen, and pushed a ten pound note under the small window.

Inside the zoo, Jenny led the way up the hill, past a series of pools containing different kinds of waterfowl, to the sea lions' enclosure. Feeding was in progress, and she seemed to stop almost in spite of herself to watch the keeper dispense fish to the three sea lions. The animals sat on the rocks, raising their small heads and adroitly catching the silver fish. Whenever the keeper paused, they began to make the honking sound I had heard earlier. We found a place at the barrier, among the other adults and children.

"Can you see?" Stephen asked Jenny. "Shall I lift you up?"

"No. I can see everything." She was observing the scene with an expression of grave attention such as I imagined she might wear when watching her teacher write a problem on the blackboard.

The largest of the sea lions raised itself on its flippers and caught a fish with special dexterity. There was a round of applause. Stephen laughed and clapped. "Good catch. Did you see that, Jenny?"

"Come on," she said. She hurried along the path to the next enclosure, and Stephen and I followed. When I looked over the low stone wall, I saw a pair of otters playing beside a small pool. The surrounding bank was trodden to mud, and on the far side was a little wooden house, like a dog kennel, where presumably the animals slept. The otters themselves were sleek, brown, and much smaller than I had remembered. One of them was playing with a penny, tossing the coin into the air and trying to catch it. The other was scrabbling in the mud at the base of the wall directly below the spot where Jenny stood. "Here, here," she called.

The otter glanced up, then continued to dig, with even greater determination. "He needs a penny too, Dad," Jenny said. "Can we give him one?" I noticed that she had decided on the sex of the animal.

"No, it might be dangerous. The people at the zoo give the animals everything they need." Stephen leaned forward, resting his elbows on the wall. "I wonder what it's digging for. Do you think it buried some food?"

"I don't know," said Jenny. "Maybe he's trying to get out."

The idea of the otter persisting day after day in such a fruitless enterprise had not occurred to me, and I found it distressing. I tried to focus on the playful animal. It rolled over on its back and ducked into the pond. Suddenly I noticed something small and yellow floating on the surface of the muddy water; it was a dead chicken, so young that the flesh was barely dusted with feathers. At once I saw that there were several more. I glanced at Stephen. He was standing beside me, absorbed in the otter's antics. Then I felt Jenny watching me. As soon as my eyes met hers, she turned pointedly in the direction of one of the tiny corpses. Hastily I stepped back from the wall. "Let's go," I said.

We passed the penguin compound. A platoon of birds was waddling up and down, squawking and waving their out-stretched flippers. They seemed to demand an audience, but Jenny claimed there were better penguins further on and barely broke her stride. She stopped again at the polar bears. Stephen took my hand, and we walked to the far end of the pool. Fifteen or twenty feet below a single bear lay sprawled on the rocks, its rumpled fur the colour of old linen.

"Do you see how low the water is?" Stephen said. "Apparently when the zoo was started the water level was much higher, and one of the bears managed to climb out. Ever since, they've given them just this puddle to swim in."

"How old is the zoo?" I asked.

"It was founded in 1909, and most of what we're seeing was built then." He smiled. "I've been here on so many school outings that I could be a tour guide. Look."

He pointed to the bear, which rose to its feet and lumbered down to the water. It began to swim across the pool. When it reached the wall of rock at the end, it heaved its head and shoulders high out of the water, opened its jaws in a kind of grimace, and, almost in the same motion, threw its huge body down into a somersaulting turn. It swam back to the other end and performed exactly the same manoeuvres. The pool was so small that each length took only a matter of seconds. As we stood watching, the bear heaved, and grimaced, and turned, over and over, with as little variation as a mechanical toy. Perhaps because of Jenny's remark about the otter, I could not help thinking of a prisoner pacing a cell.

After a few minutes Stephen stepped back, shaking his head. "This is horrible," he said. "I remember reading an article which claimed that many of the animals kept in zoos become insane. And I can see why."

We started walking again. "Somehow I thought that nowadays they kept the animals in larger enclosures," I said.

"What are you talking about?" Jenny demanded. She was skipping along on the other side of Stephen.

"We're talking about the fact that the animals don't look very happy, that they don't have enough room."

She nodded. "I like it better when we see them on television. Then they have lots of space."

We continued to make our way up the hill. I had not been

to a zoo for years, and animal after animal contradicted my puny efforts at imagination. I could not have visualised the impossibly large mass of the white rhinoceros, nor the curious proportions of the elephant. While Stephen and I meandered along, pausing in front of each enclosure, Jenny, for whose sake we were there, kept walking at a tremendous pace, as if she were on her way to her friend Anna's house and the animals, like the houses separating her from Anna, were simply to be gotten past as quickly as possible. Other children were running around, but they lacked Jenny's distinguishing air of purpose.

We caught up with her again just beyond the brown bears. She was standing in front of a small cage, which according to the sign housed the Scottish wildcat. Although the sun had come out, the interior of the cage was dim, and I searched for a moment or two before I saw the cat. It was sitting on a tree stump, washing itself. As I watched it licking its paws, I was struck by how closely the wildcat resembled my tabby, Tobias. There was something sinister about the spectacle of such an animal in captivity. The cat looked as if it ought to be a beloved family pet; that it was behind bars suggested a ferocity the more frightening for being so thoroughly concealed.

Jenny rocked forward on the railing that separated us from the cage. "We learned about wildcats in school," she announced.

"So what did you learn?" asked Stephen.

"They are native to Scotland and live in remote places. They can never be tamed. Even if you take the kittens away from the mother at birth, when they grow up they'll bite you and run away." She spoke in a singsong voice, as if she had learned these sentences by heart.

"Have you ever seen one in the wild?" I asked.

"I'm not sure," said Stephen. He turned to Jenny. "Do you

remember that time we were up near Ullapool and a cat ran across the road?"

"Mummy was sure it was a wildcat and you thought it was lost. We stopped the car, and you walked up and down the road, calling, 'Pussycat, pussycat.' " She giggled.

The cat stood up, walked slowly towards the front of the cage, and stopped just short of the bars. We were only a few feet away, but it gave so little indication of noticing our presence that we might have been invisible. The large green eyes stared unblinkingly through us into some other landscape. The three of us fell silent. Beside us a family had paused; the man carried a baby on his back, while the woman held the hand of a small boy. "Look at the kittycat, Phil," she said.

"I want to see the camels," said the boy. "You promised there would be camels."

"We're getting to them. They're at the top of the hill," said the man.

They moved on. Jenny remained staring at the cat. She was, like the animal, completely still and seemed unaware of what was happening around her. I thought how odd it was that after being impervious to the more immediate charms of bears and monkeys, she should be engrossed in this motionless animal. The cat switched its tail and returned to the rear of the cage, leaving behind in the damp sand a neat trail of footprints.

Jenny watched the cat retreat and gave a small, satisfied nod. Then she turned her back to the cage. "I'm hungry," she announced to Stephen. "Can we go to the Penguin Pantry?"

"What about the rest of the animals?" he said. "If we go to the Pantry, we probably won't have time to see them."

"That's okay. I've seen enough."

We turned back down the hill. At the crossroads Jenny bent to retie the laces of one of her shoes. I waited beside her while Stephen wandered over to look more closely at the flamingoes. From where I stood I could see the rosy-pink birds clustered by twos and threes beneath the leafless trees.

Jenny gave the knot a final twist and straightened up. As we started walking again I felt her hand tugging at mine. She often held her father's hand in a manner that seemed both childish and proprietary, but she had never before taken mine. In fact it occurred to me that Jenny had never touched me in any way before, not even accidentally. I was struck by how small and cold her hand was. She walked silently beside me. Stephen turned around to ask if she remembered the baby elephant they had seen last year. He saw her gesture, and smiled. Jenny said that she did remember. As soon as he was no longer looking, her limp fingers slid from my grasp.

It was near closing time, and the crowds were moving towards the exit. The cafeteria was empty save for a scattering of elderly people who looked as if they were waiting to be retrieved by younger, more active relatives. We approached the counter. "What would you like?" Stephen asked.

Jenny pointed to a cake, and he lifted it off the shelf and put it on our tray. Then she demanded a chocolate biscuit, and an ice cream.

"A cup of tea, please," I said to the girl behind the counter. "Won't you be having supper soon, Jenny?"

"I'm starving."

"Couldn't you get the thing you're going to eat first and then come back if you're still hungry?" I suggested. "The ice cream will melt unless you eat it right away."

"I want to eat them at the same time. Daddy always lets me have whatever I want for tea before I go home." She emphasised the word "Daddy" in a way that made it clear that I was intruding.

"It does look like a lot," said Stephen, "but if you promise to eat everything, I suppose we'd better get it now. I think they're about to close," he added, apologetically, to me.

"I promise."

We chose a table by the window. Jenny sat beside Stephen, and I sat opposite. Someone had left a box of matches on the table, and she picked it up and rasped a match along the side. A faint, sulphurous odour mingled with the smell of tea as the match burst into flame. Jenny blew it out, then struck another. She held the match vertical and watched intently until the small flame consumed the wood down to her fingertips. "Ooh," she said with a little gasp, dropping the charred stick.

She was reaching for a third, when Stephen said, "Don't, Jenny. Matches aren't a toy."

Slowly she closed the lid. She turned her attention to the cake and took a bite out of the middle.

"Do you think animals can talk?" Stephen asked, looking first at Jenny, then at me.

"How do you mean, talk?" she said.

"Talk like humans. You know, like in *Wind in the Willows* or Beatrix Potter. When I was six or seven, I was always trying to trick our pets into speaking to me."

"That's silly." There was a pause while she nibbled the chocolate off one end of the biscuit. Then she said, "What happened?"

"They never answered, but for years I was convinced that they could. They just didn't want to because I was a human."

A small puddle was forming around the ice cream where it lay on the tray. I was determined not to say anything. I sipped my tea while Stephen reminisced about the dog he had had when he was Jenny's age. Eventually he noticed the ice cream. "I thought you promised to eat everything," he said.

"But you're always saying chocolate's bad for me." She grinned with pleasure at her cleverness.

He looked at me and gave a small shrug. An elderly woman, wearing a head scarf, passed our table. She smiled down at us approvingly, and I knew that she was imagining that I was Jenny's mother and that we were a nice young family having tea. "Which was your favourite animal?" I asked Jenny.

"The wildcat," she said, without hesitation.

"Mine were the otters," said Stephen. "They actually seemed fairly content."

"Why did you like the cat?"

She gave me a pinched look, as if she did not wish the slightest sliver of expression to slip out. "Because he was alone."

She seemed to have decided that the cat, like the otters, was male. I followed her lead. "Did that make you feel sorry for him?" I asked.

I expected her to say yes and in my presumption already found that endearing, but she shook her head. "Then why?" I persisted.

"I think he's lucky." She took a bite of cake so large that her cheeks bulged.

"Lucky?" I said, mystified, but before I could question her further, the cashier called loudly, "Ladies and gentlemen, the cafeteria closes in five minutes. Five minutes."

Jenny took a few more hurried mouthfuls, and we got up to leave. I saw her look at the debris on the table with a small smile and thought that I was witnessing neither greed nor bad manners, but rather her need to be reassured about Stephen. This mess of sweetness was a tangible sign of his often absent love.

On the way out, Jenny and I stopped at the ladies'. There was a small queue, and we lined up with the other women and children. For a couple of minutes neither of us spoke. I did not realise that I was twirling my bracelet round and round until Jenny remarked that she liked it. The bracelet was the first gift I had ever received from Stephen, and as I described how he had given it to me, a surprise at supper one night, I felt myself smiling.

"Can I see?" Jenny asked.

I passed the bracelet to her, and she slid it on. It was, of course, too large, and when she pushed up the sleeve of her pullover the silver circle dangled from her small white wrist. She stood in front of the mirror, her arm outstretched, her head slightly to one side, as if she could detect more from the mirrored image than from the object itself. We were at the head of the line. A toilet flushed, and the door of one of the cubicles opened. Jenny disappeared inside.

I availed myself of the next free toilet. When I came out Jenny was washing her hands. I bent down at the basin beside her. "Could I have my bracelet back?" I said.

For a moment I thought that she had not heard me. She finished washing her hands and went to dry them. "Jenny," I said. I held out my hand.

Very slowly she slid the bracelet down over her hand and dropped it into my outstretched palm. Then she hurried from the room.

As we drove out of the zoo car park one or two of the street lights were already glowing. Stephen began to talk about the pros and cons of having the house rewired.

"We could just have the kitchen and dining room done," I suggested.

"No, if we're having it done at all, we ought to do the whole thing," said Stephen. We turned down Ferry Road. He had insisted on dropping me off before he took Jenny home. Although he seldom saw Helen on his weekly trips to their house, even the possibility of the two of us meeting made him anxious.

Jenny was sitting in the back. Throughout the journey she was so silent that I almost forgot her presence. When we pulled up outside our house I turned to speak to her. "Bye-bye. Thank you for taking me to the zoo."

"Thank you for coming," she replied, with a speed that robbed the words of their meaning. I said that I would see her next week, and she nodded; her features conveyed neither gladness nor dismay.

She came and took my place in front beside Stephen. I shut the door for her and stepped back, ready to wave. Suddenly I remembered that I had left my new shirt lying on the seat. "Jenny," I called, knocking on the glass.

She stared at me. Her eyes, always dark, appeared totally black. Involuntarily I found myself retreating before the force of her gaze; I shuffled back a couple of steps. During the months I had known Jenny, I had assumed, in spite of some difficult moments, that she was well disposed towards me; the malevolent intensity of the look she now bestowed upon me conveyed the exact opposite. It was almost, I thought, as if she hated me. I raised my hand but before I could knock again she had turned away. I saw her lips move as she said something to her father. Then the car slid forward. It gathered speed, the brake lights flared, and it disappeared into the main road. I was left standing, empty-handed, in the middle of the street.

PART II

CHAPTER 2

Only a few months before I moved to Edinburgh, the idea that I would leave London ever, let alone in the near future, would have struck me as incredible. To me the capital of Scotland was a distant northern city where occasionally friends went on holiday, and returned muttering about the weather. Even when I found myself living there, I saw the city merely as a staging post where I had been forced to halt on the way to my real destination. My destination I thought of then as being Lewis.

Lewis and I had been at university together but had subsequently lost touch. When I ran into him in a London bookshop, I had not seen him for more than eight years. I had just come into the shop and was wondering which way to turn, when I realised that the man standing at the display table was Lewis. He wore an overcoat of dark, heavy material and was bending over a large volume. His red-gold hair, which I remembered hanging luxuriously down his back, now barely grazed his collar, and from this angle it was apparent that it had receded, leaving his forehead high and smooth. While I was debating whether to speak to him—the chances of his remembering me seemed slender—he looked up. "Hello," he said. "I know you. You were at York."

As I introduced myself, I recalled that his surname was Jenkins.

"I don't suppose you know anything about gardening?" he asked. "I'm trying to buy my mother a birthday present, but whenever I find a book that seems appropriate I worry she may already have it." He held up the book he had been examining; on the cover a bush of scarlet roses illustrated the title *How to Grow a Prize-Winning Rose*.

"I'm looking for a present too. For Greg and Lynne's daughter."

"You mean Greg Turner and Lynne Harrison? That's amazing. Last time I saw them they were planning to go round the world."

"Eve is two on Monday."

"Two. My God." He seemed genuinely flabbergasted, as if giving birth were among the most unusual of human activities. "Did you know I'd been abroad for the last four years, in Hong Kong?" I shook my head. "I only came home for good at Christmas, so I'm still in the process of getting in touch with people. I keep being taken aback at how much their lives have changed. For some reason I thought no one would make any major decisions in my absence." He smiled in acknowledgement of his foolishness.

"What were you doing in Hong Kong?" I asked.

"Working for a bank. I've become one of those capitalists we used to love to hate."

"Excuse me," said a large woman in a fur coat. Lewis stepped closer to me to allow her to pass. For a moment I found myself looking into his eyes; they were blue, with unusually dark outer rims. I turned away in confusion. "I should go to the children's section," I said awkwardly.

"I'll come with you. It'll give me a chance to decide whether to buy this book or not."

While Lewis browsed, I scanned the shelves, searching for a book which Eve did not already own and which would also meet Lynne's high standards of political correctness. Finally I settled on a story about a cat who lived amicably in a church with many mice. As I was waiting to pay, Lewis came over.

"This was one of my big childhood influences," he said, holding up a book. "Do you know it?"

The title was *Horace Goes Hunting*. I shook my head.

"You missed a vital part of your education. Horace the bear is the beloved pet of a large family, whom he devours at the rate of one a day. It used to make me laugh uproariously. Maybe I should get it for Eve. When did you say her birthday was?"

"Monday, but the party's today. I'm on my way there now." I passed my book and money to the cashier.

Lewis looked at his watch. "Why don't I come along?" he said. "I'd love to see Greg and Lynne again." The cashier counted out my change, and before I could answer, Lewis had handed over *Horace* and the gardening book. "I think this is a good choice for my mother," he remarked. "She may be growing roses but she's not winning any prizes."

I was delighted at Lewis's decision. Although I had not known him well at York, now he seemed like an old friend; it was as if the cafeterias and corridors, libraries and lecture halls through which we had passed, often unaware of each other's presence, had created a bond between us. We left the shop and he led the way around the corner to a maroon car. There was a ticket lodged beneath the windscreen wiper; without a second glance, Lewis crumpled it up and stuffed it into his pocket. Then he beckoned me to the driver's side. "The passenger door hasn't opened since someone rammed into it at Hyde Park Corner."

Lynne and Greg lived on the edge of Maida Vale and soon we were heading towards the Euston Road. As we idled along behind a bus, Lewis asked what I did, and I told him briefly about my job, editing textbooks.

"That's right, you took English at York. And what else do you do?"

"How do you mean?" I was watching his hands on the

steering wheel, the pale skin, slightly reddened with cold, the golden hairs, each one distinct.

"You can't edit textbooks twenty-four hours a day. If Lynne and Greg can have a daughter, you could have a complete menagerie: sons, daughters, lovers."

"None of the above. I do have a cat who travels up and down in a basket from my kitchen window." As soon as I had spoken, I wished that I had phrased my reply differently— there was no reason to make myself sound quite so much of a spinster—but before I could emend my statement Lewis braked sharply. "Damn," he exclaimed.

An old man in a raincoat had stepped out from behind a parked car. Paying no attention to our abrupt halt or that of several other vehicles, he continued slowly towards the middle of the road.

"Have you noticed how often that happens?" Lewis demanded. "The elderly cross the street with reckless abandon, while the young and able-bodied wait cautiously at the zebra crossing."

I made some sound of agreement. I wanted to ask about his situation but he seemed intent on his speculations.

"Perhaps it's an example of natural selection," he continued. "Old people aren't going to think: now it's time I committed suicide for the good of the tribe. But nature takes care of the problem by rendering them oblivious to danger. The species can't afford to have too many unproductive members."

We were driving around the edge of Regent's Park. I watched a scruffy-looking boy trotting along the tow-path with three Dalmatians. It was perturbing to hear Lewis voice the sort of opinion that I had always attributed to bankers; at university he had been an ardent socialist. "You take the first right here," I said.

In a few minutes we had reached Lynne and Greg's. We found a place to park down the street and walked back, shielding our presents from the drizzle. As we approached I pointed out the house. The living room was on the first floor, and we paused to look up at the tall lighted windows. Various people were moving around the room, and I saw Lynne, her long hair hanging loose, talking to a man with a beard. Then we crossed the street and mounted the steps. I knocked at the door.

Lewis stood slightly behind me. "You can tell there's a proper family living here," he remarked. "Look how clean the milk bottles are."

The door was opened by Greg. "Celia," he exclaimed. He leaned forward to kiss me and, as he did so, caught sight of Lewis. "Holy smoke. Lewis Jenkins."

I stepped aside, and Greg reached to embrace Lewis. The two men followed me up the stairs, trying to remember where they had last seen each other. Greg thought it was in a pub near Paddington. Lewis reminded him of a concert at the Notting Hill Carnival. Conversation ceased as we reached the living room, where a dozen adults and almost as many small children were milling around. Some sort of game was in progress, but gratifyingly, as soon as she saw me, Eve broke out of the ring of children and ran towards me, shouting "Ceel, Ceel."

Before Jenny, Eve was the only child with whom I had had an intimate association. She was bright, good-tempered, and wildly energetic. She was also marked with an angelic beauty, which made strangers in supermarkets exclaim. I picked her up, gave her a kiss, and wished her happy birthday. Behind us, in the hallway, Lewis was hugging Lynne. I was about to introduce him to Eve, but she started to wriggle and say, "Down, down." The instant her feet touched the ground she rushed off to resume her game.

Lewis came into the room with Lynne and Greg. Introductions were performed. I recognised everyone, either from previous occasions or from remarks Lynne had made. If I had not brought Lewis, I would, as so often in the past, have been the only single person present. The smiles and hellos were barely finished before he walked over to a group of small boys and squatted down to ask about the castle they were building. For the next couple of hours he devoted himself to Eve and her contemporaries. As a strategy for meeting women, it could not have been improved upon; he seemed to be constantly involved in conversation with one or another of the attractive young mothers. While I gave Lynne a hand with organising the tea, I watched him in what I hoped was an unobtrusive fashion. Never once did I catch him looking at me.

After tea I went out to the kitchen, and began to load the dishwasher. Suddenly the door opened wide. "So this is where you are," said Lewis. He picked up some remnants of cake and popped them into his mouth. "I think we ought to be on our way."

"But Lynne and Greg have asked us to dinner," I said. In the course of the afternoon they had both remarked that they could scarcely wait for the other guests to leave, so that the four of us could talk in peace.

"It'll be ages before they're free. We can get together some other time. Unless you want to stay," he added. It was clear that if this was the case, he was not offering his company.

"No. I'm quite ready to go." I dried my hands and went to fetch our coats.

Outside, it was already dark. The indistinct dampness of earlier in the afternoon had turned to steady rain. "All those nice people," Lewis burst out, as we crossed the road. "Don't you get tired of families—the problems of child care and potty training? What's happened to adults and the fate of the world?" He shook himself, like a dog emerging from water, impatient to shake off every trace of familial life.

"I thought you liked children." Hadn't he, all afternoon, been offering himself as a play-mate to Eve and her guests?

"The children are fine; they're just themselves. It's the parents who are impossible."

"Today was Eve's birthday party. Lynne and Greg aren't usually so preoccupied with her."

"I'm not accusing them. They wouldn't be good parents if they weren't interested in their child."

He opened the door and I scrambled in. When he was seated beside me I said, "I'm sorry. I thought you were having a good time."

"There's no reason for you to apologise. As you pointed out, what could I expect, gate-crashing the birthday party of a two year old. Besides, I could always have left." On the third attempt the engine caught.

Later I came to recognise this kind of behaviour as one of the several devices by which Lewis kept me enthralled. I would be under the impression that he was enjoying himself, and then it would emerge that he had been miserable. Or sometimes the reverse; he would seem to be sunk in gloom, yet, if I made some comment to this effect, deny it vehemently. These contradictions bewildered me; I never knew whether he was happy or not.

We came to a stop at a traffic light beside Paddington Station; Lewis concluded his remarks about a wine merchant's we had just passed. "What shall we do next?" he said. "I don't suppose you have a newspaper with you?"

My surprise must have been visible. He turned towards me, smiling. "You're free, aren't you? The cat won't mind if you stay out late?"

I shook my head. "I could run in and buy a paper at the station."

"Given that I have to get out first, I might as well do the running. You can seduce any policemen that come along."

He left the engine on, and while I waited I tinkered with the radio. The smallest movement of my hand carried me from Mozart to the shipping forecast. "An unusually high neap tide off the coast of Ireland," said a male voice. "And in the North Sea we have a force nine wind and a strong probability of thunderstorms." I was so engrossed in the announcer's soothing tones that I did not notice Lewis until the door opened.

"Sorry," he said. "I thought I'd take a look while I was in the light. That French detective film is on in Camden. We could make the six-thirty show."

In the darkness, side by side, we watched the tale of deception and double-crossing unfold. The hero and heroine extricated themselves from one difficult situation after another, but I had little interest in their fate. More potent than any image on the celluloid screen, Lewis's arm lay alongside mine.

Afterwards, as he drove me home, Lewis talked animatedly about the film; he had clearly been engrossed. I gave directions and agreed with his comments. I lived not far from Camden, and we were almost at my flat when he said, "You know, the birthday cake must have worn off. I'm quite hungry."

"So am I," I said, realising with surprise that it was true. "I could make us supper, if you don't mind some variation of scrambled eggs."

"Scrambled eggs would be perfect."

We stopped to buy wine, and drove the short remaining distance to my flat. As soon as I had shown Lewis into the kitchen, I excused myself. In the bathroom I combed my hair—the dampness had made it even frizzier than usual—and patted on a little powder. Then I hastily crammed things into the cupboard. When I returned to the kitchen Lewis was standing at the counter rummaging in a drawer while Tobias wound around his legs. "Where do you keep your corkscrew?" he asked.

"Second drawer down. I can shut Tobias in the living room if he's being a nuisance."

"No, I like cats. I used to have one before I went to Hong Kong." He found the corkscrew and opened the wine. The cork came out with a small pop. "Do you live here alone?"

"At the moment. Until a month ago I was sharing with a girl who used to do free-lance editing for us, but she's gone to Geneva to work for the U.N., and I haven't got round to finding someone else." As I spoke I bent to look in the fridge.

"The older I get," Lewis said, "the less the idea of sharing a house appeals to me. I can see I'm going to be a thorough misanthrope by the time I'm fifty."

Soon we were seated on opposite sides of the table with a fried egg sandwich and a tumbler of wine in front of each of us. I asked Lewis where he lived.

"I just moved into a small house in Clapham. It's virtually a ruin, although you wouldn't think that from the price I paid."

"How small is small?"

He paused to finish a mouthful. "Two up, two down. A friend from Hong Kong who's over on a six-month course is staying in the front bedroom." He described his trials and tribulations with damp-proofing, while I wondered about the sex of the mysterious friend.

"Couldn't your friend stay home to let the workmen in?" I asked.

"Not really. The course Mike is on is like a job, nine to five, and if he misses a day it's hard to catch up." Lewis reached for the bottle and refilled our glasses. "Are you in touch with many other people from York?"

"I see Nick and Charlie from time to time and that's about it. What about you?"

We had moved in such different circles that I did not even recognise the names of most of the people whom he mentioned, but I said, "Oh, yes," and "How is he?" as if I knew everyone. I could feel the wine making my cheeks hot, making me laugh at anything remotely amusing. Lewis mopped his plate with the last piece of toast, and I asked if he would like a cup of tea.

He glanced at his watch. "I should probably go. It's quite a drive to Clapham, and Mike and I agreed that we would work on the house tomorrow." He drummed his fingers lightly on the table. Then he said, "Would you like to have supper on Tuesday?"

"Yes." I smiled and nodded.

"Why don't I ring you to make a plan?"

He noted down my phone numbers, and put on his coat. At the door he gave me a quick, friendly kiss on the cheek.

On Tuesday the office was unusually busy. Courier packages arrived on my desk almost every hour, and a number of people seemed to find my opinion indispensable, but nothing could distract me from thoughts about Lewis. As I waited for him to telephone, the minutes oozed by with infinite slowness. I made matters worse by my reluctance to leave the office; at lunchtime I persuaded one of the secretaries to bring me back a sandwich, and before going to the toilet I took the receiver off the hook. I was on my third attempt at a letter of rejection to a would-be author when at last he phoned. He suggested that we meet at six-thirty in a pub near his office, I agreed, and he hung up. The call had lasted all of ninety seconds.

Lewis's directions to The White Knight had been brief, and by the time I located it, in a little courtyard off the main road, I was fifteen minutes late. The pub seemed to be filled entirely with men in dark suits, and as I scanned the room, I wondered if I would recognise Lewis. Before I had taken more than a couple of steps towards the bar, he appeared by my side.

"Thank goodness you came and rescued me," he said, when we were out in the street. "That place is like an extension of the office. Listen, there's a program on TV about

Hong Kong. I thought we could get a carry-out and watch it at your place."

In my living room, we sat on the floor, the Indian food spread out between us. Lewis kept up a running commentary: "See that building on the left? That's where my friend Jerry lives." "The yacht club is on this bay." "This is the market where I used to buy fish." The program ended. I carried some of the containers and plates out to the kitchen. When I returned Lewis was sitting on the sofa; he motioned me to join him.

"You're terrific, Celia," he murmured, and put his hand on my knee. Through my skirt I felt the warmth of his hand. I reached out to touch him. It was not as if he were a stranger, we had known each other for years.

It was still dark when Lewis slipped out of bed, and I assumed that he was going to the toilet. Suddenly the bedside light went on. I sat up, startled. He was standing at the foot of the bed, sorting out his clothes. "What time is it?" I asked.

"Six-thirty. I'm sorry, I didn't mean to wake you. I have to be at work early."

"Do you want some coffee? Or toast?" I reached for my dressing gown.

"No, thanks. I'll pick something up on the way to work."

"It won't take a minute."

"In a minute I'll be gone. You go back to sleep, Celia."

An irritable note was creeping into his voice. I lay down and pulled the sheet higher. There was the click of buttons, the slide of a zip. I lay with my eyes closed, waiting for him to come and kiss me. "I'll give you a ring," he said. Then the light went out, and before I could speak, he was gone.

Months later I was still discovering the mistakes I had made at work that day. Changes of tense and person, monstrous inconsistencies, typographical errors, incoherent examples, all seemed, in my blissful state, fine. I was too busy imagining life with Lewis to be troubled by such minor matters. At five-thirty Gillian came into my office. She was wearing a shiny green blouse, and I guessed that she must have had a business meeting. "Are you ready?" she asked.

Ever since I had joined Fredericks, three years previously, Gillian and I had been going swimming on Wednesday evenings. Now I realised with amazement that I had forgotten what day it was. I blurted out that I had not brought my things.

"Not to worry," she said. "You can rent a suit and towel, and I can lend you a pair of goggles." She was so eminently practical that I was ashamed to confess my reluctance.

On the way to the YWCA, Gillian talked about the author she had had lunch with, and I tried to maintain an appearance of intelligent interest. I was glad to reach the pool and be released from the demands of conversation. I swam up and down, doing, with my clumsy breaststroke, one length to every two of Gillian's streamlined crawl. When I lowered my face into the water I could see the bottom with exquisite clarity, and the echoing cries which filled the air became remote and muffled. I remembered Lewis undoing my belt, and the rustling of our falling clothes. "I love the sounds," he whispered, "like wrapping paper." I must buy wine on the way home, and bread and milk.

Almost invariably after swimming, Gillian and I went out to eat and spent a satisfying evening grumbling about the idiosyncrasies of our co-workers, so it was a further sign of my distraction that I was taken aback when she suggested an Italian restaurant off Old Compton Street. We were in the changing room, standing side by side in front of the mirrors. I struggled with a knot in my hair, as I tried to gather my thoughts. "I'm sorry," I said at last, "but I think I ought to go home and work on the Wheeler manuscript. He's coming to town on Friday, and I've only skimmed it so far."

"We can make it quick. I promise not to have dessert."

Awkwardly I insisted on my need to work. Gillian glanced at my reflection; before our eyes could meet, she turned away. While we gathered our possessions together, I agonised over whether to confide in her, but I could not bring myself to do so; she had little patience with men and romance. In the street we parted to walk to our respective tube stations.

As soon as I arrived home I dialled Lewis's number. There was no answer. I took off my outdoor clothes, put away the milk and wine, and tried again. What I had told Gillian was true, the Wheeler manuscript was in urgent need of attention, but I settled instead to watching television and sewing buttons onto several shirts. Every half hour I tried to call Lewis. Finally, at midnight, I went to bed, leaving the living room and bedroom doors open to be sure that I would hear the phone. Some business associates must have kept him out late, I thought; several hours passed before I fell into an uneasy sleep.

Next morning I rang Lewis's office and left a message. For a couple of hours I felt better; then, as caller after caller proved not to be him, I lapsed into despair. Twice I rang back, and each time the secretary's voice seemed tinged with deeper disdain. I did not dare to try again. Fortunately I had agreed to baby-sit for Lynne and Greg that evening. Eve was happy to stay up late and demand my attention.

He rang on Friday afternoon as I was getting ready to go home. "Sorry to take so long to call back," he said. "I've been frightfully busy."

While he described a difficult client, I cautioned myself not to dwell upon the delay and when he asked how I was, I was able to attempt an imitation of his cheerful tones. "One of my books came back from the typesetters with hundreds of typos," I said. "I'm tearing my hair out."

"But that's not your fault," said Lewis. "Go and tear the typesetter's hair out. I'll just be a minute," he added to someone in the background.

When I had gone to babysit, Lynne had suggested that Lewis and I come to supper on Saturday. Now I was glad to have this invitation to pass on; it licenced my several phone calls.

"I'm afraid I'm going to Bath tonight. Listen, how about if we do something on Monday. I'll pick you up about eight. We can go to my favourite Chinese restaurant. Give my apologies to Lynne and Greg and have a good weekend."

When he came round on Monday, we ended up in bed, and by the time we emerged, it was too late to go out. I fetched wine and bread and cheese and we sat up side by side, eating and drinking. "Who were you visiting in Bath?" I asked, as I handed him the Brie.

"Friends."

"Oh," I said. "What did you do?"

"Nothing much. Would you like some more?" He leaned over to pick the bottle up off the floor.

I held out my glass. He filled it. I drank a couple of mouthfuls. Then I said, "You sound as if you think I'm prying."

"Good Lord, no," he exclaimed. "I'm still in a daze from the day. Celia, let me tell you about my scintillating weekend in Bath."

I looked at him.

"Come on," he said. "Ask me again who I was staying with."

"Who were you staying with?" I said docilely.

"George and Lydia. George used to be in Hong Kong with me." For several minutes he held forth in eloquent detail

about his old friends and the beauties of Bath—they had gone
for a splendid walk along the river—and I allowed myself to
be persuaded.

He stayed with me that night and the next, then vanished
again for several days. When he reappeared I had decided to
ask if he saw other women. I had worked myself up to such a
pitch of anxiety that I could not wait for an appropriate
moment; I stammered out the question in the middle of a
traffic jam on the Fulham Road.

"Of course I do," he said heartily. "There's my secretary,
Mrs. Reynolds next door, Donna at the Alpine snack bar.
What's this fellow up to?"

It would have been easy to accept his joking answer, but
now that I had blundered into speech I was determined not to
be silenced. "You know what I mean. Are you having an
affair with someone else?"

"I have some women friends, but not like you." He kissed
me. Immediately the driver behind sounded his horn.

"It seems odd," I said, "that you disappear for days at a
time, and you never talk about what you've been doing unless
I badger you with questions."

"Celia, you'd be bored rigid if I talked about what I'd been
doing. Being a banker is not like being an editor. We're
expected to be in the office at the crack of dawn, work all day,
and then in the evening entertain clients."

The traffic began to move and soon we were seated in the
Royal Court, watching a comedy about high finance. For the
rest of the evening Lewis was particularly attentive and
charming. In the morning he told me that he was going to
Geneva for a week.

We did at last have dinner with Lynne and Greg. The four of
us spent a pleasant evening reminiscing about famous parties
and demonstrations, and marvelling at the astoundingly

small amount of work we had got away with. Next day Lynne telephoned me at the office. After we had both said how much we had enjoyed the evening, she told me that she was ringing about a friend who was looking for accommodation.

"I'm not sure if I want to rent out the room at the moment," I said.

"But you were saying only a few weeks ago how expensive it is to live alone."

"I know, but Lewis has a lodger, and if I had one too there wouldn't be anywhere we could be alone together."

"Celia, I don't think you should be planning your life around Lewis."

"I'm not planning my life around him," I said defensively. Only that morning I had refused to join an office outing to the National Theatre in case it conflicted with seeing Lewis.

"Of course," said Lynne, "I don't know how Lewis is when you're alone together, but last night he certainly didn't give the impression of being about to settle down."

"What do you mean?"

She began to repeat remarks he had made about travel plans, his ambition to work in New York. "And," she said, "you'll forgive me saying this, but he doesn't seem that interested in you. I mean he obviously likes you, but if I hadn't known you were going out together, I would never have guessed."

I managed to pretend that I was needed on another line and said goodbye. For a quarter of an hour I paced around my small office, thinking furious thoughts about Lynne. Then I consoled myself by remembering that she did not have any privileged source of information. She had not seen Lewis for years.

This conversation proved to be only the first of many in which Lynne tried to persuade me that Lewis and I were not ideally suited, and I, in spite of all the evidence supporting her view, did my best to contradict her. Sometimes a whole week would pass without my being able to reach him. Then he would surface again, talking about business. He used Mike as an excuse not to invite me to his house in Clapham, but night after night I telephoned and no one answered. He rivalled Houdini in his ability to extricate himself from compromising situations. I often felt as if I had wandered into a hall of mirrors where illusion and reality could no longer be distinguished.

To Lynne, Gillian, and my other friends, my behaviour seemed like lunacy; I was too shy to explain what justified my persistence. In the dark with Lewis I experienced passions and pleasures that I had never known before, and it was this that made it hard for me to accept that he did not reciprocate my feelings. I could not grasp that for him the intensity of the event was matched by its brevity. One moment he could be sighing with passion over me, and half an hour later he was hurrying out of my flat, totally preoccupied with reaching a client in Tokyo.

As the months passed, Lewis became increasingly unreliable and I was not surprised when at the last minute he announced that he was too busy to come to Charlie and Nick's midsummer teaparty. I even welcomed his decision. His absence would give me a chance to see old friends without the sense of constraint that his presence engendered. Charlie and Nick had both been at York, and their annual party, given in honour of Nick's birthday, functioned as a reunion.

In previous years I had often met up with fellow guests at Charing Cross, but Lewis's change of plan had made me late, and I spotted no one either on the train to Maze Hill or on the short walk from the station. It was a beautiful day, warm and breezy, and my spirits lifted. As I opened the garden gate Nick's cat, Satan, who was lounging on the doorstep, rolled belly-up. Obediently I stooped to pat his slightly dusty fur.

The door was open, and I stepped inside. I found Nick in the kitchen. He was looking impressively boyish. His hair was cut shorter than I remembered, and he was deeply tanned.

He kissed me on the cheek. "We're all out in the garden," he said. "I was just making a fresh pot of tea."

"Happy birthday. You look wonderful."

"Thank you, thank you. Not a day over thirty. This was my present from Charlie." He fingered the creamy fabric of his shirt.

"It's lovely," I said, and he reciprocated with some flattering remarks about my blue dress. I followed him outside. The long, sheeted table, spread with food, was surrounded by guests; everyone seemed to be engrossed in animated conversation. I saw Greg and Eve standing off to one side and went over to greet them.

Eve hugged my knees and Greg kissed me. "We were discussing which flowers Eve could pick," he said. "Charlie and Nick keep this garden so fiendishly tidy that there doesn't seem to be a single dandelion, and scarcely any daisies either."

"Are you complaining about our garden?" Charlie said. He proffered sandwiches from two mounded plates. "Cheese and cucumber, or egg salad. Celia, lovely to see you."

"I want to pick flowers," Eve said. "I want to pick flowers for Nick."

"What a nice idea," said Charlie. "Suppose you give me a hand with taking round the sandwiches, and then we can make a bouquet together."

"Yes, please."

Charlie led the way to the table, where he swiftly made up a small plate of sandwiches for Eve to carry. The two of them set off round the garden together.

"They spoil her rotten," Greg said. "Where's Lewis?"

"He was too busy to come."

"He's always too busy. Given how much he works, he ought to be president of the World Bank by now."

Lynne approached. She was wearing a white dress made of *broderie anglaise;* the pattern of little holes in the fabric made it impossible not to wonder what lay beneath. "I've had this since we were at York," she said, "and I thought if I couldn't wear it today, then I never could." The three of us chatted for a few minutes before moving on to talk to people we saw less often. There was something enchanted about the afternoon: we were all, briefly, young and brilliant again, transported to those days at university when anything seemed possible.

After talking to one of Charlie's colleagues and several old friends, I found myself a bystander to a conversation about one of our more controversial lecturers. I had never actually met him, and after two or three anecdotes I wandered over to the table.

A short-haired woman wearing a checked shirt and jeans said hello. I suddenly recognised Mary.

"Have you tried the trifle?" she asked. "Charlie and Nick are the only people I know besides my mother who still make puddings." She ladled a final dollop of cream into her bowl.

At York, Mary, with her long blond hair and costly clothes, had seemed the acme of sophistication; ten years later she was no less formidable, although in a very different way. I asked if she was still working as a translator.

"No, I have a bread-and-butter job in a bookshop, but I spend most of my time teaching classes in self-defence for women."

"You mean like karate or judo?"

"It's a sort of grab bag of martial arts. I aim to teach skills that can be used by women of all ages and levels of physical fitness."

I described my company's new policy on sexism in textbooks, a major step forward which Mary at once condemned as inadequate. We drifted into conversation about mutual acquaintances. "Last time I spoke to Frances she told me that you and she had become neighbours in Peckham," I said.

"Twenty minutes on brisk foot. Frances is a dear. I think she worries that I'll turn into a bag lady. She's always inviting me over for a square meal. What about Lewis Jenkins?" she asked. "I thought he might be here."

What angel or demon prompted me to indicate merely vague recognition? Mary had just taken a mouthful of trifle, and there was a pause before she continued. "I work near his office so I run into him once in a while, and every time I see him, I swear he's with a different woman. A couple of weeks ago he came into the shop with someone I know slightly; she's a friend of a friend. Since then I've been wondering what to do. On the one hand I think I ought to tell her, so she'll know where she stands, and on the other, that seems like meddling."

"Perhaps they're just friends," I said. We were standing beside the table, and I laid down my plate, for fear that Mary would notice the shaking of my hands.

"No, there were too many little pats and gestures for that. They were all over each other." Mary licked her spoon in a satisfied way and laid aside her plate. She stood straighter, with her arms folded, to pronounce judgement. "I'm afraid he's a textbook case, an intelligent, charming man whom you can't trust to go to the shops for a pint of milk."

What did I say? I have no idea. Maybe Charlie came round with the teapot, or maybe Nick urged me to try the cake he had made. I left as soon as I could, pleading an evening engagement. On the train home I experienced despair, shame, fury, but also relief. I had felt at times almost mad in the face of his injured innocence. Even when I could smell the other women on him, he would be telling me that my suspicions were absurd, that I must stop being possessive and insecure. There was a bitter consolation in knowing that I was right.

Suddenly as the train rattled across Waterloo Bridge I remembered how once at York I had come into the college library late at night and seen Mary sitting on Lewis's lap. I did not think they had ever gone out together, but a certain tenderness between them might explain her vehemence. I was sure that Lewis was spending today with Mary's friend of a friend.

CHAPTER 3

During the next few weeks scarcely an hour passed without my mind swinging towards the idea of confronting Lewis with Mary's comments, and then swinging away again. When we did talk, either face to face or on the telephone, I subjected even the most innocuous of his remarks to scrutiny, and whenever he was late, or made excuses not to meet, or explained too fully what he had done the night before, I suspected the worst. He submitted to my cross-examination with a curious meekness which probably signalled that he was about to break off with me.

In the midst of these difficulties I had lunch with a former director of Fredericks. She was shocked to learn that I had still not been promoted to senior editor, and by the end of the meal she had persuaded me to apply for a job with a firm in Edinburgh. Once the letter was written and posted I did not give the matter much thought and I was taken aback to answer the telephone a fortnight later and hear a woman introduce herself as the secretary to the director of Murray and Stern. In a soft Scottish accent, she asked if I was free to come for an interview with Mr. Murray at ten o'clock tomorrow. I hesitated, and she began to apologise. "Mr. Murray's down in London for a couple of days to talk to various educational authorities. He knows it's short notice, but he was hoping that he might be able to see you at the same time." I found myself saying that I was sure I could manage.

"Super," she said. "Let me give you the address of his hotel."

The following day was unusually warm. Even early in the morning, as I walked the short distance from Victoria Station to the hotel, the petunias in the window boxes were already wilting. I had not mentioned the interview to anyone. I had asked for the day off from work, pleading various errands, and Lewis, with whom I had gone to see a film the night before, had not been in the sort of mood that inspired confidences. Perhaps the secrecy served me in good stead, for it made the prospect seem less real, and not until I entered the lobby of the hotel was I aware of being nervous.

As I approached the reception desk a voice from behind me said, "Miss Gilchrist?" I turned to find myself facing a tall, red-faced man. "Call me Bill," he said, and shook my hand. He led the way to a group of armchairs in one corner of the lobby, and we sat down on opposite sides of a coffee table. "We just got back from the south of France, where, like an idiot, I fell asleep on the beach," he said, gesturing towards his visage.

A waiter came by offering morning coffee, and we each ordered a cup. Bill asked me about my current projects. I described the new series of Victorian novels on which I was working. "The rationale for the series is to introduce students not only to the text but to a wide range of critical approaches. I'm editing *Tess of the D'Urbervilles* at the moment, and we're including examples of feminist, Marxist, and Freudian criticism as well as more traditional discussions."

"I saw the *Jane Eyre* that came out this spring," Bill said. "It's a handsome book and very nicely organised. We're hoping to do something similar, specifically with Scottish novels." We began to discuss possible projects for development. Bill put his briefcase on his knees and used it as a desk, jotting things down in a small spiral notebook. When he looked at his watch and announced that he would have to leave shortly, I was surprised to discover that we had been talking for an hour and a half.

"Have you ever been to Edinburgh?" he asked.

I shook my head.

"It's the most beautiful city in Europe. My wife and I moved there from Leamington Spa four years ago, and we've never regretted it." As he listed the attractions of Edinburgh, I suddenly realised that he must be planning to offer me the job. The idea was so startling that I had to struggle not to burst out laughing.

He smiled at me. "Of course you have projects to finish up, but from our point of view, the sooner you can start the better. You're exactly what we've been looking for, and I know you're going to be a tremendous asset. I'll get a letter off to you first thing next week, spelling out the p's and q's. If there's anything you don't like, give me a ring, and we'll do our best to fix it."

We stood up and shook hands as if sealing a contract. Bill headed off towards the stairs, while I ducked into the ladies'. I stood in front of one of the basins, holding my hands under the cold tap, and thought, an asset, a tremendous asset. The laughter, which a few minutes earlier I had managed to contain, spilled forth. "Well, somebody's happy," the woman at the next basin remarked.

At Victoria Station, I stopped to telephone Lynne. I said I had taken the day off, and she at once invited me for lunch. All the way to her house, I was smiling so broadly that strangers were noticing and smiling back. Three different groups of tourists asked me for directions, and I replied with painstaking thoroughness, even venturing into French on one occasion. When Lynne opened the door, she said, "You won the premium bonds."

"Not exactly."

"You're certainly dressed as if you had." She gave my interview suit an approving pat.

I followed her upstairs. I had mentioned the job to her in passing, and she had applauded my decision to apply. "Maybe it'll help you to get more money at Fredericks," she had said. Now while she moved around the kitchen getting out plates, cutlery, food, I told her about the interview.

"I'd have much more input into the books at every level," I said.

"You mean you could acquire books?"

"Yes, and, even better, commission them."

"It sounds like you've got the job." Lynne was standing at the counter, slicing bread for sandwiches. I could not see her face, but her tone was as even as the steady sawing of the knife across the loaf.

"I doubt it," I said. "Probably he was just being polite. When he gets back to Edinburgh he'll have his secretary write a letter, explaining that I don't have the right qualifications, or offering a minuscule salary. But it was exciting to be able to discuss my ideas with such a responsive audience." I smiled at her, wanting to coax her out of her mood of sombre realism.

"I think they'll offer you a huge salary, and the letter will be all about how much they want you." She brought the bread to the table and sat down facing me. "I'm going to miss you so much."

"I would miss you too, but they're not going to offer it to me, and even if they did I wouldn't accept. I'd only go to Edinburgh if you'd come too."

I wanted to keep talking about the interview, to mention all the bits and pieces of praise Bill had given me, but in the face of Lynne's reaction, I could not do so with abandon.

Instead I began to describe the film I had seen with Lewis the night before. I was glad when lunch was over and it was time to collect Eve from nursery school.

I did not tell Lewis about the interview until the letter came, warmly phrased, offering a substantial increase in salary. Then I telephoned his office, thinking I could at least leave a message, but for once he answered. His secretary was on holiday, he explained. I told him my news and he said, "That's wonderful, Celia. Can I take you out to celebrate? Are you free this evening?"

He sounded more enthusiastic about the prospect of seeing me than he had for months, and we arranged to meet at an Italian restaurant in Soho. I spent the remainder of the day busily at work in the city of my imagination; I erected substantial buildings with a speed that any contractor might envy. By the time I arrived at the Trattoria, I was convinced that Lewis would react with dismay, that he would save me from going to Edinburgh and from everything else.

He was already seated at a corner table. As I approached he stood up and came to meet me. "Congratulations," he said, kissing me on both cheeks.

We sat down and a waiter, so thin as to be almost cadaverous, brought over an ice bucket. After a brief struggle he relinquished the champagne to Lewis, who uncorked and poured it with a flourish. "Here's to you," he said, raising his glass.

Lewis was looking unusually handsome. He was wearing a dark blue shirt which deepened the colour of his eyes, and in the soft light of the restaurant his pale skin shone. Throughout dinner he questioned me assiduously. He had soon winkled out of me all the advantages of this new position. "It sounds wonderful," he said. "I'll have to come and visit you. I've always wanted to see Edinburgh." He polished off the last of his veal and pushed his plate to one side.

"Are you finished?" asked the waiter, looking at the heap of fettuccine on my plate. I nodded, and with an air of disapproval he cleared the table. "So you think I should take the job," I said.

"From everything you've told me, it would be mad not to. It's a small company, you'll have much more input, and you'll be virtually your own boss. I've heard you complain dozens of times that working at Fredericks is a dead-end job, that there's absolutely no possibility of promotion." He emptied the remainder of the champagne into our glasses.

"But I don't want to leave London," I said. "Especially to go to Scotland. If it was Oxford, or even Bristol, that would be different, but Edinburgh is like the end of the world."

He put his hand over mine. "It's not that far, Celia. You can fly up in an hour. Besides, you're not talking about going forever, only for a couple of years, and then you can come back to London in all your glory and get a fantastic job. I remember before I went to Hong Kong, I felt like I was going to Botany Bay, but once I actually arrived it was fine, and I could never have got my present job without the experience I gained there."

"But," I said, forcing out the words, "I don't want to leave my friends."

"Your friends don't want you to leave," Lewis said. He squeezed my hand and smiled. "We'll all visit you, and you'll visit us, and it won't be for long. I'm delighted for you. Do you want coffee? Dessert?"

Unable to speak, I shook my head. Lewis beckoned the waiter, and I excused myself. In the small pink cubicle of the ladies' toilet I admonished myself not to cry. The broad avenues and lofty buildings of my imaginary city lay in ruins, and the tears I struggled to hold back stemmed as much from fury at my own stupidity as from grief. Even to me, it was abundantly plain that Lewis had not the slightest notion that our relationship could possibly constitute a reason for my staying. I washed my hands and, in the absence of a towel, wiped them on my skirt.

Every aspect of moving to Edinburgh was made easy. In August, Bill's assistant telephoned to tell me that the sales manager was going to do a training course in Glasgow for a year and hoped to sublet his flat. I reached Malcolm at the first attempt, and in twenty minutes we had made the necessary arrangements. A week later the old-fashioned, heavy keys thudded through my letter box. With equal ease I sublet my flat to a friend of Gillian's who was coming to London for a year to do an M.A. at King's College. These arrangements made my impending exile more bearable, for they reminded everyone that I was only going away for a year, a claim that was further supported by the managing editor of Fredericks, who assured me I could have my old job back anytime.

No sooner had I arrived in Edinburgh, however, than my effortless progress ceased; it was as if I had coasted to the bottom of a steep hill, and the route ahead lay sharply upwards. When the train pulled into Waverley Station, it was raining hard, and the queue for taxis wound down the pavement and round the corner. As I shuffled forward with my suitcases I surveyed the station. At ground level a barrage of garish signs offered refreshment, but above the first storey the trappings of the twentieth century fell away. The upper part of the huge structure was grimly Victorian. Rain fell relentlessly on the glass roof. In his travelling cage, Tobias uttered piteous cries.

Half an hour passed before it was my turn to climb into a cab, which at least had the virtue of looking like a London taxi. I gave the driver Malcolm's address and settled back into my seat. We came out of the station, opposite what I guessed to be Princes Street Gardens, and turned in the direction of a forbidding mass of black buildings which stretched up the hillside towards the Castle. The pavements were thronged with pedestrians carrying umbrellas. Only a few hours earlier, I had left London in brilliant sunshine.

The expediency of departure had created a kind of excitement which had carried me through the day so far; now as the moment of arrival approached, I wished, in spite of the meter's swift clicks, that it could be indefinitely postponed. After barely ten minutes, however, the driver slowed down. "It was number sixteen you wanted?" he asked. I agreed, and we pulled up at the curb.

I unloaded Tobias and my suitcases into the rain, and the taxi drove away. I stood looking up at the building. Number sixteen was part of a terrace of houses built of dark red sandstone. There was something dourly respectable about the facade that brought to mind all the unpleasant rumours I had heard about Scottish Calvinism. It was inconceivable that I was going to live here. Only for a year, I told myself, and picked up the cage and a suitcase.

The front door opened into a short corridor that lead to a flight of stairs. The floor was stone, and the walls were painted in two colours, the bottom half maroon, the top pink. One by one I carried my bags up to the fourth floor. Not until I had everything on the landing, did I put the key in the lock and push open the door.

Like the palace of Sleeping Beauty, Malcolm's flat had the appearance of being both suddenly abandoned and neglected for a long period of time. In the living room, cigarette ends filled the ashtrays, newspapers were scattered over the sofa and the floor, coffee cups, some half full, stood on the sideboard, and the sink was stacked with dishes. A layer of dust and dirt covered every surface. The other rooms were in a similar condition: a towel hung lopsided on the edge of the bath; the covers on the bed were thrown back.

On the table was a note: "Welcome. Make yourself at

home. Sorry the place is a bit of a shambles. If you have any problems, give me a ring. Cheers, Malcolm." He had propped the piece of paper against the antiquated black telephone, as if to urge me to act on his suggestion, but when I picked up the receiver the line was dead.

By morning the sky had cleared and I woke to find the high-ceilinged bedroom filled with light. I lay in bed thinking about Lewis. During the last few weeks he had been unusually considerate, and even though I told myself that this was only because of my imminent departure, I had been seduced into remembering again how much I liked him. He had said Edinburgh was only an hour away by plane; perhaps he would fly up to see me.

Eventually I persuaded myself to get out of bed. The flat looked even worse than it had in the gloom of the previous day. As I sat drinking instant coffee at the living room table, I made a shopping list of the many domestic items I required. There would be plenty of time for cleaning on Sunday. I spread out the map of the city, which Gillian had given me as a parting gift, and tried to decide in which direction I would be most likely to find shops.

On my way out I looked quickly at the two other doors on my landing, and discovered on one side an L. Smith and on the other a Miss Lawson. From behind the door of the latter, there came the sound of shrill barking, followed by a woman's voice raised in remonstration; guiltily I hurried downstairs.

When I came home a few hours later, a tall, white-haired woman, very upright in her blue raincoat, was standing on the pavement outside the house; at her feet a brown and white Pekinese sniffed the base of the lamppost. As I moved towards the front door she said, "Hello. You must be my new neighbour. I'm Miss Lawson, and this is Rollo."

"I'm Celia," I said. I explained that I was renting the flat for a year.

Miss Lawson nodded. "Malcolm told me all about it," she said. "I must say I don't envy you. He's a nice enough young man, but I don't think he's ever heard of housework. Like most men, I suppose."

"It is a bit dirty. I've just been out buying cleaning supplies." The handles of the shopping bags were cutting into my palms, but I welcomed this housewifely exchange, my first human contact in the city. I was about to ask where one put the rubbish, when Rollo, having finished with the lamppost, began to strain at the lead and pant.

"Quiet, Rollo. I'm afraid I'm not much good at scrubbing nowadays, but if there's anything you need, let me know. We're going for our constitutional." She gestured in the direction of the local park, which I knew from my map was called the Meadows. "Why don't you drop in later for a cup of tea?"

On Sunday night I set my alarm clock with a sense of relief. The anxiety that beginning a new job would normally have aroused was held in check by the thought of having people to talk to and a working telephone. Next morning the sun was shining, and although still cold by London standards, the day was comparatively warm. I decided to walk to work. As I made my way down the hill and across Princes Street, stopping often to consult my map, I appreciated for the first time Bill's commendation of the city. I found Melville Street without difficulty. It was an unusually wide street, lined with terraces of tall, grey stone houses; halfway down was a statue, and at the far end stood a church, so large that I thought it might be a cathedral. The office was only a hundred yards from the corner. I had a few minutes to spare and I strolled down one side of the street and up the other, looking at the brass nameplates beside the doors: Campbell, Blair, Liddell, McNaughton, Stewart. I was indeed in Scotland.

The offices of Murray and Stern were on the second floor. I turned the corner at the top of the stairs and found myself in a large room with books displayed all round the walls. At the receptionist's desk a stoutish woman was watering a begonia. I introduced myself, and she put down the watering can and offered me a damp handshake.

"I'm Marilyn. Bill isn't in today, but I'll tell Clare you're here." She pressed a button and sang into the phone, "Miss Gilchrist's here." There was an indistinct mumble. "She'll be down in a minute. Clare is our managing editor. I think you may have spoken to her on the telephone."

I said that I had. While I waited, Marilyn asked me about my journey, and whether I was settled into Malcolm's flat. "Moving is a terrible business," she said. "My husband and I have moved twice in the last five years, and I always swear never again." She pinched a couple of shrivelled leaves off the begonia. "I've been on holiday for a fortnight, and I don't think the temporary receptionist knew anything about plants."

A woman dressed in white came round the corner. Unconsciously I had been expecting someone like Virginia, my former supervisor, an untidy woman in her mid-fifties, with whom I had had a pleasant friendship. Clare was my age, perhaps even younger, and her white suit was spotless and ironed almost to the point of rigidity. In her formal phrases of welcome I could not detect even the pretence of warmth.

She showed me round, presented me with my office, and suggested that I might spend the day familiarising myself with the company's books. Bill would be back tomorrow, and there would be time enough then to discuss my duties.

My office had been created by partitioning off one corner of a larger room. The ceiling was tremendously high, and when I sat down at my desk I felt as if I were at the bottom of a box. Two walls were devoted to bookshelves, now pitifully bare, and on the third wall, beside the door, was a row of battered filing cabinets. A large window provided a view of a brick wall and some rooftops.

I had been staring blankly at a grammar book for half an hour, when a woman appeared in the doorway. She was the antithesis of Clare. Her hennaed hair was tied up with red ribbons, and she wore enormous bright green earrings, a red and white striped T-shirt, and blue trousers. "I'm Suzie, the book designer," she said. "You must be Celia, our new guru from London. Bill claims you're the best thing since sliced bread. I have the office next door. Come and see."

Suzie's office was similar to mine in size, but at the threshold bureaucracy and anonymity ended. A mass of plants hung in the window, a mobile was suspended from the light fixture, and there were children's drawings all over one wall. Both the designer's table and the desk were covered with papers. Suzie gestured towards the mess. "I'm struggling with a geography book. I hated geography at school, and now I know why. It's unutterably tedious. Would you like some coffee?"

"Yes, please."

She picked up a couple of mugs and led the way down the corridor, introducing me to everyone we passed. As soon as they were out of earshot, she described their foibles. "Diana's our office femme fatale. She always dresses like she's on her way to a nightclub." "You don't want to do business with Elaine after she's been out to lunch." Back at our offices, she said, "I suppose I'd better try and organise these maps. If there's anything you need, just come and ask. The more interruptions the better, as far as I'm concerned."

Somehow Suzie's boisterous presence enabled me to begin behaving as if I were at work. I went down the hall and asked Marilyn where I could find stationery. Armed with a notebook and pencil, I began to skim through the books, making notes as I went. Soon after twelve-thirty Suzie came and asked if I wanted to go for lunch.

When I had talked to Lynne about being lonely in Edinburgh she had said, "Nonsense. You'll meet colleagues and neighbours. You'll have friends in no time." But although there were a dozen flats in my tenement, only Deirdre seemed like a possible friend. No one could fail to notice her; her small face was surrounded by a cloud of hair which reminded me of the pictures of princesses in children's books. She almost always wore a leather jacket and jeans, and I was surprised to learn from Miss Lawson that she was a schoolteacher. We had passed each other on the stairs half a dozen times before she stopped to introduce herself. We exchanged pleasantries. I told her I was on my way to the local shop, and she asked if I could get her a loaf of bread.

When I returned, she invited me in. I made some feeble excuse about work. I was afraid that my loneliness, like the mark of Cain, was visible to all, and I did not want to be treated as an object of pity.

"Don't speak to me of work," said Deirdre, opening the front door wide and ushering me inside. "I have a ton of compositions to correct."

"Miss Lawson told me you teach English."

"For my sins. We're doing *Macbeth* for 'O' level. Now do you want a cup of tea, or wine? I'm going to have wine."

"That would be great." I followed her to the doorway of the narrow kitchen and asked how long she had lived here.

"Ages. Four years. Before that I spent a couple of years in Toronto."

We settled down in the living room. Deirdre plied me with questions, but it was impossible to pursue any topic at length because of the frequency with which the telephone rang. Each time Deirdre would grimace and apologise, then talk warmly to the caller. While she was occupied, I wandered around the living room, examining her books and records. I overheard her planning a quick supper, agreeing to go to a film, and volunteering to call other people back to make plans.

She told me she had three sisters living in Edinburgh. "There's always something going on between us. At the moment, we're trying to organise a surprise birthday party for our mother."

"Do your parents live here too?"

"No, they have a house on the outskirts of Dumfries."

Before I could ask where Dumfries was, the phone rang again. After she hung up, Deirdre said, "I suppose I ought to get going on *Macbeth*. If I don't finish all the essays I can't give back any of them."

"Thanks for the wine."

"I'm glad I got a chance to talk to you," she said, as she showed me out. "We must go to a film or something soon."

Whenever I ran into Deirdre she repeated this remark, but if I made a specific suggestion, she was always busy. I blamed her for being insincere; it was easy, however, to recall too many occasions on which I had behaved in similar fashion. In fact perhaps not even as well, for when people from outside London had come to work at Fredericks, I had introduced myself in the hall and not given them a second thought.

At the office I saw Suzie every day, but she was a single parent and had other commitments, and this seemed true of everyone I met. Although there were soon several people to have lunch with at work, even to have a drink with after-wards, these social incidents, isolated and precarious, did little to alleviate my loneliness. During those first months in Edinburgh I devoted myself to my various projects, and the results brought me considerable praise, but as I had once remarked to Lynne, being an editor was like being an accompanist: no matter how great my contribution to a book, I was always overshadowed. Miss Lawson told me that there had recently been several cases of rape in the Meadows, and when I took Rollo out for her, as I sometimes did last thing at night, I would walk defiantly across the open grass, thinking alternately that I was immune from such dangers and that I did not care what became of me.

CHAPTER 4

For a number of years I had been spending Christmas with Lynne and Greg in preference to either of my parents, and even before I left London, I had arranged to return for the holidays. This plan helped to render my loneliness bearable. As I counted the days, the season took on magical properties that it had not had since I was a child. Lewis had been telephoning with surprising frequency and had even offered to meet my train. It was understood between Lynne and me that I might prove to be an erratic guest.

I caught the train down on the afternoon of the twenty-third. I passed the journey daydreaming and leafing through the various women's magazines which I had impulsively purchased at the station. As soon as the train pulled out of Peterborough I went to the toilet. In the mirror I scrutinised my face; compared to the women in the magazines I looked wan and indistinct. When I had had my hair cut the week before, the hairdresser had told me that I must always wear eye make-up. It was not easy in the swaying compartment to apply eye liner and mascara, but I did my best, and as I walked back to my seat, several men glanced up at me. I was wearing clothes that Lewis had never seen before, a bright blue pullover with a black skirt and black boots.

For once the train was on time, and as I approached the ticket barrier, I glimpsed Lewis's unmistakable red hair. He was leaning against the wall, studying the crowd. When he caught sight of me, he hurried over, took my bags, put them down, and kissed me. "You look great," he said.

Outside the station he stopped beside a white car. I exclaimed in surprise.

"I finally had to give in," he said, almost apologetically. "It had reached the stage with the other one that I was taking it to the garage every week." He put my luggage in the boot and opened the door for me. The interior smelled sharply of new plastic.

The traffic was bad, and in spite of the punctuality of the train, we arrived to find Lynne and Greg in the last stages of making dinner; Eve was already in bed. While Lewis carried my bags up to the spare room, they both kissed me and exclaimed how well I looked. "You're thinner," said Lynne. "It suits you."

We ate in the living room. Greg had lit the fire, and in one corner the Christmas tree, hung with ornaments made by Eve, glittered brightly. The meal passed in a wave of laughter and conversation. The others deferred to me, and I found myself holding forth; my life in Edinburgh became a series of entertaining anecdotes. When Lynne went out to the kitchen to make coffee I followed with a stack of dirty plates. "Did your mother really say that wearing jeans would turn Eve into a lesbian?"

"Not exactly; that would be much too explicit for her. But she did give Eve two dresses for Christmas and attach a note saying that she thought it would be healthier for her to wear these."

"Amazing."

Lynne bent over the fridge and got out a pint of milk. "If Lewis wants to stay, it's fine," she said.

I was at the sink, filling the kettle. The action served to cover my confusion. "Thanks," I said awkwardly.

As soon as we had finished our coffee, Lynne announced

that she was off to bed. "Are you sure you won't join us for Christmas?" she asked Lewis.

"I'd love to, but duty calls. My parents would expire if I told them that I'd rather spend Christmas with you."

I saw Lynne tug Greg's arm. They stood up and exchanged kisses and seasonal greetings with Lewis. When they were gone, he came to sit beside me on the sofa. The fire was burning low, and through the uncurtained windows I glimpsed the dark streets of the city. "So how's your love life?" Lewis said, putting his arm round me.

"Not brilliant. How's yours?"

"Better now you're here." He nuzzled my neck.

"Did you miss me?"

"Of course I missed you." He kissed me, and I slid my hand inside the collar of his shirt.

"When are you coming back from your parents'?" I asked. "Boxing Day?"

"I'm not coming back," he said. "Given the logistics, it makes more sense to go directly from their house to the airport."

His hand was still resting on my breast, the fire was still rustling in the grate. On the telephone Lewis had mentioned that there was some problem with his plans for a skiing holiday, but I had not understood that the new arrangements might encroach upon my visit. Once I had begun to cry, it seemed impossible to stop. Lewis fetched me a glass of water. Then he sat down at the far end of the sofa, safely out of reach, and said, "Don't cry. Tell me what's the matter."

"I thought we would spend some time together," I said. I just managed to utter this modest sentence, into which I had compressed all my hopes and fantasies.

"We are spending time together, although not as much as either of us would like." He stood up. "It's late; I should go. Celia, it's wonderful to see you. Next time we'll be better organised. Happy Christmas." He patted my shoulder and left the room almost on tiptoe, like a hospital visitor.

Although I had known Lynne and Greg for years, I had never before stayed with them, and in small, unexpected ways it proved to be a strain. My efforts to conceal my misery were only partially successful, and they were out of sympathy with my despair. When I told her what had happened, Lynne said, "But, Celia, what did you expect? Some variation of this has happened twenty times." She spoke with an exasperated sympathy which drove me to silence. In Edinburgh I had thought that there was nothing worse than being alone, but now even solitude began to seem easier than this perpetual pretence of cheerfulness.

At breakfast on New Year's Eve I said that I had been thinking of going back that afternoon; someone at work was giving a party, I claimed. As soon as the words were out I felt like a fool. In vivid detail I visualised my flat and what I would do in it, alone, for the remainder of the holidays. I bent my head over my coffee cup, waiting for Lynne and Greg to protest. I had planned to stay until the third.

The toast popped up. "That sounds fun," Lynne said. "As you know, we never do anything at New Year because it's impossible to get a baby-sitter." She buttered a slice of toast and handed it to Eve.

I wanted to say that I would much rather stay, that their company was infinitely preferable to any nonexistent party, that I would not be a burdensome guest. Eve demanded jam, and as I reached to help her, Greg said, "I wish I could come with you. They really know how to celebrate New Year in Scotland."

"You're welcome to go," said Lynne, smiling. "You and Celia can bring in Hogmanay together while Eve and I keep the home fires burning."

"I want to go too," said Eve. Lynne and Greg laughed. Pleased with her success, she said it again.

The train was packed, and many of my fellow travellers had already begun to celebrate. Three different men offered to buy me a drink, and the middle-aged woman across the aisle produced a bottle of Scotch from her capacious handbag. We arrived in Edinburgh late in the afternoon. It was fully dark, and a bitter wind blew down the platform. As the taxi turned out of the station I remembered my arrival four months earlier, when I had not known that the hill beside the Castle was named the Mound. The knowledge of what I was returning to only compounded my desolation.

The driver of the taxi, however, was anything but desolate; I was his last fare of the day. "Some of the drivers work Hogmanay and make a killing," he said, "but if you ask me, it's daft. What's the point of spending the evening with a bunch of drunken strangers? Money isn't everything."

No answer seemed to be required. Through the window in the partition, he regaled me with a detailed account of the previous New Year, until we reached my flat. Then he switched on the overhead light and turned to address me. "So you'll have great plans for tonight? Are you going first-footing?" He was smiling, but the long vertical creases in his cheeks gave his expression a melancholy quality.

"Isn't it a bit cold to wander around in the middle of the night?" I said, as I searched for my purse.

"Away with you. Nothing that a drop of whiskey can't cure. Here, have a dram, to get the evening off to a good start."

It seemed churlish to refuse. I took the open bottle he was proffering and under his approving gaze pressed it to my lips and swallowed the smallest possible amount. "Now no more nonsense about staying home. Tonight's the night you'll meet that tall, dark stranger. I feel it in my bones."

As I climbed the stone stairs I heard Deirdre's voice. "I'll get it," she said loudly. "I'll get everything. You just concentrate on the balloons." She was standing in the doorway of her flat. Pulling the door to, she turned around and saw me. "Celia," she said. "I didn't know you were coming back today. I'm giving a party. Will you come?"

I thought it was the last thing I would do, that by ten o'clock I would be in bed with a book, but I said that I would love to. Perhaps not very convincingly, for Deirdre, continuing down the stairs, called over her shoulder that if there was no sign of me by eleven she would send Big John to fetch me.

During the autumn I had grown accustomed to Malcolm's flat; now the contrast with Lynne and Greg's was unbearable. Even Tobias's rapturous welcome could not make me feel at home. Miss Lawson had been taking care of him during my absence, but he had clearly felt neglected. I put the kettle on and made a mug of tea. I drew the curtains, I went around with a milk bottle, watering the plants, I turned on the radio, I unpacked. Nothing could distract me from the fact that it was New Year's Eve. It was not that I had a history of exuberant celebrations—perhaps my happiest years had been as a teenager, when I was much in demand as a baby-sitter— but I had never before faced the turning of the year in such utter solitude.

I puttered around, telling myself that I did not enjoy parties, until eleven o'clock. Then I went into the bedroom and changed my old pullover for a black shirt. As I was brushing my hair I caught sight of the blue leather box in which I kept my amber earrings. I had inherited them at the age of sixteen from my great-aunt Marigold, and they had become a talisman, marking my entry into the adult world. I wore them only on special occasions, to bring me luck; as a small, private gesture of celebration, I put them on.

The door of Deirdre's flat was ajar, and a barrage of music and conversation greeted me. I would stay for half an hour, then slip away. As I stepped into the hall, a man came out of the bathroom. He smiled with such easy friendliness that for a moment I was sure that I knew him. "You must be one of Deirdre's neighbours," he said.

"Yes. How did you guess?"

"Because you don't have a coat, and you don't look cold."

"I only got back from London late this afternoon, and I wasn't planning to come. I didn't even bring anything to drink."

"There's enough booze here to launch the Armada. I'm Stephen." He held out his hand. The sleeves of his white shirt were rolled up, almost to the elbow, and I noticed how smooth and well-rounded his forearms were.

I told him my name and asked where the drinks were. Stephen pointed to the kitchen; it was full well beyond overflowing. "No use trying to get in there," he said. "What do you want? Wine?" When I nodded, he called out, "Hey, John," several times, until he had the attention of a large man standing next to the table. "Pour us a couple of glasses of wine." The glasses were passed above the crowd to Stephen's waiting hands. He gave me one. "I should have asked for the bottle," he said.

I drank some wine and immediately felt slightly giddy. I had had nothing to eat since breakfast. Stephen was standing quietly, smiling. "Shall we go into the living room?" I suggested.

He led the way, and I followed. I waited for him to take me over to a woman and introduce her in a manner that left no doubt as to the nature of their relationship, or to make some excuse to get away, but he guided us without stopping to the corner farthest from the stereo. Then he turned towards me. "Cheers," he said, raising his glass and clinking it to mine. Near us a woman in a brief red satin dress was dancing wildly.

"How do you know Deirdre?" I asked.

"I teach maths at her school." He was about to elaborate, but, as if she had heard her name, Deirdre appeared. She put an arm round Stephen and said to me, "You came. I was afraid you wouldn't when I saw your face this afternoon. You looked like you were arriving back at Holloway Prison after your Christmas break."

"I was worn out from the train," I said. "It was jammed with drunken Scotsmen."

Deirdre and Stephen burst out laughing. "I can guarantee you won't find any of those here tonight," said Deirdre. "I'm pissed as a newt already, but if you want anything, let me know. Right now I'll leave you in the capable hands of my big brother." She drifted out among the dancers, and reappeared in the arms of a middle-aged man, barely up to her shoulder, who in spite of the music was trying to waltz her round the room.

"Who's that?" I asked.

"That's Mr. Sutherland. He teaches classics at our school."

"You're not really Deirdre's brother, are you?"

"No, it's a joke between us. We've known each other for years, ever since teachers' training, and we were lucky enough to end up at the same school. What brought you to Edinburgh?" he asked.

"I was offered a job here."

"You mean you moved here just on the strength of having a job. You didn't know anyone?"

I nodded.

"That's very courageous," he said. "I don't know if I could stand living in a city of strangers."

I asked Stephen how long he had lived here and where he grew up. I thought he must realise that every one of my questions was really the same question, and next day, when he claimed that he had not known whether I liked him, I was incredulous. Because he was so much taller than I, and soft-spoken, because of the music, perhaps because my emotion like a high wind whipped his words away, there were all kinds of gaps in my understanding of that first conversation. If we had, at that moment, been swept apart, I would have been hard-pressed to describe him.

Later I discovered he was tall, loose-limbed, with light brown hair and eyes. He had fine, straight hair which flopped over his forehead, his nose was small, his skin was smooth and even in midwinter looked slightly tanned. Everything about him, including his horn-rimmed glasses, was sweetly rounded, he even had a dimple in his chin, and I was amazed to learn that he was several years older than I.

Suddenly the music stopped. Above the crowd I saw Deirdre standing on a chair. She stretched out her hands in a gesture of silence. "Quiet, children," she shouted. On the radio Big Ben began to chime, everyone joined hands and sang "Auld Lang Syne." As the noise crescendoed, Stephen kissed me.

For a brief interval the room, the noise, the music, the people, all dropped away. Then I heard Deirdre's voice saying, "Save some for me." Stephen released me, picked Deirdre up and swung her round. Meanwhile the man on my right seized his chance to give me a whiskery kiss. By the time I emerged, Stephen had disappeared into a round of embraces.

I went in search of a drink. The kitchen was deserted. I found a glass, rinsed it, and poured myself a substantial measure of Glenfiddich. I was suddenly exhausted. It was hard to believe that only that morning Eve had come into my room at seven A.M. to demand a story. I felt a kind of vertigo at the immense distance I had covered in the course of the day. I closed my eyes and swallowed some Scotch. Then I went into the hall, paused for another quick drink, and prepared to brave the living room.

As I stepped forward, Stephen hurried through the door.

He saw me, stopped, and smiled. "Celia," he said, "I was afraid you'd left. All hell's breaking loose here. I was wondering if you'd like to go for a walk."

My fatigue vanished. I ran upstairs to fetch my coat. In the bathroom mirror my cheeks were flushed and my eyes slightly red from drinking, but I did not linger over my appearance. I gathered up various toilet articles and put them in my bag.

When we stepped out into the street it was immediately apparent that the people of Edinburgh were celebrating the New Year. The air was filled with the sounds of car horns, shouting, and the wailing of bagpipes. As we waited on the pavement, a man stopped his car and blew me kisses through the window.

We crossed the road into the Meadows. It must have rained earlier in the day. On the wet grass our footsteps made a squelching sound and I could feel the water seeping into my boots. "It would be nice to go up Arthur's Seat, but I think that's a bit ambitious," Stephen said.

"I've never been."

"Never?" he exclaimed. "And how long have you lived here? The next fine day, I'll be your guide. I mean if you'd like."

"That would be lovely."

As we walked, the noises of the city faded, and soon even the bagpipes were barely audible. We were halfway across the Meadows when Stephen stopped. "I haven't been paying attention to where we're going," he said, "but I think if we head over there we'll get to some benches. Don't those look like trees to you?"

Dimly I could make out the dark shapes. "I think so."

In a few minutes we had found a bench. We sat down. It was cold, hard, and slightly damp. Side by side we looked out across the Meadows. Even above the grassy expanse the sky was tinged with the orange light of the city. "One of the things I hate about living in a city," Stephen said, "is that you can never really see the sky. Where I grew up, you only had to walk a short distance in any direction and you'd be out in a field. You could even see the small stars in Orion's belt without a telescope."

I followed the gesture of his hand. The Milky Way lay like a ribbon of gauze across the sky, and directly in front of us the seven stars of the Plough shone brightly. "Do you remember the part in *Tess of the D'Urbervilles* where she looks at the stars and imagines herself transported to one of them?" I asked.

"Yes," he said. "Poor Tess."

I gave a tiny shiver, so small, I thought, as to be imperceptible, but Stephen noticed. "You're cold," he said, and put his arm around me.

CHAPTER 5

We had forgotten to draw the curtains, and on the morning of New Year's Day the sunlight coming through the window woke us. Stephen's flat, like mine, was on the top floor, and from the bed I could see the outlines of slate roofs and chimney pots. In one corner of the window sill two blue-grey pigeons were cooing vigorously, filling the room with their soft rumbling.

When Stephen at last went to make us coffee, I studied the room. My first impression was of an almost feminine neatness. The bedside table was covered with a white cloth; there was nothing on it save a lamp and an alarm clock. The walls were pale yellow, and opposite the bed was a small cast-iron fireplace with blue tiles around the grate. There were a couple of photographs on the mantelpiece, and when I heard the bathroom door close, I went to look at them. One showed Stephen with a small girl, the other the same girl with an older man and woman. I presumed she was a relative: a niece or cousin.

Stephen returned, walking slowly, carrying two red mugs. He handed one to me, took off his dressing gown, and climbed back into bed. I sat up to drink some coffee. "Who's the little girl in the photographs?" I asked.

"That's Jenny, my daughter."

Suddenly I understood the careful tidiness of the room. No wonder he had been pleased to find a stranger at Deirdre's party and had refrained from introducing me to people;

everyone else knew he was married. I should have guessed that he was too good to be true.

"The other people are my parents. Both the photographs were taken outside their house in Abernethy."

I raised the mug to my lips and drank some coffee. I would have liked to leap from the bed and run out of the flat, but I was determined not to give him the satisfaction of seeing that I minded.

"Is something wrong? Are you having second thoughts about me?" Stephen asked. He was looking at me anxiously.

"You should have told me."

"Celia, it wasn't as if I was trying to keep her a secret. I didn't get round to it. She lives with her mother, and I only see her on Saturdays. Helen and I have been living apart for the last four years."

"So you're not married?"

"Legally I am—when you have a child, getting a divorce is complicated—but it doesn't mean anything. We only got married in the first place because we had to."

Stephen went on, explaining and reassuring. Once I grasped that he and Helen were safely apart, I was pleased rather than dismayed. Lewis had cured me of the notion that people could change, and I saw it as a sign of promise that Stephen had been married and had a child; it showed that such a relationship was possible for him. We slid down under the covers again. The sunlight moved across the room.

When we roused ourselves for the second time, I remembered that Tobias needed to be fed. I told Stephen, and as soon as we were washed and dressed we drove to my flat. After the revelry of the previous evening the streets were deserted, and the journey took only a few minutes. We found Tobias in a wretched state. The sound of plaintive mewing reached us while we were still climbing the stairs, and he greeted me as if he had not seen a human being for days. After I had fed him, I left the room to collect some clean clothes.

When I returned Stephen was kneeling down beside Tobias, stroking his neck. "Why don't we take him with us?" he said. "It seems particularly horrid to leave him alone on New Year's Day."

On our way back to Stephen's flat, the sight of a taxi reminded me of the previous evening. I told Stephen about the driver's prophecy.

"So I'm your tall, dark stranger," he said. "What if I'd decided to dye my hair as a joke?"

"It wouldn't have made any difference. We were in the hands of fate. Originally I was going to come back on the third, and if I hadn't met Deirdre on the stairs, she wouldn't have known to invite me."

With Lewis any avowal of affection had been a mistake; he would disappear for one week if I said I liked him, two if I hinted at love. But Stephen took my hand and smiled. "And if I hadn't happened to go to the toilet at exactly the right moment."

Later, when we were back in bed, he said, "I believe our meeting was fate too. I knew the moment I saw you that you were going to be important to me. There was something about the way you stood in the hall that made me want to put my arms around you. You were so uncertain, like an animal coming out of its burrow—you looked as if the slightest alarm would make you go back into hibernation for another six months."

Stephen had placed two candles on the bedside table, and from where I lay, I could see the outline of his face against the light. In the still air the flames hung golden and unwavering. "But I'm so ordinary-looking," I protested.

He propped himself on one elbow and gazed down at me. "I was watching your hair in the sunlight this morning; there are reddish lights in it, a sort of Stewart colouring. It made me wonder if maybe you had Scottish ancestors."

"Not that I know of."

He pressed himself against me. "Anyway, when I said there was something about you, I didn't mean something physical. I felt that I recognised you in a deep way. And you have very beautiful eyebrows."

For years I had plucked my eyebrows, thinking that they made me look like a sulky boy; only since I moved to Edinburgh had I let them grow naturally. I raised my head to kiss Stephen. Slowly I pushed my hand down his chest and over his belly. Then I followed with my mouth.

As I pieced together Stephen's history, I realised that he and I had arrived in each other's lives at exactly the right moment. My grief about Lewis had been magnified by my loneliness in Edinburgh, and I was more than ready to discard that shop-soiled emotion. In doing so, I discovered that being with him had not been a complete waste of time. Before I knew Lewis, I had always been passive, waiting for the man to make everything perfect; he had shown me how to be otherwise. Now, with Stephen, I found that I could be passionate in a way that I had never been before. I desired him and I felt free to act upon my desire. Part of the pleasure of being with him was the pleasure I took in discovering this new side of myself.

And Stephen seemed to feel something similar. Helen had been his equivalent of Lewis—beautiful, successful, sexually unreliable. "It wasn't love exactly," he told me. "It was a sickness. I never trusted her, and I never felt that I could be myself; being myself wasn't enough." He had learned from Helen to think of female beauty as a snare and a delusion, and I suspected that it was a relief to him to be with a woman whom people did not turn to stare at in the street.

Jenny had been staying with Helen's family in Reading for the Christmas holidays, and I had known Stephen for almost a fortnight before one of her regular Saturday visits occurred. When the alarm sounded that morning I was deeply asleep,

and at first I did not understand why we were being thus
rudely woken. Then, as Stephen kissed me, I remembered his
daughter. I ran my hands down his back; I loved the smooth-
ness of his body. He kissed me again and pulled away. "Helen
gets furious if I'm late," he explained.

"I suppose this is her one free day." I rolled back to my side
of the bed. I was determined to be exemplary about Jenny. In
view of the fact that they had not seen each other for several
weeks, I had suggested that it might be better for me to leave
them alone together, but Stephen had disagreed. "She likes
meeting my friends," he said. "Besides, I want you to meet
her."

He got out of bed and walked over to the window. As he
drew the curtains, I heard the turbulent beating of wings.
"The pigeons were on the sill again," he said. "We should put
out bread."

"As long as we keep the door shut so that Tobias can't
molest them."

Even as I spoke there was a scratching sound. Stephen
opened the door, and Tobias padded in and jumped onto the
foot of the bed. He tucked himself against my legs. Stephen
began to dress, picking up his clothes from the floor where
they had fallen the night before. Behind him, through the
window, the sky above the rooftops was the colour of wood
ash. "It's freezing," he said. "I'll put on the fires. Don't get up
until it's warmer." He bent down to kiss me goodbye.

I had never been alone in Stephen's flat before, and there
was a peculiar intimacy about the solitude; it made me feel
that this was my home. Almost forty minutes passed before I
persuaded myself to emerge from the safety of the blankets.
Then the sharpness of the cold drove me to carry my clothes
into the living room, where, fearing that I might be surprised
at any moment, I dressed in front of the gas fire. The bracelet
which Stephen had given me the night before was lying on the
mantelpiece. I clasped it around my wrist. The silver band

was carved with wavy lines, like running water; I thought I would wear it always.

As I buttoned my cardigan, I wandered over to the window. Beneath me in the dark street a man and a small girl were waiting to cross the road. As I stared down at Stephen and Jenny, I was suddenly aware of my heart beating with uneasy rapidity. There was no need to be nervous, I reminded myself; she was only a child. I turned away from the window and began to tidy the room, picking up newspapers and plumping up the pillows in the armchairs, until I heard the front door open and Stephen call my name. I stepped into the hall. He came over and put his arm around me. "Jenny, this is Celia," he said.

I smiled and said hello.

"Hello," she said. She looked down to unzip her jacket.

I made a pot of tea, Stephen fetched a glass of orange juice for Jenny, and we settled down in the living-room. He and I sat on either side of the fire, and Jenny knelt on the rug between us. She was wearing a dark blue pullover, with a white shirt and new, freshly ironed jeans; her hair was held back by barrettes. The overall effect was so neat that it was almost as if she were in uniform. While she sipped her juice, I searched for signs of her kinship with Stephen.

Even allowing for the disparities of sex and age, they were very different: she was pale, he was warmly coloured; her eyes were dark as pickled walnuts, his were light as the water in a burn; her hair was dark and heavy, his was the colour of honey and wispy. But as I watched Jenny I began to notice that there were ways in which she did resemble her father. She had the same habit of using her hands when she talked, and her intonation of certain words was identical to his. Stephen had told me that he knew Helen was having an affair when Jenny started to say "preposterous"—a word that neither he nor Helen often uttered.

"What's an editor?" Jenny asked.

I looked at Stephen. "You're the expert," he said.

"When people write books, I correct them before they're published so that there won't be any mistakes in them."

"What sort of books?" she asked.

"Textbooks, like the ones you use in school."

She giggled. "I never knew those were written by people. They're so boring I thought they came out of a machine."

"Sometimes I wish they did," I said. "Authors are difficult. They always think they know everything."

"Teachers think that too. Miss Nisbet will never say she doesn't know the answer. Sometimes we ask her things no one knows, to see what she'll say."

"Like what?" said Stephen. He had been sitting back in his chair, watching our exchange with a pleased expression on his face.

"Like," she said, elongating the syllable while she gathered her thoughts. "Like who was the man in the iron mask, and where is Hitler buried. Anna asks her dad what we can say."

"And what does Miss Nisbet tell you?"

"I don't remember." She spread her fingers as if the answer might be hidden between them, then shook her head. "Different things."

"I could help with this," said Stephen. "There are lots of mathematical conundrums that have never been solved, like Fermat's last theorem. I bet that would flummox her." He put down his cup. "If we're going to go to the library before the film, we should think about leaving." He turned towards me. "Jenny wants to see *Ghostbusters*. Would you like to come?"

I looked at Jenny. She was tracing the pattern in the rug with one finger. Her lips were slightly pursed. "Are you sure?" I asked.

"Of course," said Stephen. "We'd be delighted to have your company, wouldn't we, Jenny?"

"Yes," she said.

I was so absorbed in deciphering Jenny's reaction that

when the telephone rang, I started. Jenny giggled. As Stephen left the room to answer it, she said, "You jumped."

"I know. I was surprised."

Through the open door we could hear Stephen saying, "Hello, Mum. How are you?"

"That must be Granny," Jenny said, and scrambled to her feet. She went out into the hall. After a few minutes Stephen surrendered the phone to her and returned.

"That was my mother," he said. "I promised we'd go and stay the last weekend in January."

"Oh," I said.

"Is that all right? I should have consulted you, but she was so eager that I said yes. I can always ring her back."

"No, it's fine. I'm just taken aback. I didn't even know that your parents knew about me."

"Of course they know, and they're longing to meet you. We can talk about it later. Now we have to get ready to go."

While he tidied up the tea things I went to the bedroom to collect my bag. Tobias was still asleep on the foot of the bed. I had planned to introduce him to Jenny, but I could hear her talking on the phone. "So what happened?" she said. A few minutes later, when I came out into the hall, she was putting on her jacket. She stared at me as I walked towards the coat rack. "Are you staying here?" she asked.

I had my back to her and so could not see her expression, but I sensed a faint note of accusation in her voice. Before I could muster an answer, Stephen called from the kitchen, "She's visiting me for the weekend."

"I thought you had a flat."

"I do." I turned around, with my coat in my hand, and found Jenny standing immediately in front of me.

Stephen came out of the kitchen. "Jenny, you have a flat," he said lightly. "In fact you have two if you count mine, but you still go and stay with Anna sometimes. Have you got your gloves?"

Jenny nodded. She had brought her schoolbag, presumably to carry her library books; she picked it up from the floor and looped the strap diagonally over one shoulder. Then she opened the door. I followed her out onto the landing. Stephen was still putting on his jacket. "Which library are we going to?" I asked.

Jenny had already started down the stairs. "What did you say?" she said.

She was nearly at the bottom of the first flight of stairs, and I hurried after her, thinking to answer when I had caught up. She was only a few yards ahead, and I expected as I rounded the corner to find myself almost abreast of her, but she was nowhere to be seen. I heard her feet pattering down the stone stairs. She repeated her question. "Celia," she called. "What did you say?"

I glimpsed her dark head two floors below. She seemed to want to engage me in conversation and I was eager to respond. I broke into a trot; at Jenny's age I could remember never walking down stairs, and it was as if I were simultaneously imitating her and my own younger self. Suddenly, at the top of the second flight, I tripped and but for my hold on the bannister would have fallen. Lying in the middle of the stair was Jenny's bag. I picked it up and continued my descent more slowly.

In the street, Jenny was standing between two parked cars, trying to balance on their bumpers. "You dropped your bag," I said, holding it out to her.

"Thanks." Without getting down from her perch, she took the bag and looped it back over her shoulder.

I waited for her to offer some explanation as to how she had dropped the bag and why she had not stopped to pick it up, but she seemed to be concentrating exclusively on her balancing act. Finally I said, "Don't you get dizzy going down stairs so fast?"

She shook her head. "I never get dizzy."

CHAPTER 6

On the day of our visit to Stephen's parents, a storm broke over Edinburgh. The rain lashed against my office window, and Marilyn remarked that there would be snow on the hills. The forecast had predicted an improvement towards evening, but by five o'clock the sound of the wind howling in the alley had reached new heights, and the glass shook so hard in the window frame that I was afraid it would break. I had offered Suzie a lift home, and we went downstairs to the lobby to wait for Stephen. A stream of people walked past us; a few called goodbye, and the sales director made a comment about our vigorous social life.

While we waited, Suzie entertained me with stories about meeting the parents of various lovers. "They'd given us separate bedrooms so it seemed like the ideal opportunity," she said in conclusion to an account of how, while visiting Alan's parents for the first time, she had dyed her hair, ruining several towels in the process and leaving ineradicable traces of her presence on their bathroom wallpaper.

I was about to ask what had happened to Alan when a horn sounded. I stepped out of the building. Rain stung my face as I ran to the car. Stephen was holding the passenger door ajar, and I opened the back door for Suzie. We all exclaimed about the weather. Suzie gave directions, and we set off, rattling over the cobblestones. "So what will they give you?" she asked, when we stopped at a red light. "One room or two?"

"One," said Stephen. He laughed.

"Well, that's something. In my experience, it's fairly rare to cop a single room on the first visit. The anxiety I've suffered sneaking round strange houses at night trying to find the right room."

"Not everyone has Victorian parents," Stephen said.

"Everyone who fancies me does. I think I must appeal to their overdeveloped sense of sin."

She asked about the son of a friend, who was in one of Stephen's classes, and the remainder of the short journey to her flat passed in a discussion of the boy's learning disabilities. After we had dropped Suzie off, we continued out of the city along the Queensferry Road. "This was where my two great-uncles lived," Stephen said, gesturing to the left. "Number four Craigcrook Place."

His voice was low, and I leaned closer to hear above the din of the engine. "Do they still live there?" I asked.

"No, they're both dead. Norman had a stroke when I was about ten. Alexander only survived him by a few months. I used to go and stay with them by myself. I'm amazed that they put up with me. Norman had a huge nose. I would draw grotesque pictures of him and then ask him to help me write his name underneath."

"Maybe you admired his nose. One of my uncles had a wooden leg, and I was very proud of it. I would try to get him to show it to my friends. What about Alexander?"

There was a pause while Stephen negotiated a roundabout. "Alexander was the one who cooked and cleaned, so I tormented him by refusing to eat and making as much mess as I could."

"You must have had some redeeming features."

"I don't think so. The main reason I liked visiting them was because they gave me money and treats that I never got from my parents. I would actually calculate in advance how much I would get from them."

"I think all children are like that," I said. "I remember knowing exactly what each of my aunts and uncles was worth."

By now we were on the outskirts of the city, and the street lights were further apart. Stephen leaned forward to wipe the windscreen. "I suppose that's true. What worries me is the idea that Jenny has that attitude towards me. You know: 'Daddy's good for going to the cinema, and I bet if I ask him nicely he'll buy me that comic.' "

"But she doesn't. She's obviously very fond of you." The windscreen wipers limped back and forth. I tried to come up with some compelling evidence; I had only seen them together on two occasions.

"It's an odd thing to have a child," Stephen said slowly. "Sometimes I think I understand Jenny fairly well; after all, I've known her all her life. Then I remember myself as a child, and I suspect that she's a total mystery to me."

I looked over at him. It was hard in the darkness to determine his expression. A lorry overtook us, and the sudden deluge rendered the windscreen opaque. For a moment I was afraid, but Stephen held the wheel steady, and gradually the screen cleared. When the road was visible again he said, "I'm afraid this car isn't meant for torrential rain. The combination of the geriatric windscreen wipers and the heater barely working means that you need X-ray vision."

"We can drive slowly," I said. "It's not as if we have far to go."

Soon we were coming down the final incline towards the Forth Road Bridge. Ahead of us the line of tollbooths shone. Stephen pulled up beside one and rolled down his window. "Nasty night," said the attendant as he took our money.

We drove out onto the bridge. "When I was little," said Stephen, "the only way to get across here was by ferry. Then they started to build the bridge, and every time we went to Edinburgh I would watch the men swarming up and down the cables at either end. I couldn't imagine how they would ever get the two halves to meet. But one day we arrived at the ferry and there was the bridge stretching all the way from shore to shore. I remember how thrilled we were. I can't really explain why, but it was one of the things that made me want to study mathematics."

The whole bridge was capable of swaying thirty feet in either direction, and Stephen was certain that he felt it shifting; that we were swinging like a pendulum, in huge sixty-foot arcs. He slowed down until we were barely moving. "Can you feel it, Celia?" he kept asking, until I said yes.

Suspended in the darkness, high above the water, I felt anything was possible. I forgot our destination, that we had left one place and would shortly arrive in another, and wished only that we might forever, side by side, continue to drive where the light of the headlamps showed us the way.

When we were once more on land Stephen accelerated. In less than half an hour we turned off the motorway onto a country road, and from there it was only a few miles to the outskirts of the village. Stephen pulled up beside a low stone wall, and I glimpsed the facade of a house. A light above the front door shed a small pool of brightness.

"I'll go first," he said. "Wait until I get the door open." He leaned over and kissed me until I tasted, beyond the coldness of his lips, the warmth of his mouth. Then he was out of the car. I watched him hurry up the gravel path towards the light. He opened the door and turned to beckon me.

I ran through the rain. As I crossed the threshold, the door on the left of the hall opened halfway and a man squeezed out, saying, "Down. Stay. Good dogs." He patted Stephen on the shoulder. "What a frightful night," he said. "I was worried about you."

Stephen introduced me to his father, Edward. We shook hands, and Edward's whole body tilted slightly forward, in the self-effacing, almost deferential manner of a tall man who is anxious to demonstrate that he does not plan to take advantage of his size. It was easy to imagine him as the country solicitor he had been for nearly forty years.

Stephen carried our wet coats off to the kitchen, and Edward showed me into the sitting room. As soon as he opened the door, two King Charles spaniels shot out, falling over my feet in their eagerness to reach Stephen. "Sorry about the dogs. They're an absolute menace when they're excited." Edward indicated that I should sit in the high-winged arm-chair closest to the fire. A book lying open on the nearby table suggested that I was taking his seat, but I was too shy to object. I stretched out my hands to the blaze. Edward poked the fire and sat down opposite me. "How was the drive?"

"Fine," I said. "I wish we had come by daylight so that I could have seen the countryside."

"Plenty of opportunity for that in the spring. It's really rather depressing at this time of year: fields of mud popu-lated by turnip stumps and soggy sheep. I hope it will be dry tomorrow so that I can show you the garden. Not that there's much to see besides snowdrops and jasmine, but I do have an unusual Christmas rose that's still in bloom." He cleared his throat, as if checking himself. I knew from Stephen that Edward was a passionate gardener. "Now what can I get you? Whiskey, sherry, gin, vermouth, martini, wine?"

While he was reeling off this list, the door opened and Stephen came in, followed by his mother. Joyce was as round as her husband was angular, and when I stood up to greet her I saw that she was a head smaller than I. She shook my hand, and I found myself looking into her blue eyes. How was it possible, I wondered, that Stephen had failed to inherit such vivid eyes?

She settled herself in a corner of the sofa and picked up a piece of mending. "Look at Celia," she said. "She's perished. I tell you, that car is a collector's item; it takes you back to the early days of motoring. Give her a drink at once, Edward."

"I'm trying. I'm waiting for her to tell me what she wants."

"I'd like whiskey and a little water," said Stephen. He had stationed himself with his back to the fire, his heels resting on the fender.

"I'll have that too," I said hastily.

"I'll have a gin," said Joyce.

"Right you are, dear." Edward left the room in search of drinks.

"If the rain doesn't stop soon, we won't have a drive left." Joyce threaded her needle and turned towards me. "There's a farm track along the side of the house, up the hill to our garage. When there's this much rain, it turns into a stream, and then the tractors go back and forth, churning it up. We've been arguing with the local farmer for twenty years about whose responsibility it is. Stop hogging the fire, Stephen."

In response to his mother's admonition, Stephen sat down in the other corner of the sofa. "You're like someone out of Dickens, always threatening lawsuits," he said. "If Daddy had let her, she could have kept his whole firm in business single-handed."

"That's not true," said Joyce. She began to sew the hem of a blouse. "I was involved in a dispute about the nursery school; they were taking in too many children for the number of staff. Some of the parents protested, but we weren't being vindictive. What we wanted was to get more staff and a better building. The reason the track is a bone of contention is . . ." But before she could finish her defence, Edward opened the door and came in bearing a small circular tray. One of the dogs slunk in at his heels and was immediately ejected by Stephen.

"Cheers," Edward said, when we each had a drink. The whiskey made my throat catch, and I struggled not to cough. Stephen smiled. "I should have warned you how strong a drink my father pours."

"Is it too strong?" Edward began to get to his feet.

"No, no, it's just what I need to warm me up." Edward settled back in his seat, and Stephen gave me a wink.

Next morning after breakfast, Stephen and his father disappeared up the garden to the old stone building, once a stable, which Edward used as a workshop. I found Joyce bustling around the kitchen.

"Do you want some coffee?" she asked.

"Yes, please. Is there something I can do to help?"

"Keep me company."

I sat down at the far end of the table and watched while she measured flour into a bowl, threw in a pinch of salt, and poured in the foaming yeast. I was reminded of the many occasions when I had sat watching my aunt Ruth; she too was an energetic cook. "Are you making bread?" I asked.

"Yes. There is a bakery in the village, but when I've time I like to make my own. I'm sorry that Jenny couldn't come with you. I suppose it didn't suit Helen." She was looking down into the bowl, slowly stirring the ingredients together, and I could only guess at her expression.

"I don't think it was really Helen's decision. Jenny already had various plans for the weekend. I never knew how many social engagements a nine-year-old could have. She was very disappointed."

"Oh, well," said Joyce, sounding brisk again. "Next time we'll manage things better."

The kettle came to the boil. She made us two cups of Nescafé and began to beat the dough with a large wooden spoon. "I don't know if Stephen's told you, but when Jenny was a baby she spent a lot of time with us. Helen didn't want to leave her with strangers, and she and Stephen were both working. Now we hardly ever see her. I used to telephone once a week, but Helen made me feel as if I was intruding."

She gave the dough a final stir and scraped the spoon. "She doesn't seem to understand that we're still Jenny's grandparents."

A movement outside the window caught my eye. On the bird table a female blackbird was pecking at a heel of bread. Joyce emptied the bowl onto a floured board. With her short, rather broad fingers, she began to knead the dough, flattening it out and folding it up again, gradually rendering the mixture more and more elastic, as she waited for a sign that the magic expansion of the yeast was safely under way.

"I worry," she said, "that if Helen decided to move away, we might never see Jenny again. Sometimes I lie awake, I feel so helpless. Edward says that the situation will get easier as Jenny gets older, and I'm sure that's true, if she still wants to see us." Joyce sighed.

I did not know what to say, but I could not help feeling a flicker of pleasure, both at Joyce's criticisms of Helen and at the approval of me that voicing them implied. She punched the dough a few more times and rolled it into a ball, which she nestled carefully in a large china bowl. Her actions covered my silence. As she placed the bowl on the stove and draped a blue tea towel over it, there was a gentle knocking.

"Here's Raven," Joyce said. Wiping her hands on her apron, she went to answer the door and returned followed by a small boy, who padded behind her in his stocking feet. "Raven, this is Celia. She's a friend of Stephen's."

"Hello, Raven."

"Hello. I live next door." To my surprise he came over and held out his hand for me to shake. "Is Jenny here?" he asked. He remained standing, as if uncertain whether to leave or stay.

"I'm afraid she couldn't come," said Joyce.

He promptly pulled out the chair beside me and sat down.

"You're making bread," he said.

"Yes, but I only just started. It still has to rise. Did people like your loaf?" He nodded. Joyce turned towards me. "Everyone in Raven's class had to make something and explain how it worked. Raven chose bread. He drew pictures of all the stages and took the loaf he'd made to school." As she spoke, Joyce was opening and closing the refrigerator, slipping bread into the toaster, slicing some cheese. "Tomato or cucumber?" she asked.

"Tomato, please. Do you know how yeast works?"

I shook my head, and Raven launched into an explanation. Yeast, it turned out, was a fungus. Joyce set a cheese sandwich in front of him, but he refrained from eating until he was sure that I understood the whole process; then he turned to his sandwich with equal seriousness. As soon as he had finished, Joyce asked him to carry a thermos of coffee out to Edward and Stephen. He thanked her for the sandwich and went to do her bidding.

After the door had closed behind him, Joyce smiled at me. "So now you know everything about yeast."

"Yes. What a nice boy." I carried my coffee cup over to the sink. Something about Raven's initial hesitation had made me think that he was relieved rather than otherwise to find Jenny absent. "Do he and Jenny get on well?" I asked.

Joyce looked up from wiping the counter. "I think they do. Sometimes when he comes to the house Jenny is a bit standoffish. I suspect she doesn't like the fact that Raven gets to see more of us than she does; she can be quite territorial, as maybe you've noticed. Now," she said briskly, "what are we going to have for lunch?"

CHAPTER 7

When we left, late on Sunday afternoon, Joyce and Edward walked out to the car with us. "Come again soon," Joyce said. "We're always here." She put her arms around me, and briefly I was enveloped in the sweet odour of baking. She released me, and Edward stepped forward to shake my hand; he too urged me to return.

Stephen hugged both his parents. "Thank you for everything. We'll be in touch soon." He climbed into the car beside me and started the engine. We turned onto the main road. "You see," he said, "they like you. You'll have to tell Suzie that it is possible."

I smiled. As we drove through the village, I looked at the houses on either side of the road, each in the middle of its tidy garden. The approval of Stephen's parents, like the keystone of an arch, I thought, completed our union. I placed my hand lightly on his leg. "Joyce really misses Jenny," I said.

"I know. When do you think would be a good weekend to take her for a visit?"

"Maybe in a fortnight?" We had passed beyond the village, and as Edward had told me, the road was bordered by muddy fields; in some, flocks of sheep were grazing among the turnips.

"A fortnight is Valentine's Day, and I want to be romantic with you, not go home to my parents."

I leaned my head on his shoulder. "But then it will be three weeks before we can go again, unless we go next Friday."

"That's too soon. Joyce would start to get on my nerves if I saw her two weekends in a row."

"Why don't we invite her to come to Edinburgh for the day?"

"Now there's a good idea. We could go on some sort of outing together, and no one would have time to be badly behaved. Good." He squeezed my hand.

I was still sitting with my head on his shoulder, gazing out of the window, when suddenly I saw an arrow of geese flying purposefully across the grey sky. "Look," I said. Stephen stopped the car and we got out. The lonely cries of the geese filled the air, and as they flew low over the road, we could hear the whistling sound of their wings. They landed a few hundred yards away in a field of stubble.

When we reached the city Stephen drove directly to my flat. We both had work that had to be finished by next morning, and we had agreed to spend the evening apart. During the last month I had returned to my flat only to change my clothes or to pick up mail, never staying longer than a few minutes. Now, as I climbed the stairs, I found myself looking forward to spending an evening there alone.

I opened the front door. Immediately I knew that something was wrong. There was a slight ticking noise, louder and less regular than a clock, and for a moment I was sure that there was someone else in the flat. I put down my overnight bag, conscious of the minute slippage of my vertebrae, one against the next, all the way down my spine. Cautiously I pushed open the door of the living room, so that the light from the hall fell in a bright rectangle across the threshold. I listened intently until I was convinced that whatever the source of the noise, it was not human. Then I switched on the overhead light.

The high white ceiling was traced with jagged brown cracks, from which the water was slowly dripping down in half a dozen places. The upholstered chairs were sodden, the shades of the two lamps I had bought were crinkled and stained. I went over to the bookshelf and saw that the water had trickled down my books from top to bottom. When I stooped to feel the carpet, the fabric was bloated with water.

I went to the phone and dialled Stephen's number. After a dozen rings I told myself it was too soon for him to be home and hung up. I turned on the gas fire and began to take down my books, spreading them out on the kitchen counter to dry. I found myself wishing that Tobias were here; his absence intensified my loneliness.

After ten minutes I called again. The curtains were open, and from where I stood holding the phone I could see my reflection in the window. I watched my head floating in one pane, my arm in another. If Stephen had so many exercises to correct, why was he not sitting at the living room table correcting them within a few strides of the phone? What could explain his absence?

Periodically I tried again. From the beginning Stephen and I had been so much in each other's company that the telephone had never played an important role between us. Now I let the phone ring and ring, not even expecting that it would be answered, but for the bleak consolation of being able to imagine the sound reverberating through his flat.

I carried another armful of books over to the counter. Three cups on the shelf above the sink caught my eye. I had bought them in an Oxfam shop soon after I arrived in Edinburgh. They were a dark orange, almost an umber colour, with a golden filigree pattern. I had noticed them in the window and gone back several times until the shop was open. "It's a lovely pattern," the woman at the counter had said. "Too bad there isn't a set, but I'm afraid all we get here is odds and ends." I gazed around the room. Everything I saw—the books, the lamps, the pictures, the brightly coloured cushions, the plants, everything I had bought to make the room mine—struck me as pathetic and trivial. My cherished possessions were merely the remnants of other people's abundance. The steady drip of the water mocked my efforts to make this place into a home.

When Stephen answered, at last, I could only say his name.

"Celia, what's wrong? What's the matter?"

"Where have you been?"

"I stopped to buy groceries on the way home."

I managed to tell him about the ceiling, but I could not have begun to explain what it was that I was feeling, or why. Misery had been lying in wait for me, like a tiger for a lamb, and found me an easy victim. The sense of safety so strong when I left Joyce and Edward's had vanished; I was convinced that I would always be coming home, alone, to find my life in ruins.

"Make a pot of tea. I'll be over in ten minutes," he said. "We can clean up together and then you'll come and stay here."

I made tea and turned on the radio. Then I went into the bedroom and sorted out my clothes until I heard a knock at the door.

Stephen was suitably appalled. Somehow his horrified exclamations cheered me up. "This is terrible." He squeezed the arm of a chair. "The furniture will be fine when it dries out; anyway, most of it is Malcolm's. I'm certain that the landlord is responsible for whatever damage there is. We'll get Edward on the warpath."

While we were rolling up the sodden carpet and organising buckets, he suggested we should buy a house. "It's stupid to have the anxiety of looking after two flats when we're almost always together."

On my knees, spreading newspapers on the damp floorboards, I agreed. If I had blinked, tears would have run down my cheeks.

Next morning when I drew the curtains of Stephen's bedroom window, I discovered that it had snowed during the night. As far as I could see, the rooftops glistened white against the blue sky; only an occasional dark patch showed where the snow had already begun to melt, revealing the slate beneath. We had been feeding the pigeons, and they were nestling in one corner, looking up at me expectantly.

Stephen had told me that it was still too early in the year for there to be many properties on the market, but at work a few days later, glancing through the *Scotsman* while I waited for the kettle to boil, I saw an advertisement for a garden flat. I telephoned the school and managed to catch Stephen between classes. When he heard the description of the flat, he said, "It sounds exactly like what we're looking for. Why don't you try to get us an appointment to see it at lunchtime? I have the first period in the afternoon free."

"You mean today?" In my excitement I had rung him without thinking about what we might do next; I was taken aback by the immediacy of his response.

"Yes, unless you're busy."

"It does say in need of modernisation."

"That's going to be true of almost anything we can afford," said Stephen. "There's no harm in looking."

The solicitor who was advertising the flat seemed to find my haste unseemly, and only after I assured him that weeks might pass before Stephen and I were again available, did he agree to see if a visit could be arranged. He spoke so grudgingly that I was convinced the answer would be no, but when he called back he said, "Miss Gilchrist, Mrs. Menzies is expecting you at twelve forty-five. I should tell you that she is in her eighties. If you have any questions about the property, please refer them to me."

It was a cold, bleak day, and even at noon night seemed imminent. The flat was in a part of the city called Trinity, which bordered the Firth of Forth, but any romantic notions

I had about being by the sea were soon dispelled. A busy road, lined with factories and warehouses, ran alongside the water. When at last we found the address it turned out to be a quiet side street off the Trinity Road. We parked at the top end, opposite the grocer's shop on the corner, and began to walk down, searching for Mrs. Menzies' house.

"On a nice day there'll be a beautiful view from here," Stephen said, gesturing towards the water visible in the distance. Meanwhile under the grey sky, the two-storey stone houses looked dark and gloomy; the front gardens were protected by bedraggled privet hedges, and the windows were hung with lace curtains, which made Stephen mutter about suburbia. Number 54 was in these respects identical to its neighbours, except that a light was on in the front room. We paused at the garden gate.

"I think I've brought us on a wild-goose chase," I said.

"Nonsense, we have to start somewhere. We can't expect the first house we see to be perfect." He led the way through the gate and pressed the doorbell. Such a long interval passed as we stood before the faded green door that we began to wonder if, in spite of the light, there was no one home.

At last the door opened to reveal a tiny elderly woman leaning on a walking stick. Mrs. Menzies smiled up at us. "Come in," she said. "Please go into the living room. First on the left."

We did as instructed and, slowly, she followed. On the table in front of the fire was a tea tray; Stephen and I exchanged glances. Mrs. Menzies lowered herself into an upright chair next to the fire. She hooked her stick over the back of the chair and asked whether we took milk and sugar. "What a frightful day," she said when we had our tea. "I wonder if you'd mind telling me your names again. I didn't quite catch what Angus said on the telephone."

We repeated our names.

"Stephen. My husband's name was Stephen." She nodded,

smiling to herself, and began to tell us how she and Stephen had lived here for nearly fifty years. He had died four years ago, and reluctantly she was planning to move into sheltered housing in Dundee, to be near her son. "It's a bother for him and his wife to keep driving through to visit me, and as you can see, I don't get around much anymore." She looked at us in turn, her eyes bright in her deeply wrinkled face. "And are you married?" she asked.

Stephen shook his head. "Not yet," he said, with a smile.

"How I envy you young people," she sighed. "We had to get married just to be able to walk down the street holding hands. Not that I'd have done things differently; still it would have been nice to have had the choice."

"Do you think we could take a look around?" said Stephen.

"Yes, of course. What am I thinking of."

She led us slowly from room to room. The flat was arranged around the hall into which we had first entered; there was a dining room, a living room, a bathroom, and two bedrooms. The kitchen lay beyond the dining room, and through the back door provided the only access to a large garden. The decor was familiar to me from childhood visits to my great-aunt Marigold. Each room displayed a different kind of patterned wallpaper and contained twice as much furniture as necessary. Every available surface was crowded with objects: pictures, books, ashtrays, souvenirs, knick-knacks. From the kitchen window Mrs. Menzies gestured at the garden. "You can't tell now, but when the spring comes all my flowers will be popping up. Do you like gardening?"

Stephen told her about Edward. "Oh, well then," she said, "you'll be an expert."

When we tried to ask her practical questions, about the neighbours, the upkeep, she brushed them aside. "Ask Angus. He's known me and Stephen for twenty years; if anyone has the answers, he does." It did not seem to occur to her that we might not want to buy the flat. She had interviewed us for the position of successor, and we had proved satisfactory. "I think you'll be very happy here," she said as she showed us to the front door.

Back out in the street, the wind had picked up, and it was even colder than before. As soon as we had closed the garden gate Stephen exclaimed, "Celia, you're wonderful. It's perfect. Absolutely perfect. Don't you think so?"

"Yes," I said. "I mean it's virtually a museum, but all the rooms could be really nice if we fixed them up."

We crossed the street, and as we stood gazing at our new home, we both began to giggle in a fit of childish glee. "We should phone the solicitor right away. I have the feeling that she might accept an offer without trying to drive the price up," Stephen said.

On the way back to my office we enumerated the flat's advantages. Neither of us could keep quiet. I said how much I liked the idea of having both a dining room and a living room. Stephen said that the second bedroom meant Jenny could come and stay. "Until of course we need it for our triplets," he added.

PART III

CHAPTER 8

On the day when we visited the zoo I had known Stephen for a little over three months. As the hours of daylight increased, so too did our love, and, like the alterations of the season, the increments by which it grew were hard to detect. The darkness through which I walked to the bus stop every morning seemed unremitting, and then one day I would notice that a church spire, which I had not seen for several months, was again visible. Almost every day I thought that I could not imagine loving Stephen more, and then, a few days later, looking back at that moment, I would realise that already my feelings were more expansive and more profound.

By the time Stephen and Jenny left me at the house, the street lights were fully on. They drove down the street and turned the corner out of sight, but even after they had disappeared I remained where I was, transfixed by Jenny's stare. The whole afternoon had been marked by her odd behaviour. Although she had been the one to suggest going to the zoo, she had seemed ambivalent about being there. Then there had been the incident in the ladies', when I had thought she might refuse to return my bracelet. But all of this was subject to interpretation. I could have misconstrued her behaviour; she could simply have been out of sorts. There was no question of construction, however, about her parting stare. Even in memory her gaze was sharp as broken glass.

As I pushed open the garden gate, it occurred to me that although I had now been seeing Jenny regularly for several months, I knew as little about her thoughts and feelings as I did about those of the wildcat to which she had that afternoon appeared so strangely drawn.

Inside, the house was cold, and there was a distinct smell of paint. I turned my mind to the more immediate question of what to do about dinner; during the week since we moved, we had exhausted the local restaurants. Suddenly I thought that I could cook. We had made nothing more elaborate than toast and tea so far, but the stove worked and we had groceries for a rudimentary meal. The idea of surprising Stephen appealed to me. I started water to boil. Then I went to light the fire in the living room. Stephen had laid it that morning, and at the first touch of a match the paper flared. I drew the old-fashioned brocade curtains, which Mrs. Menzies had bequeathed to us, and turned on the small lamp in one corner. Although still cold, the room at least looked cozy.

I was in the kitchen stirring the tomato sauce when Stephen returned. He came into the kitchen, still wearing his anorak, carrying a bottle of wine. "You're cooking. This is amazing. What can I do?"

"It's only spaghetti. Maybe you could make a salad. We've got lettuce, tomatoes, and cucumber."

When everything was ready we carried our plates and glasses into the living room. Stephen fetched us blankets to wrap around our shoulders. We sat on cushions on either side of the fire, with our plates on our knees. Tobias had come in from the garden and lay on the sofa, purring audibly.

"Cheers," said Stephen, raising his glass. "To us and our new home."

"To us and our new home," I echoed, clinking my glass to his.

The room grew warmer, and by the time Stephen refilled our glasses we were able to discard the blankets. "I can scarcely believe that I'm going to have to teach on Monday," he said. "Sometimes I feel my life hasn't changed in fifteen years. Here I am, middle-aged, still dreading the start of a new term."

"You're not middle-aged," I protested.

"According to my doctor I am. Last year when I wrenched my knee, he quoted Dante and told me that now I had entered the dark wood I had to be more careful." He twirled up another forkful of spaghetti. "My pupils would certainly agree with him. They see me as ancient, whereas they of course are forever young."

I looked at Stephen. Sitting cross-legged on the floor, his hair falling over his forehead, his face tawny in the golden light, he could have been twenty-five. I drank some wine, holding it in my mouth to appreciate the slight tartness. "Do you think Jenny likes me?" I asked.

"Of course she does," said Stephen immediately. "What on earth would make you think she doesn't?"

I had intended to tell him what happened in the street, but now that the moment had arrived, I did not know how to begin. He often teased me about being insecure, and I could guess what his reaction would be. He would tell me that I had imagined her hostility; when I knocked on the window, she had thought I wanted to wave goodbye. Instead I said, "I felt I behaved badly at the cafeteria. It's none of my business if she wants to eat ten ice creams. I'm not her mother."

"If anyone behaved badly, it was me. On the way home I was thinking how often I let Jenny get away with things just because it's easier. I ought to behave as if I saw her every day, not try to be nice all the time."

"That's hard to do, though," I said, "when in fact you see her once a week." I helped myself to salad and passed him the bowl.

"Yes, of course, that's the excuse, but the last thing I want is to be the sort of absentee father who tries to buy his child's affection and leaves all the real work to the mother. It's so stupid. I worry that Jenny will think of me as another grown-up she can blackmail for presents, and then that's how I behave." He looked at me earnestly, his glasses glinting in the firelight. The bowl of salad sat ignored before him.

"But now we're living here, you'll be able to spend more time with Jenny in ordinary ways," I said. "There's a garden, and she'll be able to come and stay."

He put down his plate. "How could anyone not like you, silly?" he asked, pulling me towards him.

I had taken a week off work to move, and on Monday for the first time I made the journey from our new house to the office. During my absence letters and manuscripts had piled up, and although I stayed at my desk all day, I seemed to make little headway. It was after seven when I arrived home, feeling cold and tired. As I stepped into the hall, the sight of the many boxes still waiting to be unpacked overwhelmed me. For a few seconds I wished that I were returning to Stephen's old flat, where I could sit down in a clean room and discuss my day. Then I thought, but this is our home, and it occurred to me that I had never before in my adult life been able to use that word with any conviction.

Stephen was at the dining room table, a pile of exercise books in front of him. "Surely you don't give them work on the first day," I exclaimed, bending to hug him. "What a taskmaster you are."

"I gave them some problems to do in class to see how much they remember from last term. So far amnesia is widespread."

I went and stood with my back to the gas fire, warming myself. "I've been having rows all day," I announced.

"Who with?"

"Clare mostly. Do you remember the dreaded Brockbank? He refused to accept my editing, so we're ditching him."

"You mean you did all that work for nothing?" said Stephen incredulously. I had been editing the manuscript of

Brockbank's grammar book when Stephen and I first met, and for weeks he had watched me labouring over the stodgy prose.

"It wasn't for nothing," I protested. "Some authors reject seventy-five percent of my suggestions, and at least this way we're getting rid of a bad book and I won't have to work with him for months."

"I still think it's outrageous. He shouldn't have submitted the book for publication if he wasn't prepared to accept your editing. He ought to pay a fine, or something."

"I'll suggest it," I said, smiling at his indignation. "How long is it going to take you to do all those?"

He flipped through the books. "About half an hour. I thought we could go to Standard Tandoori."

"Shouldn't we do something about the house?" A slight scorching smell wafted upwards as the fabric of my trousers grew warm. I shifted away from the fire.

"I think we'll get grumpy if we try to renovate after working all day. We can live in squalor for another few days and then slave like demons this weekend."

"But if we only work at weekends it'll take ages to get everything done." On the bus coming home I had been making lists and trying to decide in what order we should approach various tasks.

"I suppose it will take a little longer, but does that matter? Aren't we going to follow in our predecessors' footsteps and stay here for fifty years?"

"Yes, we are." I walked back to the table and bent over him once more.

"You're so warm," he said, running his hands up and down the backs of my legs.

Brockbank proved to be only the first crisis of the week, and after staying late at the office several nights in a row, on

Friday I felt justified in leaving at the stroke of five. Even so, Stephen was home before me. I arrived to find him stripping the wallpaper in the dining room. He greeted me cheerfully from the top of the ladder. "This machine is great," he said. "The stuff comes off in huge strips. Look." He ran the steamer up and down the wall until the paper bubbled.

I made some tea, and Stephen came down from his ladder. We carried our mugs into the living room. "So how much does it cost to rent the machine?" I asked, as we settled down on the sofa.

"If we return it first thing on Monday, then we get the weekend special. If we keep it longer, the rate changes." His explanation was cut short by the telephone. He went out into the hall to answer it. I knew immediately from his monosyllabic answers that he was talking to Helen. "Yes," "No," he said alternately, and then, "All right. Bye."

He came back and sat down at the far end of the sofa. "That was Helen. Jenny has a cold, and Helen thinks it would be better if she didn't go out tomorrow."

"Is she in bed?" I asked.

"No, but apparently she's been coughing and sneezing for the last few days."

I was sharply disappointed. All week I had been thinking about Jenny's farewell. I vacillated between two impossibilities: on the one hand believing that she loathed me, on the other, believing that through some strange process of the synapses I had invented the whole affair. I needed to see her to find out what had really happened. "Are you sure she couldn't come?" I asked. "She'd only be outside for about sixty seconds as you bundled her to and from the car."

"I thought you'd be glad of the extra time to work on the house," Stephen said. He was frowning in the way he did when one of his pupils made a particularly incomprehensible mistake.

"We can work tonight, and we'd still have all of Sunday. I think it's important for Jenny to see your new home."

"I suppose." He leaned forward to pick up his mug of tea, then seemed to sink more deeply into the cushions.

"Couldn't you call Helen back and ask her?"

"I already agreed."

I looked at him sitting hunkered down over his cup. On a number of occasions Helen had summoned him to baby-sit at a few hours' notice, and Stephen had gone without complaint. "She only asks me if it's an emergency," he had told me apologetically, but what constituted an emergency in Helen's mind, as far as I could tell, was the possible thwarting of her desires. I did not understand why the situation could not be symmetrical. "You could at least suggest it," I said. "The worst that can happen is she'll say no."

"All right." He put the cup on the floor and got slowly to his feet. For a moment he stood gazing out of the window, his hands plucking at the hem of his painting shirt, then he plunged out of the room. I overheard him repeating my arguments in conciliatory tones. After a couple of minutes, he bounded back.

"It was fine," he exclaimed. "She'd been having second thoughts too. I'll fetch Jenny after lunch and take her back at six."

For the rest of the evening Stephen was in the best of humours; he felt that he had achieved a minor victory. By next morning, however, he had become convinced that Helen would change her mind. When the phone rang as we were finishing breakfast, he said, "Oh, God." But it was only the young man who had taken over Malcolm's flat, wanting to know what to do with my mail. After I hung up, I asked Stephen why he was so worried.

He shrugged. "Helen will probably have decided that I bullied her into changing her mind."

"You told me she agreed."

"That's the rational approach," he said, smiling at my innocence.

But the telephone remained silent, and at one o'clock he went off to collect Jenny as planned. When he had gone I fetched the white paint and began to paint the door of our bedroom. So far this was the only room we had decorated; we had stripped the wallpaper and painted the walls and ceiling the week we moved in. Now the room was a beautiful Antwerp blue. The colour was Stephen's choice; left to my own devices I would have taken the easy route of painting everything white, as I had done in London. He had paced up and down the aisles of the paint shop. "The front rooms don't get the morning sun, so we ought to paint them in warmer colours," he had said judiciously. "And we should paint our bedroom to match your eyes." I had watched with pleasure while out of a whole wall of finely gradated blues—cobalt, ultramarine, cerulean, indigo—he had chosen the perfect shade.

I was finishing the lintel when Stephen and Jenny returned. Paintbrush in hand, I greeted them. "Hello," I said to Jenny. "I hear you have a cold. "

She smiled at me. "Not really. I just sneeze a lot." She was wearing an enormous green sweater, leg warmers, and a scarf. Inside the bulky clothes she looked especially small and pale. I knew as soon as I set eyes on her that I had been wrong; in the ambiguous twilight I had misunderstood her gaze. Tobias appeared, and she bent down to pat him. He rubbed back and forth against her legs and then retreated to his place in front of the living room fire.

Stephen hung their coats in the hall cupboard, and I followed them into the dining room. Jenny surveyed the bare walls. "It was nicer before," she said. She had been to see the house shortly after Mrs. Menzies moved out and had especially admired the dining-room wallpaper, which depicted galleons in full sail against a sunset. Our stripping had reduced the glowing fleet to a few solitary vessels.

"That's true," said Stephen, "but it has to get worse before it gets better. We're going to paint it grey and pink."

"Pink." She gave a mock shudder.

"Dusty rose," I suggested. She still looked disapproving. Stephen ushered her into our blue bedroom, over which we had laboured so hard. I followed. She walked to the window, breathed on the glass, and began to trace something with her finger.

"Do you remember?" Stephen asked. "There was a dirty brown wallpaper covered with flowers."

"Yes, I remember. Now it's the same colour as Mummy's room." She wiped the glass clear and turned to face us.

"I thought Helen's bedroom was wallpapered."

"No. It's like this. Blue is her favourite colour." Like a chilly draught, her words blew through the room.

"Well," I said, "you should tell us what your favourite colour is so that we can use it for the spare room. Come and take a look." I wanted to indicate that Helen was not a delicate subject. I led the way to the spare bedroom.

"This will be your room when you come to stay," said Stephen.

"Oh," said Jenny. She glanced around, and I followed her gaze. The floorboards were rough and dirty, for furniture there was a single bed, a small desk, and a chair, the window was bare and the light unshaded.

"It won't look like this," I said.

"We thought of painting it yellow," said Stephen.

"Like my room at Granny and Grandpa's?"

"Maybe a little more primrosy. What do you think?"

"Okay." She folded her arms. "I don't suppose I'll be here much."

"It will be nice, you'll see," said Stephen. "Come on, let's go into the living room, where it's warm."

I went back to my painting. Although the living room door was closed I could hear everything that passed between Stephen and Jenny. After they had drawn a map for her history project and done a jigsaw puzzle of Edinburgh Castle, Jenny announced that she wanted to dress up. "But you don't have any clothes here," said Stephen.

"Doesn't Celia have some?"

"Of course she does, but not dress-up clothes like you have at home. How about helping me make flapjacks for tea?"

"I don't feel like it."

"Why don't you stay here and read then."

"I'm tired of reading," said Jenny in a small voice. "I'm bored."

"Jenny," I called, "if you want to play with my clothes, it's fine with me."

There was a brief silence, as if my interruption had startled them. Then Stephen repeated my remark to Jenny, and she said, yes, she would like to play with my clothes. They came out into the hall. Stephen gave me a grateful look. My hands were covered in white paint, so I explained to him which dresses he should show to Jenny. "Careful of the paint," I said.

Jenny walked through the doorway on tiptoe, keeping her elbows pressed tightly to her sides. Stephen followed. Soon he emerged and announced that he was going to make the flapjacks.

From time to time I glanced in on Jenny. Stephen had lifted down a number of dresses for her, and she was examining them with a calculating expression, almost as if she were trying to guess the price. I went off to find a screwdriver to remove the door handle. When I returned I saw that she was wearing the black silk dress which Stephen had bought for me in an antique shop in the Grassmarket. It was not among those which I had authorised him to give to her; she must have seen it in the wardrobe and taken a liking to it. I wanted to say, "No, not that one," but it seemed curmudgeonly, especially as the dress was a present from her father.

Jenny had pulled a chair over to the chest of drawers and she was kneeling on it, looking in the mirror. She pushed her face close to the glass and squinted critically at her reflection. Her gestures were those of a grown woman, and I suddenly noticed how much she resembled her mother.

I had seen Helen only once. Shortly before we moved, we had gone to a film at the Assembly Rooms, and as we were leaving, Stephen had pointed her out to me on the far side of the foyer. Even from that brief glimpse I could tell that Helen was everything I was not—slim, elegantly dressed, beautiful—and she had a job that sounded both high-powered and enviable, working in the international department of the Bank of Scotland. More than all this, there was the incontrovertible fact that Stephen had married her and had a child, and indeed was still married to her. On the way home, I had asked him again why they were not divorced.

"Helen is adamant that she doesn't want to," he said. "According to Edward I could force her, but it would be a long battle, and meanwhile God knows what would become of Jenny. At least the present situation is fairly stable."

"But why?" I repeated. "I mean you've been separated for years."

"I really don't know. Maybe she's punishing me for leaving. She won't even discuss it."

"When did you last ask her?"

"A couple of years ago. No, maybe three."

"So she might have changed her mind?"

"I doubt it," Stephen said sullenly.

We stopped at a zebra crossing, and Stephen turned to me. "I love you, Celia," he said. "Even though we're not married yet, I feel more married to you than I ever did to Helen."

Jenny had found my lipstick. I watched with fascination as she stretched her lips tight and drew in the outline of her small mouth. Then I saw that she in turn was watching me in the mirror. Hastily I stepped back to continue my painting. A few minutes later there was the clip-clop of high heels on the bare wooden floorboards. I looked up and saw Jenny walking unsteadily towards the door.

"You look very nice," I said. "Be careful of the paint."

"I'm just going to show Dad."

I stepped aside, leaving plenty of room for her to pass through the doorway. She did not look up; she was holding the skirt with both hands, concentrating on keeping her feet safely set in my shoes. As she crossed the threshold, she stumbled, slipped, and fell. The whole of her left side grazed the freshly painted white door. For a brief interval she simply looked at me, her lips pressed together in a thin red line, then she burst out crying. I put down the paint and moved to comfort her, but before I could make more than a hesitant gesture, Stephen appeared.

"Jenny, what is it? Did you hurt yourself?"

She did not answer. She let out high-pitched, gulping sobs. He kept asking if she was all right, and I stood there with my paintbrush in my hand.

As she grew calmer, Stephen asked where the mineral spirits were. I went to fetch the bottle from the kitchen. When I came back they were in the bathroom. Jenny had stopped crying and was sitting on the edge of the bath; Stephen knelt beside her. My dress lay on the floor. I handed him the bottle. "Did you bring a rag?" he asked.

"Use a towel," I said, passing him mine.

Stephen began to scrub Jenny's left arm, where there was a long graze of paint; my dress had protected her T-shirt and jeans. "Don't worry, Jenny," he said. "We'll have this off in no time. At least you didn't get it on your clothes." I heard the relief in his voice. Once when Jenny had spilled a milkshake over herself in a restaurant, Stephen had insisted on going straight home to wash her clothes. "This is the sort of thing that drives Helen into a frenzy," he had explained.

I touched up the door, then carried the painting things out to the shed in the garden. As I hammered down the lid of the paint tin I recalled an incident with Lewis. We were in my flat, and from the bathroom I had overheard him talking on the phone. "So Tuesday is fine?" he was saying. When I entered the living room, he hung up almost immediately. "I was calling Brian," he said, "to arrange a game of squash." A few days later, I asked how the game had gone; he replied that he had lost.

The following weekend we ran into Brian at the National Film Theatre. "I hear you won as usual," I said cheerfully. "Won?" echoed Brian. "Not as usual," Lewis exclaimed. "My game is improving by leaps and bounds. Are you going to the film?" Brian shook his head. "No. I stopped in for a snack." He started to say something else, then stopped, cleared his throat, and said he must be going. In the queue for tickets I caught Lewis giving me a quick, sly glance, as if waiting for something, but I raised no questions; I was still anxious to turn a blind eye.

What brought this scene to mind was that moment between her fall and her tears, when Jenny had looked at me, almost as if she were checking on my reaction before she decided what to do next. It occurred to me that her fall had not been an accident. Then I took myself to task: I was being absurd. The week before, I had knocked over a tin of paint in the middle of the dining room floor, and an appreciable length of time had passed while I did nothing but watch with appalled fascination as the liquid spread.

A thrush landed on the lawn in front of the shed and began to peck vigorously at the grass. As I moved to put the tin of paint on the shelf, it darted away.

CHAPTER 9

When I opened my eyes and saw the flowery wallpaper, only a few feet away, I had for a moment no idea where I was. Then I remembered that the night before we had moved our bed into the spare room. I rolled over. Stephen was watching me. "Is it late?" I asked.

"No, there's plenty of time. I woke up early."

I nodded drowsily. Still immersed in the dream I had been having, I got out of bed and went to the bathroom. I had an image of Stephen and me carrying a table, and then I was in my office searching the bookshelves, but I did not know what had been happening in either scene, or how the two were connected. When I returned to the spare room, Stephen was sitting up in bed, a cup of coffee in one hand, the novel he was currently reading in the other. I settled down beside him, and he handed me my coffee. "What are we doing with Jenny today?" I asked.

"I thought we could work around the house. She could help us lay the carpet and whatever else we decide to do. She's going to bring old clothes so we won't have a repetition of last week." He smiled at me. The dry cleaners had rejected my dress as beyond repair, and Stephen had promised to buy me another, even more ravishing.

"And in the afternoon we can do something fun," I said.

"We can do something fun now," said Stephen, putting down his coffee cup.

*   *   *

106

After we dressed, there was just enough time to carry the few remaining pieces of furniture out of the bedroom and carry in the roll of carpet before Stephen had to leave. "Promise not to do too much," he said. "Jenny and I will be back soon, and we can all do it together."

"I promise. I'll try to get the measuring done. That's really a job for one person."

He gave me a hasty kiss and hurried away.

I fetched the radio from the dining room and tuned it to the station that I had listened to as a teenager. I was amazed to discover the same disc jockey still compering the show. I found myself laughing at his feeble jokes, and when he played a song I knew, I joined in. I unrolled a couple of yards of the carpet and began to tack down the edge along the straight wall beneath the window. The carpet was a sandy beige colour, "Ideal if you have a family," the salesman had said with a wink.

I had one edge down and was at work on the second when I realised that Stephen and Jenny were late. Helen's flat was a twenty-minute drive away, and Stephen had left over an hour ago. Perhaps Jenny had needed to go to the library, I thought, or perhaps Helen had wanted to discuss something with him. I continued to hammer in tacks at regular intervals.

The carpet had been treated with chemicals to increase its resistance to fire and dirt, and bending over it, I became conscious of the strange fumes I was inhaling. When I stood up, I felt slightly dizzy. I opened the window and went to the kitchen to make a cup of tea. While I waited for the kettle to boil, there came into my mind fully formed, as if it had been lurking there all along, the image of Stephen with his arms around Helen.

It was true that he made only negative comments about her, but at the height of my complaints about Lewis, I had wanted nothing more than to be with him. I tried to recall how I had described that relationship to Stephen: something vague to the effect that we had not been getting on well for some time before my moving to Edinburgh ended matters. I knew I had not said that Lewis was like a virus in my blood and that only a few days before I met Stephen I had still entertained passionate hopes about him. And if this had been the case for me, how much more likely for Stephen in the face of Helen's beauty. Whatever he might say to the contrary, I had learned from my mother that beauty was a kind of power.

As far back as I could remember I had known that my mother was beautiful, but only gradually had I realised that my features, a mixture of hers and my father's, added up to something different. The first intimations I had of the disparity between us came when I was nine or ten. She had left me in the library while she went to get her hair done. When she returned I was engrossed in a children's version of the story of Theseus. One of the librarians, a plump, cushiony woman, who had interrupted me twice to ask if I was enjoying my book, looked up as my mother joined me. "She's been good as gold," she said.

My mother thanked the woman for keeping an eye on me. "It was no trouble at all," the woman replied. Then, lowering her voice to tones of conspiracy, she added, "I would never have guessed she was your daughter."

"She takes after my husband." My mother grasped my hand and drew me to my feet.

"Oh, well then," said the woman. "Still she seems a bright little thing."

Later I was finishing the story of Theseus at the kitchen table, when my mother told my father what the librarian had said. He laughed and patted my head. "Our poor ugly duckling. You'll be a swan some day, you'll see."

The kettle rumbled to the boil. I made a mug of tea and returned to work. Whatever I did, I could not make the carpet fit. There were alcoves on either side of the fireplace, which had to be specially measured, and in addition the room was slightly asymmetrical. I kept tugging and cutting and tacking, only to find, as soon as I got the carpet fitted snugly in one area, that it was creased or too far from the wall in another. I took measurements and the second I laid down the tape forgot the figures.

At school when exam results were imminent I would tell myself that I was undoubtedly twentieth out of the twenty-two girls in my class. When I came second or third, the news seemed as much a reward for my deception as for my hard work. If I stopped waiting, I thought, then Stephen would return. I began to plan the rest of my day as if he did not exist—I would go to the pub for lunch, then visit Suzie—but no car stopped outside the house, the telephone remained mute.

He had been gone now for well over two hours. All the reasonable explanations I could imagine foundered on the fact of the telephone. He must be either hurt or making love, else he would phone, I thought. But if he was hurt, someone else would phone. I reminded myself that if Stephen was with Helen, Jenny was there too, but although I knew that her presence would be an insuperable obstacle to his and my making love, I could not convince myself that she would serve as the same kind of deterrent to her parents. Then I thought of the other occasion when Stephen had disappeared, the evening I had come home to find the ceiling of Malcolm's flat leaking, and how it had turned out that he was buying groceries. There was probably some perfectly good reason for his delay.

I went out into the hall. There sat the telephone, black and obstinate as a toad. I lifted the receiver and listened to the tone, but I could not bring myself to dial Helen's number. On the few occasions when I had answered her calls, she had brusquely demanded Stephen. If he was out, she said, "Tell him to call," and hung up.

At last the phone did ring. I was back hammering down tacks, and I was so startled that for a few seconds I remained on my knees. Then I leapt up. The carpet was across the door, and I had to tug it aside before I could get it open.

"Celia," said a woman's voice.

Such was my state that I did not recognise Joyce until she identified herself. She had to make an unexpected trip into the city and wondered if she could come to tea. I told her that we would be glad to see her.

"Are you all right?" she asked. "You sound out of breath, or something."

I blamed the carpet.

"Stephen ought to help you with the heavy jobs," Joyce scolded. "You shouldn't be struggling alone."

After I put down the receiver, I felt somewhat better. Stephen could not simply disappear; we were living together, and his parents regarded me as part of the family. History does not have to repeat itself. What had happened between me and Lewis was quite different from what was happening now. Stephen was different.

For a brief interval I was reassured, but when one is waiting, time breaks down into an infinite number of discrete moments, and I was reassured for only a finite number. As I went to search for another box of carpet tacks I thought, but what does Joyce know? My own mother was almost always the last to learn of any important development in my life. Stephen might be different from Lewis, but I was still the same.

As I grew older I had become increasingly aware of the implications of the librarian's remark, and at the age of fifteen the school Christmas dance had clarified her meaning beyond doubt. The dance was a major event because the boys from our companion school would be present. For the entire autumn term we practised waltzes and fox-trots during our gym lessons. There were no boys at these lessons, and I could not help noticing that week after week the gym mistress would say, "Celia, you be a boy for today." One Saturday late in November I bicycled over to visit Aunt Ruth, and when she asked about the dance, I voiced the fear that no one would dance with me. Somehow because she was stout, red-faced, and untidy, it was all right to tell her about anxieties I would never have dreamed of mentioning to my mother.

"Nonsense, Celia," she said. "When I was your age, boys literally ran away from me. I was fat, spotty, and wore big, ugly glasses. You're not a raving beauty, but you've no reason to be afraid of the mirror. You're very pleasant-looking." As Ruth spoke, she outlined previous fatness, the magnitude of her glasses; I could believe that boys had indeed fled from her, but that in no way eased my own difficulties. She must have sensed my scepticism, and out of the goodness of her heart she offered to make me a dress. "You'll be the belle of the ball," she promised. "Just wait and see."

Throughout the next few weeks there were frequent consultations and fittings, and then, the Friday before the dance, I brought the dress home, carefully folded in a brown paper bag. My mother was sitting at the kitchen table, peeling Brussels sprouts and listening to carols on the radio. "Away in a Manger" was starting as I came through the back door.

"So let's see the masterpiece," she said.

I pulled the dress out of the bag and held it by the shoulders. My mother raised her hand to cover her mouth. Her eyebrows arched upwards.

"Do you like it?" I asked.

She laid aside her knife and came over. "Did you choose this material?" she asked, fingering the thin fabric printed with enormous green and pink flowers.

I nodded. "It's very fashionable. Look, I'll show you in my magazine."

"No, I believe you. Well, let's see it on."

My room was chilly, and I did not linger to look in the

mirror, but the brief glimpse I caught of my reflection was not encouraging. I hurried back downstairs, where my mother was singing "Once in Royal David's City." I asked her to do up the zip. Her hands, damp from washing vegetables, grazed my skin, as the zip snagged a few times and then slid safely to the top. Still singing, she turned me around, examining the dress from every angle. The carol ended, and she walked over to the window sill and switched off the radio.

"Celia," she said, "you're not really planning to wear this tomorrow, are you?"

"Of course I am. Ruth made it specially. You don't like it because it's trendy."

"No, that's not true. Come upstairs and look in my mirror."

In my parents' bedroom my mother drew the curtains and turned on the electric fire. Then she came and stood beside me in front of the wardrobe with its mirrored doors. Although Ruth was always making garments for herself and her daughter, practice had not honed her skill. As my mother pointed out, nothing about the dress was quite right: the bosom had an angular quality, the sleeves fitted awkwardly, the waist was too high and tight, and the hem of the short skirt rose and fell around my thighs. Somehow in Ruth's company these defects had been less apparent. In the mirror I could see my mother's reflection, next to mine. She was wearing a heavy white sweater and dark trousers; she had recently had her hair cut short, and in her ears were bright red earrings, the size of half crowns.

She even made me go and put on the dress which she had given me for my birthday. When I returned she said, "You look very nice. I know this dress isn't so trendy, but it's very becoming."

In Ruth's dress I had scarcely recognised myself, but here was my familiar reflection, and that was the problem: the blue dress, however attractive, left me unchanged, whereas

Ruth's transformed me. I did not have the words to explain this to my mother, but I was stubborn in my insistence that I would wear the new dress. She shrugged and said it was up to me.

The dance was held in the school gym, a room without mercy, bare and brightly lit. Non-dancing girls sat along the walls. As I sat watching, trying to resist the temptation to tug at the front of my dress, even the most graceless of my contemporaries seemed to skim by in the arms of their partners. I realised what I had known for years: that my mother was beautiful and that I was not. Neither fact in isolation would have affected me so deeply as the two together. Oddly, I did not blame the dress; rather I concluded that no dress had the power to save me. Punishing myself was infinitely preferable to admitting that my mother was right; she already had everything: beauty, power, my father's love.

I was trimming yet another half inch off the carpet, when the Stanley knife slipped in my grasp. The blade sank into my finger. Dark red blood rose slowly through the layers of skin, then flowed swift and bright. As the blood ran down my finger and across my palm, I began to cry, not so much from pain but from despair. I had turned off the radio hours before, and in the empty house my sobs were the only sound. After a few minutes I pulled myself together and went to the bathroom. As I held my finger under the cold tap, the pain lost its first sharpness and settled to a dull ache. I wound a bandage tightly round my finger.

Almost four hours after Stephen had helped me to unroll the carpet and kissed me goodbye, I heard a key in the lock. I began to hammer in tacks, in a parody of frenzied activity.

"Celia, I'm home." He came through the door.

I hit a tack so hard that it sank without trace into the carpet. Then missed a second.

"Celia," he said again.

I sat back on my heels and looked at him where he stood on the threshold, his hands hanging awkwardly by his sides. "Where's Jenny?"

"She still has a cold; she's in bed."

He was about to say more but I interrupted. All my terrors, which I had been secretly prepared to dismiss in an instant, crowded back, clamouring like hounds as the scent of their quarry grew stronger. "So where have you been?"

"I was at their flat, tidying up."

"You mean you've been at Helen's all this time?"

He nodded. "You can't imagine what it was like. I've been cleaning up for two solid hours, and the place is still a shambles."

"I don't understand. I don't understand why you didn't phone me. Stephen, I thought something terrible had happened. I couldn't imagine a situation in which you wouldn't phone that wasn't terrible." I was still kneeling in the far corner with the hammer in my hand. Looking at Stephen as he stood in the middle of the room, beneath the bare light bulb, I was certain that he was lying.

"I'm sorry," he said. "I didn't know that you would worry. I thought you would assume that everything was taking a bit longer than expected."

"You said you'd be back soon." I bent over and hammered in another tack.

"Celia, stop. Let me explain. Get off the floor and come and sit with me in the dining room." He came over and held out his hand; I ignored his gesture but nonetheless got awkwardly to my feet. He looked at me, then seemed to decide against further speech and led the way into the dining room. I sat down at the table, while he turned on the gas fire and went into the kitchen. He returned carrying a glass of water, sat down opposite me, and immediately drained the glass.

"I'm sorry I didn't phone," he said. "Once you hear what happened you'll understand. Helen answered the door in her dressing gown. It was obvious she was feeling terrible; she could hardly speak. She told me Jenny was ill too and asked if I could pick up some groceries. It's the sort of thing she does that makes me furious, but I couldn't say no; there's no one else she can ask. I went to the shops and bought basic supplies and some comics for Jenny.

"I was going to put the groceries away and leave, but when I saw the state of the kitchen, it was impossible. There were dirty dishes everywhere—on the floor, the stove, even in the oven. The place smelled like a dump. I started washing up, and that's what I've been doing for the last two hours."

"Why didn't Helen call you this morning and tell you that Jenny was ill?" I was sitting very straight, holding on to the edge of the table with both hands. More than anything I wanted Stephen to acquit himself, but I was determined not to be fobbed off with false evidence.

"Because she needed me and was too proud to admit it. Celia, don't be angry."

"But why didn't you phone? What did you think I'd think, waiting and waiting?"

Stephen shook his head in a gesture of helplessness. "I couldn't."

I waited to see what else he would say, and when he said nothing, I asked again.

"Helen would have thrown me out." He spread his hands, as if offering me a self-evident truth. "I couldn't bear the thought of leaving Jenny in that squalor. I'd have felt that I was abandoning her."

"So it's more important to you not to upset Helen than not to upset me."

"That's not what I said. If it was only Helen, it would be an entirely different kettle of fish. I'm sorry. I should have called, but I had no idea you'd worry."

"You could have made an excuse, said you needed to buy something, and slipped out to call me."

"I'm sorry," he repeated. "The whole experience was upsetting. They both looked so wretched." He stared at the empty glass between his hands.

I stood up and came round the table to embrace him. "Don't you understand?" I said. "I thought that you were making love to her."

"Celia." He held me away from him so that he could look into my eyes. "I love you. When I see Helen, I can scarcely believe that we were once involved. It's like night and day, her and you."

The idea that this might be what lay behind my anger had not even occurred to him, and that was more reassuring than anything he said. Presently I asked why he thought that Helen would throw him out if he telephoned me.

"I suppose she's jealous." He clasped his hands more tightly around my waist. "What she says is that she doesn't want to know anything about my other relationships, ever."

Stephen rose to his feet and together we moved towards the spare room. As we lay side by side, I felt the image of Helen begin to fade. She had been dwelling like a ghost in some corner of the house, and now, banished by our love, she was stealing away, as spirits are meant to do at cockcrow.

By the time Joyce arrived we had the carpet in place and had almost finished tacking it down; she was lavish in her praise. "This looks really professional," she said. "And the colour is perfect." Over tea Stephen described what had happened at Helen's. Joyce could scarcely contain herself. She wanted to go to their flat immediately, and only Stephen's firmness persuaded her that Helen might regard this as an intrusion. "They're fine for now," he said. "It would be better to telephone when you get home and see if they need help tomorrow, or on Monday."

CHAPTER 10

At work the controversy over Mr. Brockbank's manuscript continued; almost every day Clare received a letter or telephone call from him. She was convinced that we were morally obligated to publish the manuscript, while Bill and I maintained that to do so would only injure both his and our reputations. The situation was further complicated by the fact that we had already published half a dozen books by Brockbank, several of which were coming up for new editions. On Friday afternoon I was looking through a list of permissions when Suzie came into my office. "If I were you," she said, "I'd go and lock myself in the toilet."

"Why?"

"I just saw Brockbank in reception. I bet you'll be receiving a summons any moment."

"Oh, no. What is he like?"

"He's what you'd expect from his books: an old-fashioned schoolteacher. It won't be so bad. You told me that Bill was on your side." She leaned over and patted my shoulder.

"I know, but I'm not used to criticising people face to face. I do it in the margins. If there's a confrontation, I may behave like an idiot and start telling him how good his manuscript is."

"Don't you dare," said Suzie. "Getting rid of that old fart was a stroke of genius." Even as she spoke the telephone on my desk began to ring.

My first thought as I stepped into Bill's office was that

Suzie's description did not do Mr. Brockbank justice. He was an extremely large man, not in the least like the puny school-teachers I too often encountered. He dwarfed the easy chair in which he sat, and it was easy to imagine him terrifying generations of small boys. Bill introduced us, and he gave a kind of abbreviated bow. I sat down in the chair near the door.

Bill launched into a speech about recent trends in secondary education. "In teaching grammar nowadays, there are a whole new set of factors to be taken into account," he said. "For a significant percentage of children English is a second language. Your book is eminently suitable for public schools like Fettes and George Watsons, but we have to aim for a much larger market."

There was a pause. Bill looked at Mr. Brockbank enquiringly. I studied the pad of paper I had brought, as if about to take notes. Finally Mr. Brockbank said, "It's well known that Fettes and George Watsons are the jewels in the crown of Scottish education, yet here you are trying to tell me that a book which is good enough for them is not fit for publication. I will have to consider whether I can continue to be associated with a company that puts mammon above learning."

He glared at us both and, without a word of farewell, rose slowly to his feet and left the room.

Bill grinned at me. "Thank goodness that's over," he said. "We deserve a drink."

I was thinking about this encounter on my way home when I ran into Mr. Patterson coming out of the corner shop. He lived two doors down from Stephen and me and was the friendliest of our immediate neighbours. The day we moved in, he had appeared at the door with a tin of homemade shortbread. Now we exchanged greetings, and I asked if he needed a hand with his groceries.

"I may be an old man, but I'm not so far gone that I'm

going to let a woman fetch and carry for me." He drew himself upright and swung his shopping bags, to demonstrate how light they were. As we started down the street, I matched my pace to his.

"Have you had any word of Mrs. Menzies?" he asked.

"No, it's my fault. I said I would write, and I haven't."

There was a pause, filled by the rustlings of Mr. Patterson's bags. "I've never been much of a correspondent either," he said. "It's a shame, though. She was a keen gardener in her younger days."

Mr. Patterson's own garden was immaculate; even Edward had praised it. His privet hedge was so symmetrical that it looked as if he had measured each individual snip of the sheers. As we paused at his gate, I glanced along the road to where the thin, disorderly strands of our hedge reached out to snag unwary passers-by. "I'm afraid we've been neglecting the garden," I said. "There's so much to do in the house."

"I noticed you were going for the uncultivated look," Mr. Patterson remarked with a sly grin. He tipped his cap to me and opened the gate.

His comment was more than justified. Except for picking daffodils or occasionally uprooting a weed on our way to the washing line, neither Stephen nor I had touched the garden; both the lawn and the flower beds surrounding it were lushly overgrown. Next morning when Stephen left to fetch Jenny, I decided to cut the grass.

Our only gardening equipment came from Mrs. Menzies, who had left us the contents of the garden shed. Edward had called her implements museum pieces, and as I sorted through them I understood why. There was an old-fashioned sieve, a wooden wheelbarrow of the kind seen in photographs of village life at the turn of the century, a pair of long-handled shears, a rake, and several forks and spades. The mower was right at the back, behind our paint supplies and everything else; it took several minutes to manoeuvre it out of the shed.

I unravelled the skeins of dead grass twined around the wheels and began to push the ancient machine around the lawn.

The grass was thick with dandelions and daisies, and I soon took off my pullover and hung it over the washing line. The mower, dark green, wooden handled, with a sort of bonnet attachment to catch the fresh-cut grass, was exactly like the one my parents had owned when I was a child, and as I trudged round and round, I had a sudden image of my father. It was from him that I had acquired the habit of mowing in circles rather than strips. "I hate to keep retracing my steps," he had said, when Uncle James enquired about this method. "At least this way I feel that I'm getting somewhere, zeroing in on something."

On the day I was remembering, I had come home late after school and found my father cutting the grass. The lawn was in shadow, and he was wearing a white shirt hanging open over a pair of khaki-coloured shorts; his long bare feet were covered with bits of grass. He had been away in London, and now he was back. "Come and help me rake the grass," he said.

Under my father's directions, we divided the lawn into quarters and began to rake the grass into four heaps. As we worked, he questioned me about school; he was always particularly concerned to hear what I was studying in maths and science. When we had finished raking, he held the sack open and I scooped the grass in, two-handed. "You're dropping most of it," he kept saying, which was true, but I could tell that he was not annoyed. We were working on the fourth pile when my mother appeared. "What a good job the two of you have done," she said. "I was wondering if there might be enough strawberries for dinner."

While my mother and my father held aloft the green plastic net, I crawled over the strawberry bed, retrieving the ripe fruit. They took turns drawing my attention to possible berries, but I was the final arbiter. "No, it's only ripe on one side," I would say, and rotate the berry in order to present the hard, greenish underbelly to the sun.

I emptied the bonnet and continued to circle the lawn. That summer evening I must have been roughly the same age as Jenny, which meant that my father had been only a few years older than Stephen. Maybe that was why, although his feet were vivid, I could not visualise his face; to the little girl who was there he was indefinably old, whereas to my present self he would have been a young man.

When I had finished going round the lawn once, I fetched a wrench, adjusted the mower blade to the lowest setting, and began to go round again. I was so engrossed that I did not notice Stephen until he was almost beside me. "Hi," he said.

I stopped in my tracks. Looking over his shoulder, I saw Jenny peering into the shed.

"I thought this was an antique. I didn't know you could actually use it." He bent down to examine the mower.

I found a Kleenex in my pocket, and blew my nose. "You can after a fashion."

"Woo-woo-woo." Jenny was patting her hand against her mouth. She ran across the lawn towards me, and before I knew what was happening she had flung herself against my knees. Perhaps she merely meant to take me captive, but in my surprise I fell with a thud onto the freshly cut grass. Jenny stood over me; one foot dug sharply into my side. She stared down, with a slight grimace on her face, as if she found me ridiculous. Pointing her finger at me, she shouted, "Bang, bang. You're dead."

I lay there, the grass pricking my cheek. I suppose it was a phrase that any child might use, that I had probably used myself, but something about the way in which Jenny said the words made it impossible to ignore their literal meaning.

"Here comes the cavalry," yelled Stephen. "It's a surprise attack."

Jenny made a run for cover. From the shelter of the shed, she exchanged gunfire with Stephen for a couple of minutes. He staggered and fell. She ran over and placed a foot on her father's back. When she saw me looking, she tossed back her hair and chanted, "I won, I won."

Then Stephen sprang up with a yell and grabbed her and tossed her into the air. She let out squeals of genuine, delighted terror.

The three of us set to work. Stephen took over the mower and I began to clip the edges with the shears. "What can I do?" asked Jenny.

"You could do some weeding," I said. "The flower beds are terribly overgrown."

"Okay." She walked to the far end of the herbaceous border that ran along one side of the garden and began to pull out clumps of groundsel and chickweed. When I had clipped the edges as best I could, I went to help her. There was already a substantial pile of weeds lying on the grass. "Don't pull that one," she told me. "It's a flower. Grandpa grows them."

We worked in silence for a few minutes. I uprooted a dandelion and brought up several small bulbs in its wake. "Are you feeling better?" I asked.

"Yes. I wasn't really ill, not like Mummy. She's been going to bed at the same time as me all week."

"What about this one?" I pointed to a tall, feathery cluster of leaves.

"I don't know."

"I'd better leave it just in case. You seem to know a lot about plants. Do you and Helen have a garden?"

Jenny shook her head.

"Then you must come and help often." I tugged at some groundsel.

"I don't specially like weeding." She stood and walked away to where Stephen was bending over the lawnmower.

*   *   *

After lunch, I retired to the bedroom to work on my current project: a new edition of *Sunset Song*. Stephen was putting up shelves in the kitchen, and at intervals throughout the afternoon when I emerged to make a cup of tea or to see how he was getting on, I found Jenny fidgeting around. Stephen had said she could help him, but that consisted mostly of holding screws and screwdrivers until he needed them. It was hard to ignore the fact that our adult activities were boring to her. When Stephen said that it was time to go home, she ran to get her jacket.

I continued to work for half an hour and then set out for Standard Tandoori, where Stephen and I had arranged to meet. It was still warm, and I walked with my jacket open, enjoying the sense that summer was approaching. My mind was busy with thoughts of Jenny. From her point of view the day had not been a success. She was used to doing special things with Stephen and to being the focus of his attention. It was too much to expect her to suddenly adjust to such humdrum activities as weeding and carpentry.

The restaurant was almost empty. As the door closed behind me, the owner, Chandor, looked up and waved. During the last few weeks we had eaten frequently at Standard Tandoori and had become friends with Chandor and his family. He finished pouring water for a couple of elderly Indian men and came over to shake my hand. "Hello, stranger. Now you have your own kitchen, you desert us."

"No, we've just been so busy. When we don't come here, we starve."

"Tonight we'll make up for your absence. I promise a feast. Are you alone?"

"Stephen will be here in a minute."

"Good. I will alert the kitchen." He led me to a table by the window.

Chandor's family was camped out at the large table near the back of the room, and I had barely sat down when his youngest son, Banu, came over. "Will you look at my homework?" he asked shyly. He held out a blue notebook. While I read his account of shopping with his father, his large eyes remained fixed upon me.

"On Saturday," he had written, "I go with my father to my cousin, Rasiks. Petunia is asleep among the vegetables. We buy carrots, onions, potatoes, peas, and tomatoes. They go in the boot of the car. She tries to come too."

I thought of Mr. Brockbank and wondered what he would make of Banu's tales of family life. As I began to explain about apostrophes, I heard the sound of the door opening. Stephen came in. I waved, and he nodded and made his way across the room. "Hello, Banu," he said. He sat down on the opposite side of the table. "Have you ordered?"

"No, I've been too busy. Let me finish explaining this." While Banu stood at my elbow, listening intently, Stephen studied the menu as if he had never seen it before. In a minute Chandor came and dispatched Banu back to the family table. "He wants to be prime minister," he said. "Although I tell him in England that's a job for women."

"Can we order?" Stephen asked. Normally he would have responded to Chandor's joke, asked to see Banu's homework, leaned across the table, and squeezed my hand. When Chandor had taken our order and brought lager and papadums, I asked what was wrong.

Stephen broke a papadum onto the white tablecloth. He looked down, fingering the larger pieces so that they broke into smaller ones. "Jenny and I were arguing on the way home," he said, "and she accused me of hating Helen."

"What were you arguing about?"

"It wasn't important. She wanted to invite Anna to come over next Saturday, and I told her we were hoping to go to Abernethy." His tone was brusque, as if I had deliberately misunderstood him, and still he did not raise his head.

"You did get quite absorbed in your shelves," I said, trying to tease him out of his gloom. "We can't expect the house to be as interesting to her as it is to us."

He put out his hand to silence me. "Did you say something to Jenny?" he asked, looking up into my eyes.

"What do you mean?"

"I asked Jenny why she thought I hated Helen, and she said you had told her."

"Stephen, I would never do that. I don't think I even mentioned Helen today. No, maybe I did when I asked if they had a garden. I do try to make occasional comments about her because I don't want Jenny to feel that her mother is a forbidden topic, but I would never dream of saying anything about you and Helen." I waited for Stephen to nod understandingly or reach out with a smile to take my hand. "You can't believe that I'd tell your daughter that you hated her mother."

"I know you wouldn't use those words, but you might have said something negative about Helen without thinking." On his face was an expression I had never seen before, a mixture of embarrassment and determination.

"I definitely didn't."

He raised his glass to his lips. He swallowed some lager, lowered the glass, wiped his lips. A long time seemed to pass. At last he spoke. "I'm not accusing you, Celia. You probably made some remark that Jenny misconstrued. Sometimes she seems so intelligent that it's easy to forget she's only nine."

Chandor appeared, carrying several dishes. His arrival was timely; I would not have known what to say. There seemed no way to defend myself against the charge that I had said something which Jenny had misinterpreted; it was, in spite of Stephen's protestations to the contrary, an irrefutable accusation. Banu brought the rice, and we began to eat.

CHAPTER 11

On Sunday, Stephen and I worked on the bathroom. Every available surface was coated in a shiny green paint which had probably been chosen by Mrs. Menzies in the first months of married life. It took us most of the day to sand the walls and apply undercoat. As the hours passed, the proximity imposed by the confined space seemed to increase rather than lessen our estrangement. The first fissure had appeared in our union; only a hairline crack, faint as those that seamed the green paint, but nevertheless a blemish on what had previously been perfect. He had forgiven me, which implied that there was something to forgive.

For once I found myself looking forward to going to work, and on Monday I was at the office even before Marilyn. I covered my desk with piles of paper to camouflage my inactivity and then sat gazing out of the window. In the alley below, two men were unloading boxes from a van. Their voices came to me in muffled bursts. I tried to imagine what had happened on the drive to Helen's flat. Perhaps Jenny in an outburst of anger had exclaimed, "You hate Mummy and me." Stephen had replied by saying that of course he didn't: why on earth would she think that? And Jenny, searching for an answer that would serve simultaneously as a pretext and a reason to press the question, had said, "Celia told me." Next week I would ask her what she thought I had said. But then I remembered her standing over me, shouting, "You're dead," and I knew there could be no question of questioning her.

The sound of footsteps in the corridor roused me; Clare whisked by. I wished there was someone with whom I could discuss the situation, but even with Suzie, my closest friend in Edinburgh, I felt reticent. If only Lynne were not at work, I thought, I could telephone her, and then it occurred to me that I could write. I wound a sheet of headed note paper into the typewriter and began to type at top speed. I covered two pages almost without pause. When I stopped to reread what I had written, however, I felt less confident of Lynne's allegiance. I suspected she might reply by pointing out the difficulties of Jenny's situation. For my anxiety to make sense, I would have to explain that what had happened on Saturday was not an isolated event but the latest in a series of incidents, each in itself trivial but all suggesting that, contrary to the appearance she maintained most of the time, Jenny did not like me. I was wondering whether to go into more detail, when Suzie came in to ask my opinion about the design of a maths book.

She put the manuscript down on my desk and pointed out different kinds of examples and headings. "I have no idea whether we should distinguish between the various subheadings, or what format we should be using for the examples."

"Didn't you ask the author to identify each kind of heading?" I asked.

"Yes, and he did after a fashion. But when you study his notes, he's completely inconsistent: sometimes he distinguishes between two identical headings, sometimes he conflates two or three different kinds."

We began to look through Chapter Six, which Suzie had chosen as having the greatest variety of examples. After we had come up with several different lists of headings, she suggested that we take a coffee break. We went down the corridor to the kitchen. While we waited for the kettle to boil, I asked what she had done at the weekend.

"I seemed to spend most of my time arguing with Tim

about his hamster. It was a birthday present from his father."
Suzie shook the kettle impatiently. "Tim insists on having the
cage in his room, but then he can't sleep because the hamster
is a secret exercise fanatic and makes a terrific din on its
treadmill all night long. No wonder it's comatose during the
day."

"Couldn't you oil the treadmill?"

"I've tried. I drenched it in Mazola but that didn't make the
slightest difference, and it seems cruel to take the wheel away.
The whole problem would be solved if Tim would agree to let
the hamster spend the night in the living room, where it
would be out of earshot, but he won't hear of that."

"Maybe you could drug the hamster." I spooned Nescafé
into the cups and poured on water.

Suzie giggled. "I'm not going to share my drugs with a
rodent," she said.

She returned to her office, and I settled down to finish my
letter to Lynne. I was reaching for another sheet of paper
when the idea came to me: we could buy Jenny a pet for her
birthday, which was only a fortnight away. Although she
liked Tobias, he was too much mine to be really satisfying.
The advantages of the plan ranged before me: Stephen's
pleasure in the suggestion would raise the temperature between us back to normal, and the ownership of a small animal
would work a kind of alchemy for Jenny, transforming our
house into a home for one day a week. I tore up the letter and
at lunchtime wrote Lynne a cheerful postcard.

The walls of the pet shop were lined with cages. Near the
front there were mice, rats, hamsters, and guinea pigs, and,
further back, away from the draughts: canaries, parrots,
mynah birds. On the floor were a couple of pens similar to
those used to confine small children; there were puppies in
one and kittens in the other. I knelt down to look at the latter.
A Siamese kitten walked over to rub itself back and forth

against the bars. "I can see this might be fatal," Stephen said. "It wouldn't be fair to get Jenny a pet I planned to completely monopolise, would it?" The kitten raised a paw and patted my finger. "Anyway, Tobias would never forgive me."

A heavyset young woman wearing a green apron appeared from the back of the shop. She walked over and stood beside us, resting her plump hands on the edge of the pen. "He's a charmer, and he knows it," she said. "We call him Prince. He's had all the shots."

"He's beautiful," I said.

"Do you want me to lift him out?"

"We're really here to buy something for a ten year old, not a dog or a cat," Stephen explained, straightening up.

"Inside or out?" the woman asked briskly. She looked from Stephen to me, and when it was clear that neither of us understood, said, "Do you have a garden where a pet could live for at least part of the year?"

"Yes," said Stephen.

"In that case, I'd recommend a rabbit. They're more fun than hamsters or guinea pigs, and much less delicate." She led us over to a large cage which contained half a dozen rabbits, ranging from pure black to pure white. "These are does," she said. "Put your hand in and see what they do."

A small, light grey rabbit with a splash of white under her chin came fearlessly to sniff Stephen's fingers. He stroked her, and she was quiet under his hand. "She's pretty. Don't you think so, Celia?" he said.

"Yes, she's sweet."

The woman lifted her out and offered her to me to stroke. Her fur was soft as thistledown, and her large ears twitched towards me like antennae searching the air waves.

On Saturday morning I was sitting at the dining room table, consulting a cookbook, when Jenny arrived. She followed Stephen into the room, barely nodded in response to my greeting, and stalked out again. "Is something wrong?" I asked Stephen.

He sat down at the opposite end of the table. "She's annoyed that we're not going to Abernethy for the day." He tried to shrug as if Jenny's pique were a minor matter, but I could see from the set of his mouth that he was unhappy.

"But Joyce and Edward are coming to lunch. Isn't that as good?"

"Apparently not. I'd forgotten that she wanted to invite Anna today. Now she thinks that I cheated her out of Anna's presence by pretending that we were going to Abernethy and then not telling her that we'd changed our minds."

"She'll cheer up when she sees the rabbit," I said. It was still ten days until Jenny's birthday, and there was no reason for her to suspect a surprise.

"Yes, of course." Stephen smiled. "Let's give it to her now."

He left the room, and I overheard him asking Jenny to help him tidy up the garden shed. She muttered something in-audible.

"I meant now," he said.

He came back in, and slowly, dramatising reluctance with every step, Jenny trailed after him out to the garden. On the pretext of hanging a couple of dish towels on the washing line, I followed. Stephen opened the door of the shed.

I could not see Jenny's face, but I heard her whisper, "A rabbit," almost as if to speak aloud would make the vision vanish. She knelt down and put her fingers through the bars of the hutch. Over her shoulder I saw the rabbit, sitting in one corner; her blue eyes were wide and alert, and her nose quivered. She showed no signs of coming closer. After a minute or two Jenny pushed past Stephen and me into the garden, to pick a handful of grass. Then she came back and pressed the greenery through the bars; the rabbit hopped over and began to munch.

"What's its name?" she asked.

"It doesn't have a name," Stephen said. "You'll have to choose one."

"Is it a boy or a girl?"

"It's a girl."

"Oh," said Jenny, and then fell silent. She remained kneeling, engrossed in watching the rabbit eat the grass, until Stephen suggested that they move the hutch out into the garden, where they could build a run.

I left the two of them debating which corner would be most suitable and went inside. During the next couple of hours, whenever I looked out, they were engrossed in building the enclosure. At one o'clock I went to tell Stephen that his parents were late. "Good," he said. "Maybe we can get this finished." He continued to hammer in a stake. Jenny was busy adjusting the wire netting. I returned indoors. A few minutes later, while I was mixing the salad dressing, the doorbell rang.

"Celia, I'm so sorry we're late," Joyce exclaimed. "We stopped at a market garden, and you can guess what happened."

Edward's arms were full of plants. He had bought us basil, columbine, and delphiniums. We trooped through the house, with Joyce commenting on all the improvements, and out into the garden. As soon as Jenny saw her grandparents, she dashed over and seized Joyce's hand. "Come and see my rabbit," she said.

"A rabbit," said Joyce, sounding properly surprised. "Goodness, where did that come from?"

"Dad got it for me. For my birthday."

Edward had paused beside the herbaceous border. "Some of these will fit nicely here, I think. I'll put them in after lunch." He set down the bedding plants and surveyed the garden. "I must say I wouldn't fancy having a rabbit in a garden as nice as this. Think of the damage it could do."

"I don't think it can get out. Stephen and Jenny are building it a run."

Reluctantly Edward left the plants and followed me over to the far corner of the lawn. In the course of the morning Jenny and Stephen had constructed a large wire-netting run, which stretched in front of the hutch. There was even, Jenny demonstrated proudly, going to be a gate.

"It still needs a few finishing touches," said Stephen, getting to his feet.

"It's wonderful," I said. "Now she has lots of space, and nothing can hurt her."

"What could hurt her?" asked Jenny.

"Oh, I don't know. A dog?" I felt foolish. I had been thinking of my childhood, when even close to town there had been talk of foxes and weasels.

"But how could a dog get into the garden?"

"It couldn't," I said.

"What's her name?" asked Joyce.

"Her name's Selina." Jenny spoke as firmly as if she had had a divine revelation of the rabbit's name.

"That's a pretty name," said Edward, but she vouchsafed no hint of its origin.

Jenny had to be cajoled into coming inside for lunch. She ate at top speed, then begged to be released. Edward was almost as anxious to get back to the garden, and he and Stephen soon followed Jenny, leaving Joyce and me to clear the table. When we were settled over our coffee, Joyce described the terrible state in which she had found Helen's flat a fortnight earlier. "Helen's never been keen on housework, but the mess was unbelievable." She spread her arms wide to suggest the scale of the disaster. "I ended up coming through on the Monday with Mrs. Blair, my daily. Between us we got the place clean."

"Stephen was quite upset about it," I said. Even though I believed his story, I was glad to have Joyce's confirmation.

"I don't wonder. Well, the situation should be easier now. I always liked Stephen's old flat, but it wasn't good for Jenny, whereas this place is ideal." She drained her cup and stood up. "I didn't come here to spend the whole afternoon blethering. You must set me to work. I brought an old shirt and a pair of trousers in case you wanted me to do some painting."

Soon she was ensconced in the bedroom, painting the window frame, which we had left for last and never got round to doing. As I washed the dishes, I glimpsed Edward's tall form stooping over the herbaceous border and heard the sound of Stephen hammering. I began to cover the kitchen shelves with lining paper. When teatime came, I carried out a tray and spread a blanket on the grass. Joyce, Edward, Stephen, and I drank Earl Grey and discussed central heating. All Jenny wanted to do was play with Selina. She poked grass and dandelion leaves through the wire netting, and Selina obligingly twitched her nose and ate everything that was offered. I felt pleased with myself.

After tea, while Joyce and Edward went to wash and change, Stephen showed me what Edward had done in the garden. In the course of a few hours he had tidied up the entire border; he had staked the taller plants, cut back some of the bushier ones, and weeded vigorously. Stephen was explaining how we should water the new plants, when his parents reappeared.

"Jenny," called Joyce, "it's time to go." She and Edward had offered to drop Jenny off on their way home.

"Oh, no. Do we have to? Can't we stay a little longer? Just half an hour?" Jenny pleaded.

"Helen will have supper ready," Stephen said. "You'll see Selina next week, and we promise to take good care of her."

"She'll miss you," said Joyce. "But she'll be here waiting." She walked over to where Jenny knelt beside the hutch and put her arm around her. Reluctantly Jenny allowed herself to be led away.

We all went out to the street to exchange thanks and farewells. In the back seat of the car, Jenny wound down the window. "Daddy, don't forget to feed Selina," she called.

"We won't," said Stephen. He and I stood side by side, waving, until they were out of sight. Then he turned to me. "The rabbit was the ideal gift. Now our only problem will be persuading Jenny to go home." He smiled and squeezed my hand.

"That doesn't sound so bad," I said.

CHAPTER 12

As soon as I woke, I knew from the dull, grey light seeping through the curtains that the sky was overcast. If it was raining, I thought, we would not be able to go for the picnic we had planned to celebrate Jenny's birthday; she was ten on Tuesday. I turned to Stephen. He lay motionless, with his back towards me. I could not hear him breathing. I reached out to touch him, and as I did so I remembered Lynne making a similar gesture. Soon after Eve was born, the three of us had gone for a walk in the park. We were strolling along beneath the horse chestnuts when, in the middle of a remark about her mother, Lynne had suddenly stopped, reached into the pram, and put her hand on Eve's back. She turned to me and smiled. "Just checking," she said. From then on, I had imagined her bending over the tiny body of her daughter a dozen times a day to verify the astonishing presence of life.

Under my hand I felt Stephen warm and breathing. I edged out of bed and as quietly as possible gathered up my clothes and went to the kitchen. Through the window above the sink I saw that the flagstones behind the house were dark with water and the rose bushes were drooping. It had rained heavily during the night and was still drizzling slightly.

As was so often the case in Edinburgh, however, the beginning of the day was not a promise of its maturity. Even by the time I had dressed and drunk a cup of tea, the dense ceiling of cloud had lifted; there was a slight breeze and a substantial patch of blue sky. I scarcely needed my jacket to walk to the corner shop, and when Mr. Murgatee, who was behind the counter, claimed that it was a grand day, I agreed.

I arrived home to find Stephen in the kitchen. He was standing in his dressing gown, looking out of the window. "I think the rain's going to hold off, don't you?" he asked.

"Yes, it's a grand day," I said blithely.

He laughed. "You're turning into a proper Scot when you can call this a grand day, but as long as it isn't actually pouring, I think it would be fun to go to the island."

"It's not going to pour, you'll see."

"All right," he said, "you're the expert. Did you feed Selina?"

"No. Will you? I want to start on the cake."

"I'll do it as soon as I've put some clothes on." He made us each a mug of coffee and went to put his words into action.

I found the recipe I was planning to follow; the instructions seemed simple enough, and in the photograph on the facing page the cake looked magnificent. I began to measure out flour, salt, sugar, and baking powder. Tobias prowled around my feet, meowing hopefully whenever I opened the fridge. The last person for whom I had made a birthday cake was my father. We had been alone together—my mother was away taking care of an aunt who had slipped a disc—and I had decided to surprise him. After an energetic search I had managed to find all the necessary ingredients tucked away in various cupboards; some, like the tin of baking powder speckled with rust, looked as if they were as old as I was. My mother never baked, but I had often watched Ruth. Full of urgent importance, I measured and mixed; like the perfect cake, my father's affection for me would rise.

Perhaps the ancient ingredients had lost their power, or the frequency with which I opened the oven door may have had something to do with it, but the cake remained obstinately concave. Even when the sides had not only risen but turned from golden to dark brown, the middle was still sunken and moist. In such circumstances, Ruth always said, "What the eye doesn't see . . . ," cut off the burnt bits, and concealed the various imperfections by the lavish use of icing. I endeavoured to follow her example.

My father behaved perfectly. He was surprised, ate two slices, and claimed that the cake was delicious. Although I was struggling with my own portion, I was happy to believe him.

The following day when I came home from school my mother was back. I rushed into the kitchen. "I made a cake for Daddy's birthday," I said.

"I didn't know you could cook." She cocked her head to look at me as if I had revealed some astonishing new accomplishment.

"Ruth showed me."

"Good old Ruth. As long as you're not wasting time doing domestic science."

While she made tea for herself, I cut us each a substantial slice. We sat down at the kitchen table, and she asked what had happened at school.

"Mrs. Pomfret was ill, so we got to go to the library instead of having a history test. And in English we're doing *The Merchant of Venice* and I'm Jessica."

"Jessica," said my mother, wrinkling her nose. "She's such a Goody Two-shoes." She looked closely at the cake, took a small mouthful, and burst out laughing. "Oh, dear, it must be hereditary. You're as bad at baking as I am." She went and tipped her slice into the dustbin and came back with a packet of chocolate biscuits.

In spite of twenty years, fresh ingredients, and an electric beater, Jenny's cake too was slightly concave. I covered it with white icing, wrote the number "10" in Smarties on the top, and placed candle holders around the perimeter. The result was lopsided but colourful, and Stephen praised it exuberantly.

We were not collecting Jenny until two, and for once, to save time, I accompanied Stephen. While he went inside, I sat in the car, reading the newspaper; I wanted to give the impression to any observer that I was perfectly at ease. I had finished the front page and was in the middle of a review of a book about Florence Nightingale, when a tapping sound made me look up. I let out a stifled gasp. She had pressed her face against the glass. The nose was flattened into a grotesque white blob, the lips into a reddish wound; two dark eyes stared at me. Then Jenny stepped back, giggling. I pulled myself together and rolled down the window. "Hello, how are you?" I said.

"Okay."

Stephen opened the driver's door and asked if Jenny could sit in front; she was prone to carsickness on longer journeys. I climbed out and paused to take off my jacket. As I stood on the pavement, twisting my arms out of the sleeves, a woman appeared in the doorway across the street. "Jenny," she called, and held up an article of clothing.

Half in and half out of my jacket, I stood as still as I had in childhood when we played statues; if only a small cloud could descend and render me invisible. At the sound of her mother's voice, Jenny, who was standing beside me, turned. She was about to dash across the street, but Stephen said, "Wait! There's a car coming."

Several cars passed, and then Helen, bright and decisive in her purple cardigan and grey trousers, ran across the street. "You forgot your sweater," she said, handing Jenny the garment.

She turned to me, smiling, and held out her hand. "Hello. I'm Helen."

I extricated myself from my jacket and found myself shaking her hand. The knowledge that I was blushing intensified my embarrassment. "Hello," I managed to say.

"Jenny's told me lots about you," she said. "Have a nice

day, you three." She nodded her head to include Stephen and her daughter, as well as me, in her wide smile, then ran back across the street, with light tripping movements that seemed designed to draw attention to her grace and good humour. In the doorway she paused to wave.

We all got into the car. Stephen gave me a quick smile; the three women in his life had met, albeit briefly, and there had been neither shouts nor blows. I was scarcely aware that the engine had started and that we were pulling away from the curb. I felt that in some mysterious fashion Helen had got the better of me. I was the second wife, a temporary amusement, graciously admitted to the family by the senior wife.

In the front seat Stephen was telling Jenny about the picnic. "What about Selina?" she asked.

"You'll see Selina later. We have to have the picnic first because we're going to the island at Cramond."

"Oh, will we go by boat?"

"No, there's a causeway we can walk across, but only at low tide. We'll have to be careful not to get cut off."

"Then we'd have to stay until we were rescued," Jenny said, gleefully.

The sun had come out, but dark clouds were massing in the very quarter towards which we were heading. Stephen announced that we must, as his family had done at the beginning of every trip, sing "The sun has got his hat on."

"What happened if it was raining?" Jenny asked.

"We had to sing even louder, so that the sun would hear us behind the clouds and know that he had a duty to shine forth."

We sang the song twice through, and by the time we reached the shore the ominous clouds did seem to have thinned. Stephen parked by the side of the road, and we unloaded the picnic basket and the rucksack. The island was only a few hundred yards from the mainland, and at low tide, the causeway stretched intact from shore to shore.

Jenny scampered over the rocks to the water's edge. She sat down to take off her socks and shoes and then set out for the island. I had hoped that there would be a chance to speak to Stephen about Helen, explain how the encounter, apparently so friendly, had nonetheless upset me, but he stuck close to Jenny; any private conversation would have to wait until evening. The causeway was covered with barnacles and occasional tufts of seaweed. I walked carefully, avoiding the pools of water that still lingered in some places.

When I reached the shore, Jenny was putting on her shoes and Stephen was skipping stones. "Hey, Celia," he said. "I've managed four bounces."

I set down the picnic basket and looked for a suitably flat stone. I found a thin, grey one and spun it out over the water; it bounced once, then sank. "Come on," Jenny called. "I want to see the rest of the island."

A path wound up the steep grassy bank and she led the way, followed by Stephen, then me. At the top of the rise we saw a middle-aged couple sitting over their picnic. We said hello. The woman looked up from pouring tea out of a thermos. "Hello," she said. "We were just saying we could be on a desert island. You're the first people we've seen all afternoon."

"A desert island," exclaimed Jenny with pleasure.

As we continued along the path, a low concrete structure came into view. "What is it?" Jenny asked.

"I think it must be one of the lookout posts that they built during the Second World War when they were guarding the coast," Stephen said. "They probably had soldiers here keeping watch."

Jenny charged down the slope towards the building. Several sheep scattered in alarm and then resumed their grazing a few yards away. The door was sealed shut, and she asked Stephen to lift her up to one of the narrow slit windows. I peered in through another. It was too dark to see anything, but on my face I felt the damp coldness of the interior. I walked round the building. On the wall overlooking the sea the words "Terry and Rita forever" were written in white paint; several beer cans lay scattered on the ground below. It was hard to believe that within living memory people had seriously prepared to defend this island and the city that lay behind it.

In the next small valley were the remains of several houses. Amid the stone walls nettles grew to an astonishing height. We left the main path and headed to the eastern shore. In a few minutes we were standing at the top of a grassy bank, which sloped gently at first, then more steeply, down to the water. The breeze had dropped, and it was almost hot. Stephen pointed out the Bass Rock, a dark knob on the horizon.

"Shall we stay here?" I asked. On my cheek I felt the faint tickling of an insect.

"What about over there?" Stephen pointed vaguely along the shore.

"It's nice being under the birch trees," I said. He at once put down the rucksack. I shook out the blanket. It billowed like a counterpane and descended onto the knee-high grass. From behind me, without warning, Jenny dived, with a whoop. She rolled over onto her back, pulling the blue and red checked fabric around her. "I'm a caterpillar."

I looked down at her small, pale face, the straight hair neatly braided back. "Why don't you grow up and fly away?" I demanded. I was taken aback by the anger in my voice.

"No. This is my cocoon."

I bent down and seized the edge of the blanket, about to pull it from under her. Then Stephen raised his hands to his mouth and let out a strange screech; he was blowing through a blade of grass. "Come on, Jenny," he said. "Come and look at the sea."

She scrambled to her feet. "I want some grass too."

"Over here. Can you manage without me?"

I nodded, and he led Jenny off in search of the ideal blade of grass. I began to unpack the picnic. Plates, containers of sandwiches, glasses, and bottles of lemonade stood topsy-turvy on the uneven surface of the blanket. I could no longer see Stephen and Jenny, but from the direction of the shore came occasional squeals. Around me in the long grass the insects buzzed and hummed.

"Stephen, Jenny," I called, when everything was ready.

They appeared almost immediately. "It's time for surprises," I said. "Jenny, you have to go over to that rock and promise not to look until we call you."

"What sort of surprises?"

"You can't ask that, else it wouldn't be surprising."

Jenny scampered over to the rock I had indicated and buried her face in her hands. "You get out the presents," I whispered to Stephen. "I'll do the cake." I lifted the cake out of the plastic container. It was only slightly more misshapen than before. I pushed the candles into the holders and held a match to each in turn, but I could not keep them all lit simultaneously; even while I was lighting one, another, already lit, flickered out.

"Can I come?" called Jenny.

"Not yet," said Stephen. He knelt beside me and shielded the cake with his jacket. As I held the match to the tenth candle, he called out, "Jenny." We began to sing loudly and slightly off key, "Happy Birthday."

After tea Jenny announced that she wanted to play hide-and-seek. Stephen looked at his watch. "It'll have to be a quick game," he said. "The tide was already turning when we came out here."

"You be it, Celia," said Jenny. She smiled at me.

"The island's huge," I protested. "I'll never find you."

"Yes, you will. Daddy and I will hide together. You have to

count to two hundred slowly. And you mustn't look." She took Stephen's hand and pulled him to his feet. "Close your eyes," she said.

The sun was shining. I lay back on the blanket. Once when Lewis and I had gone to Brighton for the day, we had met a group of blind holiday-makers, tapping along the pier with their canes. Lewis had remarked how pointless it was to take the blind to the seaside. But as I lay there, listening to the soft slapping of the water on the rocks below, breathing in the salty air, I understood that the sea was unmistakable to every sense.

I climbed down to the shore and began to search among the large rocks that lined the water's edge. The salty smell, which had wafted to me so pleasantly as I lay in the sun, was here transformed into a more dubious odour. After walking a hundred yards in either direction without finding anything besides an old lobster pot and the corpses of fish and seagulls, I scrambled back up to the blanket. I paused uncertainly. Surely they would not hide anywhere too distant; part of the fun of hide-and-seek was the possibility of discovery. Then I thought of the ruined settlement we had passed. It was the perfect hiding place. I made my way back along the narrow sheep path.

There were the remains of what looked to have been four houses. Only the exterior walls still stood; the interiors were filled with rubble and the rapacious nettles. I wondered how long it was since people had lived here. As I walked round, peering through the empty doorways, I kept expecting Stephen or Jenny to burst out from behind one of the low stone walls; the only sign of life was a wren running along a fallen branch.

I did not know where to look next. From what I had seen, there were not many places to hide on the island; there were few large trees, and although the long grass and uneven ground would probably conceal anyone from a short distance, I was sure that they would not choose such an unfair method.

"Stephen, Jenny," I called.

I stood still, listening. I heard nothing save the wind rustling in the trees, and the occasional bleating of sheep.

I tried again, cupping my hands to my mouth. "Stephen, Jenny. I give up."

We had made no contingency plan, but the most sensible course of action seemed to be to circle back to our picnic place. I would wait there, and surely they would find me. I set off, shouting periodically.

The picnic basket and blanket were exactly where I had left them, but the sight of these familiar objects did not reassure me. Something about their appearance made me think that the moment before I came into view Stephen and Jenny had been sitting here. Although I knew this was absurd, I glanced around uneasily and called their names. The answering silence only made me feel more abandoned. It was almost five o'clock. I was not sure when we had begun playing, but at least half an hour must have passed. What could have happened to them? Could they have been swept out to sea or trapped in a cave? Suddenly I had a more realistic fear. Every minute the tide was rising. We were in danger of being cut off, just as Jenny had imagined.

If they were not back in five minutes, I decided I would carry our things across the island to where we had come ashore. I sat down and immediately stood up again. I wandered around, unable to keep still. A minute passed. Then another. Stephen had told me that it was the Babylonian astronomers who had introduced the minute, but how had they been able to measure something so subjective without mechanical means? No two ever seemed to pass at the same rate.

At last five minutes stammered by. I felt reluctant to leave the one place where I was sure that Stephen would be able to find me, but there seemed nothing else to do. Perhaps they had assumed that we would rendezvous by the causeway. I had neither pencil nor paper, but I arranged three branches in the shape of an arrow pointing back the way we had come.

Then I set off, the rucksack on my back, the basket in one hand. As I hurried along the path, my panic increased; I did not know if I was in flight or in pursuit. Several times on the rough ground I almost fell. The journey which in the company of Stephen and Jenny had been comparatively short now seemed endless. I was afraid that I had lost my way. At last I spotted the lookout post. I struggled up the final incline, hoping that I might find the middle-aged couple. They were gone, and as I came over the top, I saw why. Between the mainland and the island lay an unbroken sheet of water.

Slowly I began to walk down towards the shore. I told myself it was ridiculous to be afraid—I was in sight, almost within sound, of humans, cars, civilisation—but I was terrified. At every step it seemed that the earth might swallow me. I passed a sheep; it raised its head and stared at me with callous yellow eyes.

Suddenly I heard a faint sound. I stopped. It could have been only the cry of a gull. The sound came again, and I made out the syllables of my name. Frantically I turned around, looking back the way I had come. Then a movement on the mainland caught my eye. I saw our car and, at the water's edge, a figure, waving. Stephen began to wade towards me. The water reached barely above his ankles.

I watched his progress. In his light blue shirt and jeans he seemed to glide over the rippling surface of the water, and as he grew larger, I moved from fear to anger as easily as I might have crossed the threshold from the kitchen to the dining room. I continued to walk down towards the shore.

"Celia," he said, when only a few yards separated us. "Thank goodness you brought everything. I had no idea the tide would come in so quickly."

"Why did you leave me behind?" I demanded. I had meant to ask the question loudly, but my voice came out as an absurd squeak.

Stephen launched into an apologetic story. Jenny had suggested that they hide by the lookout post. When they arrived there, she had announced that she wanted to get something from the car. He had given her the keys. She had dropped them on the far side, and he had gone over to help her look for them. They had found them a few minutes ago. "I'm dreadfully sorry," he said. "I shouted for you. When there was no answer, I didn't know what to do. I thought if I didn't find the keys, we'd never get home." He held out his hand. "Give me the rucksack and let's wade across before the water gets any deeper."

I took off my shoes and rolled up my trousers. As I followed Stephen through the water I felt cheated of my anger. He had deprived me of my justification; he did not even need to tell an elaborate story. The name "Jenny" rolled over my objections, like a wave over a sand castle, obliterating them without a trace.

On the shore Jenny was waiting. "You were nearly cut off, Celia," she said, hopping up and down.

"But we rescued her," said Stephen, hugging me close.

CHAPTER 13

As if our song exhorting the sun to shine had had some permanent effect, each day following our visit to the island was hotter than the one before. The city took on a summery guise; even the blackest of buildings seemed to grow lighter in shade and softer in outline. Weather was the major topic of conversation; everyone commented upon the heat and what measures they had taken against it. Stephen wrestled with his pupils; exams were imminent and still no one could concentrate. Suzie came to work in bright red shorts, provoking disapproval from Clare and envy from Marilyn, myself, and the rest of the staff. The manuscripts over which I laboured grew limp in my hands. The sun did not set until almost eleven, and when darkness finally came, Stephen and I lay down to sleep covered by a single sheet. With each passing day the sky grew less clear, and by Thursday the sun was invisible beneath a lemony haze.

That afternoon everyone who did not have some urgent task on hand left the office early, but Clare had asked me to check through a biology manuscript because the science editor was on holiday. There were innumerable figures and photographs, and it was almost five-thirty by the time I escaped. Outside, the air was heavy with moisture, and the pavements seemed to shimmer with heat. As I walked to the bus stop I could feel my blouse sticking to my back. When the bus arrived, there were no window seats. I perched uneasily beside an elderly woman who was fanning herself with a newspaper.

"You look hot," she remarked.

"I am, but I'm on my way swimming."

"Swimming. How lovely. I'm afraid I never learned." Now that I had shown myself receptive, she continued to talk about the weather, past and present, until we reached my stop. "Bye-bye, dear," she said, as I rose to leave. "Enjoy your swim."

The bus pulled away. I began to walk down the hill. A group of children passed me, exclaiming over their ice creams. I was tempted to stop and buy one, but I told myself it would be a mistake so soon before swimming. I kept walking. I turned into the narrow street where the pool was. When I rounded the bend, Stephen came into view. He was sitting on the steps of the baths, wearing a white T-shirt and brown shorts; he was staring straight ahead and did not notice me. I stopped mid-stride. Nowadays I hardly ever saw him from a distance, and I remembered, almost with surprise, how good-looking he was. Then I moved; he caught sight of me, jumped up, and came to meet me.

"I'm sorry I'm late," I said.

"It's fine." He put his arms round me. "You're all sweaty," he said. "Nice."

As we stepped through the outer door of Glenogle Baths the smell of chlorine fell over us like a blanket. The baths were on the upper floor and, with every step we mounted, the heat and the odour grew more intense; by the time we reached the turnstile, I felt dizzy.

"Two adults," said Stephen, holding out a five-pound note to the woman in the office.

"One pound forty. The adult session doesn't start until six-thirty. You don't want to go in there with them. Listen." She gestured towards the pool, from which came an immense, muffled din.

We climbed another flight of stairs and passed through the doors onto the spectators' balcony. We sat down on a wooden bench overlooking the pool. The shouts of the children echoed around us and beneath the opaque glass roof the water was dazzlingly bright. The edge of the pool was ringed with old-fashioned cubicles; I was reminded of the pool where I had learned to swim and of Mr. Brown, the formidable Liverpudlian, who had taught me. I was describing his draconian methods when a voice behind us said, "Stephen."

We turned round. A plumpish man with a dark beard was smiling at us. "Julius," Stephen exclaimed. "What are you doing here?"

Julius came forward and shook Stephen's hand energetically. "This is my local pool."

"Ours too," said Stephen. "Celia and I moved into a flat in Trinity a couple of months ago. Celia, this is Julius."

Julius said hello and sat down beside me. "So how are you?" he asked. "Still with the same school?"

"Yes," said Stephen. "Deirdre and I are now the oldest members of the staff. It's a little worrying."

"You mean the longest serving," said Julius. "You can't possibly be the oldest."

"We certainly feel like the oldest some days. What about you? Are you still working with young offenders? Julius is a social worker," he explained.

"No, I've moved on to junkies. I work in a clinic in Leith. We have no money, no accommodation, and a flourishing AIDS epidemic. At least with my young offenders, I had occasional success stories. Now I never get any cases that aren't desperate. On average I go to a funeral a week." He spoke rapidly as if anxious to hurry over these unpleasant facts. When he finished, we were all silent for a moment. Below us some young boys were storming the inflatable crocodile which was tethered in the middle of the pool.

"That sounds terribly hard," I said.

"It is. The only way I can cope is by trying to forget about it when I'm not working, but that's not easy." He shook his head, then turned to Stephen. "How's Jenny?" he asked.

"She's fine. She just had her tenth birthday, and she's showing signs of being good at languages, like Helen."

"Has she grown?"

"She's still small for her age, but incredibly poised."

"She always was." Julius turned to me. "I lived with Helen and Jenny for a while. I'm afraid that Jenny never really became reconciled to my presence."

"She's much happier now," said Stephen. "She and Celia get on very well together."

"Good for you," said Julius. He sounded as if he thought such praise was seriously earned.

A woman in a striped T-shirt and shorts came to the edge of the pool and blew several loud volleys on a whistle. There was a general splashing towards the sides, save for a couple of boys who disappeared underwater. "Everyone out," she shouted.

One by one the children disappeared into the cubicles around the edge. Gradually the water grew still, and the reflected light from the ceiling came together in one smooth rectangle. The lifeguards removed the inflatable and set up lanes. "Come on, Ceel," said Stephen, pulling me to my feet. "Let's go and make waves."

Julius followed us downstairs. "Nice to run into you both," he said. "The best of luck." He smiled at me.

After the steamy atmosphere the water felt cold, and I shivered as it closed around my thighs. I adjusted my goggles and pushed off. Julius's remarks about Jenny had made me think again of the visit to the island, and as I swam up and down, I remembered that awful moment when I had looked out across the empty water and known myself abandoned. And it was true that but for the chance of my walking over to the causeway I would probably have been stranded on the island for the next eight hours. Stephen would not have risked leaving Jenny alone on the mainland to search for me. That evening we had gone round to see his friends, Molly and Ian, and in talking to them my narrow escape had become a humourous narrative: the perils of Pauline. I had succumbed to the bantering, even embellished the episode, but in my heart I felt that Stephen had failed me; he ought not to have left the island without me, and his apologies had been insufficient. I wondered what it was that Jenny had wanted from the car; no one had thought it worth mentioning.

At the shallow end I collided with a pregnant woman. She swam on unperturbed but I stopped and stood up. On the far side of the pool I saw Julius swimming doggedly up and down. Stephen surfaced beside me. "How are you doing?" he asked.

Without his glasses his face looked peculiarly vulnerable; his hair was dark with water. "All right," I said.

"Shall we do six more lengths?"

I nodded. He pushed off, and more slowly I followed. By the time I finished my six lengths Stephen had already got out. I was wading towards the steps when ahead of me Julius swam up to the bar. Before he could turn, I had reached out and touched his shoulder. He stood up, coughing. "Celia," he said. "Sorry, was I in your way?"

"No." I had not known what I was going to say, but his expression was so kindly that I found myself asking, "I wondered what you meant about Jenny."

Julius looked around the pool, and I realised that he was searching for Stephen. Then he said, "I feel awkward saying this. There were just lots of small mishaps. Jenny always seemed to be spilling her paints over my desk; I would find drawing pins in my shoes; once she even set fire to my briefcase. I could never prove that she did any of this deliberately—I mean she was only six—but it caused a great deal of friction between Helen and me." He smiled. "It was soon after Stephen and Helen separated, and Jenny was obviously having a hard time. We all were. I'm glad she's settled down."

"Thank you," I said. And then, although it seemed foolish, both of us waist deep in water, I held out my hand to Julius.

In my cubicle I dressed quickly, conscious that Stephen was waiting. When I emerged, he was standing in the hall, reading the notice board. I apologised for being slow. He said that was fine, and I thought, with relief, that he had not seen me talking to Julius. We descended the stairs and stepped outside.

Evening had brought no lessening of the heat. The grey sky still covered the city like a lid, and as we headed towards home the sweltering streets took on an almost surreal quality. Stephen told me about his day; a girl had burst into tears at the results of a test. We were walking along in the shadow of the high stone wall which surrounded Warriston Cemetery, when I asked what had happened between Julius and Jenny. "It sounded like they didn't get on terribly well," I said. I tried to appear only moderately interested.

He shrugged. "I don't really know. Jenny was so young that she couldn't explain her unhappiness, and for obvious reasons I wasn't particularly close to either Helen or Julius. I suspect that he rather overdid being a stepfather. He'd read all the right books, and he couldn't leave Jenny alone."

"When did he start living with them?"

"As soon as I left. Julius and I virtually passed each other in the hall."

Stephen had always made it sound as if he had been the one to initiate the separation and move out; now, hearing the edge in his voice, I realised that although he had indeed moved out, he had not necessarily done so willingly. I experienced one of those moments, comparable to the morning I had learned of Jenny's existence, when everything I knew about him shifted. A feeling akin to anger prompted me to praise Julius. "He seemed a nice man," I said. "I'm sure he meant well."

"I'm sure he did," said Stephen, sighing. "Christ, I hate this humidity." He pushed his hand through his damp hair and gave me a small, apologetic smile.

Suddenly it occurred to me that I was behaving with Stephen as I had so often behaved with Lewis, saying less than I knew or wanted to. I stopped, seized his arm, and pulled him to me. I should not hold it against him that he had been unable to leave Helen, nor that he was an indulgent father. He was as frail and human as myself. I buried my face against his chest; through his T-shirt I could smell the odour of chlorine still clinging to his skin.

We were in bed and had just turned off the lights, when the storm finally broke. The first rumbling of thunder was so faint that neither of us was sure of having heard it until a few seconds later, when the room was lit by lightning. Then came another roll of thunder, markedly louder. We both began to count, measuring the distance of the storm. Each successive flash of lightning was followed more closely by thunder, and each clap of thunder was louder than the one before. When the storm was only two miles away, I heard a new sound, a slight rustling. The window was wide open, and the air was trembling in the fabric of the curtains. Suddenly there was a bang so loud that the house shook, and then in the silence came the whispering of rain. Stephen touched me, and as the rain grew stronger, we began to move together.

The heat had caused a surge in our garden; overnight it seemed the vegetables had shot up and with them the weeds. Next evening after supper Stephen went out to do some weeding, while I did the washing up. I was scrubbing a particularly stubborn casserole dish when the telephone rang. I wiped my hands on my jeans and went to answer.

"Hello, Celia," said Helen. "How are you? Jenny had such a good time at the picnic last Saturday. She said you made a wonderful cake."

I was so startled that all I could think to say was: "I'll get Stephen." Then I accidentally dropped the receiver, and the clatter seemed to reinforce my brusqueness. Somehow Helen was always one step ahead; now her politeness shamed me, as her earlier rudeness had taken me aback.

Stephen was digging the vegetable bed at the far end of the garden. I could, by raising my voice only slightly, have drawn his attention, but I walked over the grass and did not speak until I stood beside him.

"What does she want?" he asked. He sounded irritable, but already he was stabbing the fork into the soil, going off obediently in the direction of the house. I began to dig in his place, turning over the soil between the rows of lettuces, carrots, and spinach. Above me, on the telegraph wires that stretched across the garden, the swallows sat and twittered.

Sometimes as a child when I was bicycling in the country I would stop to listen to the wooden telegraph poles that lined the road. When I pressed my ear against the rough, creosote-smelling wood, a faint hum was audible; I believed this to be the distillation of a thousand conversations. I was always hoping to overhear something meaningful, but no matter how long I listened, I was never able to decipher a single sentence. I was sure it was different for the birds who perched on the wires, that they understood everything. When they twittered they were discussing significant pieces of human news, and it was boredom that drove them to flight.

I bent down to remove a piece of earthenware which had wedged between the prongs of the fork and added it to the small pile of stones Stephen had made in one corner. The swallows were fidgeting, unfolding and refolding their wings. They were expressing their annoyance, I thought, at the conversation between Stephen and Helen, a conversation to which I was no more privy than if I had been still standing beside a telegraph pole, my bicycle lying in the grass at my feet.

The minutes passed. The entire bed had been forked over, but I felt awkward about going back into the house. If I had been there all along, it would have been fine, but now it seemed that my return must be significant of anxiety, or curiosity.

I wandered around pulling out weeds, snapping the dead heads off the roses. Our swimming costumes and towels hung motionless on the line. The birds vanished; Selina had retreated inside her hutch; the air seemed colder. The earth turned on its axis, bringing even that endlessly light summer sky a little closer to darkness.

I was examining the runner beans when I felt Stephen's gaze upon me. As soon as I saw his motionless figure, standing in the kitchen doorway, I knew that all was not well. I walked over and put my arms around him. One step above me, he stood still for a moment in my embrace, and then his arms closed around me.

CHAPTER 14

We went for a walk, but where we walked I do not know. I was aware of a crack in the pavement, the zigzagging flight of a bat stitching the sky, a clematis in full bloom, an elderly man in shirt sleeves and braces watering his garden, every detail shimmering and distinct with life, yet as to which streets we crossed or turned up or down, I was oblivious. I did not ask what was the matter; I said to myself that Helen had upset him, as she so easily had the power to do, and he would tell me soon enough.

We were crossing a bridge over the railway line when Stephen at last spoke. "Helen's going to Paris." He uttered the words so softly and the conjunction of the names was so like a joke that I asked what he had said, even as I realised that I knew.

"Helen's going to Paris," he repeated.

"For a holiday?"

"No, to work for a year. The bank has a branch in Paris. They find her a place to live, and she'll get almost twice as much money, compensation for being on foreign soil."

Fifty-two weeks, I thought, without Jenny. Or at least only for holidays, and those, like the fixed buoys in a harbour, would be easy to negotiate. "It sounds wonderful," I said. I was about to say a wonderful opportunity for Jenny, but I did not trust myself. With the prospect of release, my dislike of the present situation blossomed like a genie suddenly freed from the confines of his bottle.

"Yes, she's very happy. She's talked of doing something like this for years. In fact she was actually offered a job abroad shortly before she found out she was pregnant." He had taken my hand, and I felt his palm burning against mine.

A van was approaching. We paused on the edge of the pavement, and the sheet of dark metal rushed by a few feet in front of our faces. In its wake the words "She's not taking Jenny" appeared, not as if they came from Stephen, but like an aural hallucination.

We stepped into the road. He had not spoken; I had conjured the words out of my fear; like the sound of the van, they would disappear.

On the far pavement, Stephen stopped. "She just told Jenny today."

I did my utmost to practise the magic of denial. "Jenny must be thrilled," I said. "Going to Paris will be a big adventure."

Stephen reached out and took my other hand in his. "Jenny isn't going," he said. "She's coming to live with us. I mean of course it depends on you, but that's what Helen has offered." He spoke slowly and simply; there was no mistaking his meaning.

I stood looking up at him. His face was tense with suppressed emotion. At first I thought he too was upset, and then, as he returned my gaze, I realised that his reaction, as extreme as my own, lay in the opposite direction; the corners of his mouth twitched; he was trying not to smile. He was so happy he wanted to grin like an idiot.

I pulled my hands out of his clasp. In what sense did it depend on me? I wondered. Nothing depended on me. I would not say one word. But even as I had this thought, the words burst out of me. "Why can't she take Jenny with her?"

"Celia," said Stephen, "what's wrong?"

"One minute she'll hardly let you see Jenny. The next she

tries to dump the whole business onto you. It seems so unfair, both to you and to Jenny."

"Helen admitted on the phone that she has been difficult. She even said that one reason she applied for the job was because she knew that she and Jenny were too close for comfort."

There was a clicking sound. I looked up and saw a young man bicycling towards us. He caught my eye and smiled. "I thought she was worried about another woman replacing her in Jenny's affections." I remembered how much friendlier Helen had been recently, how much easier about arrangements; this was no will-o'-the-wisp of an idea but a carefully considered, well-established plan. I began to walk again, and Stephen fell in beside me. We passed a garden with a hedge so overgrown that we had to step into the street.

"Everything she's heard from Jenny makes her think you'll be the perfect stepmother," he said.

"I can't imagine what she's heard," I said angrily. I was not seeking the information but repudiating it. All the attempts I had made to befriend Jenny, to make her feel at home, rose up to mock me. Bitterly I recalled the satisfaction I had taken in Selina.

Stephen put his arm around my shoulders. As if following my thoughts he said, "You take a lot of trouble with Jenny. Since I've met you my relationship with her has improved enormously." He paused, then, before I could respond, continued. "I can understand you being shocked. I'm still stunned. When Helen announced that she'd got this job, I was convinced that she was about to tell me that I wasn't going to see Jenny for a year."

A group of people was coming towards us: a very tall man, holding the hand of a small girl, followed by a woman and a slightly older girl. All four of them said good evening, and Stephen replied.

"So why isn't she taking Jenny?" I asked again. This time

I kept my voice calm; I wanted Stephen to answer me.

"It's partly a practical decision. She's going to be working very hard, and it would be difficult for her to spend much time with Jenny. And, as she said, I'm now in an excellent position to take care of Jenny. I'm living with you; we have a house and a garden." He squeezed my shoulder. "This couldn't have happened at a better time. Jenny's young enough to accept the switch, whereas in a year or two, when she's a teenager, it would be much harder."

As we made our way home he continued to enumerate the advantages: his parents would be pleased, it would be good for Jenny to have a normal relationship with him and to be less dependent on Helen. All the reasons were irrelevant. Jenny was Stephen's daughter. Helen did not need to insist that Stephen take care of her; Jenny, by her mere existence, insisted.

Night after night since New Year's Eve I had squatted down to put in my diaphragm. That night as I held it up to the light, scrutinising the thin hemisphere, I paused. Why not, I thought, put it back in its case and replace the case on the shelf. Who would be any the wiser? The chances of anything happening were remote, but there would at least be a possibility, and that seemed desperately appealing. I imagined a sweet-smelling baby, whom Stephen and I would take everywhere.

Suddenly I thought of Helen. Perhaps Jenny had been conceived not accidentally but out of some such fleeting impulse. I knew from Stephen that Helen had planned to have an abortion and then changed her mind. That life, existence, depended upon such tiny moments was terrifying. A pinprick in a piece of rubber, the contraction of a woman's heart as she waited for her womb to be scraped clean: was that all that was needed? Maybe the fetus, even tiny as a minnow, could sense these twists and hesitations, and this was the root of

Jenny's difficulties; she had always known that her presence was provisional. I opened the tube of jelly and bent down.

Given her momentous announcement, I had thought that Helen might want to spend Saturday with Jenny, but in fact it was she who suggested that Stephen take Jenny and Anna to the Chambers Street museum, where there was a special children's exhibition of flora and fauna. I decided to stay at home. I told Stephen that I wanted to keep an eye on the plumber who was coming to install the washing machine. The truth was that I did not think that I would be able to sound suitably enthusiastic about the prospect of Jenny's living with us; I needed some respite.

Shortly after Stephen left, the doorbell rang. I opened the front door and found Barry, the plumber, standing on the step, a tool box in one hand and a cassette player in the other. He smiled shyly and said something complimentary about the garden. Soon he was lying on the kitchen floor, with his head under the sink, playing Buddy Holly at full volume. I spread newspapers on the floor of the spare room. We had prepared the walls and bought the primrose yellow paint almost a month before, but from week to week we had postponed the task. Now our decision to devote this weekend to painting the room took on an ironic quality. I must learn, I thought, to call it Jenny's room.

I filled the roller tray with paint and set to work. There was something oddly soothing about the mechanical act of running the roller up and down, and as I moved along the wall, my anger and dismay began to subside. I was sorry for Jenny. Beyond the fact that Stephen and I were going to be so greatly inconvenienced, I could imagine that she must feel abandoned. When I thought back over the conversation of the night before, I was struck by how little part Jenny had played in the discussion; she was after all the one most affected, yet we had barely mentioned her reactions. I poured more paint into the tray and edged my way round the corner. I was so much under Stephen's influence that I had always thought of his leaving Helen as an unmitigated blessing. Now it occurred to me that Jenny's grief about her parents' separation might be no less than my own had been.

My parents had broken the news to me soon after I went to university. I had been there for only a few weeks when my mother's letter arrived. All unsuspecting, I had carried it into breakfast; my cornflakes had grown limp before me as I tried to make out what she was saying. "I'm sure you won't be surprised," she wrote, "to know that your father and I have decided to separate. He's going to stay on in the house, at least meanwhile, so it won't make much difference to you. Your old room will be waiting. I'm going to live with Harry."

For years Harry had been an avuncular presence in my life. He played in the same chamber group as my mother and often gave her lifts to concerts. He would sit in the kitchen, dressed in evening clothes, chatting to my father or me, until my mother appeared wearing a long black dress. Then off the two of them would go, set apart from us by their elegant appearance and lofty destination.

There must be some mistake, I thought. I could still picture my parents standing side by side on the station platform, waving goodbye to me. I hurried to the nearest telephone. When my mother answered, I announced that I was coming home. I had the idea that my mere presence would restore normality.

"Didn't you get my letter?"

"Yes," I admitted.

"Then you'll understand that now isn't the best time. Everything's in an uproar. If you want to come in a couple of weeks, after we've sorted ourselves out, that would be lovely. Harry's terribly fond of you. We're both looking forward to seeing you in the holidays."

In retrospect it seemed unbelievable, but only at that moment, when I heard my mother unite herself with him in the first person plural, did I begin to grasp that she and Harry were something more than friends.

She had begun to talk about the difficulties of packing. "It's amazing how much junk I still have. Listen to me," she said, "prattling away as if you were in the next room. Phone this evening, or sometime very soon, and we'll have a long talk."

I went back to my room and lay down on the bed. Thoughts fluttered around my brain, like a bevy of pigeons startled out of their dovecote. My mother had a lover, had been having an affair, was Harry's mistress. I had never used those words before except about characters in books. Day after day that summer I had come home from my job at Marks and Spencer's to find her sorting through her possessions; she had given a dozen bags of clothes to Oxfam and thrown out as many more. "I'm sick of not knowing where anything is," she had said. I had never known her to be tidy, but it did not seem implausible. How could I have guessed what was going on, I thought, when she did everything to ensure that I would not? What was the subterfuge for, if not to deceive me?

That my mother was not utterly oblivious to my telephone call was revealed by the postcard that arrived a couple of days later. She suggested that as the Christmas holidays were only a few weeks away, there was no point in my coming home for a weekend. I did not need to read between the lines to see that I played an exact and limited part in her life. She had borne me, raised me, and she would do her best by me, but there was no reason for unnecessary sentiment or sentimentality.

I had been eighteen the year that my parents separated. Jenny had been five when Stephen moved out, but who was to say that her agony had not been as great as mine. It was easy from my present adult perspective to reduce her emotions to black and white, but if I thought back to my own childhood,

I knew that at her age I had experienced a range of feelings as wide and subtle as the spectrum of paints from which Stephen had so carefully chosen the primrose yellow I was now applying to the walls of her room.

I had almost finished the bottom half of the first wall when Barry put his head round the door. "Nice colour," he said. "Is this the future nursery?"

"It's the room Stephen's daughter will use." I concentrated on running the roller smoothly up and down.

"At least she has good taste. My daughter Linda has an absolute bee in her bonnet about having everything pink."

I remembered how Jenny had shuddered at the thought of us painting the dining room pink. "How old is she?" I asked.

"Linda's thirteen and Margaret's fifteen. Proper little madames, the pair of them." He shook his head. "I just wanted to let you know that I have to turn the water off."

I thanked him and went to fill the kettle and a couple of saucepans.

Later, while we were eating sandwiches at the dining room table, Barry told me that he was a single parent. I asked who took care of his daughters when he was working.

"My sister does her best, but of course they're convinced that they're too old to need minding. I always thought things would get easier as they got older, but actually it's harder. Nowadays I can't tell them to do anything."

"They'll be grown up soon," I said. "And you won't have to worry about them anymore."

"I wish it were that simple. Wait until you have children. Then you'll see." He sighed and took another bite of his ham sandwich.

In an effort to distract him from what seemed to be a painful topic, I enquired about the plumbing. There was a problem with the valves, and for the rest of the meal Barry described the intricacies of our sink, sketching in the air for me the nature of the difficulty.

I went back to my painting. As I opened a new tin of paint, I thought about what Barry had said. In the past when people had made remarks about their children being intractable, I had secretly harboured the opinion that they had only themselves to blame, but in getting to know Jenny I had learned that a child could be as stubborn and determined as any adult. I felt a terrible wave of apprehension at the thought of living with her; it would not be like living with an adult, who would come and go and have her own life. She would have our life.

By the time Stephen returned, I had begun work on the fourth wall. He stood in the middle of the bare yellow room, looking around admiringly. "This is great," he exclaimed. "I thought you were only going to do a little bit. You must have been working all day."

"I wanted to finish it," I said. I smiled at him over my shoulder and continued rolling up and down.

"I'm glad you didn't, else I'd feel guilty. Tomorrow you can stand around and direct me while I do the ceiling." He walked over and tentatively touched the paint near the window. "What about Barry?" he asked.

"He needs a couple of parts. He'll be back on Monday."

"Oh, well, we thought that might happen," said Stephen. "I bought you a present." From behind his back he produced a poster tube. "It's for your newly painted walls." He unwrapped it and held it up for me to see. The poster was titled "How the World Began—Part I" and showed various kinds of rocks and fossils.

"Thank you. We'll have to put it up when we finish painting." Even as I spoke I remembered that this was Jenny's room; it was not for Stephen and me to decide what should go on the walls.

"Why don't you stop now? I can tidy up." He took the roller out of my hand and gave me a little push in the direction of the door.

*   *   *

While we were making dinner, I asked how the day had gone. "It was fun," said Stephen. "The exhibition was very nicely laid out, and there were lots of games and questions for the children. Did you know that you shouldn't feed birds during the spring?"

I shook my head. "Why not?"

"Apparently, stale bread isn't good for them when they're nesting. I suppose it's like eating only chocolate when you're pregnant."

He was sitting at one end of the dining room table, cutting up vegetables. I was standing at the opposite end, grating cheese. "That makes sense," I said. "Did Jenny seem upset?"

"No, she was fine. Of course Anna was there, so there was lots of girlish giggling and no chance for major conversations, but she seemed her usual self. She did tell me about a dream she'd had in which she and Helen and I were living in our old flat."

"And what happened?"

"Nothing, as far as I know. She only mentioned it in passing. I was glad because it suggests that she's forgotten the strain of those last six months."

"Perhaps she didn't realise how much of a strain they were." I pushed the cheese against the grater and watched it emerge out of the holes in soft strings.

"Of course we tried to shield her—we would have furious arguments entirely in whispers—but it's impossible to keep that sort of thing secret. You can't lie to someone you live with, or at least not for long." Stephen smiled at me and reached for a pepper.

"I'm not sure about that," I said. "Look what happened with my parents. I would have been prepared to swear on the Bible that they were happily married. Even when they told me they weren't, I didn't have that experience of everything suddenly making sense. In fact it was the reverse: everything suddenly made nonsense."

"From what you've told me, it doesn't sound like your parents were lying," Stephen said. "They were happy; they just weren't happy to be married to each other." He began to dice the pepper, bringing the knife down through the green flesh.

I returned to the kitchen to beat the eggs and pour them into the frying pan. As I stood at the stove, watching the yellow liquid bubble and solidify, I thought of the other main example of deceit in my life: Lewis. But that had been different from my parents; I had wanted so badly to believe him that no one could have hoped for a more willing collaborator. I added the mushrooms and cheese and turned down the heat.

CHAPTER 15

After the initial shock, Helen's phone call ushered in a period of comparative calm. Everyone seemed happy that Jenny was going to live with us. Stephen wanted to be a full-time father; Joyce and Edward were ecstatic to have their granddaughter back; even Suzie, when I told her the news, jumped up and hugged me. Probably the only person who shared my reservations was Jenny, and she, like me, had no voice in the matter.

There was, however, little opportunity to gauge her reactions; in the weeks that followed we scarcely saw her. School ended and she visited her maternal grandparents in Reading for a fortnight, spent another fortnight with Joyce and Edward, and then went with her mother to the seaside town of Nairn for a week. Stephen too was on holiday, and he began to renovate our house at a furious pace. His diligence gave me a pang. He no longer spoke of our having fifty years to get all the work done; now he wanted everything to be finished before Jenny moved in. He employed a couple of boys from his school, and with their help the house was rapidly transformed. In the evening I came home from the office to find the house smelling of paint, and Stephen waiting to show me what he had done that day.

In August I took a fortnight's holiday. We found a local teenager to take care of Tobias and Selina, and drove south. We spent the first week with Lynne and Greg, who were renting a cottage on the coast in East Anglia. Beforehand I had fretted as to whether Stephen and they would like each other; almost immediately it was apparent that the three of them were going to be friends. Lynne and Stephen had long discussions about education, and Greg, who with Lewis had tended to talk about work, became in Stephen's company relaxed and playful. The slight tension that had existed between them and me since Christmas eased.

The week that had seemed so long in anticipation passed swiftly. We spent the days on the beach or exploring the countryside. At night we took turns cooking, and after dinner played games or went to the local pub, where we could sit outside and read Eve stories until she fell asleep. The only flaw in my pleasure was that I was never alone with Lynne for more than a few minutes; I had imagined that there would be ample time for long conversations, but we were always in a foursome. Not until the last day of our visit, when Greg and Stephen took Eve shopping, was there an opportunity for us to talk at length.

When they had finally gone—Greg had come back for the shopping list and Stephen for Eve's favourite book—we went out into the garden to pick raspberries for supper. It was midafternoon, and as we walked across the lawn our shadows followed us, razor sharp in the bright sun. The raspberry canes were at the bottom of the garden, next to the hedge, and a slight breeze carried the scent of hay from the neighbouring fields. Lynne handed me a basin, and we set to work on opposite sides of the first row of canes. The plants were so tall and leafy that we were entirely hidden from each other, and the berries hung in juicy plenitude.

All week we had been exchanging news in snatches over the washing up or on the beach, and now that it was possible to talk at length, I scarcely knew where to begin. We both commented on how good the raspberries tasted. Then I said, "It's amazing how much Eve has changed since Christmas."

"Yes, going to kindergarten has really made her grow up.

Especially in the first few months, she learned something new almost every day."

"This morning she told me that she liked Stephen and that she thought we were very compatible." I reached for an especially large cluster of berries.

Lynne laughed. "I don't know where she picked up that word, but she's inordinately proud of it. What class is Jenny in?"

"She'll be starting junior six next term," I said.

"And the plan is she'll move in with you when you get back?"

"Yes. She'll be living with us from the end of August until next June."

"What about seeing Helen?"

"She'll go to Paris in December. We haven't talked about Easter yet, but I'm sure she'll go then too." During our fragmentary conversations I had become aware that Lynne now regarded me as having motherly concerns similar to her own; I realised that unless I exerted myself she would happily spend our whole time together discussing children.

"That seems awfully hard," she said. "Three months is endless when you're Jenny's age. What I don't understand is how Helen can bear it; I begin to fret when I don't see Eve for a few hours."

An overly ripe berry turned to pulp in my hand. I licked the sweet juice from my fingers and thought I must speak. "It seems endless to me too," I said. "I worry about how I'll manage. If Jenny had been living with Stephen all along, then it would be different, but as it is, it's going to be a huge adjustment."

There was a pause. The leaves stirred, marking Lynne's passage. Then she said, "I can remember worrying before Eve was born that she'd come between Greg and me. After all, we'd no longer be free to jump into bed at a moment's notice.

But having a child changes you in ways you can't imagine in advance. I would never have believed that we would often feel closest when we're doing something ordinary, like feeding the ducks with Eve."

"You're Eve's mother. She loves you," I said indignantly. "That's not how Jenny feels about me. She would like nothing better than to see me vanish."

"That's absurd, Celia. You're great with children, and according to Stephen, Jenny worships you."

Ahead of me between the canes hung a dark cloud of gnats. I stood staring at the minute, quivering insects. I had expected to find in Lynne an ally, who would understand my predicament with Jenny, and her optimism only increased my despair. I had barely touched upon my true fears. I remembered all the occasions when we had argued about Lewis. Then it was I who had claimed that everything was going to work out and she who had raised objections. "Stephen doesn't know," I said. "She really dislikes me."

"You're too sensitive," said Lynne. "You know the quarrels I have with Eve, and in the present situation there's bound to be friction between you and Jenny. It can't be easy to share her precious father when she only sees him one day a week, but once she's living with you, that will change."

"No. Things have happened." I stopped. In my head I had rehearsed the incidents which had convinced me of Jenny's antipathy, but now that I was on the verge of reciting the list, I was suddenly aware that everything—the dress, the lie Jenny had told to Stephen about me, the curious events of her birthday picnic—could be perceived as mere accidents. Even Julius's troubling remarks did not count as evidence.

I hoped that Lynne might question me further, but she ignored my remark; perhaps, given the low voice in which I had spoken, she had not even heard it. Instead she asked if Stephen and I planned to have children.

Although she could not see me, I nodded as if the gesture

conveyed more certainty than speech. "The only question is when. Given present circumstances, it's hard to make a plan."

"There's no hurry," said Lynne. "I'm sure Stephen will be a wonderful father. Do you think we might have picked enough by now?"

I showed her my berries, and we agreed that we had plenty. We emerged from the canes. A robin landed on the edge of the lawn. Keeping its bright eyes fixed upon us, it bobbed cautiously forward. In the field beyond the hedge the cows were lowing, and from the copper beech tree in the far corner of the garden came the liquid sound of a thrush in full voice.

"I wish we never had to go back to London," said Lynne. "Recently I've been feeling more and more strongly that I want to move to the country. I hate all the restrictions that living in a city puts on Eve." The robin retreated a few steps, then took flight.

"Your house must be worth a fortune by now."

"It is, but everything within a hundred miles of London costs a fortune. And then what would we do for money? Greg grumbles about being in advertising as if he would quit at the first opportunity, but the truth is he loves it. I just wish he would admit it." She pushed back her hair, leaving a faint smear of raspberry juice across her forehead.

"You should come to Edinburgh," I said. "The city is beautiful, house prices are low, and it's easy to get out to the country."

"It sounds perfect," said Lynne. "I envy you."

I felt a flush of pleasure; in the entire history of our friendship, Lynne had never envied me anything.

Next morning Stephen and I drove to Oxfordshire, to stay with my mother and her family. I had always found my visits to them an ordeal, but now, as with Lynne and Greg, Stephen's presence made everything easier. His reaction to my mother was perfect; he thought she was selfish and not particularly beautiful. In the face of these criticisms I was able to admit that she and Harry did have some good points, not least that they immediately liked Stephen. For the first time as an adult I enjoyed my mother's company.

The biggest change, however, was in my attitude towards my half-sister, Julia. A year after the separation my mother had telephoned to announce that she was going to have a baby. "A baby!" I had said incredulously. "How could you?" She had laughed. Months later when she rang from the hospital to tell me that I had a sister, I said I was too busy to visit. I could not forgive her for all those years of longing, when a sibling would have transformed my life, nor for the indecency of having a baby at the age of forty-one. Julia herself had not improved the situation by inheriting my mother's beauty and both her parents' musical abilities. In the past I had remained stubbornly aloof; now I was eager to befriend her, and she responded gladly to my attentions. Every morning she brought Stephen and me tea in bed. She showed me secret places, asked me to read to her, taught me games, and generally made much of me. She was a year older than Jenny and almost six inches taller. I could not help thinking what a sweet little girl she was.

Julia was particularly excited about the fact that my birthday occurred during our visit. That morning she brought us a lavish breakfast tray, decorated with nasturtiums. "You're going to get a surprise," she said, giggling, as she left the room.

In spite of this warning, I had no suspicion of intrigue when Stephen suggested that we go into the village to collect some groceries. I was amazed on our return to find my father laying the table for lunch. "Happy birthday," he said. He picked me up and swung me round as if I were a child. I was still exclaiming over his presence when Stephen came in, followed by Harry, Julia, and my mother. The three musicians serenaded me with "Ode to St. Cecilia," followed by "Happy

Birthday." Then we sat down to lunch. My mother had made artichoke soup, Harry had prepared smoked salmon, and Stephen had baked a cake. My father had contributed the champagne, of which we all drank too much.

When the cake was served it was time to open gifts. Year after year my mother had unerringly given me presents that made me feel inadequate—records of operas that I could not understand, clothes that I did not have the nerve to wear—but this year when I opened the bulky package, I found a beautiful Le Creuset casserole of the kind usually given as a wedding gift. "With love from Evelyn, Harry, and Julia—for your new home," the label said. My father gave me a subscription to *The Economist*. Stephen gave me a handbag of soft black leather; inside was a card with the inscription "I love you utterly."

Late in the afternoon, when lunch was finally declared over, we went for a walk in the Chiltern hills. My mother and Harry walked hand in hand, and I followed with my father and Stephen. They were discussing the controversial photographs taken by the spaceship Voyager III. I listened and talked to Julia. From time to time she ran over to show me something: an oddly shaped stone, or a spotted beetle.

In many ways it was the perfect birthday, but that night as I lay in bed the gaiety of the day evaporated and I felt instead a sense of loss. My father was so at home in my mother's household. If it were not for their conversation, I might have dismissed my entire childhood as a mirage. He and she talked freely about the past. "Oh, that was the year we went to the Lake District," one of them would say, and the other would respond, "Yes, and we argued the whole time." He treated Julia as a favourite niece or godchild, and she called him "David" and held his hand.

Stephen was the only person I had ever known who seemed to understand why I found the amicability of my parents' separation hard to bear; I felt that it robbed me of not one but both parents. After my mother's letter I had spent the remainder of the university term indulging the fantasy of a new life with my father. I thought that he would turn to me for solace; at last he and I would have the kind of companionship I craved. When I went home for Christmas, however, it was only too apparent that he was flourishing in his new single state; he had turned into a competent cook, rearranged the furniture, and seemed suddenly to have a host of friends. Like my mother, he had been longing for change, and during the decade that followed, I watched him, grey-haired, no longer lean, become involved with a succession of women half his age. He loved to teach, and I came to suspect that what he sought was not so much physical but didactic pleasures.

On Sunday Stephen and I drove north along the M1. I watched the newly harvested fields flash by and thought that in less than forty-eight hours Jenny would move in. I had hoped, especially with Lynne, to find sympathy for my situation, but instead I had encountered, as I did in Edinburgh, a massive, inflexible wall of approval. My mother, my father, even Harry and Julia, were all glad that I was about to become a stepmother. There was nothing to be done except to make the best of the situation. Perhaps Lynne was right in claiming that our difficulties stemmed from Jenny's not having sufficient time with Stephen. Once she was living with us, she would relax.

"Penny for them," said Stephen.

"I was thinking about Jenny. I hope she's going to be happy with us."

"I'm sure she is," said Stephen. "Of course she'll miss Helen and be homesick to start with, but she'll soon settle down." He spoke with an absent-minded conviction that did not invite discussion. For a few minutes we were both silent. Then he said, "I was wondering if I was all right with your family and friends."

I stared in surprise. He so seldom asked for reassurance that it had not occurred to me that he might feel insecure. "You were perfect," I said. "They all want to come and live with us. I was positively bored listening to them sing your praises. But what about you? Did you like them? Did you have a good time?"

"It was great being with Lynne and Greg; they were so easy. With your assorted parents it was more complicated. I think if I'd met Evelyn and Harry and David on, say, a train, I'd be going around telling everyone about these three fascinating people. But they're not strangers on a train, they're your parents, and I kept wanting them to behave better towards you. You know," he said, "the whole time we were there, neither of them paid you a compliment."

"That would be quite out of character. They believe in praise where praise is due; none of this parental gushing. Nothing is ever enough for them." I looked over at Stephen. He sensed my gaze and reached across to pat my thigh. "It makes me feel better to hear you say these things," I said. "Most people think I'm lucky to have such interesting parents."

"I think they're lucky to have such a wonderful daughter."

It was six in the evening when we arrived back in Edinburgh. The sun was shining, and in our small front garden the roses were in bloom. We stood on the pavement, looking at our flat. "The trouble with home improvement is that you can't stop," Stephen said. "Don't you think we should paint the window frames?"

"You're too perfectionist. They're fine." I squeezed his hand and pulled him over to the gate. "Come and smell our roses. Aren't they splendid? They're even better than Mr. Patterson's."

"They are beautiful." He kissed me.

I took off my sunglasses and smiled up at him. "You know, I was just thinking that it's less than a year since I moved to

Edinburgh. I remember I felt as if I was setting out to find the source of the Amazon."

"So did your heart sink as we crossed the border?"

"No," I said. "Quite the reverse. I felt that I was coming home."

We unlocked the front door and went inside. I bent to pick up the mail that lay scattered on the floor and saw at a glance that most of the envelopes were bills. "Tobias, Tobias," I called. He rushed out of the dining room. I picked him up. For a few minutes he purred rapturously in my arms. Then, as if suddenly remembering that I had abandoned him for two whole weeks, he jumped down and walked very deliberately back into the dining room. Stephen had finished decorating the hall only shortly before we left, and during our absence the smell of paint had reasserted itself. As we went from room to room, opening windows, everything seemed both familiar and strangely pristine.

Stephen went to fetch our bags. I put the remains of our picnic away in the fridge. When I came into the bedroom, he was gazing out of the window. "Look at the poppies," he said. "They must have seeded themselves."

All along the edge of the herbaceous border the vivid pink and red flowers were in bloom; the grass was strewn with petals. Stephen was wearing a blue shirt with snap fastenings. One by one I pulled them open.

PART IV

CHAPTER 16

We had returned to Edinburgh at the last possible moment. On Monday we both had to go to work, and on Tuesday Jenny was moving in. At the office, chores had piled up during my absence. So many of the staff had been on holiday simultaneously that there had been no one to take care of my projects. Almost as soon as I sat down at my desk, Clare stopped by to talk about the autumn sales conference. It was in a couple of weeks, and I would be responsible for presenting several of my books. I took notes and tried to conceal my anxiety behind intelligent questions. Last year I had attended the conference solely as a spectator.

After Clare left I began to sort through my mail, trying to divide tasks into more and less urgent categories. The editor of *Sunset Song* was delighted with my editing; Mr. Brockbank sent a letter, written in beautiful sloping copperplate, announcing that he was looking forward to our collaboration on a new edition of *Introduction to Scottish Poetry;* there were problems with the permissions for a primary-school anthology. And to my dismay, the biology book on which I had worked while the science editor was on holiday seemed to have become my property. There was a note from Bill asking if I could check through it with particular care; the last book we had published by this author had resulted in a steady flow of complaints from teachers up and down the country.

For the rest of the day I scarcely left my desk, and by the time Stephen picked me up, at six-thirty, our holiday seemed to have taken place in the distant past. We had talked of doing something special, given that it was our last evening alone together, but after supper we were both too tired to do more than pay a visit to the pub. We had one drink and then returned to bed. Just before I fell asleep, it occurred to me that however ordinary the evening we had passed, such evenings would, in the course of the next few months, become a rarity.

Next day I came home from work to find a note on the dining-room table: "Daddy and I have gone shopping. Jenny." The door of the spare room was ajar, and I looked inside. The floor was strewn with bags and boxes, and on the yellow walls were posters of a ballet dancer, a pop group, a pony jumping a fence. Jenny had not yet passed a single night beneath our roof, but already she had made this room her own.

She and Stephen arrived home with three parcels of fish and chips, which we ate out of the paper at the dining room table. Afterwards Jenny showed me the stationery she had bought for the new school term, and I admired her notebooks and brightly coloured pencils. Then Stephen announced that it was time for her to go to bed. While he helped her to get organised, I sat in the living room reading the *Scotsman;* the Edinburgh Festival had just begun, and I circled events that struck me as interesting. When Stephen returned, I said, "I can't believe how many things are on during the festival."

"Weren't you here for it last year?"

"I arrived in the middle. It made moving even harder. There were all these interesting shows and no one to go to them with."

He came and sat down beside me on the sofa. "This year we'll go to everything your heart desires."

"I was wondering about the Polish theatre company. The review makes them sound fantastic."

"Deirdre was talking about that. She went at the weekend and said they were wonderful. We should definitely go." He looked at the page of reviews and advertisements that I had been studying. "This would interest my father," he said, pointing to an exhibition on the history of the Scottish garden. His head was close to mine, and I reached to kiss him. As our mouths touched, there was a slight noise. Stephen pulled back, and following his gaze, I saw Jenny standing in the doorway. She seemed to be staring directly at me, but then I thought that of course she was looking at both of us. She wore a white nightdress patterned with red flowers, which made her appear particularly small and waif-like.

"Daddy, I can't sleep." She closed the door behind her and went over to sit in the armchair on the other side of the fireplace. She curled her legs up, as if settling herself for a long conversation. "What are you doing?" she asked.

"We're reading the newspaper. Now come on," said Stephen. "It's nearly nine-thirty." Not knowing what expression to assume—a smile of complicity with Jenny, a frown indicating solidarity with Stephen—I pretended to be engrossed in the newspaper. There was a small pause, then Jenny slowly got out of her armchair and trailed out of the room.

"Shall I try to get tickets for Friday or Saturday?" I asked. "I could telephone from work."

"Perhaps you should wait until we've organised a babysitter before you do anything definite," he said quietly.

The door opened again. "I'm thirsty," said Jenny. Ten minutes later she had an itchy foot. On the fourth occasion, before she could say anything, I stood up and left the room. I had not myself dared to try my parents' patience in such a fashion, but I remembered vividly the awfulness of being confined to bed, especially in summer, when it was still light outside and so apparent that life was going on without me. I wandered into the kitchen with no particular purpose in mind. The sink was stacked with yesterday's dishes, which Stephen had promised to do. I pushed up my sleeves and set to work. When I had finished and even the worst of the saucepans had been scrubbed clean, the murmur of voices from the spare room was still audible. On impulse I began to lay the table for breakfast. As a teenager, last thing before bed, I had laid three places at our kitchen table, but since I left home, breakfast, whether eaten in haste or leisure, had never been a meal to prepare for in advance.

Stephen came into the dining room as I was putting out the cereal bowls. He closed the door behind him. "Maybe this is it," he said. "We had a long talk about Helen. About why she's doing what she's doing and when Jenny will see her again. Helen's gone over and over this, but in an odd way I don't think Jenny fully realised until today that she would be living here and Helen would be far away." He spoke softly, and in his low tones I heard the pressure of Jenny's presence.

"It's an awful lot to adjust to all at once," I said. "The first evening we moved in, it took me ages to go to sleep." I lined up the knife and spoon at Jenny's place.

"I remember when I went to stay with my great-uncles I would be up and down like a yo-yo. It was partly that I had to find out what I could get away with. Of course," he added, "they were hopelessly indulgent." The dining room door opened, and Jenny padded in, rubbing her eyes.

The following night I attended a workshop on the use of computers in publishing and did not get home until almost eleven. I let myself in quietly. The light was on in the hall, and the doors of both bedrooms were ajar. Without pausing to take off my coat, I tiptoed into our room. Stephen was sitting up in bed, reading. "How did it go?" he asked. "Have you worked out how to replace authors by silicon chips?"

"Not quite, but we're getting closer." I sat down on the edge of the bed. "You're wearing pyjamas," I said in surprise.

"Yes, in the interests of paternity, but with a little encouragement I'll throw them aside."

"I'll try to provide it." I stood up and took off my coat.

"I think the worst is over," he said. "There was only one request this evening, for a glass of water."

"Can I close her door? I'm worried that I'll wake her."

Stephen shook his head. "She insists on having it open, but don't worry. She's used to sleeping through noise."

I went to hang my coat up in the hall cupboard and then to the bathroom, where I performed my toilette as quietly as possible. When I had finished I stole back into the bedroom and closed the door. Stephen switched off the light; we turned to each other. He groaned my name and whispered words of passion. I slid my hand up under the jacket of his pyjamas and kissed his neck. But I could not forget that only a thin layer of wood kept the noises of our mouths and bodies from travelling to Jenny; I tried to be quiet, to bury my face against Stephen or in the pillow, as I had done, during the last couple of weeks, when we made love in other people's houses.

On Saturday morning, while Stephen did the washing, I took the car to Safeways. I was used to having Jenny around on Saturdays, but months of weekly visits had not prepared me for how different it felt for Stephen and me to divide the household tasks between us, sensibly, out of necessity, and without the respite of Sunday in our immediate future. Just before I left I had asked Stephen again about the Polish theatre, and he had said that he thought it was premature to leave Jenny with a baby-sitter. He urged me to go by myself. "There's no reason why you should stay at home," he had said. I agreed, but I did not relish the prospect of making solitary arrangements; it was too reminiscent of the previous year.

In Safeways I wandered up and down the aisles, unable to make decisions. Which kind of cereal did Jenny prefer? I could not remember. Was there any point in buying ingredients for ratatouille when she hated it? Should I buy more chocolate biscuits, given the rapidity with which they disappeared? The shop was thronged with people, and whenever I paused for more than a few seconds, someone would say, "Excuse me."

Finally I had all the items on the list and made my way to the front of the shop. The cashier was deep in conversation with the girl at the next register about a new kind of diet. "It works by enzymes," she explained. Without pausing in her conversation, she rang up my groceries; I owed seventeen pounds and sixty-three pence. I opened my purse, and as I counted out the money, I discovered that ten pounds was missing.

I arrived home to find Stephen in the kitchen, organising a third load of washing. We had both remarked on the amazing amount of extra laundry that Jenny's presence had created in only a few days. "You were gone a long time," he said. "I hope it wasn't fiendishly busy."

Tobias ran to meet me, purring loudly. I put the box of groceries on the counter and bent to pet him. "Not especially," I said. "I've lost ten pounds."

"Maybe you spent it. That's what usually happens when I think I've lost some money. Or I've stuffed it into a pocket." Stephen smiled; he was going through the pockets of a pair of jeans.

"I went to the bank at lunchtime yesterday, and I haven't done anything since then except take the bus home."

"And you're sure the cashier gave you the correct amount?"

"It was only fifty pounds. She counted the notes out in front of me, and I counted them again." I had been going to the Royal Bank of Scotland, round the corner from the office, since I moved to Edinburgh, and I knew all the cashiers by sight. The day before, the dark, plump woman with gap teeth had given me my money. I had noticed a new ring glittering on her well-manicured hand.

"A note must have fallen out," Stephen said. He began to

scoop the rest of the clothes off the floor into the machine. I felt that he was giving me only a fraction of his attention, and I was irritated by his suggestions; I had already, while driving home, considered all the obvious alternatives. Rather tartly, I said that I did not see how I could lose one note out of five. Tobias padded off towards the garden.

Stephen straightened up. "Well then," he said, "perhaps someone took it."

I stared at him in amazement. "But I've only been here and at the office, and I can't believe anyone at work would steal. Besides, why not steal the whole lot?"

"I don't know. Ten pounds is not a great deal of money, Celia. I expect it will turn up." He closed the door of the machine, set the dial, and pulled the knob. I watched the water rushing into the tub. He was being so reasonable that I did not know how to explain my distress. I was vexed not by the loss, which as he pointed out was small, but by my ignorance of where or how it could have occurred.

He moved over to the counter and looked inside the box of groceries. "What nice apples. You can actually smell them."

He picked one up, bit into it, and then held it out for me to see; the flesh beneath the skin was tinged with pink. I took the apple out of his hand and sank my teeth into it. The back door swung open.

I left Stephen to put away the groceries and went to the bedroom. Although I had no recollection of doing so, it was possible that I had tucked the money away in a pocket. As I searched through the clothes I had worn the day before, I remembered how often I had mysteriously lost things as a child. "Be sure not to lose it," my mother would say, giving me a letter to post, a shopping list, money, and the occasions when I neglected her injunction were many and tragic. She thought I was careless; on the contrary, I was always taking great care, thinking about whatever must not be lost, the piece of paper clutched in my hand, the action to be performed. But almost inevitably, it seemed, I would be distracted—I would see a comic in a shop window, or someone would talk to me—and the precious object would disappear. Often hours, even days, would pass before something would bring it back to mind and I would, with a start, realise my loss. Then terrible, panic-stricken searches would ensue, before I was forced to confess. At least nowadays, I thought, there was no one to be angry with me. My search yielded a total of twenty pence.

Over lunch Stephen told Jenny about the money. "You didn't see it by any chance?" he asked.

She shook her head. "I'm sure I can find it," she said to me. "Mummy always asks me to help when she loses things. She says I'm lucky. In Nairn I saw a five pound note on the bumper of a car. And last term I found a ring in the school cloakroom. Where did you lose it?"

"I'm afraid I've no idea. It seemed to vanish between the bank and the supermarket."

"That makes it harder," she said judiciously, "but I expect it's in your bedroom somewhere. If I find it, can I have a reward?"

"Of course," I said. "That's only fair."

"How much?"

I had been thinking of a trip to the cinema, or a book, and this blunt demand for remuneration startled me. "I don't know. What do you think?" I said, turning towards Stephen.

"Ten percent?"

"That sounds right." I looked back at Jenny to see what she thought.

"So, do you know how much Celia's going to give you for finding her money?" Stephen asked.

"A pound," she said flatly, not at all as if she were glad to be able to answer his question.

When we had finished eating, Jenny quizzed me again

about my movements. Together we searched the house, but all we found were the kinds of things that are always under pieces of furniture: dust, paper clips, hairpins, tissues. Jenny was even more persistent than I. "Could we lift the bed?" she asked. "Did you look under the chest of drawers?" She only agreed to stop when Stephen announced that it was time to leave; we had tickets for a matinee of *Winnie-the-Pooh*.

As I sat watching Pooh and Eeyore frolic around the stage, my attention wandered. Stephen's suggestion that someone could have stolen the money pricked me, like a burr caught in my clothes. At the office, in spite of occasional memos about security, I had followed Suzie's example. I kept my office door open, and I often went out leaving my handbag unguarded. It was hard to imagine that someone I saw every day would steal from me, but of course there were always strangers wandering around.

That evening after Jenny had gone to bed Stephen and I settled to work at opposite ends of the dining room table. He was preparing a test. I was editing Brockbank's *Introduction to Scottish Poetry*, which, in spite of my reluctance, we were reprinting. The room had been silent for some time, except for the roar of the gas fire and our intermittent sighs, when Stephen burst out, "Damn, how can I teach algebra when I can't solve this problem myself? So far I've got three different answers."

"With difficulty," I said, and giggled.

"How's old Brockbank doing?"

"Some parts are fine. His biographical notes, for instance, could be published as is, but his critical introduction is nothing more than a paean to his favourite poets."

"I've never heard anyone actually use the word 'paean' before. Would you like some more?" He picked up the bottle of red wine that stood in the middle of the table.

"Yes, please." I pushed my glass towards him. "There was

something I wanted to ask you," I said. "Do you think you could you tell Jenny not to go into our room? A couple of times I've found her peering into the wardrobe, or examining the things I keep on top of the chest of drawers. It makes me uncomfortable."

"You should ask her to leave," Stephen said energetically.

"I feel awkward telling her what to do."

"That's absurd, Celia. It's your room, and even if it weren't, you're perfectly entitled to tell Jenny what to do."

I ran my finger up and down the edge of the manuscript. "You don't think it will seem like I'm trying to take Helen's place."

"Of course not. You're the adult, she's the child. You shouldn't have any compunction in bossing her around." He stood up and came round the table to hug me. "I love you," he said.

CHAPTER 17

We were having breakfast on Tuesday when Stephen broke the news to Jenny that he would be working late. The previous term Deirdre and he had decided to set up a tutoring program at their school. Every Tuesday, he explained, senior pupils would volunteer their time to help those in the lower forms who were having difficulties. He and Deirdre would preside over the whole occasion and act as consultants. Tonight was the first session of the program.

"How will I get home?" Jenny asked.

"Celia's going to leave work early and pick you up from school."

"When will you be home?" She had been pouring cereal into her bowl. Now she put down the box carefully, as if it were important to position it in exactly the right place.

"Not until you're fast asleep. I'll see you tomorrow morning."

He spoke in a jolly tone which took for granted Jenny's good-humoured compliance in the arrangements. Watching her, I felt less confident of her reaction. The corners of her mouth were tucked in, and for a moment I was worried that, like a much younger child, she would refuse to stay alone with me. "It'll be fun," I said. "We can make supper together."

"Can I have the milk, please?" she asked. When Stephen passed her the jug, she poured an exact amount into her cereal, then deftly raised the jug so that no drip trickled down the side.

*   *   *

Stephen had drawn a map showing the way to Jenny's school, but I must have taken a wrong turn. Just as I expected the school to come into view, I found myself on the edge of a housing development; half a dozen multistorey buildings rose out of a wasteland. A boy in a raincoat was standing at a zebra crossing, and I stopped to ask for directions. "Let me think," he said several times. "Langton Road. I know it's right around here." I was about to drive off in despair, when a middle-aged man wearing shorts came jogging along. "Excuse me," I called loudly. He stopped and between gasps gave directions. The boy in the raincoat nodded accompaniment. "That's right enough," he kept saying.

My hands were sweating, and I knew without glancing in the mirror that my cheeks were red. I drove as fast as I could, using the horn on several occasions to warn pedestrians and fellow motorists. Outside the school the pavement was empty, save for the small, solitary figure of Jenny. She was standing in front of the gates, and as I approached I saw her looking anxiously up and down the street. She caught sight of the car, and ran over and climbed in. I apologised for being late.

"That's okay," she said. "I knew you didn't know the way."

"Will you tell me how to get home?"

"First you turn round. Then go left at the main road." In between directions she told me about her classes. In English they were learning "Ode to Autumn," in history they were studying the Vikings. Miss Nisbet had asked her to read her composition to the class. "The one about Edward and Selina?" I asked.

"Yes."

Ahead of us a man on a bicycle was pedalling furiously up the slight incline. He carried a briefcase in one hand and wove erratically from side to side. I slowed down to give him a wide berth.

"Turn left at the church." Jenny pointed. "In gym we got to play netball."

"I was always terrible at netball. I much preferred hockey."

"Hockey's easy if you're big," she said. "Then you can bash everyone; but if you're small, netball's better. Even though I can't shoot goals, I can sneak around, getting in the way and passing the ball."

When we reached home, we both went to our rooms to change. I had been worrying all day about how Jenny and I would manage, but her lively conversation was dispelling my anxiety. As I put on my jeans, I realised that I was looking forward to spending a few hours alone with her. How could I expect us to become friends if our intimacy depended entirely upon Stephen?

By the time I came into the kitchen Jenny was already there. She was standing on the stool she used to reach the cupboards, inspecting the contents of various tins. "What would you like for tea?" I asked.

"Tea and toast and honey." She lifted the loaf out of the bread box.

While visiting her maternal grandparents during the summer, Jenny had acquired a taste for tea, and she now insisted upon drinking it at every opportunity. The kettle boiled. I filled the teapot and carried it into the dining room. When I came back to the kitchen, she was buttering the toast. "I've done two slices each," she said.

We agreed that we would read at tea. I settled for the newspaper, and Jenny produced a *Bunty* annual. She read the comic every week. I remarked that I had not seen the book before. "I bought it today," she said. She did not raise her eyes from the page. I knew that there was a newsagent's near the school that she and her friends sometimes patronised in their lunch hour.

After tea we went out into the garden to feed Selina. She was crouched in one corner of her run, nibbling the grass. "Selina," Jenny called. The rabbit raised her head and took a couple of hops in our direction.

"She knows her name," I said.

"I think it's more that she knows my voice," Jenny said. "Fred," she called.

Selina, who had resumed her grazing, looked up again. Jenny reached in for her dish and walked off towards the shed, where the rabbit food was kept. Meanwhile I knelt down and poked some grass through the wire netting. Selina gazed at me; her eyes were the same shade of delicate blue as the forget-me-nots in the herbaceous border. She ate the grass I held out to her until Jenny returned and set down the dish brimming with pellets. Then she hopped over and began to eat the pellets daintily, one by one. Jenny squatted down to watch her, and I went back indoors.

The *Bunty* annual was lying open on the dining room table. I picked it up and found myself reading about the four Marys. Except for their hairstyles, they seemed exactly the same as when I had followed their adventures twenty years before. I read a couple of pages with amusement. As I put the book aside I noticed that the price was six pounds ninety-five pence. It was a considerable sum of money for someone who got only twenty-five pence a week in pocket money.

I settled down to work on the introduction of *Sunset Song*. The author had agreed to my editing with tremendous zeal, which I had initially welcomed. Now that I studied her comments more closely, I understood that she was in effect washing her hands of the manuscript and it was up to me to solve the many problems that remained. When Jenny came in I was pondering a particularly incoherent paragraph. "What are you doing?" she asked.

"I'm working. Do you have homework?"

She nodded. "I have to do arithmetic, and I have to read a chapter about the Vikings."

"That doesn't sound too bad."

She left the room, and I assumed that she had gone to work at her desk, but she returned in a couple of minutes with her satchel and seated herself at the far end of the table. For a few minutes there was silence. Her head was bent over her books, and I could not see her face. She wrote something. I turned my attention back to the manuscript. Suddenly the table shook slightly. Jenny was rubbing something out.

"I don't understand this," she said with a small sigh.

"What?"

She stood up and brought her notebook to show me. She was just beginning fractions, and her homework consisted of ten problems in addition and subtraction. "Can you do this one?" I asked, pointing to the first question: $\frac{1}{2} + \frac{1}{4} = ?$

Jenny shook her head.

"You can only add fractions that have the same denominator. The denominator is the bottom number. Suppose this was a half plus a half, then what would the answer be?"

"One," said Jenny doubtfully.

"That's right. So what did you do to get one?"

By a series of questions I coaxed her into translating a half into two fourths. "Two fourths plus one fourth is what?" I asked.

"Three fourths?"

"Yes."

She looked at me, as if waiting for something more. "That's the answer, Jenny. Write it down."

As we worked down the list of problems, I realised that I was using the same technique with Jenny that my father had used with me. He had been an enthusiastic teacher. I remembered how he had come home one afternoon and found me attempting to draw a triangle in which the sum of the angles did not equal one hundred and eighty degrees. The floor was littered with my attempts. I had drawn triangle after triangle, making the apex severely acute, gapingly obtuse, imagining each time that I would take the third angle by surprise, and occasionally, for a moment, it seemed that I had succeeded. Closer scrutiny of the protractor, however, always revealed that the amount by which the sum varied was too small to be above suspicion.

"What are you doing?" my father asked. He stood in the doorway of my room, undoing his tie.

Reluctantly I explained. I had wanted to surprise him.

"But that's impossible, Celia," he burst out. He did not seem to understand that that was the point; there would be no glory attached to showing that a square had four equal sides. "What did Miss Grey tell you about the sum of the angles in a triangle?"

"That they always add up to a hundred and eighty degrees."

"Didn't she show you why?"

I shook my head.

My father walked over to my desk, seized a pencil and a clean sheet of paper, and drew a very ordinary triangle. "Now let's call the angles a, b, and c." He drew a line at the apex parallel to the base. "What size is this angle?" he asked, indicating the angle between the line and the left-hand side of the triangle.

"I don't know."

"Yes, you do. This line is parallel with the base."

Grudgingly I gave the right answer. In a few minutes he had led me through the steps of the proof. At every stage I knew what my father wanted me to say, and I said it, yet I remained unconvinced. Whatever he had proved, that did not mean that I had to believe it. Although I stopped trying to draw the magic triangle, it was only because I saw that he would be irritated by my persistence.

Jenny, however, seemed more amenable to the Socratic approach, and by the last few sums I was merely affirming her answers. I was pleased by her new skill and especially by the fact that we were managing without Stephen. When she had written out the answers neatly and finished the Vikings, I put aside my editing. Together we made macaroni cheese. At Jenny's suggestion we ate in front of the television.

After supper I returned to *Sunset Song,* but I soon realised that I was too tired to do anything useful. I put the manuscript back in my briefcase and went to the bedroom. The day before, Marilyn had posted an appeal at the office asking for donations of clothes for a jumble sale; it seemed a good opportunity to get rid of various garments. I opened the door of the wardrobe and began to slide the hangers along the rail. Tucked away at one end was the blue dress which I had last worn to Nick and Charlie's party. I lifted it out and, holding it up against me, turned to the mirror. As I gazed at my reflection, I remembered with amazement the grief I had suffered over Lewis. It was as if he had transported me to a foreign country, where nothing made sense. Now that I was home again, that emotion, which had once loomed large as a mountain, seemed no bigger than a mole hill. I was still pondering this amazing transformation, when Jenny came in.

She asked what I was doing. I explained, and she walked over to join me. Side by side we scrutinised the contents of the wardrobe. "Why aren't any of Daddy's things here?" she asked.

"He keeps them in the hall cupboard."

"Oh," she said. She pulled out a pair of brown trousers and held them up in front of her. "These are horrid. Like mud."

"Jenny, I just bought those. I've never even had a chance to wear them. I thought they'd be useful in winter."

"They can be useful to someone else." She put them down on the foot of the bed. She pointed towards a striped blouse, with a bow at the neck. "Do you ever wear this?"

"Sometimes," I admitted. "If I'm meeting authors."

"It's not very nice." She wrinkled her nose.

I took the blouse and placed it on top of the trousers. There was soon a sizeable pile. Jenny had strong opinions about my clothes, and few of them were favourable. Rather than argue, I decided to sort through the collection again after she had gone to bed. Meanwhile I announced that we were finished. Jenny moved towards the door, then stopped. "You're not getting rid of this, are you?" she asked.

She was pointing to the blue pullover which I had bought a few days before to console myself for returning to work. "No, of course not," I said. "I forgot to put it away."

"Good. It looks really nice on you." She smiled at me. She swung back and forth on the door handle, watching while I put the pullover in the appropriate drawer, then left the room.

When I came into the living room a few minutes later, she was lying on the floor, watching a program about Whipsnade Zoo. Tobias lay stretched out beside her. "Tobias recognises the lions," she said. "Watch." A few minutes later, when a lion roared, he did indeed seem to glance at the screen. "There," said Jenny triumphantly.

"You're right," I said. "Did you know it was eight-thirty?"

She stood up and went off to her room without a single protest. I heard her moving around, going to brush her teeth, then she reappeared in the living room. To my surprise, she came over and kissed my cheek. I could smell the warmth of her body.

After a suitable interval, I returned to the bedroom. I did succeed in rescuing a few items from the pile of condemned clothing, but not as many as I expected. Even my favourite shirt seemed tainted by her disapproval, and when I tried it on, I was forced to acknowledge the justice of her criticism. As I folded the clothes into carrier bags, I thought of the summer my mother had given half her wardrobe to Oxfam.

For weeks the hall had been crowded with bags, each one, I later understood, another step in her preparations to leave my father and me. I had always held this careful planning against her. Now it occurred to me that she and Harry had probably wanted to live together for years and had refrained from doing so only on my account. Maybe some day I could ask her about the ins and outs of her decision.

CHAPTER 18

On Saturday afternoon Jenny asked if we could go to Victoria Park so that she could try out her new roller skates. They had been a birthday present from Helen, but with all her travelling over the summer, Jenny had scarcely had an opportunity to use them. The sun was shining, and not until I stepped outside did I realise that there was a nip in the air. I told Stephen and Jenny to go on ahead, and let myself back into the house. When I opened the drawer where I kept my woolens, I saw my new pullover lying on top. For a moment I hesitated. Then I thought that I was long past the age when I was going to climb trees, and hastily put it on.

Stephen and Jenny were waiting for me at the corner. Jenny held a roller skate in either hand. She was swinging them back and forth, banging them together like cymbals. "You're wearing your new pullover," Stephen said, as I drew close.

"It was the first thing I saw."

Jenny had paused while I spoke; now she spread her arms and brought the skates together with a furious bang.

"Careful," said Stephen. "You might bend them out of alignment. It looks very nice."

"Thank you." I took his hand, and we turned down Craighall Road. Jenny ran ahead.

"I can scarcely believe that two weeks ago we were walking in the Chilterns," I said.

"God, is it only two weeks? That's amazing," said Stephen. "I know with six weeks holiday I can't complain, but I feel as if I've never been away from school. Even the kids in my new class are already distressingly familiar. This is the time of year I always think about quitting."

"What would you do instead?"

"Live off you," he said, smiling. "I do enjoy teaching, but so many of the children are in trouble of one sort or another, and algebra doesn't necessarily seem like the solution. Sometimes I think I'd like to do social work, be able to help in a more direct way."

"Maybe you should look into it," I suggested.

He shrugged. "I'm afraid any career change is out of the question until Jenny is older. Besides, you remember what Julius said: everything is being cut back except for the problems."

There were several benches just inside the entrance to the park. Jenny sat down on one of them and with Stephen's help began to put on her skates. I wandered off across the grass in the direction of the playground. Two grown men were playing football with a group of small boys, and I stopped to watch. One of the men almost scored a goal but was foiled by a chubby, sandy-haired boy who intercepted the ball with surprising speed.

For a Saturday the playground was fairly quiet. A line of children stood at the bottom of the slide, waiting to go down, and two girls in skirts were exhorting their father to play on the seesaw. I sat down on the swing nearest to the slide. As I pushed myself idly back and forth I watched Stephen and Jenny on the far side of the park. Jenny was dressed as usual in dark colours, and at this distance it was Stephen's bright red pullover that made them vivid. She held his hand, and they began to move along the tarmac path which ran round the perimeter of the park. The leaves were just beginning to turn, and the air was exceptionally clear. I felt as if I could suddenly see twice as far.

Jenny was gathering speed, and by the time they reached

the playground Stephen was jogging briskly to keep up. "You go round by yourself," he said, and walked over to the swings. "Like a push?" he asked.

"Yes, please." I raised my feet off the ground and held my legs straight out in front. Stephen took hold of the swing and pulled me backwards as high as he could. He let go, and I swooped forward. He kept pushing me, higher, higher: the sky, the grass, the tarmac, the football players, the distant figure of Jenny, all swung back and forth, until I said, "Enough." Stephen sat down on the swing next to mine. When I was at a standstill he said, "Did you know that there was a hole in your pullover?"

"A hole? How can there be?"

Jenny approached unsteadily on her roller skates, her arms outstretched for balance. She paused, holding on to one of the supports of the swings. "Will you run with me, Daddy?"

"Okay," said Stephen, sliding off the swing. "We won't be long."

Jenny took his hand, put her feet together, and crouched down. "Run, Daddy. Run," she said. Obediently Stephen set off at a slow trot down the path, towing Jenny behind him. I stood up and removed the pullover. In the back was a hole the size of my fist.

"Excuse me," said a voice. "Are you using this swing?" A woman and a small boy stood before me.

I shook my head and went to sit on the low wall that surrounded the sand pit. I peered at the edges of the hole; perhaps there had been a weakness in the wool and it had snapped, or a knot had come undone and the wool had unravelled, but where the wool itself had gone I could not imagine. I remembered the many physics lessons in which we had chanted, over and over, "Matter is neither created nor destroyed." On the far side of the park Jenny and Stephen had stopped; Jenny was doubled over, presumably to adjust her skates, and Stephen was standing beside her. It was a beautiful day.

I set out to meet them, carrying the pullover as if it were now unwearable. They were moving again, although more slowly than before, and our mutual progress brought us quickly together. Stephen's cheeks were flushed, and his glasses were sliding down his nose. He released Jenny, and she continued to skate along in the same direction. We followed slowly.

"This is great exercise," he said, breathing hard.

"I can tell. What am I going to do with my pullover?" I asked.

"You got it at that shop on Saint Stephen Street, didn't you? Why don't we walk over there and ask them to exchange it?"

"But I don't have the receipt."

"I'm sure that doesn't matter. It's obviously brand new." He sounded so calm and reasonable that I at once felt better. Order was about to be restored. He called to Jenny, and she stopped and waited for us to catch up with her. Stephen explained our plan.

"I thought you just got it," she said.

"I know. The hole must have been there all along. When you look at the front, you don't notice it."

"Can I see?" she asked. I held up the pullover, and on her skates she moved cautiously forward. She lifted her hand and ran her finger round the edge of the hole. Her cheeks, like Stephen's, were flushed, and her eyes were dark. "Why are we going to the shop?"

"Because I'm hoping that they'll exchange it."

"Oh," she said. It was hard to tell if she was on the verge of smiling or pouting. She moved off towards the nearest bench and sat down to unlace her skates.

*   *   *

As we turned the corner into Saint Stephen Street the shop was immediately in view. Several striped pullovers hung next to the open door, swinging back and forth in the breeze. Inside, the shelves brimmed with brightly coloured objects—socks, gloves, scarves, wooden toys, hand-dipped candles—and the air smelled of sandalwood and lanolin. There was a knitting machine in the back, and as I approached the counter I heard the soft clicking of the needles. Suzie, who lived round the corner, had told me that the shop was run by a collective of women.

Jenny and Stephen disappeared behind the central display. The woman at the counter smiled and asked if she could help me. I remembered her from the day when I had bought the pullover. Her fair hair was braided into a single pigtail, which hung almost to her waist. I told her what was wrong. As I spoke, the smooth openness of her face contracted into a frown. She took the pullover out of my hands and examined it. "I don't understand how this could have happened," she said. She went to show the pullover to the woman who was operating the machine. Together they scrutinised the hole.

Both women looked up, and the woman from behind the counter pointed to me. I went over. "I'm sorry that I didn't notice sooner," I said. "The hole's at the back, so even when you're wearing the pullover, you don't see it."

"We don't make clothes with holes in," said the woman at the machine. Her face was shadowed by unruly hair, and it was hard to detect her expression, but her tone conveyed ample disapproval.

"Perhaps a customer damaged it, here in the shop," the fair woman said doubtfully.

"They'd have to have been trying pretty hard. As far as I can see," the other woman said, "the only way this could have happened is if someone took a pair of scissors and cut out a piece."

Stephen had left Jenny examining the toys and come up behind me. "Who would do that except a manic tourist?" he asked. I wondered if he too understood that I was being accused.

"Sometimes people do strange things," said the machinist, staring at me.

"This is exactly the pullover I want," I said. "If there's any way you can repair it, I'd be perfectly happy."

The two woman exchanged glances. "I believe we have a very similar one on the shelf over there," said the first woman. She spoke with grudging resignation. Some customers approached the counter, and she went to serve them. The machinist did not take her eyes off me.

"Let's have a look," said Stephen. He seemed oblivious to the tensions of the situation.

The second pullover was a richer, deeper shade of blue than the previous one and fitted perfectly. As Stephen was praising it, the woman from the machine approached. "Suppose you give us fifteen pounds for the new pullover, to defray some of our costs," she said. "And suppose we all check it together very carefully to be sure that it's in perfect condition before you leave the shop."

Fifteen pounds seemed a small price to restore good will, but as I got out my purse Stephen said, "That doesn't seem fair. Celia bought the pullover in good faith. It isn't her fault if there's a problem. If you bought a new camera, and the first time you tried to use it the shutter jammed, would you think you were to blame? No, you'd blame the manufacturer, and you'd expect the shopkeeper to assume responsibility."

"And what if you were the shopkeeper and you were sure that the camera had been in perfect condition when it left your shop, and that for whatever reasons the customer had damaged it herself?" the woman asked. She folded her arms and frowned up at Stephen.

"Stephen," I said, "I didn't check the pullover properly." I would have given any amount of money to get out of the shop without further argument.

The woman turned away without looking at me. As I stood at the counter writing out a cheque, the knitting machine started up again, and now the needles seemed to make a fierce, admonitory sound. I hurried out into the street. Stephen and Jenny joined me. "That woman behaved like we were criminals," Stephen said. "Doesn't she know it's bad for business to accuse your customers of lying?"

"It is puzzling, though," I said. "The hole was so large, and I'm claiming that I didn't see it when I bought the pullover." Jenny was walking between us, trying not to tread on the cracks between the paving stones. Suddenly I noticed that there was something different about her. "What happened to your skates?" I asked.

"Oh." She raised her hands and examined them, as if surprised to find them empty. "I must have left them in the shop."

While Stephen and Jenny went to retrieve the skates, I sat down on a wide flight of stone steps in front of an antique shop. In the window a row of Victorian dolls, their eyes fixed in wide china stares, ignored me. It would be a long time, I thought, before I would be able to go into the knitwear shop without feeling embarrassed.

Jenny and Stephen were coming down the street. Jenny was swinging her skates, looking up at her father. He was talking, pointing to something I could not see on the far side of the road. A black dog, which was tied to the railings, began to wag its tail as they approached. They stopped to pet it, and I stood up and went to join them. We bought ice creams and walked home, talking about other matters.

Later, when I was in our bedroom, I caught sight of my reflection in the mirror. Without doubt the new pullover was more becoming than the old one, but I did not take as much pleasure in it. Although Stephen and I were about to go out alone together for the first time since Jenny moved in, I felt a kind of heaviness descend upon me. I wished that we could spend a quiet evening at home, but it would be almost as hard to cancel our plans as it had been to make them. Charlotte would be arriving shortly to baby-sit, we had tickets for a play at the Traverse Theatre, and besides, there was Jenny. She had greeted the news of our absence with an enthusiasm that made Stephen's earlier anxiety seem absurd; she would clearly be disappointed if we were to stay at home. I picked up my hairbrush and began to brush my hair, stroke after stroke, until my scalp tingled.

Stephen and I were watching the news on television when Jenny ushered Charlotte into the living room. We said hello. Charlotte smiled shyly and muttered something. I had rarely heard her speak, but Jenny, who had met her a couple of times in the corner shop, assured us that when we were not around Charlotte chattered nineteen to the dozen. She had answered our advertisement for someone to look after Selina and Tobias while we were away, and, as Stephen remarked, it would be hard to find a teenager with better credentials; her mother was a nurse, her father a policeman, and she lived only a few houses away.

Stephen turned off the television and began to brief her. "There's macaroni cheese in the oven. It'll be ready at seven. You can eat in here, but be sure to take everything back to the kitchen afterwards."

Listening to Stephen's instructions reminded me of my own career as a baby-sitter. The best part had been having the run of an entire house; as I wandered from room to room, I could almost taste what it would be like to be an adult, to be free, and never to be in the wrong. Suddenly I wondered if Jenny would avail herself of our absence to explore our room. Stephen had told her that it was out of bounds, but I knew that when I was her age I would sneak into my parents' room at every opportunity, to smell my mother's lipstick, run my father's comb through my hair. I guessed that whatever it was that made us a family was going on here, and I scrutinised my parents' possessions in the hope that they would yield up the secret.

I looked at the two girls. Charlotte was gazing at the floor and wobbling back and forth on the sides of her feet. Although she was only fourteen, her large breasts and wide hips made her look, at first glance, like a woman. Jenny was standing beside her, and the contrast between the two made the difference in their ages seem much greater than it actually was; Jenny's body still showed no hint of the coming of puberty.

"Jenny has to be in bed at eight-thirty," Stephen said, "and she can read until nine. We should be home by eleven."

As soon as Stephen finished speaking, Jenny said, "Come. There's something I want to show you." She skipped out of the living room, and Charlotte, with a quick nod to us, followed. A moment later shrieks of laughter erupted from Jenny's bedroom. We called goodbye. "Bye-bye," they called back in unison.

"What if something goes wrong?" I asked Stephen as we got into the car.

"What could possibly go wrong?"

"Once when I was baby-sitting for Aunt Ruth her son Adam fell and cut his face. Jenny could hurt herself. Or," I said, casting around, "there could be a fire."

"Celia, what a worrier you are. Nothing's going to happen, but if anything does, Charlotte will ring her mother. I spoke to Irene, and she's going to be in all evening. Now stop it." He began to talk about a review he had read of the play, and I forgot my fears.

When we arrived home, shortly after eleven, Jenny's room was in darkness, and Charlotte was curled up on the sofa, reading a book. As we came in, she hastily slid it into her bag, but not before I glimpsed on the cover the hero and heroine exchanging a passionate embrace. While Stephen escorted Charlotte home, I took a quick look around. In the kitchen, not only their supper dishes but the ones we had left were washed and the table was set for breakfast; there were no signs that anyone had been in our bedroom.

Next morning we rose late, and as soon as we had finished breakfast it was time to start preparing lunch for Joyce and Edward. It was their first visit since Jenny moved in, and we were determined that for once they should behave like guests and not spend the entire afternoon working on our house and garden. Stephen ran out to buy eggs and I tidied up. Nowadays the house seemed to be perpetually strewn not only with Jenny's possessions but also with Stephen's and mine, as if we no longer had the time or inclination to be neat. I went through the living room and dining room, picking up books and newspapers and articles of clothing that we had discarded during the week. In the living room there was an old painting shirt of mine, a jacket of Stephen's, and a pair of Jenny's socks. I put the socks on Jenny's bed and took Stephen's and my clothes to our room.

As I opened the bottom drawer of the chest of drawers, something caught at the back of my throat. A dreadful pungent smell surrounded me. Trying not to breathe, I hurried to the window. I pushed up the sash to its fullest extent and leaned out. I was desperate to expel from my lungs every vestige of the peculiar odour.

Outside the air smelled very faintly of wood smoke. I took several deep breaths and then, holding the last one, plunged back into the room. From the open drawer the smell rose around me like a swarm of insects. As hastily as possible I began to shake out the articles of clothing. From between two T-shirts something small and furry tumbled out. It was the corpse of a mouse in an advanced stage of decomposition. Vomit came into my mouth and I swallowed. The idea of touching the tiny carcase made me hurry from the room.

I went to the kitchen to fetch a bag and a pair of rubber gloves; if I didn't look too closely, I thought, I could put the mouse in a bag. On my way back to the bedroom, I met Jenny in the hall. "There's a funny pong," she said, wrinkling her nose.

"Yes," I said. "I found a dead mouse." As soon as I had spoken I regretted it; for some reason I did not want Jenny to know what had happened.

She gave a small shudder. "How gross. What are you going to do with it?"

"Put it in the dustbin."

I managed to pick up the mouse by what remained of its tail and dropped it into a polythene bag. I tied the top, then put that bag inside a paper one. When I came out into the hall, Jenny was still standing there. She said nothing as I hurried by, carrying the paper bag by the tips of my rubber-gloved fingers. I deposited my burden in the dustbin.

Leaving the back door ajar, I returned inside. As I stepped through the dining room door, I saw that Jenny did not seem to have moved. "What are you doing?" I asked.

"Nothing." She squeezed out the two syllables in a way that suggested it was none of my business and that she was perfectly entitled to stand in the hall for as long as she pleased.

"Sorry about the cold," I said. "I'm trying to get rid of the smell."

When I reemerged carrying the drawer, she followed me through to the kitchen, and stood in the doorway watching as I emptied the contents of the drawer into the washing machine. I set the machine to hot and added as much bleach and soap powder as I thought the garments could stand. "These clothes are going to be cleaner than they've ever been," I said.

The sound of Stephen's return saved Jenny from the need to respond. She ran to meet him. I started the machine and began to scrub my hands.

"It smells like a hospital in here," said Stephen, as he came into the kitchen. "I knew you were doing some cleaning, but I didn't know you thought it was necessary to sterilise the house before my parents set foot in it."

"She found a mouse," Jenny said. She was standing on tiptoe at the counter peering into the bags of groceries.

I explained what had happened. "I don't understand why neither of us noticed the smell before," I said. "I mean we open the drawers all the time and it must have been there for quite a while."

"Grapes," exclaimed Jenny. "Can I have some?"

"No," said Stephen. "They're for after lunch. I imagine Tobias is to blame."

"He might have killed the mouse, but how could he have put it into a drawer?"

"Maybe he drove the mouse to take refuge there, and it died of shock. Anyway you've got rid of it now."

"She put it in the dustbin," said Jenny.

Stephen turned to her. "Will you give me a hand with lunch?"

"Okay. What do you want me to do?" She popped a grape into her mouth and turned to face him.

"You could wash the potatoes."

"Ugh, I always get the potatoes. Why can't I do something else for a change?"

I went into the living room and knelt down in front of the hearth. As I raked the poker back and forth over the grate to shake down the ashes, I kept thinking about the mouse. Harmless in itself, the tiny corpse seemed like a bad omen, linking me with the dark side of life. Into my mind came a picture of Jenny standing in the hall. She had worn an expression rather similar to that with which she had regarded the hole in my pullover the day before. She was not, I thought, sorry to see misfortune befall me. Suddenly I remembered the money I had lost a few weeks earlier. Where could it have gone, I wondered. I spread a newspaper open on the hearth and began to shovel the ashes onto the printed page.

At twelve-thirty the doorbell rang. I went to answer and found Joyce and Edward, bearing a bottle of wine and a bunch of russet-coloured chrysanthemums. "Flowers for the lady of the house," said Edward, handing them to me.

"Thank you. They're beautiful." They were the largest, most perfectly formed chrysanthemums I had ever seen.

Joyce explained that they had come directly from church; it was the Harvest Festival. She was in the middle of describing the wonderful array of fruits and vegetables, when Jenny appeared from her room. She ran to hug her grandparents. Before doing anything else, she insisted they must come and visit Selina. As she led them towards the garden, I heard her recounting the composition she had written about Selina and Edward. "My goodness," Joyce said.

Stephen opened the wine, and I put the chrysanthemums in water. We both bustled around, and by the time the three of them returned from the garden, everything was ready. We all sat down. I served the quiche and the potatoes, Stephen poured the wine. When everyone had taken salad and was poised to eat, Edward raised his glass. "Here's to you and your new home," he said, looking in turn at Jenny, Stephen, and me.

"To you," Joyce echoed. She beamed round the table and gave Jenny, who was sitting beside her, a hug.

"Thank you," said Stephen, smiling. In the brief pause I drank some wine. Jenny had already begun to eat.

"The house looks wonderful," said Joyce as she picked up her fork. "And so clean."

I was suddenly afraid that Jenny might say something

about the mouse, but she seemed absorbed in her food. Stephen began to talk about the tutoring program, and the moment passed.

"What a good idea," said Joyce. "I must mention it to our school."

"I should think the tricky part is getting the bad students to come forward," said Edward thoughtfully. "People don't usually like to admit that they have problems."

"Do you think you'd be interested in doing something like that, Jenny?" Joyce asked.

She shook her head. "I don't like trying to teach people. Even if I'm older than them, they don't listen to me. Anyway it's boring." She patted her mouth with a napkin.

"What about if you need help?" Joyce persisted.

"Then I ask Dad or Celia."

"You're lucky to have them," said Joyce. "Lots of children have no one at home who can help them with their homework."

"Mother," said Stephen, "have some more quiche. You haven't said a word about my pastry. I thought you'd be praising it to the skies."

"I'd love a small piece. It's delicious."

After lunch we decided to go for a walk. The weather was not as fine as the day before. The sky was largely overcast and there was a keen wind but, as Edward remarked, that would keep off the rain. "Look at those roses," Joyce exclaimed, pointing to the blooms in our front garden. "Ours are almost over. You wouldn't think forty miles could make such a difference."

"Perhaps being close to the sea helps," I said.

"That's probably the only way I could ever get Edward to consider moving, by suggesting a place with a longer growing season. He does tend to get cranky in winter." We passed a young woman peering under the hood of a car. "I can't tell you how glad we are that Jenny's living with you," said Joyce.

The two men had already drawn ahead, but Jenny was only a few paces in front of Joyce and me. "Look at the cat," I said loudly, pointing to an animal lying asleep on a doorstep. "Jenny, why don't you go and ask Stephen if we can go by the allotments." He and Edward were by now some hundred yards ahead.

"Why don't you go?" she said. She did not stop walking or turn around; I was certain that she had heard and understood her grandmother's remark. The set of her shoulders beneath the navy blue anorak and the scissoring of her legs conveyed fury and despair.

Beside me I sensed Joyce's disapproval. "Please, Jenny," I said. I stared at her back, willing her to do as I asked. She paused, and I caught a glimpse of her pale face as she gave a swift, sharp glance over her shoulder; then she began to run at top speed.

"I've never known her to be rude," Joyce said. She had stopped walking and turned to face me.

"I think she may have overheard you and thought you were criticising Helen."

"Oh, dear." Joyce's blue eyes widened in remorse. "It's not easy to know how much Jenny understands. She's changed in the last few years—she used to be such a sweet little girl, and now, I can't really explain, but she seems different, as if she had something to hide. I'm sure it all has to do with the separation. Once she's settled in with Stephen and you, she'll become her old self." She smiled.

A gust of wind blew my hair across my face; I closed my eyes against the grit. When I opened them again I saw Stephen, Edward, and Jenny standing at the corner. The two men were talking together; between them stood Jenny. She was holding on to her father's hand with both of hers, but her head was turned in our direction.

CHAPTER 19

All weekend I had postponed thinking about the sales conference, but as soon as Joyce and Edward left I began to prepare. For the next thirty-six hours I spent every available moment making copious notes, rehearsing aloud, practising jokes. When I woke on Tuesday morning, however, all this frantic activity seemed irrelevant compared to the crucial question of what I would wear. I had collected my suit from the dry cleaners the night before, and as I lifted it out of the wardrobe, I could smell the faint whiff of methylated fumes. The mere sight of the immaculate folds reassured me. When I was fully dressed and stood in front of the mirror, a strangely adult woman stared back at me. I experienced one of those rare moments of satisfaction in my appearance. As a final touch I clipped on my amber earrings.

I went into the dining room. Stephen was sitting at one end of the table reading the newspaper, while at the other Jenny ate cereal and finished her homework. Neither of them looked up as I came in. I stood waiting. "I'm going," I announced.

"Don't you want some breakfast?" Stephen asked. He gestured towards his own plate as if about to offer me the slice of toast that lay there.

"I can pick something up. The sales conference starts at ten, and I want to go through my presentation one more time."

"Oh." He seemed taken aback. "You'll be there to collect Jenny, won't you?"

"Of course," I said. I saw her write something in her notebook.

Stephen smiled. "See you later then."

It was raining hard, and as I stepped through the garden gate the wind blew my raincoat out behind me. I was glad to have the use of the car. I sat there letting the engine warm up and thought about Stephen's smile. He had not even wished me luck or commented upon my appearance. The important thing was that I should collect his daughter; that was why he smiled at me. At some point I must have started driving, but I had no recollection of the journey until I found myself turning into Melville Street and looking for a parking space.

I decided to go to the restaurant round the corner from the office. I was about halfway there when the wind turned my umbrella inside out; I ran the last hundred yards as best I could in my tight skirt. The restaurant was almost empty. I ordered a cup of coffee and a scone and carried them over to a table by the window; the raindrops dribbled down the grimy glass. I opened my briefcase and spread my notes before me. "Number one: Choice of authors," I read, but all I could think about was Stephen's silence. As I reached for my pen, I caught sight of the silver bracelet clasped around my wrist. Nowadays I was so accustomed to wearing it that I seldom noticed it.

I was staring at the silver band when Suzie bounded in and sat down opposite. She had spied me through the window. "Good morning," she said brightly. "You look down in the dumps."

"My umbrella's broken. I got wet. I'm nervous about my presentations."

"Oh, dear." Suzie laughed. "You can borrow my umbrella. You can use the hand dryer in the ladies' to dry your hair. And the presentations will go fine. The sales staff aren't critical. The main thing is to say something that they can quote. How many books are you responsible for?"

"Two poetry books—one 'O' level, one primary school—and the collection of essays."

"The essays will sell themselves. It's the first book we've published besides the critical editions that I actually read for pleasure." I watched Suzie's head bobbing up and down as she offered reassurance; she had hennaed her hair at the weekend, and the colour was especially vivid.

I finished my coffee. "We should get going. It would be stupid to be late."

As I stood up, Suzie exclaimed, "Celia, you look fantastic! What a great suit!"

"Are you sure?" I asked. "Stephen didn't seem to notice." When we were out in the street, I told her what had happened.

"He probably saw you for a total of five minutes before you rushed off. If you relied on me for praise first thing in the morning, you'd expire."

"But he remembered that he needed me to collect Jenny. Why couldn't he remember the conference?"

We stopped at the curb, waiting for the light to change. Suzie held her golfing umbrella low over our heads. "When you're a parent," she said, "you're programmed to remember those sorts of things. I have this absolute mass of trivia about Tim at my finger tips: swimming, haircuts, doctors, art supplies, birthday presents for his friends. It's not like I even make an effort to remember: they just come to mind. At the same time I'll do things like forget my mother's birthday or be half an hour late to meet Derek last night."

The light changed, and we started across the road. "Derek took me to this pub where they have a talent night. It was hilarious," Suzie said. She began to entertain me with imitations of the performers.

The conference was being held in the Caledonian Hotel. It

was only a few minutes' walk from the office, but in spite of Suzie's umbrella, I arrived windswept and dishevelled. I hurried to the powder room, where I found Clare applying mascara with immense concentration. As I listened to her fuss over her appearance, I felt less nervous. Ever since the episode with Mr. Brockbank, when Bill had sided with me rather than her, there had been a shift in our relationship; she treated me more cordially, and I, having glimpsed that her daunting manner was in part a facade, was less easily intimidated. Now she too complimented me on my suit, and when we went into the meeting room, she held the door open and ushered me in before her. In the course of a year I had come to know a number of the sales people, at least by sight, and several turned to greet me.

Bill welcomed us, gave an account of sales over the last year, and talked about the proceedings of the meeting. The editors would present the books. Then there would be a coffee break, after which we would reconvene to discuss marketing strategies until one o'clock, when a buffet lunch would be served. Surreptitiously I wiped my hands on my skirt. "Celia," he said, "would you like to kick off?"

I began to describe the collection of essays. This had been my first independent project in Edinburgh; I had had the initial idea, found an editor, made suggestions about the contents. The essays were grouped under six headings—the individual, the family, the community, work, play, politics—and I had put considerable effort into finding pieces that I thought would appeal to Scottish teenagers. Around the table people scribbled briskly. I felt my words take hold, and when it came time for questions I had no trouble in answering them. To my amazement I realised that I was enjoying myself.

It stopped raining shortly before I left to pick up Jenny. This week I found the school without difficulty. I drove up in time to see a crowd of parents and children milling around the gates. Jenny was in the middle of a cluster of girls, and I was reminded of how small she was, compared not merely to older girls like Charlotte but to her peers. I saw her glance over at me. Then she said something and laughed. I turned the car around and stopped a few feet from where the girls stood. Jenny made no move. She kept her back resolutely towards me; she seemed to be having an animated conversation. I was beginning to wonder whether I would have to go and fetch her, when she detached herself from the group.

"Didn't you see me?" I said as she opened the door.

"Sorry." She put on her seat belt with a snap. "I was asking about homework."

I thought of the old adage "Ask a stupid question, get a stupid answer." After all, I had seen her seeing me. I decided not to pursue the matter. I waited for a couple of cars to pass and pulled out into the street. When we were on the main road, I asked how her day had been.

"Okay. Can we stop at the park and see if there are any chestnuts?"

"Isn't it too early?"

"No. Dad and I found a few when we were roller-skating on Saturday. And it's been jolly windy today."

"I suppose there's no harm in taking a look," I said. On the way to the park Jenny chattered about school, her friends, Anna and Sheila, and apparently anything else that came into her head. I did not need to say a word, in fact she seemed anxious that I should not, and this was the only aspect of her behaviour that could be construed as a sign that she was not entirely at ease. Since Sunday I had been so busy that I had scarcely seen her, and when our paths crossed she had been excessively polite as if to make up for her brief spurt of rudeness. "Anna has a new record by Mel and Kim," she said. "She's going to bring it to our house when she comes to see me."

Not until we were in the park, walking towards the chestnut trees, did she fall silent. The grass beneath the trees was thickly strewn with nuts. They were newly fallen, and the spiky cases were still green and hard to open. We began to fill our pockets. As a child I had gathered chestnuts every autumn and arranged them on my window sill, where, during the course of the winter, they gradually dulled. I pressed my thumb along the seam of an especially large nut. "Look at this," I said to Jenny, holding out the shell for her to see the two matching kernels with curious piebald markings.

"Can I take them out?"

"Of course."

I watched as she popped the nuts out of their shell and cupped them in her palm. "They're like Tweedledum and Tweedledee," she said. She slipped them into her pocket. Then she bent down to pick up a feather.

The feather was bright blue, the barbs still perfectly smooth. "It's pretty," I remarked. "I expect it comes from a jay."

"Here," she said, handing it to me. "It matches your eyes."

I must be going mad, I thought, to have believed her capable of wickedness and hatred. As we walked back towards the car I was certain that the worst was over, the fever had broken, and we had embarked at last on a healthy relationship, independent of Stephen.

We were on our way into the house when something lodged in my left eye. As I fumbled with the keys, tears ran down my cheeks. Jenny asked what was the matter. "I wear contact lenses," I said. "If dust gets in my eyes, it's very painful."

"What are contact lenses?"

"They're pieces of plastic you wear in your eyes to help you see."

"Plastic in your eyes?" said Jenny. She started to giggle.

"I'll show you."

In the bathroom, she perched on the edge of the bath

watching with interest as I took out the lens, rinsed it, and reinserted it. "How do they make you see?" she asked.

"Sort of like glasses, but I'm not exactly sure. You'll have to ask Stephen." I felt abashed. I was utterly dependent on my lenses and yet could not give a simple account of the mechanism. While I dried my hands, Jenny examined the lens case and the various solutions. Then, putting the case back on the shelf, she announced that she was going to make tea.

By the time I had changed out of my suit and lit the fire, she had everything organised. We carried our tea through to the living room, and I settled down on the sofa. I began to leaf through a cookbook, trying to decide what to make for supper. Jenny lay on the floor in front of the fire, petting Tobias, eating toast, and reading. Suddenly there was a small, sharp bang. A spark flew onto the hearth, and Tobias fled.

"What's the matter?" Jenny asked.

"Tobias is terrified of fire. I think once when he was a kitten a spark must have landed on him."

"Oh," said Jenny. "Poor Tobias." She stood up and, calling "Toby, Toby," walked over to the far corner of the room. She returned with Tobias in her arms, murmuring consolations.

I moved on to the egg section of the cookbook. I was contemplating a soufflé, when Jenny said, "Celia, do you know what amber is?"

"It's fossilised resin. Haven't you seen it in the museum? They often have lumps of amber with insects inside."

"No," she said. "In my book it just talks about how the Vikings used amber as money."

"Wait a minute, I'll show you." I had taken off my earrings when I changed. Now I fetched the basket in which I kept my jewellery and sat down on the rug beside Jenny. I opened the little blue leather case. "This is amber," I said.

She picked up one of the earrings and looked at it closely. The piece of amber was about the size of a shilling, but thicker and slightly irregular in shape. "It's like honey," she said. "Are these old?"

"The amber is very old, but I don't think the earrings are. Maybe a hundred years. They came from Egypt and belonged to my great-aunt Marigold."

"Egypt," she echoed. "Can I try them on?"

"Of course." My ears were pierced and the earrings were among the few that I owned with clips. Jenny hurried from the room. A minute later she returned.

"What do you think?" she asked, holding back her hair.

"Pretty."

When Great-Aunt Marigold showed me the earrings, I had behaved exactly like Jenny, putting them on and running to look in the mirror. Then I would beg Marigold to tell the story of the earrings one more time. She would demur briefly and give in. Her best friend's brother had brought them home from Egypt. "He gave Lucy and me each a pair," she said. "It was a kind of joke between us. We would wear them and pretend to be twins. But then our friend Joanie was given an amber brooch with a fly in it, and we were terribly envious. We gave Maurice an awful teasing about not bringing us the kind with flies in. 'I thought you girls were afraid of creepy crawlies,' he would say. 'Not when they've been dead for thousands of years,' Lucy and I would explain."

She was not sure how the flies got into the amber, but my father knew the answer. When I told Marigold his explanation, that slow-witted flies were trapped in the resin, she chuckled. For years I had gone around with my eyes fixed on the ground, trying to break open likely-looking rocks to see if they contained amber.

I told Jenny all this, and she giggled as I used to do. "They do hurt a bit," she said. When she unclipped the earrings, her ears were pinched to redness. "Who gave you the beads?" she asked, pointing to a coral necklace.

"My godmother, Rose, gave them to me for my christening. She was a close friend of my mother's, but I never met her. She sent me handkerchiefs every Christmas and birthday, and I would write her a thank-you letter claiming that they were just what I'd always wanted."

Jenny nodded her head vigorously. "It seems silly to write thank-you letters for awful presents. Then people never learn to do better."

"I suppose we're thanking them for the thought."

"Why should we thank people for having stupid thoughts? What's this?"

"It's a Saint Christopher. It was given to me by a boy named Richard Lamb. His father kept a jewellery shop, so he probably got it half price."

"Was he your boyfriend?"

"Not really. He was away at boarding school, so I only saw him half a dozen times. He wrote to me."

When every piece had been examined and discussed, I put them all back in the basket and carried it to the bedroom. Jenny followed. She sat on the edge of the bed, swinging her legs, while I hung up my suit.

"Do you think Dad would let me join the Brownies?" she asked.

"If you want to, I'm sure he would. Aren't you a bit old, though? I should have thought you were ready for the Guides."

"Anna's a Brownie. She's my age."

"Why haven't you joined before?"

"Mummy thought it was stupid."

I looked at her and saw that expression I had seen before at difficult moments, when her face became blank and smooth as a tightly wrapped parcel. I caught sight of my cat socks, lying on top of the chest of drawers. "Did you see these? They were a present from Tobias," I said. I passed them to her.

She took the nest of socks and unrolled them. Each sock showed a black and white cat sitting on a wall. "They don't look like him," she said.

"Well, it's hard to find socks with cats on."

"Where did you get them?"

"In London."

"Where you used to live," she said. "Do you think you'll ever go back there?" She spoke absent-mindedly, as if all her attention were on the socks; she had pulled one on over her hand to examine it better.

"I don't know. Not for a while certainly. Stephen and I both have jobs here, and you're here." I picked up a pair of tights from the floor and put them on the chair.

We made the soufflé together, and it rose to stunning heights. Afterwards, at Jenny's suggestion, we played Pellminism, a game at which she excelled. Not only did she remember the position of every card we turned over, but she was also spectacularly lucky. When she had won three games in a row, I called a halt and said that it was time for bed.

I was watching television when Stephen came home. He hurried into the living room, still wearing his jacket. "Hello," I said. "You're home early."

"Deirdre gave me a lift."

"But she didn't come in?"

"She had a mysterious date. You know what a hectic schedule she has." He sat down beside me. "Listen, I feel terrible. I forgot to wish you luck today. I tried to ring you at your office, but you'd already left. I'm awfully sorry."

"That's all right," I said.

"No, it isn't. If you hadn't rushed off quite so early I would have remembered, but that's no excuse. Tell me all about it. Did the sales people praise you to the skies?"

"Pretty much. They seemed to really like the idea of the essay book. Bill started dropping hints about a series."

"I can see it already. 'The Gilchrist Series of Improving Books,' it will say on the cover in big letters. All over the country, teachers will be saying, 'Now turn to page three hundred of your Gilchrist.' " We both laughed. "And how about the poetry?"

"That went fine. There are so many poetry books that it's more a matter of coming up with the right comparisons."

Stephen bent forward and rummaged in his briefcase. "I bought some wine," he said. "To toast your success."

CHAPTER 20

Suzie and I were on our way to lunch when she asked if I would be interested in going to a second-hand shop. She was looking for a sofa. "Danny is a bit erratic," she explained, "but Friday is a good day to catch him."

"That would be great," I said. "I want to buy a desk for our room. When I was preparing for the sales conference, it was very aggravating having nowhere to work besides the dining room table." We were walking down Melville Street. At the far end the church was sharply etched against the blue sky and the trees were in full yellow leaf.

"I thought you had a desk."

"We do, but Jenny uses it."

"How's she getting on?" Suzie asked. "You seem to have been in a better mood these last few days."

"I didn't know it was obvious." I smiled. "I think she's finally settling down. Initially the only thing we had in common was Stephen, but now that we've spent some time alone together, we're becoming friends."

"That makes sense," said Suzie.

We turned off Melville Street and began to make our way through the side streets in the direction of Haymarket Station. At first sight of Danny's, it was hard to believe Suzie's claim that she had found some nice pieces of furniture here. The sign over the front of the shop was so faded as to be illegible, and the windows were shuttered; only the open door suggested the possibility of commerce. Inside, furniture was piled high. Suzie led me between wardrobes, chests of drawers, and beds to the back of the shop, where Danny sat in an old armchair beside a single-bar electric fire. "Hello, girls. What can I do for you?" he asked.

"I'm looking for a sofa, and Celia's looking for a desk," Suzie said. "How have you been?"

"Not perfect." He began to describe some problem with his digestion, and I wandered away. As my eyes adjusted to the gloom I was better able to distinguish Danny's wares. I was examining a rocking chair when I spotted, balanced on top of a dresser, a white table with two drawers.

Danny was shaking his head about a sofa in which Suzie had expressed interest. "It's a piece of junk," he said. "It needs rewebbing, and the upholstery is covered in cat hair. There's sure to be something better by and by."

"How much is that table?" I asked.

He squinted in the direction of my gesture. "The white one? I'll give it to you for ten pounds. Mind you that's a bargain. If you strip it, you could sell it for forty."

"Show me," said Suzie.

Together we lifted the table down; I tried the drawers and checked to see if it was steady. "You should take it," Suzie said. "Ten pounds is hard to beat."

I went over to Danny and got out my cheque book. He shook his head. "Cash only," he said. When I offered a twenty pound note, he drew out of his pocket a sizeable wad of fattened notes.

Next morning Stephen and Jenny went to fetch the table and came home with it tied to the roof of the car. While Jenny carried in the drawers, Stephen and I untied the table and manoeuvred it into the house. It fitted perfectly in front of the bedroom window.

"Sit down," said Stephen. He lifted our clothes off the chair and placed it in front of the table. Obediently I sat.

"What is it for?" asked Jenny. She was kneeling on the edge of our bed.

"It's for Celia to work, so she won't always have to chase us out of the dining room." He put a book down in front of me, to simulate working conditions.

"I used to use the desk in your room." I turned to look at Jenny.

She smiled. "Before I came to live with you," she said, bouncing slightly up and down.

"That's right," Stephen agreed. He rested his hand on my shoulder. "This will be a nice place to work. You can gaze at the garden and daydream. I'm going to make the shopping list. Can you think of anything we need?"

"I'll have to come and check," I said.

"KitKats, raisins, peanut butter," said Jenny. She followed him out of the bedroom.

In the gloom of Danny's shop the table had looked fairly clean, but in broad daylight it was apparent how dirty it really was. I decided to take the drawers out and wash them at the kitchen sink; the rest of the table I would clean in place. When I came into the dining room, Stephen was standing by the side-board, reading the list. "Orange juice, butter, cheese," he said. "Do we need more flour?"

Suddenly Jenny sat down at the table and put her head in her hands. "My tummy feels odd," she said.

"Odd how?" asked Stephen. He hurried over and knelt down beside her.

"Like I might be sick."

Stephen put his hand on her forehead. "I don't think you have a temperature, but maybe you should stay here. If you're feeling sick, being in the car will only make it worse. Why don't you get into bed for a bit?"

"Okay," said Jenny. She walked slowly out of the room, followed by Stephen. I carried the drawers into the kitchen and began to wash one of them in the sink. Presently Stephen returned. "She's in bed, reading," he said. "I don't know what can be the matter. She seemed fine earlier, and all she's had to eat today is cereal and toast."

"Perhaps moving furniture doesn't agree with her. Will you get a couple of lemons?"

I finished washing the drawers and propped them against the back-door steps to dry. Then I went and tapped on the door of Jenny's room. "Come in," she said in a quiet voice. I stepped inside. The curtains were drawn, and the room was lit by the bedside lamp. Jenny was sitting up in bed. As far as I could see, she was still fully dressed. "Can I get you anything?" I asked.

"No. I feel sleepy."

"I'll be in the bedroom. Just shout if you need me."

She nodded and slid a little further between the sheets.

I filled a bucket with warm water and carried it with other cleaning supplies to the bedroom. The table was covered in a heavy white gloss paint which would not be easy to strip, but it could at least be clean. I turned on the radio and began to scrub one of the legs. In a few hours, I thought, Stephen and I would have the house to ourselves. Jenny was going to stay the night at Anna's, and we would not see her again until tomorrow afternoon, when Stephen had promised to take both girls swimming.

I finished washing the second leg and decided to fetch fresh water. As I stood up, I glanced out of the window. Jenny was in the garden. She must be feeling better, I thought. She was standing at the far end of the lawn, with her back to the house, brandishing a stick at a flower bed. I assumed she was playing some sort of game. Then she took a step forward, and Selina appeared from among the lupins. She ran across the grass towards her hutch, and Jenny darted after her, bringing the stick down as she went.

When she reached the run, Selina stopped beside the wire netting, as if seeking admittance, then the stick came down,

Jenny was almost upon her, and she fled for cover behind the shed.

I ran from the bedroom, through the dining room and the kitchen. As I flung open the back door and stepped into the garden, there was a scream, a piercing and terribly human sound. I felt the hair rise on my head. I knew at once that Jenny had not uttered such a cry.

I ran across the grass. Jenny had cornered Selina behind the shed. She had her arm raised, ready to bring down the stick once more, when I seized her wrist.

"What are you doing?" I shouted. I held her as hard as I could.

"You're hurting me." She did not even glance at me; she kept her face turned towards Selina, as if intent upon her prey.

"What are you doing?" I did not slacken my grip.

"Selina escaped. I'm trying to catch her."

Selina lay next to the compost heap, pressed as close to the earth as possible; save for the faint tremors that shook her, I would have feared she was dead. On the several occasions when we had let her out of her cage, she had proved docile and friendly, unwilling to stray too far and easily lured back into captivity with offers of food.

"How did she get out?"

"I don't know. I was in the shed. Then I looked and she was hopping across the grass."

"She's never got out before." Within my grasp Jenny's wrist was no thicker than the stick she held, and it seemed that I might as easily snap it in two. I squeezed harder.

"Let go of me," Jenny said. At last she looked up, her eyes dark and wide. There was a thumbprint of colour in the middle of each cheek, and she was breathing hard.

The urge to hit her rose inside me, brimming right to the edge of overflowing. I was so angry that I could scarcely speak, while she, although excited, seemed entirely in control.

I jerked the stick out of her hand and threw it over the garden wall. "Come on," I said. "We're going inside."

I led her across the grass, as if she were a criminal and I the jailer. Only when we reached the dining room did I release her. As soon as I did so, without my saying anything she went to her room and closed the door. I took refuge in the bedroom. The radio was still playing, and I turned it off. I wanted to be able to hear if Jenny dared to leave her room. The house hummed with silence.

I stood gazing out of the window, hoping to see Selina hop out, unhurt, from behind the tool shed. I was still breathing hard, and my heart was racing as if from some tremendous exertion. There was a movement in the herbaceous border. Tobias appeared. He looked right and left, walked swiftly across the empty grass, sprang up onto the wall, and vanished. I reminded myself of acts of cruelty I had committed when I was Jenny's age. At school it had been the custom to torment our maths teacher, a woman with a slight lisp, whose prominent teeth were often smeared with bright red lipstick. On several occasions my class had successfully reduced her to tears, the sight of which only whetted our appetite for more. Then there were the other children, whom we attacked with random ferocity.

Suddenly I remembered that I had once been one of those casual victims. Four children who lived at the far end of our street had ganged up against me and every time I came out of the house had pursued me with sticks, thrown stones. I could not tell my parents, for according to our code of conduct there was nothing worse than being a tell-tale, but I began to stay in my room; even the garden, which had always been my kingdom, no longer seemed safe.

The feud had been in progress for several days when my mother asked me to go to the shops. I argued that I had homework to do, but she insisted. "It'll only take a few minutes," she said, handing me the list and a five pound note.

I paused at the door to retie the laces of my gym shoes, and set out. I was running down the street as fast as I could, hoping to pass by my enemies unnoticed, when the first stone hit my shoulder. The children appeared, two on either side, closing in on me. Then, as another stone fell at my feet, one of the boys started to run in the opposite direction. "Stay right there," called my father. "Aren't you on your way to the shops, Celia? You'd better get going."

The most remarkable effect of my father's intervention was that afterwards the children were friendlier to me than they had been before they commenced their attacks.

Jenny must have been watching from her window for Stephen's return. Suddenly I heard her running out into the hall, and flinging open the front door. "Daddy, Daddy, Selina escaped. You've got to help me get her back."

"I thought you were in bed," said Stephen. "How are you feeling?"

I came out of the bedroom just in time to see Jenny's startled expression—she had forgotten her illness—but she quickly regained her poise. "I'm better. Come and help with Selina."

"I don't understand how she could get out." Stephen handed her a bag of groceries to carry.

"She had a little help," I said.

"It's not true. She got out by herself."

"When I looked out of the window, Jenny was chasing her round the garden with a stick. After what happened, it'll be amazing if Selina doesn't die of shock."

Jenny stood on one side of Stephen, holding the bag he had given her, staring fixedly at him. She did not once look at me, where I stood on his other side. And he remained in the middle, turning his gaze, first on one of us, then on the other.

"I didn't mean to chase her," Jenny said. "I was trying to make her go back in. Can we go and catch her now?"

"When I saw you, you weren't making the slightest attempt to catch Selina." I wanted to grab her, to force her to at least look at me, but her father stood between us.

"We can talk about this later, Celia," he said. "The main thing now is to put Selina back in her run and get Jenny some lunch. I promised I'd have her at Anna's by two o'clock." He gave me a quick smile, then put his hand on Jenny's shoulder and steered her in the direction of the dining room.

I retreated into the bedroom and went to the window; I kept to one side, in the shadow of a curtain. There was still no sign of Selina. Jenny and Stephen came out of the back door, and Jenny led the way across the grass. They disappeared from view behind the shed. After a couple of minutes they reappeared; Stephen held Selina in his arms. I saw his lips move. Jenny nodded and tentatively reached out her hand to stroke Selina.

Cleaning the table gave me an excuse to remain in the bedroom, and I emerged only when summoned to lunch. The meal was brief, and conversation between Stephen and Jenny camouflaged my silence. They talked about her history project. It was on Napoleon, whom she liked, she said, because he was small and French; she and Anna were going to work on it this afternoon. I wondered what kind of syllabus took one from the Vikings to Napoleon in a week, but I did not feel inclined to enquire. While they got ready to leave, I cleaned up the lunch things, and when Stephen called, "We're off," I called back, in what I hoped was a sufficiently cheerful tone, "Bye-bye, Jenny. Have a good time."

The door closed behind them. I finished putting things away in the fridge, then I went into Jenny's room. A book lay on the floor, and even as I bent to pick it up, I knew that it must be the one about Napoleon which she had made such a fuss about getting from the library the night before.

I felt an almost paralysing tiredness at the prospect of talking to Stephen. He had suggested that we go out for the evening, but I had argued that it would be more romantic to eat at home. We so seldom had the house to ourselves that it seemed a pity to waste Jenny's absence by our own. Now I wished that we had decided to go to a film or to have supper with friends, anything to avoid the inevitable confrontation.

When Stephen returned, I was sitting on the sofa in the living room, the book about Napoleon open on my lap.

"Hi," he said, putting his head round the door. "What are you doing?"

"Nothing."

"Nothing?"

"Well, maybe I'm reading a book about Napoleon." I held it up so that he could see the map of Europe on the cover.

"Oh, damn. I forgot to remind her to take it. I suppose she'll manage without it." He came into the room and sat down in the chair on the opposite side of the fireplace.

"I'm sorry about the ruptions this morning."

"What do you mean?" I asked. The word "ruptions" seemed a splendidly neutral choice.

"The business with Jenny and Selina. I can imagine what happened. As soon as she felt better, Jenny sneaked out into the garden to see Selina, accidentally on purpose let her out, and then panicked about getting her back in."

"Is that what she told you?"

"You heard what she said. You were there."

"You might have discussed it with her in the garden, or on the way to Anna's." I wanted to say, "Your daughter was trying to kill her rabbit," but the notion of telling Stephen what he so clearly did not wish to hear only deepened my fatigue. When he saw that I was not going to speak, he rewarded my silence by crossing the room to sit beside me.

"She was really upset at the thought that she had scared Selina," he said. He put his arm around me and gave a small, apologetic smile. "I feel that I didn't handle matters very well. I was flustered. I didn't mean to sound as if I were contradicting you."

I tried to return his smile. Perhaps I had been mistaken, I thought. Perhaps all I had seen was Jenny trying too vigorously to drive Selina back into her cage. But then, as Stephen embarked on a list of suggestions as to how we might spend the afternoon, I remembered the scream. No amount of vigour could have elicited that heart-rending sound.

CHAPTER 21

For two days following the attack on Selina, I succeeded in avoiding Jenny. On Sunday afternoon I excused myself from swimming on the grounds that I had a headache, and by the time she and Stephen returned home my lie had become a self-fulfilling prophecy; I had retired to bed. Next morning I hurried to work, pleading an early meeting. I could not bear the thought of treating Jenny as if nothing had happened; to do so seemed tantamount to forgiveness. Not until Monday evening did I find myself cornered in the kitchen. I was getting potatoes out of the vegetable basket when I heard her voice.

"Can I help?" she asked.

"There isn't anything to do," I said. I did not turn around.

There was a brief pause, during which I continued to feign absorption in the vegetables. Then Jenny said, "I could peel the potatoes."

As a rule she complained vehemently about this chore, and I saw no way to refuse her offer. She fetched the potatoes and carried them over to the sink. They were a gift from Edward, thick with mud, and I would have liked to caution her that they needed to be washed with especial care, but I did not want to utter a single unnecessary word. I remembered how the headmistress of my school had had the gift of apparently effortless silence, in the face of which I had always found it impossible not to rush into speech. For a moment I wondered if my silence might have a similar effect upon Jenny; then I thought that was absurd. I was much more likely to give in than she was. I kept my back to her and concentrated on slicing mushrooms. From the sink came the sounds of scraping and the tap going on and off.

Presently I heard footsteps. Her hands appeared in my field of vision. She laid the potatoes next to the board on which I was chopping the mushrooms. "Celia," she said. "I'm sorry about Selina."

I said nothing. I was determined not to accept any more of her lies and blandishments.

"It was sort of a game, to start with. I was pretending that she was a wild animal and that I was an animal tamer. I forgot she was only a rabbit. I didn't mean to hurt her."

"But couldn't you see you were terrifying her?"

She nodded. "In a way," she mumbled.

What would I have said, I wondered, if someone had asked me why I took pleasure in reducing the maths teacher to tears? I could imagine only too well my halting answer. I looked down at Jenny's hands, her small fingers reddened by the cold water, her nails neatly bitten down to the quick.

"Do you want me to cut up the potatoes?" she asked.

"Yes, please. I'm going to roast them. If you cut them into little pieces, then they won't take too long." I tipped the mushrooms into the frying pan. "Do you have any ideas about what we should have for supper tomorrow?"

"Maybe I could make us an omelette."

"I didn't know you could cook," I said.

"Just omelettes. Oh, and fudge, but sometimes that turns out like bullets."

She began to cut the potatoes, measuring each slice as if it were a piece of a mosaic. When she had finished, she returned to the sink. I watched as, standing on her stool, she leaned over to scoop out the peel and grit with which the drain was stopped.

*　　*　　*

The relief that I experienced immediately following Jenny's apology soon gave way to another concern. Since she had vindicated my account of events with Selina, I felt that Stephen in turn owed me, if not an apology, at least an acknowledgement that I had been right. But there was no opportunity to talk. On Tuesday he arrived home late. On Wednesday I was just settling down at my desk when Suzie came into my office to ask if I wanted to do something that evening; Tim was visiting his grandparents.

I hesitated. "I'm not sure," I said.

"Come on," said Suzie. "You're always telling me how you and Stephen don't go out anymore. We could eat, see a film, whatever."

She sat on the edge of my desk, swinging her legs, looking at me eagerly. I picked up a pencil and began to twist it in the sharpener, trying to shave off the wood in one continuous spiral. After a couple of revolutions the coil snapped. "Okay," I said. "It's Stephen's turn to cook. I expect he'd be relieved if I was out. Then he could make cheese dreams for himself and Jenny without guilt."

"Oh, good. I'll buy a newspaper at lunchtime, and we can consult." Suzie slid off my desk and bounced out of the room.

We left the office shortly before six. It was a cold, clear evening, and as we crossed Queensferry Street the moon, slightly fuller than half, was coming up behind the Castle. Suzie said that she thought we might have frost tonight, and I agreed. We walked briskly to Hendersons, where we were going to have supper before the film. I had vowed not to discuss Jenny, but as soon as we were seated in the restaurant with our food before us, I found myself telling Suzie about the events of Saturday. "The worst thing was that Stephen seemed to believe Jenny rather than me."

"But I thought you were saying you believed her too,"

Suzie said. She sliced down into her lasagne.

"I believed her when she finally apologised to me, but I didn't believe what she told Stephen."

"All parents have differences, though," said Suzie. "If you and Stephen had a child together you'd argue about how to treat him or her and what was fair and all kinds of things. Given that you're both new to being full-time parents, it sounds like you do remarkably well." She gestured towards my untouched plate. "You should eat before your food gets cold."

I picked up my knife and fork. There was a pause while we both ate in silence. At the next table a couple of young men sat down. They began to discuss a bicycle race for which they were in training.

"You know," I said, "it's really a strange experience living with Jenny. She's so unpredictable: some of the time she's angelically sweet, and then at other times it's as if she can hardly stand to speak to me. She reminds me of the man I was going out with before I moved to Edinburgh. I never knew from one day to the next how he was going to treat me."

"Jenny doesn't have to like you just because her father is in love with you. Tim thinks some of my boyfriends are idiots, but if they stick around he usually becomes friends with them, and if he doesn't that's his prerogative." Suzie paused to drink some wine. "When you told me about Harry you made him sound like an understudy for Hitler."

I stared at her, dumbfounded. Suzie saw my expression. "Sorry," she said. "Of course it's different. I only meant you don't like everyone, and not everyone has to like you."

"Jenny lives with us," I exclaimed. "Your boyfriends don't have to share a house with someone who wishes they were dead."

"Celia, you're getting carried away. I'm sure Jenny does sometimes wish you would get run over, but that's normal. I can remember having long daydreams in which my parents

238 · Margot Livesey

were painlessly killed in a car crash or drowned at sea. Half the stories in my comics were about girls who had lost their families, and I thought being an orphan was incredibly glamorous."

She took another mouthful of salad and chewed thoughtfully. "It's hard to accept a lover having a child. At least I know it would be for me, and it certainly is for some of my boyfriends. I can be head over heels in love, but I still have to be home by eleven so that the baby-sitter can leave. Whatever happens, Tim comes first."

I knew that Suzie meant to be consoling, but her reaction only strengthened my desire to explain. "I do find it hard to suddenly have Jenny living with us," I said, "but that's mainly because of her attitude. When I first learned that Stephen had a daughter, I was pleased. I was sure that she and I would become friends. Now I don't feel that I can trust her." I held my knife and fork tightly and leaned across the table, as if I could wrench understanding and agreement out of Suzie.

"But it's only been a few weeks," she said. "It's not surprising if Jenny is moody. After all, she's adjusting simultaneously to a new home, her father's presence, and her mother's absence, never mind you." She smiled at me. "I have to go to the loo." She headed off in the direction of the ladies'.

While she was gone I counted over the various mishaps that had befallen me since I met Jenny. From that first day, when she had dropped her bag on the stairs, my life had been full of small disasters. I thought again about the ten pounds I had mysteriously lost; then I remembered how shortly afterwards Jenny's expensive new book had appeared. I raised my glass of wine and emptied it. All at once I was convinced that she was responsible, for the theft of my money and for everything else. There was no other explanation. The zeal with which she had helped me search for the money was simply a ruse.

"Did I tell you about Kate?" Suzie asked as she sat down

again. I shook my head, and she began to describe her latest encounter with the new editorial assistant, a massive woman who terrified everyone at the office with her intimidating manner and irreproachable typing.

We went to see a film by a new Indian director. To my own surprise, in spite of the conversation over supper, I was engrossed, and afterwards, as Suzie and I walked to the bus stop and sat on the bus, neither of us could stop talking about the characters and their tribulations. We were still deep in discussion when we reached Suzie's stop; she tried to persuade me to get off and have a drink, but I said I was too tired. She kissed me goodbye and hurried to the exit. As the bus moved on, I saw her disappearing across the street.

Two elderly men were sitting in front of me, and now that I was alone, I could hear their conversation. They were discussing a football match; each was convinced that his team had been unfairly penalised. As they argued back and forth I found myself thinking about my father, who had been the first to teach me that knowledge depends on the eye of the beholder. I had asked him to help me prepare for a chemistry test. To begin with, all went well. "Which element has the simplest molecule?" my father asked. "What happens when you pass an electric current through water?" I answered his questions promptly, proud of my expertise.

"Good." He turned to a new page in my notebook. "Now about subatomic particles." He frowned. "Who told you that electrons and protons are the smallest kinds of particles?"

"Mr. Fergerson."

"God knows what he's thinking of. This is thirty years out of date. They've already discovered several smaller kinds of particles, and who knows what else they may find." He wrote a list on a piece of paper, which he taped into my book. In the test I answered with the exotic names he had taught me.

At the end of the next class Mr. Fergerson said, "Celia, I

want a word with you." As the other girls trooped out of the
room I approached his desk; it stood on a raised dais, and my
chin barely reached the top. "Where did you get the answers
you gave to questions six and seven?" Mr. Fergerson demanded, looking down on me through his bifocals.

"My father."

"Your father." He let the word hang in the air so that I
could appreciate fully its inadequacy. "Well, Celia, quarks
may or may not exist, but in this classroom my answer is the
right answer. Is that clear?"

I knew better than to mention the incident at home; my
father was perfectly capable of complaining vociferously to
the headmistress. Instead I began to keep in my head two
parallel systems of knowledge: what I learned from my father
and what I learned at school. When asked a question, what I
wanted above all was to please my questioner.

As I walked down our street, I saw that the light above the
front door had been left on. Inside, however, the house was in
darkness, and for fear of waking Stephen, I undressed in the
bathroom. I climbed into bed as quietly as possible. He leaned
over and stroked my arm, then turned his back towards me.
I lay sleepless beside him. The conversation with Suzie had
brought home to me the strength of my own convictions,
which had previously lain hidden beneath a smooth facade of
common sense. My desire to talk to Stephen was intensified.
It seemed crucial to tell him what I knew as soon as possible,
but when would that be? I wondered. It was true that we were
ostensibly alone most evenings—nowadays Jenny seldom dis-
turbed us after she had gone to bed—but her mere presence
was inhibiting. I could not quell the fear of being overheard or
interrupted.

I got up to go to the bathroom, and as I washed my hands
I had an idea: I would suggest to Stephen that we go out for

a drink tomorrow evening. If he did not want to leave Jenny alone, then Charlotte could come over. Back in bed, I fell quickly asleep.

The Star was thronged with people, and as I pushed my way through the crowd I wondered if perhaps it had been a mistake to come here for an intimate conversation. Then I saw Stephen, sitting by the window. I kissed him and sat down. He had already bought us each a drink.

"Thanks, Celia," he said, raising his glass of lager to me.

"Thanks for what?" I asked.

"For suggesting we go out together." He smiled. He was still wearing his teaching clothes, but he had undone the top button of his shirt and loosened the knot of his thin red tie. "We had this terrible scandal at school today. Someone wrote 'Fuck you' on the door of the headmaster's office. He was furious. He lectured the whole school about it for ten minutes during assembly. I didn't dare to look at Deirdre."

He leaned forward, describing the headmaster's circumlocutions. A juke box, or radio, was playing quietly in the background. I felt my sense of purpose wavering; one part of me wanted to relax into Stephen's good mood. But as he continued to put forth various theories as to who might be the culprit, I had a sudden vision of the tiny, shrivelled corpse nestling among my clothes. I raised my glass and drank to steady my purpose. When he paused I said, "I wanted to talk about Jenny."

"Oh," said Stephen. He sat back, crossing his legs and clasping his hands as if to ensure that no involuntary gestures would escape him.

As calmly as possible I described what had happened with the money. I mentioned the other accidents that had occurred since Jenny moved in, and then concluded by telling him what she had told me about Selina. Stephen listened with a frown;

several times he seemed on the point of interrupting but refrained. When I finished, he leaned over and took my hand. "Celia, I wish you'd talked to me sooner. About the *Bunty* annual, there's nothing mysterious. I gave Jenny the money. I mean it was her money, but I was keeping it for her."

He smiled, waiting for me to respond, but I could not utter a word. I was in the grip of furious embarrassment such as I had not suffered since childhood. Not only had I made a mistake but I had made a profoundly foolish mistake. I had accused his daughter of being a thief because she had purchased a new book; that was what it amounted to. If only I had kept silent, or could board a boat to China and never return.

"As for the hole in your pullover," he continued. "I've no idea how that happened, but I'm sure that Jenny had nothing to do with it. Of course accidents happen, but she would never do anything like that deliberately." He was similarly sensible about the mouse.

I was so mortified that I could not attend to the details of his conversation, but I grasped the general drift. He was saying how glad he was to have the matter about Selina sorted out; how he had worried about Jenny treating Selina badly. I looked over his shoulder out of the window; the sky was already dark. When we were waiting to hear if our offer on the house had been accepted, I had remarked how different Stephen and I were: I was on tenterhooks, while he seemed entirely sanguine. I had said then that I imagined his brain like a very orderly city, all the streets signposted and running at right angles, every intersection with a traffic light. Whereas my brain was like a maze. Or like a city during the war, when all the street signs had been taken down to confuse the enemy; cars were constantly running into each other, turning into cul-de-sacs, going the wrong way down one-way streets. "So we complement each other perfectly," Stephen had said, and kissed me.

Now he was watching me. Although the expression on his face was calm, he was fidgeting nervously with his tie. "There's nothing for you to worry about," he concluded.

"I'm sorry," I said. "I don't know what came over me. It's a difficult adjustment to make, living with a ten year old." Suzie's reasons seemed the only excuse I could offer for my absurd accusation.

"It is difficult," said Stephen, a little too quickly. "Even though Jenny is my daughter, there are some days when there's nothing I want more than for her to be magically transported to Paris. But overall I feel fortunate. I'm getting a second chance at being a father, and after this year, I think, whatever happens, Jenny and I will be friends."

I thought then of my father and how hard I had wished that I might matter in his life. I reached for Stephen's hand, curling my fingers tight around his.

CHAPTER 22

On Friday night it rained heavily, and in the morning when Stephen and I walked to the corner shop the privet hedges were still beaded with water and the street gleamed. Mr. Murgatee was behind the counter. "Good morning," he said. "It's a grand day." I had never heard him speak ill of the weather. Without being asked, he passed us our bag of rolls. We had got into the habit of buying half a dozen of the soft, white Edinburgh baps for breakfast on Saturdays. They were still warm, and I held them close as we walked back towards the house. In this direction, we could see clear across the Forth and into Fife.

"You know what we should do this afternoon?" Stephen said. "We should go to the camera obscura."

"I didn't know there was one in Edinburgh."

"It's at the top of the Royal Mile. You get an amazing view of the city. We'd be able to see all this." He waved his arm to embrace our house, the street, the line of hills shining on the far side of the water.

"I'd love to go," I said. "My father told me how they work, but I've never been to one."

We had paused beside the garden gate, and Stephen was still staring off into the distance. "If I ever get rich," he said, "I'd like to build my own camera obscura. Maybe when you edit a best-seller."

"That'll be the day. Come on." I opened the gate. Jenny was looking out of her bedroom window. I smiled, and she waved.

*   *   *

We set out for the camera obscura after an early lunch. As we were leaving, Stephen suggested that we take the bus into the centre of town. "You know what it's like trying to park on a Saturday afternoon," he said.

"What if we want to go somewhere else?" Jenny asked. The car was parked immediately in front of the gate, and she stationed herself beside it.

"Like where?" asked Stephen.

"Like Arthur's Seat. Or suppose you and Celia see something you want to buy."

"Yes," I said. "Suppose we want to go to Holyroodhouse."

"You two are worse than my third form." Stephen held up his hands in a gesture of surrender. "All right, I give in."

While Stephen drove, we played I spy. "I spy with my little eye something beginning with *B*," said Jenny.

"Bus," I said.

"No."

"Butcher," said Stephen, pointing to a shop on the left.

"No."

"Boy," I suggested.

After about twenty guesses, Jenny revealed the answer: a bulldog that had been waiting to cross the road with its owner when she first spoke.

"That's too difficult," said Stephen. "You have to choose something that we can see for a while."

"Okay," she said. "It's your turn."

Stephen spied something beginning with *C* and after half a dozen attempts Jenny solved it: Calton Hill. Then it was my turn. "I spy with my little eye something beginning with *F*."

"Flags," said Jenny immediately, pointing to the several fluttering above Princes Street.

"That's right," I said.

"Well done," said Stephen. "I'd never have guessed that."

We reached the Grassmarket and joined the queue of cars

driving slowly round and round in search of a parking space. Just as Stephen was saying for the second time that he knew we should have taken the bus, a Range Rover pulled out. "There," said Jenny. "What did we tell you?" Stephen handed her three ten pence pieces, and she slid them into the meter with obvious pleasure. Then she led the way towards the stairs up to the Royal Mile. Like me, Jenny had never been to the camera obscura, but she knew where it was because when her class made a map of the city, Miss Nisbet had marked it in.

The steps brought us out a little below the Castle, and we crossed the street against a coach party of tourists. "There it is," Stephen said. A small sign advertising the camera obscura hung from one corner of the white house, but otherwise the building looked identical to the other tall stone houses lining the cobbled street. I understood how in my explorations of the city I had failed to notice it. We went inside. A woman, seated at a table, took our money and told us that a showing would begin shortly. Stephen led the way up a narrow spiral stair which wound unevenly past a number of small rooms. Quite suddenly we were on the top floor. On one side of the landing was the camera obscura, the doors still closed, and on the other a terrace overlooking the city. We stepped outside to wait. We were facing towards Princes Street, and from this distance the ceaseless flow of pedestrians and traffic looked almost motionless.

"Isn't that the church where you and Mummy got married?' said Jenny, pointing.

I had always assumed that Stephen and Helen had gone to a registry office. Now I suffered a sharp, double-edged pang. He had already done everything with her, I thought, and whatever he did with me could only be a feeble repetition. At the same time I was reminded of how much I did not know about Stephen; getting married in a church was a major fact, and yet he had not bothered to mention it. While he and

Jenny tried to distinguish the spire, I moved across to the far side of the terrace. The Castle rock was only a few hundred yards away. Stephen had told me that almost every year someone fell trying to climb up to the Castle, and seeing the rock from this angle, I could easily imagine the hordes of enemies who had faltered and perished on those flinty heights.

The doors of the camera opened, and half a dozen people emerged, blinking in the light. A young man summoned us inside. Stephen, Jenny, myself, and a middle-aged couple filed into the small room and stood in a circle around a convex disc, not unlike a round table. The young man closed the doors, leaving the room in darkness save for the light of a dim red bulb. The image of the city on the disc grew sharp.

He began to describe how the camera obscura worked. In the ceiling above us was a periscope, with a lens that reflected the image onto the disc below. The original camera had been built in the 1850s by an optician named Maria Theresa Short and then restored more recently. He angled the periscope in such a way as to show the area immediately surrounding the Castle. The enormous black facade of the Tolbooth Kirk loomed beneath us. The flags flapping on the Castle battlements were flapping in the room. A bird flew behind Saint Giles. The young man handed Jenny a piece of paper folded into a *V* and told her to hold it in the path of a bus. She did so, and the bus appeared to go up and over the paper. "Oh," she exclaimed.

"One time when I was doing this," the young man said, "a boy spotted his family's car parked on Johnston Terrace, and as we were watching, a man got into the car and drove away. Of course there was nothing they could do, except run to the phone."

"Hear that, Jim," said the woman standing beside me. "I told you we should have parked in a car park."

In the darkened room the streets and houses upon which

we had gazed a few minutes before lay seemingly within our grasp, the same in every detail but quite different. Looking at the image on the disc was not like looking through a window or a camera lens, although it did have something in common with each of these. What we were seeing was simultaneously a created image and the real world. As I watched the constantly shifting picture, I began to understand the vast popularity of camera obscuras; prior to the invention of film, this was the only kind of moving picture.

The guide tilted the lens again, and suddenly, as Stephen had predicted, we could see the water of the Forth, blue in the sunlight, and on the far side the soft outline of the hills of Fife.

Stephen and I made pizza for supper. During the meal, Jenny entertained us with descriptions of her science teacher's attempts to do experiments. She knelt on her chair and, using the wine bottle and her glass, imitated Mr. Laing's attempts to dilute a solution. "Well, girls," she kept saying in a deep voice, then collapsing in giggles. Afterwards the three of us played Monopoly. Jenny and I joined forces to drive Stephen out of business.

In the morning I lay in bed dozing, while Stephen rose and dressed. We had no plans and I felt the pleasure of having an entire day at my disposal. Perhaps we could do something decadent, like go to a matinee. Eventually the smell of coffee lured me out of bed. As I went to the bathroom, I could hear Stephen and Jenny talking in the dining room: first his muffled tones, then Jenny, higher pitched and more audible, exclaimed, "Daddy, you always say that." I washed my face and hands, and opened my contact lens case. Gently I picked up the right lens with the tip of my finger and reached for the cleaning solution. I always performed these actions in exactly the same order. Suddenly I noticed a familiar smell. I sniffed once, twice to be sure, then I laid the lens carefully on the shelf above the basin and picked up the storage case; instead of the clear, odourless soaking solution, the case was full of a slightly pinkish liquid. It was malt vinegar.

I put my head round the dining room door. "Stephen, could you come here?" I said.

Jenny looked at me, and even though without my lenses I could not see her clearly, I knew, without doubt, that she knew. Stephen, however, was cheerfully oblivious. "What is it?" he asked, as he came out into the hall.

"I want to show you something." I was about to usher him into the bathroom, when Jenny opened the dining room door, her eyes bright with curiosity. For a moment I thought of confronting her, demanding an explanation then and there, but I was not so far gone in anger as to abandon all caution. "I want to speak to Stephen alone," I said.

Her eyes widened. She stepped back, closing the door very quietly.

I led Stephen into the bathroom and locked the door behind us. "Go and look at my lens case," I said.

He stared at me and then stepped over to the basin and picked it up. "Vinegar," he exclaimed. "How on earth did this get in here?"

I looked at him, waiting for him to answer his own question.

There was a pause. He sniffed the liquid again, then dipped his finger in it and raised it to his lips to make sure. "Celia, was there some sort of mix-up? Did you use it by mistake?"

"I filled the case last thing at night with soaking solution, just as I always do. Did you touch it during the night?"

"No, of course not." He stared at me, taken aback by my accusation. Then his eyebrows rose, and his eyes widened still further. "You think Jenny did this?" he asked.

"Who else? Imagine if I hadn't noticed. It would have been excruciating." I waited for an explosion of rage, but he was not angry. He was frowning slightly with what I judged to be mild anxiety and bewilderment.

"It's ridiculous," he said. "Of course she wouldn't do a thing like that."

"So you think it's more likely that either of us did it than that she did. Whenever something goes wrong you take her side." I launched into a vehement speech, enumerating his betrayals. At the height of my tirade—I was talking about the island—there was a knock at the door. Jenny called plaintively, "I need to use the bathroom."

"In a minute," Stephen said. Then he turned to me. "Celia, I cannot believe Jenny would try to hurt you, even if she did dislike you, and in fact all the evidence is that she enjoys your company. Maybe there have been some accidents, but children . . . " He stopped, seeing the expression on my face, and said, "Look, we'll ask her."

He opened the bathroom door. We came out into the hall, and Jenny hurried in. Stephen went to make coffee. I sat waiting at the dining-room table. Without my lenses everything was vague; I stared through the window at the indistinct landscape. At last I had caught Jenny out. Now Stephen would understand what had been going on, and I felt almost sorry for her; I knew how dearly she valued his good opinion. She seemed to take an inordinate length of time, but presently she returned and sat down at her place. Stephen came in with two cups of coffee. He passed one to me and sat down. "Jenny," he said, "did you by any chance touch Celia's contact lens case?"

She hung her head, and behind the wings of hair, the colour came into her face. "How did you know?" she mumbled.

"This morning it was full of vinegar. If Celia hadn't noticed, it would have been terribly painful."

"I'm sorry. I was playing hospitals yesterday. I meant to empty it, but I forgot."

"How could it have been when you were playing yesterday?" I demanded. "I only put the lenses away when I went to bed. You must have got up in the middle of the night and put vinegar in."

"No," said Jenny. "It was while you and Dad were cooking."

"You shouldn't play with Celia's things," Stephen said gently. "Her contact lenses aren't a toy; they're something medical."

"I'm sorry, Celia," she said. "I won't do it again. I promise."

I pulled my chair closer so that there could be no mistaking Jenny's expression. "I filled the case with fresh soaking solution last night long after you were in bed. Whatever you did, you did while Stephen and I were asleep. It wasn't a game."

Jenny shook her head. She looked at me wide-eyed, the picture of innocence. "Really, it was when you and Daddy were cooking. You saw how I had my dolls out. They were my patients."

"She did," said Stephen. "You were tired last night. It is possible that you wouldn't have noticed."

I got up without saying another word and went to the bathroom. I washed the lenses, over and over, until every trace of vinegar was gone. As I held each lens in turn under the cold water, I saw that my hands were trembling.

When I came into the bedroom, Stephen was sitting on the edge of the bed. He stood up and closed the door. Then he turned to face me. "Celia," he said, "I can understand why you're so upset about the vinegar, but you have to remember what children are like. They live in a world of their own, and sometimes that makes them terribly thoughtless. Jenny's really sorry. The last thing she wanted was to hurt you."

As he spoke, he took my hands and looked into my eyes. His voice sounded strange. Suddenly I remembered when I had heard him use this tone before. He had been arguing with his mother, and he had adopted a special voice, brisk and light, like a doctor handling a difficult patient, and paid no attention to the points Joyce was making. All he had wanted was to terminate the conversation as rapidly as possible. If I explained again that Jenny could only have filled the case during the night, he would not listen. He would remind me once more of my fatigue, mention how I had jumped to a false conclusion in the case of the book.

"It would have been very painful if the vinegar had got in your eyes, but thank goodness it didn't. Jenny will never touch your contact lens things again. Once she knows that something is out of bounds you can trust her absolutely. I think you ought to forgive her."

This must be what it feels like, I thought, to be a sane person locked up in an asylum; if everyone assumes you are mad, then proving your sanity becomes well nigh impossible. It was not Jenny's behaviour that worried Stephen, but my own. My attempts to enlighten him only increased his blindness.

He was still holding my hands, and as he reached the word "forgive," the pressure of his grasp increased, crushing my fingers together. "All right," I said. "I'll try." Immediately he released me.

When I looked at Jenny, with my lenses in, I saw that her hair was especially glossy and her eyes were clear. She had a plump, sleek look, as if during the night she had fed upon some secret source of satisfaction.

At work next day I shut my office door, pleading urgent proofreading, but the sheafs of paper lay ignored before me as I tried to follow the thin thread of reason through the labyrinth of confusion. When Stephen told me that he had given Jenny the money for the book, I had, in my embarrassment, been ready to discount all the other incidents that had persuaded me of her antagonism; now my earlier conviction flooded back. What was especially frightening about the vinegar was not merely the cruelty of the act but the cunning of the confession. I had always assumed that Jenny did not want her father to find out what was going on and that her fear of his doing so was my main weapon. But there could be no accident about the vinegar in my lens case and no mystery about the author of the act. That was why my hands had begun to shake. Apart from anything else, Jenny had shown me that my ultimate deterrent was useless. I could talk to Stephen about almost everything, but on the subject of his daughter, there was a barrier between us which so far I had been able neither to scale nor demolish. That he should doubt my word rather than believe her capable of wrongdoing terrified me.

The telephone rang, startling me back into the present. I answered, and Marilyn told me that there was a package waiting for me in reception. I said I would be along to collect it soon.

After I hung up I found myself thinking about the remark Suzie had made at Hendersons, about how I hated Harry. At the time, I had repudiated the comparison between Jenny and myself, but when I stopped to think, I had to admit that Suzie was right: Jenny and I were both, roughly speaking, step-daughters. Harry had always been kind to me, and for years I had rewarded him with rudeness and disdain. As far as I was concerned, he had stolen my mother. If I had felt this way at twenty, how much more so must Jenny feel at ten? Not only had she been abandoned by her mother, but in addition she was forced to share her father with a stranger. No wonder she was unhappy. If only, I thought, I could find a way to make her happier, then she would stop behaving badly.

When I put myself in Jenny's place, I knew at once what I must do. I must allow her time alone with Stephen. Before my advent in her life she had seen him less often, but at least when she did, she had had his undivided attention. Now, save for an hour or so after school, she could seldom rely upon having him to herself. As I thought about all the ways in which I had come between Jenny and her father, I began to feel more cheerful. If I had behaved perfectly, then there would be real cause for grief, for there would be nothing I could do to improve the situation; as it was, a course of action lay plainly before me. There was even an immediate opportunity for me to put my new strategy into operation. The following weekend was Guy Fawkes, and we had planned to go to Abernethy. I resolved to let Stephen and Jenny go alone.

I had reached this point in my deliberations when the telephone rang again. Kate, the formidable assistant, announced that she had finished my typing; she hung up while I was in the middle of thanking her. I went off to fetch my package and on the way stopped to tell Suzie about Kate's latest piece of rudeness.

When I announced my decision at supper that evening, Stephen at once offered to stay and keep me company. "Jenny's old enough to take the bus to Perth alone, aren't you?" he said.

Jenny did not reply. She seemed absorbed in her baked potato. "I'm staying behind to work," I said. "Even if you were here, you wouldn't see me. I'll be going into the office both days."

"But you'll have to emerge for meals. I could cook and be supportive."

"Stephen, Joyce and Edward are expecting you. Just because I have to change my plans doesn't mean that you or Jenny should."

With some difficulty I convinced him to go. While he and I settled her fate, Jenny's face took on an air of polite interest. No wonder she resents me, I thought. Only the day before, I had been oblivious to what effect this sort of behaviour must have upon her.

By dint of careful planning I managed to stay out of her

way for most of the week, and when I arrived home on Friday, she and Stephen had already departed; only Tobias came to greet me. He wove around my legs, purring at full throttle as I took off my coat. Throughout the evening, he shadowed me, following me from room to room and leaping onto my lap whenever I sat down.

I had never spent a night alone in the house before, and I had worried that I might feel uneasy. On the contrary, I found myself enjoying the unusual freedom of not having to take anyone else into account. I had lived alone for most of my adult life, and there were certain solitary pleasures that I missed and was glad to recapture briefly. Perhaps it was my imagination, but when Stephen and Jenny returned on Sunday, the atmosphere seemed lighter. By letting them go alone, I had acknowledged that there was a bond between them in which I had no part. They both said that they were pleased to see me. Over supper they took turns telling me about the fireworks.

CHAPTER 23

During the days following Guy Fawkes, domestic life continued to run smoothly; Stephen made supper, or I made supper,
we worked, and watched television, and played games. At last
Jenny seemed to be learning to accept the present situation
and my role in her life. Christmas was coming. She would be
away for a fortnight, and then in the new year, as the days
grew lighter and Helen's return grew closer, everything
would become easier. Meanwhile I was determined to pursue
my policy of making sure that she and Stephen spent time
alone together. When Stephen announced at breakfast on
Saturday that he and Jenny were planning a trip to the ice rink
in the afternoon, I said that I had to go shopping. I was in
urgent need of a new coat.

"But it'll be so busy," he said. "Why not wait and go on
Thursday evening?"

"It's just as busy then, and I'll be tired from work. Besides,
I'm terrible at skating."

"So am I. That makes it more fun."

"Maybe next time," I said, reaching for the butter.

After breakfast Stephen went to do the weekly shopping at
Safeways. I fetched my blue pullover and began to wash it at
the kitchen sink. I was adding the soap, when a sudden noise
made me look round. Jenny was standing in the doorway.
"Oh," I exclaimed. My skin prickled. Then I pulled myself
together and managed to laugh at my own surprise. "You

startled me. I thought you'd gone shopping with Stephen," I explained. At breakfast she had said that she wanted to go to make sure that he bought things she liked.

"No. I had to get my homework done." She held up the notebook she was carrying. "What's nine fourths times one third?" She carried the book over to the counter and sat down on her stool.

"What did your teacher tell you to do first?" I was not entirely sure that I remembered the technique myself.

"I don't know," said Jenny.

I shook the water off my hands and came and stood beside her. "Didn't she give you an example?" Over her shoulder I peered at the list of sums. "Turn back a page." She did so, and there were three examples of how to multiply fractions. We went through them and then returned to the first problem. "Now do you see what to do?" I asked.

"Maybe I should divide nine by three?"

"That sounds like a good idea."

While I emptied and refilled the basin, Jenny scribbled furiously. "Do you think the answer could be three fourths?"

"Yes. Well done." I finished rinsing the pullover and announced that I was going to hang it up outside. Jenny nodded.

I opened the back door. A thrush was standing on the flagstones with a snail in its beak. It had been hammering the shell against the stone and was poised for another blow. As I stepped forward, the bird dropped the snail and flew over the wall. I bent down; the topaz-coloured shell was badly cracked, but perhaps not fatally. I moved it to the herbaceous border in the hope that it might recover.

I draped a dish towel across the washing line and hung up the pullover. There was a good breeze, and if the rain held off, it would be dry in a few hours. Then I went to the vegetable patch to examine the Brussels sprouts which Edward had planted a couple of months before. Beneath the dull green leaves the knobs were still extremely small.

Jenny had left the kitchen when I returned. I put the soap away, rinsed out the basin, and dried my hands. I reached for my bracelet. I had left it on the window sill. Stephen had been going over the shopping list, and I remembered as we talked sliding the bracelet over my knuckles and placing it in one corner of the sill. Now the sill was empty.

I almost ran across the dining room and into the hall. Without knocking, I pushed open the door of Jenny's bedroom.

She was sitting at her desk, writing in her arithmetic notebook, and nothing could have made me more certain of her guilt than the fact that she did not look up. If she had been twenty years older, I might possibly have believed that monumental concentration rendered her oblivious to my noisy entrance, or alternatively that she was desperate to hold on to some fleeting thought long enough to get it down on paper. But at her age I could not believe in this pretence over homework.

"Where's the bracelet?"

"What bracelet?" She looked up at last, but kept one finger resting on the page to mark her place.

"The bracelet I always wear."

"I don't know. Did you lose it?" She turned her attention back to the page; her pencil was poised.

"Jenny, look at me."

She raised her eyes again, as if it were only now dawning on her that I was upset. Faintly she smiled.

"I put the bracelet on the window sill. Now it's gone. I thought you might have tried it on and forgotten to put it back."

"I didn't touch it. I've been busy doing my homework. Maybe you forgot where you put it."

She was as smooth as ice. If I had turned my back, it would have been easy to imagine that I was conversing with an adult. "Jenny," I said, "I'm going to give you five minutes to produce that bracelet. If you don't, it'll be the worse for you."

"I don't know what you're talking about," she said indignantly. "How would I know where your stupid bracelet is?"

"There's only the two of us here; there's no point in lying. I'm going to the corner shop. It had better be on the dining room table by the time I return."

I walked swiftly from the room and out of the house. She will put the bracelet on the table, I thought, and later I will talk to Stephen, and we will make a plan for how to deal with his daughter. She has to be made to understand that her behaviour is unacceptable. I had not paused to put on a jacket, and by the time I reached the shop I was bitterly cold.

There was a queue at the register. I went around the counter to the biscuit display. I picked up first one package and then another, looking at the pictures of biscuits, glistening with chocolate or sticky with jam. Finally I shook myself out of this trance-like state, bought some chocolate digestives, and agreed with Mrs. Murgatee that we mustn't grumble about the weather.

On my way home I saw Charlotte and Irene coming down the street towards me. From a distance they looked more like sisters than mother and daughter, an illusion that was fostered by the matching anoraks they wore. "Where's your coat?" asked Irene, as they drew close.

"I just came out for some biscuits. I didn't know it was so cold."

"That's how you catch a chill," she admonished. Charlotte nodded to me and skipped off down the street; meanwhile Irene began to talk about the neighbourhood association petition for more street lights in the local park. I stood there with my arms wrapped tightly around myself, trying to take in her remarks about wattage and maintenance. "They have to agree that it's their responsibility," she was saying, when suddenly it occurred to me that once again I had been outmanoeuvred. I shivered.

"Goodness, what am I thinking of," said Irene. "Hurry home and get warm. We can talk some other time."

I ran down the street as fast as I could, and through the open gate. I turned the handle of the front door. Nothing happened. In my haste I had left the lock on the latch and not brought a key. I rang the doorbell and pounded my fist against the wooden panel. A terrible, choking sense of panic assailed me. I was locked out, and it seemed perfectly possible that Jenny would refuse to let me in. Why had she locked the door? It could only be in order to do something terrible.

I pounded with both fists as hard as I could. "Jenny, let me in. Jenny, let me in," I shouted.

I was about to go and look through the window of her room, when the door swung open. "I was in the toilet," she said.

As I pushed past her, I heard the sound of the cistern refilling. "Why did you lock the door?"

"Mummy always told me to lock the door when I was alone." She knew Helen was sacrosanct. I thought of reminding her of all the occasions on which she had failed to follow her mother's advice, but I had other preoccupations.

She closed the door behind me and returned to her bedroom, closing that door too. I walked into the dining room. The table was bare. I stood there; my anger, like a stone in my mouth, rendered me dumb. Then I turned and went into Jenny's bedroom. She was back at her desk, pretending once more to do her homework.

"Where is it?" My voice was thin and harsh, quite unlike any sound I had ever heard myself produce, but Jenny did not seem to notice.

"What?" she said. The single syllable, bloated with insolence, hovered like a balloon between us.

I went over, took hold of her shoulders, and began to shake her. At that moment I could have done anything: hit her, banged her head against a wall, kicked her in the stomach, squeezed the breath out of her body. She did not say a word, utter a sound, beyond a small gasp. If she had still been acting, she would have protested innocence and bewilderment, but things were too far gone for that. We had both abandoned our disguises.

I stopped because I was afraid, not of what I might do to her—I would happily have left her for dead—but of what I glimpsed in myself. I let go. My breath came and went with an ugly rasping sound. Jenny stood before me. Her head was level with my chest, her face was pale and smooth as an unwritten sheet of paper. Without looking at me, she went back to her desk and sat down.

"Stand up."

She got to her feet immediately. This was the ultimate act of disobedience: to go through the motions in everything save what mattered. I knelt in front of her and ran my hands up and down her arms and legs, over her front and back.

"Go and stand there."

She went meekly to the corner by the window and leaned against the wall. I riffled through the papers on her desk, throwing them onto the floor. Nothing. I felt her eyes on me, and although her expression did not change, I could imagine the pleasure my frantic helplessness gave her.

It was stupid of me to have gone out and left her the leisure to find a secure hiding place, but I had to give her a chance to return the bracelet. I wanted Stephen to know that I had dealt fairly with his daughter. In fact, because of her age, it had to be more than fair.

Jenny picked up a book that lay near her on the floor and bent her head over the pages. I began to search her room. I no longer cared how much mess I made. I tipped all the dresser drawers out on the bed, then I sorted through the mass of clothes, tossing them onto the floor. I moved the dresser and looked under it. I stripped the bed and found nothing but a sock and a stuffed animal. I ransacked the bookcase, piling the books onto the floor. And Jenny stood there, with a small smile on her face, looking at the book: she even turned a page. It was intolerable that the one thing I needed to know was sitting in her head, like an egg in a nest.

I was working on the bottom shelf of the bookcase, when I heard the front door open. Jenny dropped the book and, before I could stop her, darted out into the hall.

"Daddy," I heard her say. "Celia's lost her bracelet, and she's very upset."

"It can't be far away. Would you give me a hand with this?"

At the sound of their voices, chiming one against the other, I saw what I had done. The room was in chaos, the floor strewn with Jenny's books and toys and clothes. In my determination to find the bracelet, I had lost sight of the fact that Stephen could return at any moment. I had believed that the bracelet, which had been his first gift to me, would save us from Jenny; that it would provide the incontrovertible proof necessary to convince him. His voice shattered the illusion. There was no reason why he should believe me; how could the loss of the bracelet prove to him Jenny's malice when even the sight of my contact lens case filled with vinegar had failed to do so?

I pushed the dresser back against the wall and crammed the clothes into the drawers, managing to get them all smoothly shut. I seized the books and placed them higgledy-piggledy on the shelves. I scooped all the papers off the floor and onto the desk. When Stephen came in I was gathering up an armful of sheets. "Jenny told me you'd lost your bracelet."

"It disappeared. Maybe later you could help me look. I thought I'd do a load of sheets."

"It just started to rain."

"It'll probably clear up. I've been saying that I'd do them for a week." Jenny was standing in the shadows behind him, and I could not judge her expression.

"This would be a good chance to clean your room," Stephen said to her. "If you pick everything up off the floor, I'll fetch the Hoover."

"I was doing my homework."

"This won't take more than fifteen minutes. Come on, if Celia can be bothered to wash your sheets, you can surely tidy up."

While Stephen spoke I had been slowly putting the blankets on the end of the bed. Now I moved towards the door, where Jenny stood. At this moment, she and I were infinitely closer to each other than to Stephen; our secret knowledge linked us as surely as it excluded him. He was the outsider whose innocence we prized. As I passed with her sheets in my arms, Jenny and I exchanged glances; such was the intimacy between us that we were almost smiling.

Then she bent reluctantly to pick up a pencil, and I moved out into the hall. I stripped our bed and piled all the sheets into the washing machine. The noise of the water filling the machine meshed with the undulating roar of the Hoover. I stood there with the sounds of domestic life loud in my ears.

The bracelet could be hidden anywhere: in a bag of flour, buried in the garden, at the back of a cupboard, behind a book. There was no point in searching; the only way I would ever find it was by trying to imagine what had gone through Jenny's mind. She knew that I was on my guard. It had been foolish of me to think that she would hide it in her room, for if it was found there, she would have no excuse. How stupid I had been.

I was sitting on our unmade bed, inching through these thoughts, when Stephen came in, pushing the Hoover. He stopped, as if surprised to see me. "I thought I might as well do our room too," he said, one hand still resting on the handle.

"I'll go and tidy up the kitchen."

"Celia, what about your bracelet?" There was a slight hesitation in his voice. Perhaps something in my expression made him pause.

"I took it off when I was doing some washing. Then I looked for it, and it was gone." Let him find the explanation, let him call me mad, I thought.

"It can't be far away. It's sure to turn up," he said, moving, plug in hand, towards a socket.

In the kitchen I put away the breakfast dishes and cleaned the sink, the top of the refrigerator, the counters. As I performed these tasks I tried to make my mind float out of my body and into that of a child with pale skin and dark eyes, several inches smaller than her peers, who knew even so early in life that she would need cunning to survive.

I got down on my knees, so that my head was at the level of her head, and looked around, trying to see the room as she did. I looked in the oven, the fridge, I shook the box of soap powder, I took the lid off the bin—taking out the rubbish was one of Jenny's tasks, and I often had to remind her to do it. Suddenly I felt certain that in among the egg shells, potato peels, and coffee grounds I would see a glimpse of silver; Jenny would enjoy the irony of my asking her to throw out the rubbish and thereby the bracelet.

I began to transfer the rubbish from one bag to another. I was lifting out an empty orange juice carton when Stephen said my name. Above the throb of the washing machine, I had not heard him approach. "Guess what, Celia," he said. "I found the bracelet in the bedroom. It was on the chest of drawers. You must have put it down without thinking and then forgotten."

Smiling, he held it out to me where I knelt beside the rubbish, and smiling, I slipped it back over my right hand.

What could be more likely to convince Stephen of my madness than to hide the bracelet where I always put it?

Once when I was shopping for my mother, the fishmonger had offered to show me a surprise. "Take a look in there," he had said, pointing to a bucket in the corner. I tiptoed over and peered inside. What I saw made me jump back in terror. The bucket contained a mass of eels. In the confined space they writhed and undulated; such was their constant motion that it was impossible to know where one dark, slippery body began and another ended. Since Stephen had handed me the bracelet, my mind seethed in similar fashion. I could not tell where one thought ended and another began. I knew I had put the bracelet on the window sill. And yet there it was in the place where I laid it automatically, night after night. For a split second I wondered if I could have been mistaken. Then I remembered Jenny's behaviour; over and above my own memories, there was my proof. I was bursting with speeches I wanted to make, not to him but to her.

At lunch I announced that I would like to come ice-skating after all. In the circumstances, my plan to be more considerate towards Jenny seemed absurd, and I could not bear the thought of being alone.

"Great," said Stephen. "It'll be good for my ego to have someone even worse than me around."

"I can show you how to skate," said Jenny, smiling. Her equanimity did not surprise me; it was part of her strategy to be especially friendly not only before but also after a fracas.

We were in the hall, getting ready to leave, when the telephone rang. As usual Jenny answered. "Hello," she said. "I'm okay." She passed the phone to Stephen.

"Hello," he said. "Deirdre." He was silent for a moment. "We were about to go skating." There was another pause, and then he said, "Let me check with Celia." He cupped his hand over the receiver and turned to me. "It's Deirdre. She wants me to help her carry up her new bed. She says that she'll give me a lift to the rink as soon as we're finished."

"That's fine. We can manage without you, can't we, Jenny?" I zipped my jacket up tight and turned to smile at her. I saw the reluctance in her face, but it was too late to feign illness or a change of heart; we were dressed, on the point of departure. She gave a stiff little nod.

As I drove, Stephen talked about one of his pupils, who had been suspended for starting a fire in the cloakroom. "Yesterday his mother came to see me. We were talking about Kenny, and she burst into tears. I thought she was going to tell me that he'd had nothing to do with the fire, but it turned out quite the contrary. She'd come to see me because she's terrified of having him around the house, and she wanted to know if there was any alternative."

"Poor woman," I said. "What did you tell her?" I had negotiated the Saturday hubbub of Princes Street and was driving up the Mound towards the black spires of the Assembly Hall.

"I recommended a couple of organisations, but Kenny won't go to them. I'm afraid there's nothing to be done until he's caught shoplifting and becomes a bona fide delinquent."

"Why did he start a fire?" asked Jenny from the back seat.

"Just to make trouble," said Stephen. "Or maybe he has a grudge against the school. I don't know. I'm not sure anyone even bothered to ask him."

We passed various university buildings and turned onto the road that circled the Meadows. On the far side of the green I spotted Miss Lawson in her blue raincoat, walking Rollo; briefly a twinge of guilt distracted me from my thoughts about Jenny. I must visit her soon.

"Did you know Celia used to live here?" Stephen asked, as I drew up at the curb.

"Why doesn't she live here anymore?" said Jenny.

"Because," said Stephen, "she's living happily ever after

with you and me." He leaned over to kiss me, then got out of the car, leaving his door open. He opened the back door. "You get to sit in the front," he said to Jenny.

In the rear-view mirror I saw her sitting absolutely still; then her head bobbed, she vanished from the mirror, as she did her father's bidding, and appeared beside me. "Have fun," Stephen said. "I should be there in half an hour."

I drove slowly round the cobbled crescent and turned left onto the main road. The needle on the speedometer hovered at twenty-five; I looked in the mirror, signalled, manoeuvred with pedantic care, as if taking a driving test. "Jenny," I said, "we need to talk." Ahead of us a bus pulled up at the stop. A young man got off, and the conductor leaned down to talk to him. "It can't be easy for you living with Stephen and me, but until Helen comes back you have no choice. It's stupid not to be friends."

"I'm going to Paris for Christmas, and Mummy's coming back in June."

"June is seven months away. That's a long time if you and I keep behaving like we did this morning. More than two hundred days." We were at a red light. I glanced at Jenny; she was fiddling with the knob of the glove compartment, giving the least possible indication of listening. "I know you've been upset, and I must seem like an interloper, but none of what is happening is my fault. I didn't make Helen go to France. I'm not your enemy." I paused.

She was turned away, resolutely absorbed in what lay beyond the window. Still there was no reply. Like a prisoner in a fairy tale, I kept hoping that I would stumble upon the magical word or phrase which would release me from her animosity.

"The light's green."

As I put the car into first gear, my foot slipped on the clutch; we stalled. Behind me a car honked; beside me Jenny giggled. I felt myself blush. When we were once more in motion, I said, "Stephen doesn't know what's been going on. It would be a pity if he found out. He trusts you."

Jenny had breathed on her window and in the mist was drawing or writing something. I looked at the back of her head and knew with a feeling of discomfort that she had measured exactly the force of my threat. "Say something," I said.

"We're nearly there."

"Jenny, don't pretend you haven't heard."

"I heard you, but I don't know what you're talking about."

"I'm talking about you being a thief and a liar."

"We turn here," she said.

"We're not going skating until you answer me." We came to a roundabout and I went resolutely straight ahead. I pushed down the accelerator, cutting off a young woman who was hesitating on the edge of a zebra crossing. I had a sudden image of us driving in silence all the way to Glasgow.

Jenny continued to look out of the window. "Whenever something goes wrong, you think it's my fault." She spoke in a small, even voice. "It's not fair. It has nothing to do with me."

"Nothing?" I said. "So it's a series of coincidences." My earlier thoughts of patience vanished; my temper was up, and I longed to wrest the truth from her.

"I don't know what it is," she said sullenly. "Where are we going?"

Anger pressed me towards speech, but I was determined to resist. I switched on the radio. "Don't miss your only chance," the announcer urged, in a soft Scottish burr, "to catch U2. They're playing at Meadowbank next Friday and Saturday." He introduced their latest record and I turned up the sound.

"Mum really likes them," Jenny said. "She has all their records."

I pushed my hair back and shifted my hands on the steering

wheel. We came to a row of shops. I wondered briefly if Jenny would tell Stephen what I had done, and then dismissed the thought. We were nearing the outskirts of the city. The two-storey stone houses that lined the street were set well back behind large gardens; in the distance I glimpsed tall, leafless trees and bare hills.

"This is stupid," said Jenny. "We'll never get to go skating. What will happen to Daddy?"

"I'll telephone Deirdre." As if by magic I saw on the other side of the road a call box beside a garage. I pulled over and reached down for my bag. "I'll just be a minute." I opened the door and got out.

A lorry was approaching; it rumbled by, followed by a line of cars. I was certain that Jenny was watching me, but I did not look. I paid attention only to the business of crossing the road, waiting for the moment when I could make my way to the other side.

A green bus passed, and the road was clear. I ran across. The call box was empty. Inside, it smelled strongly of urine. I wedged the door open with one foot and got out my address book to look up Deirdre's number. I did not know what I would say to Stephen, but I thought that when I heard his voice something would come to me. I lifted the receiver.

"Celia." She spoke through the crack in the door.

I balanced a ten pence piece in the slot.

"Please," she said. Her lips were moving. Above the noise of the traffic, her specific words were inaudible, but the sense of them reached me, something about "trying," about "friends." It was almost irrelevant; the fact that she had crossed the road was sufficient.

I turned into the car park of the ice rink and stopped beside a red Cortina. Before I had even switched off the engine Jenny had climbed out and was running towards the entrance. I sat there looking after her small figure zigzagging between the parked cars. On the playing field behind the rink, three boys were playing football. The orange ball flew back and forth across the dun-coloured grass.

In the ladies' changing room Jenny was bent over, lacing up her second skate. "Will you look after my shoes?" she asked when she saw me. I nodded and went over to the counter, where I exchanged my boots for a pair of grimy white skates. When I turned around, Jenny was hobbling on her skates out of the door. I put our shoes and my bag in a locker and sat down. I loosened the laces of the skates all the way down, then pulled on the left skate. In spite of my thick socks, the leather felt hard and cold. Beside me a stout woman in a pink pullover and blue stretch trousers was taking off her shoes. "You're not lacing them tightly enough," she said.

"I don't know if I can do them any tighter."

"You've got to really pull. If they don't feel uncomfortable to start with, something's wrong." She demonstrated with her own skates.

I did my best to follow her instructions. Nevertheless, as soon as I stood up, my ankles began to shake. I made my way unsteadily across the rubber mats to the edge of the rink, where at least I could hold on to the barrier. As I stood clutching the rail with both hands, the woman who had supervised my lacing walked past. She reached the ice and set off into the millrace of skaters. I saw her on the opposite side, twirling along, entirely at home in her new element.

I put one foot onto the ice, then the other. I did not let go of the barrier for an instant but, holding tightly to the rail, eased my way forward until I was no longer right beside the entrance. I searched the ice for Jenny. Two boys whizzed by, crouched low in racing posture, then a girl in a short skirt and purple tights came looping past. I could see no sign of Jenny. For a moment I wondered if she had run away, was even now hitchhiking towards Paris. I remembered that I was her guardian, the adult in charge of her physical safety; if anything happened, I would be held accountable and even worse, hold myself to blame.

Then I caught sight of her on the far side of the ice. She was wearing a white pullover and grey trousers; against the whiteness of the ice she seemed shadowy and indistinct, a small succubus, gliding with uncanny ease between the other skaters. She disappeared again behind a man in a black pullover. Suddenly she was beside me. "Come on," she said. "I'll show you what to do."

When Stephen joined us, we were skating hand in hand.

PART V

PART 2

CHAPTER 24

I thought of my rapprochement with Jenny as a triumph. By overcoming the timidity that had made me avoid such confrontations in the past, I had brought peace between us. I ought to have spoken to her weeks before, instead of relying on Stephen as a go-between. Although he knew nothing of what had occurred, he seemed to sense that Jenny and I were at ease, and for the remainder of the weekend the three of us were unusually jolly. On Sunday, Suzie and Tim came to lunch; we all laughed so hard at Suzie's stories that we could scarcely eat. Jenny had not met Tim before, and she at once took charge of him. While we grown-ups sat over our coffee, she introduced him to Selina and taught him to play a game called "Haunted House." In the afternoon we put on jackets and scarves and went for a walk in the botanical garden. Even this late in the year, there were a few flowers. We strolled around admiring the hardy blooms until the cold wind drove us home.

Back at the house, Suzie insisted on making scones for tea, and Jenny volunteered to help. The two of them put on aprons and set about consulting recipes.

"Do you think we should follow the Good Housekeeping one or the health food one?" Suzie asked.

"Good Housekeeping," said Jenny. "It's quicker." She climbed onto her stool and began to get out utensils and ingredients. As I listened to Jenny being charming and helpful, I thought Suzie must find my complaints about her even more absurd now than when I had voiced them. Then I reminded myself that such difficulties were purely historical. I was determined to let bygones be bygones.

While the scones were baking, Suzie ran to the corner shop to buy cream. Tim and I laid the dining room table. The five of us sat down. We were almost silent with greed as we devoured the scones, straight from the oven, with cream and strawberry jam. From time to time Jenny reached under the table to give Tobias a fingerful of cream.

"These are the best scones I have ever eaten," said Stephen. He leaned back and patted his stomach appreciatively.

"Yes, they are," said Tim. "Thank you very much."

"It was a pleasure," said Suzie. "We can't tell you the secret of our success, but we'll be happy to oblige again in the near future." She winked at Jenny.

Next morning at breakfast I caught Jenny looking critically at her slice of toast. "What's the matter?" I asked.

"I wish we had some scones left," she said.

"So do I," said Stephen. "They were delicious." He turned to me. "I couldn't get over how well behaved Tim was."

"You sound surprised," I said.

"Well, one wouldn't necessarily pick Suzie as a model parent." He was about to say more, when we heard the snap of the letter box. Jenny, as usual, slid from her chair and ran out of the room.

"Why not?" I demanded. I felt an immediate stirring of indignation on Suzie's behalf.

"I suppose she's always struck me as rather scatter-brained—the way she talks, how she does her hair. You know what I mean." He spread marmalade on his toast and pushed the jar in my direction. "Have you noticed how much earlier the post is arriving since we got a younger postman?"

"Oh, is that the reason?" I was about to continue my defence of Suzie when I felt a cold draught and realised that although Jenny had left the door open, I had not heard the slightest sound from the hall. What was she doing to be so silent? Was she holding the envelope up to the light, hoping to make out the contents; was she squeezing it between her hands, like a shaman attempting divination? Stephen picked up the newspaper. I was on the point of going to see what was happening, when she walked in, holding before her a single letter. "It's from Mummy," she said, and handed it to Stephen.

Occasionally Helen included notes to Stephen in her letters to Jenny, but this was the first time that she had written directly to him. "I expect it's to both of us," he said, putting down the newspaper and picking up the letter. Jenny stood beside him, watching intently.

At such moments, when I saw how desperately she missed her mother, I could understand any extremity of bad behaviour. I tried to pretend to be absorbed in my toast. From the bulky envelope Stephen drew out several pages. He scanned them quickly. "It's just to me," he said. "But she's writing to you soon."

Slowly Jenny sat down. She inched her chair closer to Stephen's end of the table. As he read the first page of the letter, his mouth twitched in a smile. His eyes reached the bottom of the page, and he began to read it again. Then, without finishing, he folded the pages in half and put them down beside his plate.

"What is it, Daddy? Aren't you going to read what Mummy says?" The letter lay within her reach; I thought I saw her hand quiver with the effort of restraint.

"I'll read it later." He looked up, and then, as if realising for the first time how much all this mattered to Jenny, offered some additional information. "It's about her job."

"What about her job?"

I tried to create a diversion by standing up and asking Jenny if today wasn't the day when she needed her swimming things. I could have been silent, invisible, for all the attention she paid me.

"She wanted to tell me about some difficulties at work," Stephen said. "She's fine. She sends you lots of love and says she'll write very soon. Come on, we have to get ready to leave."

I knew that he was lying and that Jenny also knew but, as an adult, for once I had the advantage. I could demand to be told the contents of the letter, even perhaps to read it for myself, whereas she must make do with whatever Stephen cared to divulge. She stood staring at her father as he stuffed the letter into the pocket of his trousers, then turned aside to carry her plate into the kitchen.

I was in the middle of a conversation with the marketing manager, when Stephen telephoned to ask if we could meet for lunch. For the remainder of the morning, ideas of what Helen might have said sprouted, avid and resilient as the weeds that spring up in the cracks between crazy paving. She missed her daughter too much and had decided that she wanted Jenny to come and live with her. At the end of term we would pack up all Jenny's belongings and put her on a plane to Paris. Or, I improvised further, Jenny would spend Christmas with us, to keep the balance, and on Boxing Day we would drive her, with her newly opened presents, to the airport. Maybe at Easter, Stephen and I could visit her in Paris. I had not been there since a school trip when I was seventeen. Periodically I chided myself—the letter could be about any number of topics—but after drawing a couple of deep breaths of the cool air of reason, I dove back into my hothouse fantasies.

I arrived at the café before Stephen. While I waited I looked around the shop at the front, where they sold books, cards, and crafts. The brightly coloured merchandise reminded me of the knitwear shop on Saint Stephen Street. I had that morning put on what I still thought of as the replacement pullover. Suddenly I found myself wondering if Jenny really had taken a pair of scissors to the original pullover. Since the idea first occurred to me, I had gone back and forth so many times that I no longer knew what to believe. I walked over to look at the display of dolls' house furniture. There was a bookcase filled with dummy books, a miniature telephone, a fridge, a stove, a cradle, as well as the more conventional tables, chairs and beds with which I had played during my childhood.

I heard the bell on the door chime and looked up to see Stephen. "Sorry I'm late," he said. "I couldn't find a place to park."

"I've only been here a few minutes. Isn't this sweet?" I held out my hand to show him a tiny bed.

Stephen joined the queue for food, and I went to find us a table. The café was housed in what I thought of as a rotunda, a circular room with the tables arranged around the perimeter. I sat down next to two middle-aged women, both wearing hats. "It's not as if I don't have plenty to complain about," the one sitting next to me remarked, "but I do try to look on the bright side, whereas Linda, you'd think she was in the poorhouse."

"I know what you mean." The woman facing me nodded. "I'm sick to death of her doing nothing but grumble."

I was watching Stephen as he waited to be served. He had taken off his glasses and was polishing them on his handkerchief. He did not seem especially happy, but then few of my daydreams of the morning would be cause for rejoicing on his part. In a few minutes he carried over our plates of food. He sat down and gave me a quick smile. There was a pause while he seemed engrossed in shaking out his napkin, rearranging his cutlery. I could not fathom his expression.

Finally I said, "So tell me what Helen's letter was about. I'm dying to know."

"Do you remember a month ago Jenny announced that Helen had a new boyfriend?"

"Jean-Paul?"

"Jean-Pierre. Last week Helen found out that she's pregnant. Of course it was an accident."

I felt envy so strong that I could not speak. Helen had everything, and now this too. The expectations which I had nurtured in the course of the morning seemed unbearably pathetic. Beneath the table I clenched my fists. "Is she going to keep it?" I asked.

Stephen stared at me, initially as if he had no idea what I meant, and then as if I had said something shocking. "Yes, they're both delighted. Helen says this is her chance to repeat her life and do everything right." He shrugged at this unflattering view of their marriage, but I was in no mood to offer consolation.

"So Jenny is going to have a sibling," I said slowly.

"I nearly blurted it out at breakfast. She'll be thrilled. She's always wanted a brother or sister." He smiled in anticipation of Jenny's pleasure, picked up his knife and fork, and began to eat.

It seemed useless to suggest alternative scenarios. Our companions had dispensed with Linda. The more soft-spoken of the two was recommending a gallery in Aberfeldy where she had bought some lovely gifts. "What's going to happen about Christmas?" I asked. I too picked up my knife and fork, but I could not bring myself to eat.

"That's what the letter is mostly about. They're spending Christmas with Jean-Pierre's family, and Helen doesn't think that it would be a very good idea for Jenny to come. She says it'll be hard enough to meet her new in-laws without bringing one and a half children along. She suggests that Jenny go over on the twenty-seventh, and fly back on the third. It means we'll be able to spend Christmas together."

Above my mushroom quiche the steam trembled. I thought

of the difference in our vocabularies, that for him the word "we" embraced one more person than it ever did for me. "But then Jenny will only be going for a week."

Stephen nodded. He chewed and swallowed. "She starts school again on the fourth. I suppose she could miss a couple of days, but given that Helen would be at work, there doesn't seem much point. I can't wait to tell Joyce and Edward. They'll be delighted."

Even as he spoke, my mind had leapt from the immediate disappointment of Christmas to the much more crucial question of Helen's long-range plans. Everything I had taken for granted was suddenly in doubt. "What about later?" I demanded.

"Later?"

"Is Helen coming back from Paris? Will she ever want her daughter back? Or are Jean-Pierre and his baby the perfect replacement?"

Stephen stared at me. "Of course Helen isn't replacing Jenny. All we're discussing is a slight change in the dates of Jenny's Christmas holiday."

"But what's going to happen?" I persisted. "Where are they going to live, and is Jenny going to live with them?"

"Helen didn't go into much detail. The baby is due in June. She plans to come back with Jean-Pierre at the end of April to look for a house to buy. She doesn't mention arrangements about Jenny, but I imagine that she might be amenable to something more like joint custody." He reached out and touched my cheek. "Celia, tell me what's bothering you. Is it the change of plan, or is there something else?"

I looked at him and saw the anxious, eager expression with which he waited for my answer. How could I voice my fears when what I was most afraid of, that Jenny would live with us forever, was something that he would welcome. To cover my confusion, I began at last to eat. Beside us the two women pushed back their chairs and rose to their feet. As they straightened their hats, they kept their eyes fixed on each other for guidance.

Trying to sound calm, I said, "We seem to be entirely at Helen's mercy. When we first met, she would only let you see Jenny between ten and six on Saturdays; even taking her to Abernethy for a weekend was problematic. Then she got a job in Paris, and suddenly Jenny was living with us. What would she have done if we hadn't had the flat? Now she's having a baby, and who knows what she'll want next. I feel our preferences, your preferences, count for nothing." By the final sentence a note of urgent bitterness had crept into my voice. I could not blame Jenny, and so I laid upon the mother all the sins of the daughter.

"That isn't true, Celia. Helen can be awkward about arrangements, but she has taken care of Jenny virtually single-handed for the last five years. However much I wanted to, I'd have found being a full-time parent very difficult. I'm sure it's no coincidence that Helen has fallen in love for the first time when she doesn't have Jenny to worry about." He put out his hand and covered mine. "You realise," he said, "that there's a good chance she'll want a divorce."

A month ago such news would have made me ecstatic. Now Stephen was holding my hand, gazing into my eyes, and all I could think was that even marriage would not protect me from Jenny, for a marriage could be broken. Finally I said, "That would be wonderful."

My halting answer seemed to satisfy him. He squeezed my hand, looked at his watch, and said that he ought to be going. Outside on the pavement he offered me a lift back to the office. I said that I would rather walk. He kissed me quickly on the cheek, then hurried across the street. I stood looking after him, wondering if he would turn to wave, but all I saw was his back rapidly disappearing from view. I started up the stairs to the Royal Mile. A few weeks before, I had climbed them hand in hand with Stephen as Jenny led the way to the camera obscura, and that night she had stolen out of her bed and poured vinegar over my contact lenses. Yesterday I would have claimed to be reconciled to Jenny's presence, but now that equanimity peeled off like a thin veneer, revealing my true feelings of dismay. On the second landing, a pool of brownish vomit lay splashed across the stone. I stepped around it.

When I reached the street, I hesitated. This was at best a circuitous route back to my office. Through the open doorway of a pub I caught sight of a telephone, and I thought, if it works, then I will take the afternoon off. I picked up the receiver, there was a dial tone, the slot accepted my money, and Marilyn answered. I said that I was not feeling well, and she at once exclaimed how peaky I had looked that morning. She was glad I was being sensible and going home.

I continued walking down the Royal Mile. The wind cut through my thin jacket, and as I drew near Saint Giles the first drops of rain began to fall. I pushed open the heavy wooden door of the cathedral and stepped inside. I had been here once before, with Stephen, on a bright June day when the sunlight coming through the stained-glass windows had made brightly coloured patterns on the stone floor. Today the building was almost in darkness; the few lights scattered high above the nave were sufficient only to illuminate the extent of the cavernous gloom. I had borne the vicissitudes of the last few months by reminding myself that the situation was temporary. Now that security had been torn from me, and I did not know which way to turn.

As I stood gazing despairingly upwards into the vaulted dark, I felt the icy air wrap itself around my bones. This was no place of refuge. I hurried down the nave, past the bronze statue of John Knox, to the east doorway. In the shelter of the eaves, I paused. The raindrops were bouncing off the cobblestones. I had no destination. I could not return to my office, I did not want to go home. For a moment I felt nostalgic for my old flat, where I could come and go as I pleased. Then it occurred to me that the Chambers Street museum was not far away. I set off, half running, along the rainy streets.

Stephen had told me that the museum was a favourite meeting place among Edinburgh teenagers, but on this weekday afternoon there was no one, bar the attendants, to be seen. As I walked across the main hall, I could hear each footfall, separate and distinct, echoing up to the glass ceiling, four stories above me. I went through a doorway in the far corner and found myself in a room full of old-fashioned glass cases containing groups of stuffed animals. I walked along, looking absent-mindedly at the elk, zebras, bison, and antelope, all somewhat shabby. The next doorway led into a much larger room, labeled "British Mammals." Here the Victorian ambience gave way to the twentieth century. The room was newly decorated, and the animals were displayed posing freely among rocks and tree trunks. I saw a badger, a fox, and then, loping along in one corner, a wildcat.

As I bent to examine it, I recalled the visit we had paid, many months before, to the zoo. The glass-eyed gaze of the stuffed cat reminded me of the fixed stare with which the living animal had looked upon us. I remembered Jenny's peculiar interest in the cat, and the chilling moment in the street when I had glimpsed her true feelings towards me. Suddenly I heard footsteps and the sound of soft whistling. I turned and saw that a guard had come in. He was carrying a bottle of cleaning fluid and a duster. "Quite lifelike, isn't it?" he said, gesturing towards the cat. I noticed that he looked a little like Lewis. He had the same red-gold hair and fair complexion.

"Have you ever seen one?" I asked.

He shook his head. "You only find them in remote regions." He repeated what Jenny had learned in school. Wildcats can never be tamed; even a kitten, separated from its mother soon after birth and accustomed to humans, grows up to be wild. As he spoke, I studied the animal's face. The taxidermist had drawn the lips back into a ferocious snarl, which made it easy to believe this account of innate savagery.

The guard began to dust the horns of two white oxen. I moved round to look over his shoulder. According to the label, the oxen were actually wild cattle. Several hundred years ago these beasts had roamed the north of Scotland; now the only survivors were to be found in the park of an English stately home. I caught the guard's eye and asked if the museum was always so quiet.

"No, this is unusual, even for a rainy weekday." He gave the cattle a final flick and turned to face me. "So which are you? Unemployed or depressed?"

I stared, wondering if I had heard correctly. "Why should I be either?" I demanded.

"During the week we only get four kinds of visitors: students, old age pensioners, the unemployed, and the depressed. You don't look like either of the first two."

"What makes you think that the people who come here are depressed?" I felt a curious lightness, as if I might say anything.

"Of course I can't be sure, but when I see someone standing in front of a moth-eaten stuffed animal for half an hour, then I form the impression that at the very least they're less than deliriously happy."

"Maybe there's something consoling about a museum," I suggested. "It puts your problems in a historical perspective."

"Is that what you find?" He stood before me, grinning, the duster dangling from one hand.

Perhaps as a man, I thought, he would not have the same prejudices in favour of children. I was on the verge of telling him everything, when there was a slight crackling noise. From his pocket he produced a walkie-talkie and held it to his ear. "I'm summoned," he said, as he returned it to his pocket. "It was nice to talk to you."

*   *   *

I let myself into the house. Immediately I was aware of activity on all sides: from the living room came the sounds of the television and voices, and from the kitchen the smell of cooking. After the solitude of the afternoon I was returning to the bosom of my family. I put my head round the living room door and saw Jenny and her friend Anna sitting on the floor watching television. Anna said hello and Jenny nodded. I withdrew and went to the kitchen, where Stephen was standing at the stove, stirring something. "Hi," he said. "I was beginning to think about calling your office."

"I missed the bus."

As soon as the words were out I wished I could recall them. On the way home I had been vacillating over whether to tell Stephen how I had spent the afternoon. To do so would reveal the extent to which I was upset, which would in turn lead to another conversation about Jenny, a conversation which, even in anticipation, seemed doomed to failure. But whenever my thinking had approached the alternative—that then I should lie—I had drawn back. All afternoon I had been brooding about Jenny. Now it was borne in upon me that over and above my own difficulties with her, she had a profound effect upon my relationship with Stephen. That I should lie to him, especially about something so trivial, was a measure of the distance that had grown up between us. The faint crack of dissension had widened to a fissure, and I saw no way to prevent it from widening still further. I felt like weeping. As Stephen sympathised with my missed bus, the dining room door swung slowly open. The noise of the television carried clearly—a man's voice followed by laughter—and Jenny came in.

CHAPTER 25

I had expected Stephen to tell Jenny about the change in her holiday plans, but apparently Helen had asked him not to; she wanted to break the news herself and would telephone on Thursday. Meanwhile, during the intervening days, Jenny suffered an agony of suspense. She kept mentioning Christmas and Paris at odd moments, watching us closely to gauge our reaction. Stephen commented that she must know something was going on, as if her ability to guess that the letter contained news of more than ordinary importance was remarkable. Once again it occurred to me how little he knew his daughter. As a teacher Stephen often came across difficult children, such as Kenny, the boy who had set fire to the cloakroom and terrified his mother, but if I were to say, "I am afraid of your daughter, in the same way as Kenny's mother is afraid of her son," he would have no notion what I was talking about. To him Jenny was a nice little girl composed entirely of sugar and spice. It was true, I thought, no one has a keener motive to understand you than your enemy; your friends can afford to take you at face value.

At the office I did my best to go through the motions of work, but by Thursday the papers on my desk were at a standstill; the very air was thick with anticipation. I thought of Brockbank's Scottish war poets and their descriptions of the sinister lull before they went over the top. I caught an earlier bus home than usual, but after I got off, I walked along the main road and down our street with increasing slowness, each step more hesitant than its predecessor, until, when I reached the front gate, I came to a complete halt. I could no more have stayed away than I could have stopped breathing, and yet I was deeply reluctant to witness whatever was going to occur. Through the drawn curtains of the living room the lights cast an amber glow which to any stranger would have suggested warmth and safety.

The sight of Mr. Patterson coming down the street drove me through the gate. I put my key in the lock and opened the door. There were the usual sounds and smells. Jenny was doing her homework. Stephen was making dinner. As I stood in the hall, taking off my coat, I felt that rather than divesting myself of encumbrances I was shouldering a new burden, one both heavy and fragile, and I could no longer foresee a time when I would be free to relinquish it. I hung up my coat in the hall cupboard, took off my boots, and went into the kitchen. "It smells good," I said. "What can I do to help?"

"Nothing," Stephen said. He was chopping parsley vigorously and seemed in good spirits. "Guess what Deirdre told me today. She's going to move in with John."

"Big John?"

"No, good heavens. John Eliot, the architect."

"He seemed nice that time we met him," I said. I had always concealed from Stephen my slight jealousy of Deirdre.

"Yes," said Stephen. "I'm very happy for her. In all the years I've known her she's never lived with anyone, so this is a big step."

I nodded and went off to change. I was in the bedroom, stepping out of my skirt, when the phone rang. "Hello," Jenny said, and then, almost a squeal, "Mummy!"

"I'm okay," she said. "I'm going to Joyce and Edward's tomorrow, and Joyce said we would go riding. There are only thirty-one days until I come to see you."

The door of the bedroom was ajar. I could have closed it,

I could have emerged and gone to join Stephen, but I felt as if my life depended on hearing what Jenny said in this unguarded moment. There was a long pause.

"A baby? How can you have a baby?" Jenny demanded. She began to cry.

On the bed the overhead light cast a clear circle of light, and I sat on the perimeter, listening. I remembered the incredulity with which I had asked my mother the same question. The window was open, and the room was very cold. I realised that I was shivering, and with each tremor that passed over me, my anger towards Jenny lessened. There was nothing particularly startling or revealing in what she said, but the note of anguish in her voice rang out above the commonplace phrases. She was only a child; in all the important aspects of her life she was helpless; to regard her as an enemy or rival was madness.

Now she could not speak for sobbing. Stephen came into the hall. "Helen," he said. And then a pause. "Jenny's going to Abernethy this weekend. Why not call back next week?" he suggested. "All right. Good night."

I heard the click of the receiver being replaced in its cradle. "She had to go," he said, "but she'll call again soon. Come on, Jenny, don't cry. There's no reason to cry, none at all." He talked on and on, as one might talk to a frightened animal, making a stream of sound to wash comfortingly over his small daughter.

At last Jenny spoke, her voice still twisted by tears. "She always said we were the perfect family, that we didn't need anyone else."

At Stephen's suggestion we ate in front of the television. Jenny was pale and woebegone, but calm. As soon as supper was over, Stephen ran her a bath, and she went off to bed.

I was doing the washing up when he came into the kitchen.

Without a word he picked up a dish towel and began to dry a plate. I continued to scrub a saucepan. When I could bear the silence no longer, I asked, "How's Jenny?"

"She's still upset. I'm not really sure what the problem is."

"She isn't going to see her mother for another month," I said. "You know the chart she has on the wall by the head of her bed. She'd calculated to the minute when she was going to Paris."

"Yes, I realise that she's been counting the days, but I thought she would be happy at the prospect of spending Christmas with us, that it would be like having the best of both worlds. God knows exactly what Helen said; I wish I'd told her myself." He spoke brusquely, as if impatient with Helen, Jenny, me.

"At least this way Jenny knows you're not to blame," I offered.

"I suppose." He picked up a handful of cutlery.

Above the sink I could see in the dark window my own reflection, and behind me Stephen, the white collar of his shirt shining. "Perhaps it wasn't the best plan for Helen to tell her about the baby," I said tentatively.

"How do you know she told her?" he asked.

I turned in surprise. After all, Stephen had heard Jenny's remark about the perfect family: what could he have thought she meant? He was standing motionless, staring at me. I felt myself blush. "I was in the bedroom," I said. "I couldn't help overhearing."

"Oh, so what happened?"

"I heard Jenny say, 'How can you have a baby?' Then she began to cry and demand that Helen come home. I'm sorry. The only way I could have avoided hearing was if I'd covered my ears."

"It doesn't matter," he said. Without another word, he began to put away the dry dishes, clattering them one against the other, opening and shutting the cupboard doors with unnecessary force. Once, I thought, not so long ago, I would have known what was troubling him, or he would have told me, but now I was baffled. Even if he guessed that I had eavesdropped deliberately, I did not understand why that would upset him. He closed the cupboard sharply and hung the dish towel up beside the stove.

"I remember," he said, "one winter Jenny had this terrible flu. She would be sick in the middle of the night. I would bathe her and change her nightdress and make the bed with clean sheets. Then I would hold her until she fell back to sleep. I felt that I was a god in her life. I could make everything better, or almost." He kept his eyes averted as if the mere sight of me might distract him from this vision. Although he was within arm's reach, I did not dare to touch him.

Later, in bed, I lay beside Stephen, and it seemed that the darkness was pouring into my body, filling me up, like sand, or like water. There was nothing to be done, no way out; I could no longer say at every difficult turn, "Well, only a few months to go, an accountable number of days and hours." I remembered, as if it were another life, the day when I had been laying the carpet and how I had worried that Stephen had succumbed to Helen. Now I almost wished that my suspicions had been justified.

By the time I came home on Friday, Jenny had already left to spend the weekend with Joyce and Edward. As I walked down the street I was lighter of heart and fleeter of foot than I had been all week. The prospect of being alone with Stephen made everything seem bearable. Like a hidden magnet, Jenny, by her mere presence, distorted our actions and our very selves; only in her absence could we recover our true direction. I found Stephen seated at the dining-room table, drinking tea. He stood up and put his arms around me. He slid his hands down my back, and I pushed against him. His mouth opened into mine.

Fully dressed, we climbed beneath the covers. We delved among each other's clothes, unbuttoning, unzipping, discarding, until we were both naked. Stephen lay on top of me and covered me perfectly, so that I felt every inch of him.

When I woke he was looking into my eyes. "I was asleep," I said.

"Yes, you were dreaming. I felt you trembling. I talked to you, and you grew quiet. Do you remember?"

I shook my head. Whatever the terrors of sleep, they were nothing compared to those of my waking life.

"Stay here," he said, sliding his limbs away from mine. He left the room, and I lay without moving in the warm hollow our bodies had made. I gazed at the blue walls, trying to think only about their blueness; I was determined not to let my thoughts stray down dark avenues. Stephen returned, and I asked what he had been doing. "I was lighting the fire," he said. He placed two glasses on the bedside table, and then, sitting up in bed, opened a bottle of red wine. "By the time we've drunk this, the living room will be warm. I bought us take-out food, a kind of picnic."

"You're wonderful," I said. I leaned out of bed, picked up my T-shirt from the floor, and pulled it on. Stephen was holding out a glass. "Here's to us," he said.

"To us," I echoed.

We spent most of the weekend in bed, and as the hours passed, I began to realise that whether Jenny was present or absent, something had changed between Stephen and me. There was a subtle shift in our lovemaking, which made me suspect that, at some level, he too was aware of what was happening. We had always been passionate together, but our passion had been mixed with gentler emotions: affection and friendship. Now we made love almost to the point of pain, bending each other into new positions, riding the crest as long and hard as we could, crying out in strange tongues. Sometimes when Stephen came, above or beneath me, his face was so greatly altered that I did not know him.

CHAPTER 26

On Monday evening when Joyce brought Jenny home, I was in the bathroom, and by the time I came out, Jenny had already disappeared into her room. Stephen and Joyce were standing in the hall. Under the bare light Joyce's hair looked almost white, and this made her face appear unusually girlish. I kissed her warm cheek.

"Let me take your jacket," said Stephen. "Come and have a drink."

"I ought to get back."

"You can't stay to supper?" I asked. "We could eat early. It's almost ready."

She looked at her watch and shook her head. "I have a meeting to go to at nine, and I left Edward in charge of two pork chops, but thank you anyway."

"Thank you for having Jenny. I hope she wasn't too much trouble," Stephen said.

"She was no trouble at all; she was as good as gold. You'll have to get her to tell you about the pony trekking. She and Raven put me to shame. I hope you two lovebirds enjoyed yourselves." She smiled from Stephen to me. There was a slight rustling behind us. The door of Jenny's room was ajar, and I was sure that she was listening to every word.

Stephen put his arm round me. "We didn't do anything very special, but it was nice not to have to worry about baby-sitters and arrangements."

"Well, anytime," said Joyce. "It was a pleasure for us." She

294

shifted her keys from hand to hand and took a step in the direction of the door.

"Jenny, come and say goodbye. Joyce is leaving," Stephen called.

She shot out of her room like a jack-in-the box. "I thought you were staying," she exclaimed. She ran over and flung her arms around Joyce.

Joyce reached down to embrace her. "Thank you for coming to visit. You were the perfect guest, and I hope you'll come again soon."

Jenny did not release her, and after a slight pause Joyce gently loosened her grip and turned to leave. Stephen opened the front door. "Don't come out. It's chilly," Joyce said, but Jenny clung to her. While Stephen and I remained on the doorstep, she walked with Joyce to her car.

"She always claims that Edward is perfectly competent in the kitchen, but she doesn't really trust him," Stephen remarked.

From the street came the sounds of departure, the car door opening and closing, the engine catching. The car drove away, and Jenny reappeared. She paused at the garden gate, staring at us where we stood in the lighted doorway; her pale face glimmered in the twilight. Then she walked slowly down the path towards us. "Are you going to unpack?" asked Stephen, as she brushed past.

"I already have," she said. "I'm going to feed Selina."

At supper Jenny answered her father's questions in a subdued manner. Stephen asked what she had done, how was Raven, what was the name of the pony she had ridden. Several times he began remarks with phrases like "Next time we're there" or "When we go in the spring," as if he were determined to demonstrate at every possible opportunity that Jenny could look forward to a secure future with him. I felt in comparison the futility of the assurances he gave to me.

*　　*　　*

Next morning Suzie summoned me to her office. "Did you have anything to do with this?" she asked, gesturing towards the pages laid out across her drafting table: "Fowler and Hayes: *Industrial England*."

"No. It's one of Clare's projects."

Suzie was pointing to a poorly drawn sketch of a small boy; he had enormous eyelashes and a rosebud mouth. One hand rested negligently on a dark mass of machinery. "They decided to do the illustrations themselves, and this is the result," she said.

I turned over a few pages. The justice of her complaints was all too apparent. "But why would they do their own illustrations?" I asked.

"Art has always been a hobby of hers, so she thought she'd have a go. She's going to make a tremendous fuss when we tell her these are unusable." Suzie snorted impatiently. "Well, how was the romantic weekend?"

"Okay."

"That's not exactly a glowing report." She put aside the manuscript and turned to look at me.

I moved towards the door, rubbing my eyes as if there was something in them. "I don't know. It was lovely to have the house to ourselves. I found it hard when she came home."

"Has she calmed down about Christmas?"

"She hasn't said anything, but who knows what that means. It's never easy to know how she feels."

"Poor kid," said Suzie, shaking her head. "Why don't you send her to Paris for a weekend? I bet there are cheap fares for children."

"That's a brilliant idea!" I exclaimed. I clasped my hands together, almost as if applauding. Then I rushed over and hugged her.

"You'd think you were the one going." She laughed.

At my desk I called a travel agent. It seemed remarkably

easy to fly to Paris and not as expensive as I had feared. I made a list of times and prices to give to Stephen.

Outside Jenny's school the orange beacons of the zebra crossing shone like Halloween lanterns in the late afternoon. As I pulled up at the curb I spotted Jenny. She was standing between two much taller girls, a little apart from the main crowd. One of them, a brawny girl wearing a very short skirt, was holding Jenny's arm. She said something; Jenny shook her head, pulled away and ran over to the car.

"Who were those girls?" I asked.

"They're in my class."

She did up her seat belt, then stared out of the window. I did not press her further. I turned around and drove back towards the main road. I had grown accustomed to thinking of Jenny as the aggressor, but now it occurred to me that her life at school might be the complete reverse of her life at home. I remembered how the girls in my class had gone through a phase when during lunch hour or break they would gang up on someone. Four or five of them would sit on top of the luckless girl and tickle her mercilessly, then strip her to her underwear, even beyond. Afterwards the victim, flushed, disheveled, often looked pleased, as if the ordeal survived conferred some odd kind of favour. To my heartfelt relief, I was never singled out in this way. I tried to recall at what age this behaviour had taken place; it seemed to me that we had been a couple of years older than Jenny, but children were more precocious nowadays, I thought.

We stopped at the corner shop to buy chocolate biscuits. "How was school today?" asked Mr. Murgatee.

"Okay," said Jenny.

"What did you learn?"

"We learned a poem: 'The Charge of the Light Brigade.' "

"Good," said Mr. Murgatee, smiling. He turned to me.

"Every day I ask my daughter what she's learned. After all, that is what school is for."

I held out a pound for the biscuits. As we drove down the street, I congratulated Jenny on being so quick to answer him. "I wouldn't have known what to say," I said.

She smiled. "I made it up. Actually we did that weeks ago."

Over tea she told me that they had had a visit from a career counsellor.

"A career counsellor," I exclaimed. "Isn't it a bit soon to be thinking about your career?"

"Not really," said Jenny, taking a bite of her toast and jam. "She asked everyone what they wanted to do. Anna said that she wanted to be a doctor. Rita and Joan both said they wanted to get married and have children."

"What did you say?"

"I never want to get married." She licked her finger and ran it round the rim of her plate to catch up the crumbs.

"Don't you want children?"

"No," she said with agonised vehemence. "Never." She looked at me, as if challenging me to admit that I did not understand.

"Why not?" I asked gently.

"Because."

I would have liked to mention the possibility of her going to Paris, but I did not dare. Instead I offered some vague platitude about how she would change her mind as she grew older. Jenny shrugged and changed the subject by asking if I wanted more toast. We passed the evening quietly. As soon as she had finished her homework, Jenny curled up on the sofa and read her Chalet school book at a tremendous rate.

I was convinced that Suzie's suggestion, so obvious and so surprising, could be our salvation. Everything was arranged with amazing speed. When I spoke to Stephen, he seized upon the idea with gratitude. He telephoned Helen next day. Apparently she too was delighted, and there was no need for Stephen to offer to pay for the ticket; I had said to him that perhaps it could be part of our Christmas present to Jenny. In truth I would happily have borne the entire expense myself.

Jenny was grating the cheese for macaroni cheese when Stephen told her about the plan. "So you'll go tomorrow afternoon after school. I've already spoken to the headmistress, and then you'll come back on Sunday evening."

I was sitting at the dining room table. I knew at once from the long silence that all was not well. She should have been squealing with pleasure. I moved to the other side of the table, in order to be able to see into the kitchen. Jenny was standing next to the fridge. "Do I have to go?" she said at last in a small voice.

"You don't have to, but don't you want to see Helen? She really wants you to come. She misses you a lot. It's still nearly a month until Christmas."

Now Jenny was crying openly. "I don't want to go. I want to stay here with you," she kept saying over and over again between her sobs.

Stephen knelt down beside her. He took the grater out of her hands and drew her to him. "Don't cry," he said. "There's nothing to cry about. Nobody's trying to force you. Listen, you don't have to decide this minute. Why don't you think about it and see how you feel in a few days. You could go the weekend after this one. Come on, stop crying."

"Promise you won't send me away," she said. "Promise."

"I promise," said Stephen. He patted her cheeks with the dish towel.

As she exhorted Stephen, Jenny looked at me, and I knew that she meant his answer for my ears. When he straightened up from drying her face, she was still staring at me; I understood that nothing would help, no amount of cajoling, or pleading, or reasoning.

After supper the three of us played Cludo in front of the

living room fire. I had last played the game with my parents, when I was about Jenny's age. While I plodded along, trying to ascertain whether Colonel Mustard could have done it in the library with the revolver, they had joked around, making inspired guesses. In Jenny I saw a reflection of my youthful seriousness, although she took greater risks than I had done. She was sitting on the floor in her dressing gown, and I noticed her smooth, bare legs. I thought of how much time I spent plucking and shaving, trying to return myself to such a soft, hairless state. For months after the first dark hairs had appeared on my body, I had shaved them off with my father's razor every time I took a bath. My mother's cheerful descriptions of puberty had in no way prepared me for this transformation.

"I suspect Miss Scarlet in the conservatory with the revolver," said Jenny.

Stephen showed her a card. I stared blankly at the pile of tiny murder weapons—the inch of lead pipe, the doll's-size noose. I could not keep my mind on the game, and Stephen too seemed absent-minded. Jenny won every round, correctly attributing murder and method to Miss Scarlet and Mr. Plum.

That night I dreamed that Jenny was in our room, that while Stephen and I lay sleeping, she had come in to get something, I did not know what. In the morning the conviction of her presence lingered. Casually I mentioned my dream at breakfast. Jenny said nothing, and Stephen made a joke about the effects of Cludo.

I was too preoccupied with Jenny's reaction to the invitation to Paris to give the matter another thought. Given her love for Helen, there was something sinister and unnatural about her adamant refusal. I could not understand what would motivate her. Was it possible that she was so angry with Helen that she wanted to punish her?

Then I thought that perhaps I was looking at things the

wrong way round. It was not that Jenny did not want to go to Paris, but rather that she was determined to remain in Edinburgh. It was as if I had drawn a knife from its sheath. The idea lay before me, hypnotic in its gleaming sharpness; I shrank from touching it, even as I reached towards it. If it was true, then what I had taken for peace was merely an armed truce. But what harm could she do? I was determined not to come between Stephen and her, and if she wanted to ride roughshod over my clothes and belongings, I would endure in silence. I would not let possessions damn me. All day I searched my mind from attic to cellar, and I came to the conclusion that without my collaboration there was no way Jenny could hurt me. As long as I remained aloof, she was helpless.

It was late in the day when I roused myself. The office was emptying fast, as it always did on Friday afternoons, but I had several letters that had to be sent out before the weekend. After my hours of daydreaming, I did not finish until almost eight. By the time I arrived home, Jenny was in bed. Stephen had saved some stew for me, and while I ate he told me about an invitation he and Deirdre had received to describe their tutoring program at a conference of Scottish schoolteachers.

"That sounds great," I said. "Did you manage to speak to Helen?"

He nodded. "She thought we'd been too precipitate and that I should wait until Jenny had got used to the idea and then ask her again. She could go next weekend, or even the one after."

"So she wasn't upset by Jenny's refusal?" I asked.

"I suppose she was, but she was quite calm about it. She said that in a way she wasn't surprised. We ought to have remembered that Jenny hates changes." There was a note of satisfaction in Stephen's voice. I realised that he was pleased rather than otherwise by Jenny's refusal. Soon after I finished eating we went to bed.

At first I did not know what had woken me. Stephen was sleeping quietly beside me, and I could tell, without looking at the clock, that it was the middle of the night. Then I heard the slightest of sounds. I wondered if it could be Tobias, but I knew that he was as usual safely shut in the kitchen. I lay still, listening. It was possible on the carpeted floor to move almost soundlessly, but suddenly I was convinced that Jenny was in the room. I measured each breath in and out, trying not to betray that I was awake. After a few minutes a small white figure flitted past me. I heard her feet tapping lightly on the bare floorboards as she moved across the hall.

I could feel my heart shaking in my chest. What could this mean? I was certain now that the night before, Jenny had also come to our room. She was up to something, she had some scheme in mind, but I could not imagine what it might be. I kept feeling that I was on the point of understanding what she was about, and then, like the remnant of a dream, the thought would vanish before I could fully grasp it.

In the morning Jenny slept late. Stephen and I had finished breakfast by the time she came into the dining room. I was sitting at the table, pretending to read the newspaper while I waited for her. Stephen was putting up cup hooks in the kitchen. As Jenny sat down, he called to me, "Will you come and see if these are spaced right?"

I got up and went to look at his handiwork. "Yes, they're fine."

He began to hang up mugs one by one on the neatly spaced white hooks. On the counter beneath was a row of tiny piles of sawdust.

I returned to the dining room and stationed myself in front of the gas fire. I had gone back and forth as to whether to mention the events of the night; I was afraid a confrontation might be exactly what she wanted, but I also feared that my silence might licence her to proceed with impunity. Too often in the past I had been silent at the critical moment. "Were you ill last night?" I asked. "You came into our room, but you left before I could say anything."

Jenny paused in the middle of pouring out her cereal. "I don't know," she said. "I woke up, and I was in your room. Then I went back to bed."

I had spoken loudly so that Stephen would hear my question. Now he appeared in the kitchen doorway.

"What time was this?" he said. "I didn't hear anything."

"It was about twelve-thirty," I said. "Jenny woke me by coming into our room."

"I don't remember anything, except going back to bed, and my feet were cold."

"You must have been sleepwalking," said Stephen. "I did that occasionally when I was your age."

All alone in the middle of the table, Jenny sat looking at her father with an expression of interest. Here he was providing her with the perfect explanation. I was struck dumb. Sleepwalking had never occurred to me, either as reality or as fiction; Jenny had, if nothing else, been much too purposeful. Then I thought that the news of Stephen's exploits had not come as a surprise to her. Such family stories are often repeated, and most likely she had been reminded of this one on her recent visit to Joyce and Edward's.

"Where did you sleepwalk?" she asked.

"Once I woke up in the garden. Another time Joyce found me in the pantry, and everyone teased me that it was a way to get late-night snacks."

"That wouldn't work for me because the cupboards are all too high." She voiced this standard complaint with mock grumpiness.

"Maybe you could try the fridge," said Stephen. Jenny giggled and wrinkled her nose. "Have you ever done this before?" he asked.

"I don't think so, but perhaps I wouldn't know. Maybe I could walk somewhere and get back to bed without waking up." She smiled at me. "Did I scare you?" she asked.

"Yes," I said. I looked at her without smiling; she knew that I spoke the truth.

Later, when Stephen and I were drinking coffee in the dining room and Jenny was in her room, he said, "Tell me again what happened."

"There's nothing to tell. I woke up, Jenny was in the room, and before I could say anything she had gone back to bed." I held my cup tightly. I wanted to say, "There's no reason to believe she was sleepwalking," but I knew that from Stephen's point of view there was every reason.

"She must be really upset about Helen." His face was frowning and intent.

"Why did you sleepwalk?"

"I think it was the summer my parents announced that I was going to boarding school; I felt as if I was being sent into exile. Anyway the question is not why I walked in my sleep twenty years ago but why Jenny does now."

"The two might be connected. Maybe sleepwalking is the sort of thing that's hereditary, so Jenny is more likely to sleepwalk than most people, and if you walked in your sleep for no very traumatic reason, then maybe she is too."

He shook his head. "It still seems too much of a coincidence." He straightened his glasses, drank some coffee, and stared off out of the window. Jenny's decision about Paris had vindicated Stephen. For the first time she had chosen him over Helen.

Danger was close; I could smell it, I could feel it fanning our hair. And Stephen too, in spite of his pleasure in Jenny's choice, sensed that something was awry, but like a befuddled lighthouse keeper he kept looking in the wrong direction, beaming the signal inland, unaware of the ships drifting onto the rocks below.

*   *   *

When Jenny emerged from her room she announced that she wanted to go to the library. Stephen was working, and I said I would go with her. While she looked at the children's books I consulted the young, dark-skinned man seated behind the information desk.

"Sleepwalking," he murmured. "I imagine the best place to look is under 'Sleep.' I can show you where that is." He came out from behind his desk, and I followed him to a far corner. He indicated half a dozen books on the bottom shelf. I thanked him and pulled out a paperback called *Sleep*. There were several entries for sleepwalking in the index. I turned to the first one.

"Sleepwalking as an occasional event is normal for most children. There is a strong tendency for it to run in families. Among some children it is an indication of emotional disturbance. The child may walk about with a blank expression, mumbling to himself. He may fumble with objects and bump into things but generally avoids major obstacles. He may appear distressed and preoccupied. Attempts to waken him meet only very gradually with success. Left to himself he will return to bed after some minutes. In the morning there is a complete lack of memory for the events of the night. Occasionally he may have injured himself and the sleepwalking is not without danger through a liability to falls through windows or down stairs."

I was gazing at these words when Jenny came up behind me. "I've got my books," she said.

I checked out *Sleep,* and we walked home together. Jenny chatted animatedly about what she was going to give Joyce and Edward for Christmas. Her liveliness was the antithesis of my heaviness. All my limbs seemed to be at a great distance from me. On the surface a young woman and her stepdaughter were enjoying each other's company, and just below the surface something terrible was happening. The disparity made me feel as if I were going mad. Worst of all, there seemed nothing to be done. I knew now, beyond doubt, that there was no point in talking to Jenny. I was reminded of the last few months with Lewis, when I had ceased to plead and argue. He would insist on talking cheerfully, on touching me as if he loved me, when in fact he was denying me everything that mattered; the contradiction was harder to bear than any truth he might have told me.

Later, when Jenny was out in the garden playing with Selina, I showed Stephen the passage in the book. "So you were right," he said. "It is hereditary. I'm glad that we don't have any stairs or low windows."

At my suggestion, Stephen and I watched the late night film on television. I thought I would foil Jenny by keeping us up until after she fell asleep. Just before midnight, however, there came the sounds of doors opening and closing, the toilet flushing. I spent the last half hour of the film gazing unseeing at the screen. When it ended, at twelve-thirty, Stephen stretched and announced that it was time for bed. I had no plausible excuse to delay him further. While he went to the bathroom, I tiptoed across the hall and listened at the open door of Jenny's room. I heard nothing.

Her hands on my face woke me. Without thinking, I switched on the light. Jenny was standing beside our bed, bending over me, her eyes shut.

She screamed.

Stephen sat up. "What is it?" he demanded loudly, not at all in the muffled tones of someone who had been asleep. He saw Jenny. At once he reached over to turn out the light. Then he jumped out of bed. I saw his dark form moving swiftly towards his daughter. In a moment he had picked her up and carried her from the room.

I did not turn the light back on. The moon was full, and the window was open a crack; the moonlight rippled round the edges of the curtain. I looked at the clock. It was a quarter to two.

Stephen climbed back into bed, and I turned and pressed against him, wanting to drive out the cold. "Is she okay?" I whispered.

"I think so." He lay in my embrace, his arms folded against his chest. "You shouldn't have switched on the light, Celia," he said.

"I had no idea what was going on. When she woke me, I assumed she was ill and needed something."

"I know you were startled, but if it happens again, please wake me quietly." On the pretext of returning to sleep, he moved out of my arms.

On Sunday I stayed at home while Jenny and Stephen went skating. I spread my current manuscript out on the dining room table, but I could not keep my mind on one page. Supposing that my suspicions were justified—that Jenny deliberately got paint on my dress, lied to Stephen, tried to strand me on the island, damaged my pullover, deposited a dead mouse among my clothes, put vinegar in my lens case, stole and gave back my bracelet—what lay behind these deeds? Of course they were all evidence that Jenny disliked me, but there seemed in addition some subtler motivation, else why not steal more money, or keep the bracelet?

The question rose before me like a high, smooth wall. I got up from the table and went into the living room. The fire was burning, and I picked up the tongs to put on more coal. Suddenly I remembered the attack on Selina. I had done my best to forget that troubling incident. All the evidence, before and since, was that Jenny loved Selina. I pictured again the white-faced, determined fury with which she had attacked the rabbit. At the time I had thought that I was spoiling her game.

Now I realised that I had done exactly what she wanted; she had arranged everything in order to make sure that I would witness her attack. It was not Selina that Jenny had been trying to hurt, but me. She wanted to sow dissension between Stephen and me, and she would go to enormous lengths to accomplish that, even hurting what she loved, even not going to see her darling mother.

I had never spelled it out so clearly before, and, still holding the tongs, I sank down onto the sofa, overwhelmed by the clarity that had come upon me. In spite of the fire, I felt my flesh rise into goose bumps. I was desperately afraid. I tried to say to myself the phrases which anyone in whom I confided would say—she's only ten, she'll get over it, she'll settle down—but such stock comments had no bearing on the reality of the situation. It had taken me many months to arrive at some understanding of Jenny's true nature, and now that I had done so, I could derive no comfort from her age, nor from the idea of her hatred being a passing phase; I had never met anyone less malleable.

I got up to put more coal on the fire. The flames disappeared beneath the bank of coal. Still I did not understand how pretending to sleepwalk could further her aim. I kept wondering, why wake me, only me, when I was sceptical and unsympathetic, whereas Stephen would have made a huge fuss over her. But I thought, if it is analogous to Selina, then she wants Stephen and me to quarrel. All I have to do is to turn the other cheek, to keep still.

That evening we went to bed at our usual time; I was tired, and it seemed pointless to resist. We were in the bedroom, undressing, when Stephen said, "Jenny asked me today if people who weren't married could have babies."

"What did you tell her?" I asked. I froze with my hands on the top button of my shirt.

"I told her the truth, that babies were the result of making love, not of marriage, but that usually people waited until they were married before having a baby. She knows all this—Helen's sister, Barbara, had a baby without the slightest sign of male intervention—but the biology doesn't really make sense to her yet, so she asks me to repeat it one more time."

"And what did she say?"

"She asked what making love was. I said it was something grown-ups did in bed together. I'll have to get her a book soon."

"Did she ask you to be more specific?" I wanted to get down on my knees, to beg him to repeat every syllable of their conversation. Stephen was telling me an amusing story, and I was in fear of all my life and happiness.

"She said, 'In bed at night?' and I said, 'Yes.' Then she asked again about people having to be married. I know that Helen's boyfriends used to sleep at their flat, but I'm not sure Jenny ever took in that there was a difference between her having a friend to stay and Helen having a man to stay."

In bed we made love. I knew his body so well that it was not hard to comply. Afterwards, almost immediately, he fell asleep, and I lay there. The shadowy outline of Jenny's plan was growing clearer; it loomed over me, huge and dark, but still I could not see it clearly.

I must have fallen asleep. Her hands were groping across the bedclothes, over my body, touching my face—a soft pattering not like any human touch I had ever known, more like a small animal, a rat, running over my skin. I cannot describe the feeling of horror that it gave me. I felt as if I were being excoriated, the skin peeled back, until every nerve lay exposed and writhing. Yet I kept still. I was determined not to give her the excuse to wake Stephen. Then she touched my eyes, very delicately, with the tips of her fingers, and I cried out.

Stephen said drowsily, "What is it?"

At once Jenny spoke, as if she were the one who had cried out. "Daddy, I couldn't find you. I thought you'd left me." She withdrew her hands.

Immediately he was alert. He hurried to her side. "Jenny, it was only a dream. Look, here I am, I won't leave you. I'm right here. There's no reason to cry."

As I lay waiting for him to return, I remembered, almost as if it were an event in my own life, the night when Angel Clare sleepwalks with Tess in his arms. At first she is glad, thinking that he has forgiven her, then she discovers that Angel believes himself to be carrying her corpse; as far as he is concerned, she is dead.

Next morning as the bus bumped slowly up the hill towards George Street, I suddenly thought, Stephen and I are finished. She is invincible. All the way to my stop I entertained the notion quite calmly; I considered what we would do with the house, whether I would return to London. I walked down the familiar street and climbed the stairs to my office. Only when I was settled at my desk did I fully realise what it was that I was thinking. Then pain seized me, like a hawk its prey, and began to shake me back and forth.

The following night, Jenny did not come into our room, but when I woke and found that it was morning, I was not reassured; too often in the past I had been lulled into a sense of security. Now I thought of the troops outside the beleaguered city who take time before the final battle to wash and shave, to smooth sweet-scented oils into their limbs, to put on fresh linen, to listen to music, to savour what they know they are about to accomplish.

Even when that night's peace stretched into a second's, and a third's, my fear did not diminish. On Friday evening Stephen and I went out to dinner. I drank with determination; it was the only way I knew to be cheerful. We came home around eleven. While Stephen escorted Charlotte home, I went into the bathroom. I removed my lenses, brushed my teeth, inserted my diaphragm. By the time I came out of the bathroom, Stephen was back. He took only a few minutes to get ready for bed.

Our light was still on, Stephen was on top of me, when I heard the slightest of sounds. Turning my head, I saw the handle of the door move very, very slowly. I could do nothing. Degree by degree, the handle turned. Stephen was in me, utterly absorbed. I had always thought of our lovemaking as a kind of conversation, conversation at the deepest level, where comprehension was sure and almost instantaneous, perhaps not so much a dialogue as a duet. Now I saw how fanciful this notion had been, for here we were, joined but entirely separate. I was in terror, and he was oblivious.

The door came open, and around it appeared Jenny's head. As her eyes met mine, her father groaned, "Oh, God." I shut my eyes and turned my head away—thinking, there is a tiny chance that she will retreat without speaking, thinking, oh, protect me.

"Daddy?" she whispered.

I felt Stephen jerk, as if electrified. "Jenny?" He was out of me, pulling the sheets up to hide the slightest glimpse of flesh, all his grace gone into clumsiness as he struggled to sit up, to retrieve his pyjamas, to dispel the faintest odour of sex and darkness.

She had been miscalculating; thinking that making love and sleeping were simultaneous activities, she had been investigating our behaviour in the middle of the night, when it seemed that something so secret was most likely to occur. She stood there rubbing her eyes. "I don't know what's happening. I was having a dream. I woke up and you were making a strange noise."

"It was nothing," said Stephen. He got out of bed. His pyjama trousers were already on, and as he walked around the bed towards her he bent to pick up his dressing gown from the floor. He took her by the shoulder and propelled her from the room. I heard him saying, "Go back to bed. I'll get you some water."

I pulled the sheets up over my face. As I began to cry, I breathed in the smell of our bodies, a commingling of scents, unique and indescribable, which had grown as familiar as my own skin, but which soon, I knew, I must leave behind.

When Stephen returned to bed, I pretended to be asleep.

CHAPTER 27

In the morning the click of the bedside lamp woke me. The first thing I saw was Stephen's back as he got out of bed. While I lay watching he put on his dressing gown and began to gather up his clothes. His movements were stealthy as a thief's, and never once did he glance in my direction. He was almost at the door when I spoke his name.

Then he turned to look at me, a shirt in one hand, and although in the dim light it was hard to read his expression, nothing in his mien invited intimacy. If only he would come and put his arms around me, I would know what to say, but in the face of such tangible reluctance, words fled. At last I said lamely, "Is everything all right?"

"Of course. I didn't mean to wake you. Would you like some coffee?"

"I'll get up," I said. I had arrested his departure, but only for an instant; the words were barely out of my mouth before he hurried from the room. I heard the bathroom door close.

I rose and dressed in the first garments that came to hand. In the bathroom mirror I looked coldly at my reflection: my eyes were dull, my skin pale, and my features still misshapen from sleep and the lack thereof. By the time I entered the dining room Stephen and Jenny were already in their places. The room smelled of toast, and the radio was tuned to the Saturday morning show. It was after nine o'clock, but the sky was barely light. I poured myself some coffee and sat down.

"Do you know what day it is?" Jenny asked, looking at Stephen and me in turn.

"The first of December," said Stephen.

"Yes, so I can start my calendar." She jumped up and fetched her Advent calendar off the sideboard. Joyce and Edward had given it to her on her most recent visit, and she had been waiting impatiently to open the first of the twenty-four doors. Without hesitation she opened the door marked "1." She showed the picture to Stephen. "It's you getting ready for Christmas," he said.

She moved around the table and offered it to me. "Look, Celia," she said.

I stared at the dark-haired girl playing with a doll and nodded.

"Our concert is less than a week away," Jenny announced.

"Are you nervous?" asked Stephen.

Jenny thought for a moment. "Yes," she said, and giggled.

After breakfast Jenny and Stephen went off to do the shopping. I walked around the house, from one room to another. In the living room the curtains were still drawn. A newspaper lay open on the rug before the fire. Jenny's room was strewn with books, toys, clothes, the walls were thickly covered with posters—just as a ten-year-old girl's room ought to be. When I went into our room I saw that Stephen had made the bed. If only, I thought, the turbulence of the night before could be smoothed over as easily as the sheets and blankets. I looked around the room. Everything within these blue walls had been chosen by Stephen and me, and yet my eye rested on nothing with which I felt any kind of kinship. Only Tobias, sleeping on the end of the bed, was dear and familiar. I bent to stroke him, and he pushed his golden face against my hand.

In what sense, I wondered, was this house my home? It was Stephen who had made the down payment, using the money from the sale of his flat; at the time there was so much good will between us that any arrangement had seemed fine. Now it occurred to me that I could move out as easily as I had from Malcolm's, in fact perhaps more so, for I would not have to worry about finding a replacement.

I went over to the bedroom window. It had rained heavily during the night, and the sodden landscape seemed to mirror my gloomy thoughts. Beyond the wall at the end of the garden, the slate roofs of the houses in the next street merged with the leaden clouds. A volley of pigeons was circling the spire of Saint Columba's Church, and I found myself remembering the pair of pigeons that had lived on the window sill of Stephen's old flat and filled our bedroom with their soft cooing. A movement in the garden caught my eye. I glimpsed Selina. I did not remember Jenny going to feed her this morning.

I put on Wellington boots and a jacket and went outside. Selina was sheltering in her hutch, but when I reached into the run to lift out her dish she appeared in the doorway. I filled the dish from the sack of pellets in the tool shed and carried it back to the run. She hopped over and began to eat. As I watched her nose twitching with pleasure, the rain ran down my face. I stroked her damp fur. "Selina," I said softly. She stopped eating and looked at me with her pale-blue eyes.

When Stephen and Jenny returned, I was sitting at the dining room table, making lists of people to send cards and gifts to. Jenny went off to watch television. Stephen put away the groceries, then came and sat down at the opposite end of the table. I kept on checking through my address book. Suddenly he said, "Celia, I spoke to Jenny, and she's absolutely definite that she doesn't want to go to Paris for a weekend."

I looked up in surprise; it had not occurred to me that he would pursue the matter. From Jenny's first protest I had known that there was no chance of her going. In some mysterious way, her behaviour had become transparent to

316 · Margot Livesey

me. Her defeat in Paris was inevitable, and however much she missed her mother, there was nothing to be gained by a visit. Like a wise general, she was employing her forces where they could be most effective: to keep control of her single remaining parent. All this was clear to me, but I was curious to learn how Stephen interpreted her refusal. "Why doesn't she want to go?" I asked.

"She said that she liked living with me—with us, that is." He smiled. "I was so glad. All along I've had the feeling that she was unhappy here and that I was just a poor substitute for Helen. Now it's clear that she thinks of this as her home." He spread his hands in a gesture of welcome or inclusion. "None of this would have been possible without you, Celia."

He stood up and came around the table to hug me. At first I resisted, then I clung to him. He was so warm and solid, and for a brief moment, within the circle of his arms, I hoped that everything might still come right. "About last night," I said.

Immediately I felt Stephen stiffen and pull away. "She was asleep. She doesn't remember anything."

He was retreating towards his end of the table, when suddenly he stumbled. "Damn," he exclaimed. From beneath his feet Tobias fled with an indignant cry.

"Sorry. I think I'll go to the corner shop to pay the paper bill." He left the room. I heard him say goodbye to Jenny, and then the front door opened and closed. Looking down at my list, I saw Mrs. Menzies' name, and on impulse I decided to write her an early Christmas card. I told her about the garden and the neighbours and that she was missed. I wanted to recapture the wonderful ease with which we had bought the house, the sense I had had of all the difficulties in my life dissolving, and the pleasure it had given me to feel that the happiness she and her husband had shared still lingered here. I was reading over what I had written, wondering what to tell her about Stephen and me, when the door opened. Jenny hovered on the threshold. "What are you doing?" she asked.

"I'm writing to the woman we bought the house from. She and her husband lived here for fifty years. He was called Stephen too."

"Like Daddy."

"Yes."

Jenny came fully into the room, closing the door behind her. She went and stood in front of the gas fire; it was turned to low and made only a slight hissing sound. I waited with my pen poised over the card.

"Celia," she said, "can we go shopping sometime soon for Daddy's Christmas present?"

"How about next Saturday? Would that be a good time?"

"Oh," she said. She looked down, and I followed her gaze to where one of her small slippered feet scuffed back and forth across the carpet.

"Are you doing something else on Saturday?" I asked.

"I don't think so. I wasn't sure you'd be here then." She spoke in quiet, sad tones.

"Of course I'll be here," I said automatically, and was about to ask if she had any idea what she wanted to buy, when the implications of her remark dawned upon me. Christ, I thought, and then in terror, could think no further.

She raised her head and looked directly into my eyes. For a moment I stared back at her. Then she smiled. "Couldn't we go after school on Tuesday? The shops won't be nearly so crowded."

"All right," I said.

"Goody." She skipped out of the room.

I rose and walked over to take her place in front of the fire, trying to warm myself.

Each day was shorter than the one before, and I came and went to the office in darkness. For months, I had been inching my way along like Ariadne, assuming that the thread I followed through the dark passages led out into the light. Now

318 · Margot Livesey

I had reached the end, and I found myself in a cave darker and more remote than any I had imagined. Day by day Jenny was severing the woof and warp of the many ties that had linked Stephen and me. I remembered the conversation we had had the day after we learned that Jenny was coming to live with us; Stephen had claimed that it was impossible to lie to someone you lived with. I watched him closely, trying to decide how much he knew, but he seemed happier than he had ever been. The only sign he gave of his distress was in bed, where he never turned to me save in the deepest hours of night. Then I would wake to find him taking me in a kind of frenzy.

On Tuesday we went shopping. Jenny knew exactly what she wanted to buy—a tie from Marks and Spencer's—and the expedition did not take long. When we arrived home she announced that she was going to hide the tie in the tool shed.

"Won't it get damp out there?"

"No. It'll be safer," she said, and hurried out of the back door.

We ate pizza for supper in front of the television. Afterwards Jenny asked for my help in devising her costume for the school concert. Her class had written a play about a rich, bad child who was lonely and unhappy and a poor, good child who gave away the little he had and was amply rewarded. Jenny was a needy street sweeper who gratefully received a pair of gloves. We found a dark, gathered skirt of mine and adjusted the waist; on Jenny it reached the floor which seemed appropriate for the Victorian flavour of the enterprise. With it she wore a plain white blouse and my grey shawl. She covered her hair with a kerchief. When she was dressed she went to look at herself in the mirror in our room.

In a couple of minutes she returned to the living room. "Do you think I could borrow your earrings?" she asked.

"But your ears aren't pierced."

"I mean the ones from Egypt. You don't need to have pierced ears for them."

"Oh, the amber ones. It's true they have clips, but no one will see them. You'll be too far away."

"They go with my costume, though. Come and see."

I stood up and followed her to our room. The blue box containing the earrings lay on top of the chest of drawers. "Let me put them on for you. They're a bit awkward," I said. I lifted out the earrings one by one and gently clipped them onto her small lobes.

She stood in front of the mirror, studying her reflection. The effect of the earrings and the costume together was to make Jenny appear, even more than she usually did, to be a miniature grown-up. "They're brilliant," she exclaimed. "Can I borrow them, please, Celia?"

I did not have the strength to argue. I nodded a minimal assent and immediately Jenny headed towards the door, still wearing the earrings. "Leave them here for now," I said. "I'll give them to you on Friday morning."

"I have to take everything to school tomorrow. Miss Nisbet is going to check through the costumes to make sure they're okay."

"The earrings aren't really part of your costume."

"I promise I'll be careful of them. Please." She looked at me appealingly.

I shrugged. "All right," I said, "but don't lose them." Before I could change my mind, she ran from the room. Tobias padded in; he stared at me for an instant, then disappeared under the bed. I drew the curtains and left the door ajar so that he could leave when the spirit moved him.

After Jenny had gone to bed, I fetched myself a glass of wine and settled down beside the living-room fire. The events of the evening, harmless in themselves, hung over me like the sword of Damocles. I stared into the glowing coals and

320 · Margot Livesey

thought how deftly Jenny had organised me to do everything
for which she needed my help. Now that my usefulness was
over, there seemed no lengths to which she might not go.

I drank some wine and cast around for a means to extricate
myself from the web of fear which Jenny had spun around
me. I could not dwell upon the present nor contemplate the
future. Only the past seemed to offer refuge. I found myself
remembering the year when I too had been involved in a
Christmas play. Soon after Guy Fawkes, my teacher, Miss
Dobbey, had announced that we were going to write a nativ-
ity play; everyone must bring a Bible to school.

"A Bible?" my mother had said when I told her. "I don't
know if we have one, darling."

"But I have to have one," I said.

My mother looked up from her book. "Ask your father
when he comes home."

While I waited, I struggled with my homework. I had
twelve problems in division, and although I understood the
principle, I could not keep things straight in my head. The
number 14, for example, remained obstinately opaque, as
opposed to disclosing its separate parts of 2 and 7. I sat at the
kitchen table, chewing the end of my pencil, writing numbers
down and rubbing them out, until at last I heard my father. I
rushed to meet him. "Daddy, do you have a Bible?"

"What's this?" he demanded. "Are you turning into a
Christian?"

"It's for school. We're writing a play. Do you have one?"

"Of course I do. Let me get a drink first, Celia."

I was staring at the next problem, $360 \div 9$, when my
father came in, carrying a drink in one hand, a book in the
other. "Here you are," he said. "Be careful of it. It belonged
to my mother."

The Bible was the most beautiful book I had ever seen. It
was small and heavy and bound in soft black leather with the

words "Holy Bible" inscribed in gold letters. The pages were edged in reddish gold, and the paper was tissue fine. I opened the book and stared at the flyleaf in wonder. There, written in black ink, was my name: Celia Gilchrist.

"Look," I said to my father.

"Yes, it was my mother's," he repeated.

I had known before that I was named after my grandmother, but I had never understood what this meant. I could not help being troubled at the idea of sharing something that I had thought of as uniquely mine.

Every day we worked on our play. First we discussed an episode, and then we wrote a scene. We took turns reading our work aloud, and Miss Dobbey always seemed to single out my efforts for praise. "Well done, Celia," she would say. "That's very nice." As the weeks passed I grew increasingly certain that I was going to be Mary. I worked extra hard at her speeches, and at night I fell asleep imagining myself in a blue dress, hugging Baby Jesus and pretending to ride a donkey.

Finally the day came when Miss Dobbey announced the casting. I was not Mary; I was not even an angel; I was a shepherd. Instead of a blue dress I would wear a beard. A tediously pretty girl named Lucinda would be saying the eloquent speeches I had written. Once rehearsals were under way I minded less. I spent several happy afternoons making my flock by sticking cotton wool onto cardboard boxes. And my mother was going to play the piano for the performance; I basked in her reflected importance.

The play was on a Wednesday afternoon, and my father had promised to attend. As I left for school that morning I reminded him that I would be the shepherd in green. "That sounds very pastoral," he said. "Good luck."

When I was dressed in my robe and beard I joined the rest of the cast, peering round the curtains. My mother was playing "The Holly and the Ivy," and I found myself murmuring the familiar words as I searched the audience for my father. He was not there, but people were still arriving.

"Children," called Miss Dobbey, "we're beginning in three minutes. Go to your places."

A tall man wearing a raincoat came in. I felt a spurt of hope, until he turned to face the stage.

"Celia," came Miss Dobbey's voice, "go and join the other shepherds." I clung to the edge of the curtain. A couple of women in head scarves hurried in. I gave the audience one last despairing glance. With sudden conviction I knew that he was not coming. If I had been Mary, I thought, he would have come. I watched my flock, I talked to the angel, I knelt down in front of the Holy Family, all in a daze. I did not remember saying a single one of the speeches I had so painfully memorised.

That evening my mother and I were in the living room when my father came home. "So how did it go?" he asked.

"It was fun," said my mother. "Miss Dobbey had done a very nice job with the children. Celia made an excellent shepherd."

"It's too bad that I couldn't be there," said my father. "Lunch with the Petries seemed to go on and on. Did you have fun, Celia?"

I nodded.

"Don't forget to bring the Bible home," he said. "It's a family heirloom."

Next morning as soon as I arrived at school I sorted through my desk, arranging the papers in neat piles. There was no sign of the black leather binding. I looked wildly around the room, then ran to Miss Dobbey. "I lost my Bible," I burst out.

"It can't be lost," she said. "You never took it out of this room. Let me have a look."

Such was my confidence in Miss Dobbey that I fully

expected her to produce the Bible, but she too rummaged through the books and papers to no avail. "Someone must have taken it by mistake," she said. "Does it have your name on?"

I hesitated.

"Now, Celia, you know the rule. Everything you bring into the classroom has to have your name on, and it's precisely so that things won't get lost."

"It has 'Celia Gilchrist' written in it," I said.

"In that case it's sure to turn up."

Quite how it was that the inscription of my name would bring this about was unclear, but temporarily my anxiety was allayed. Towards the end of the afternoon Miss Dobbey came over to where I was tidying the class library. "Was the Bible important?" she asked.

"It belonged to my grandmother."

Miss Dobbey shook her head. "I don't suppose you took it home and forgot about it."

"No," I said. My eyes filled with tears.

When I arrived home I told my mother what had happened. "Oh, dear." She shrugged. "Never mind. I'm sure your father wouldn't have given you anything valuable to take to school."

"Will you tell him?"

"I think you ought to," she said.

By the time my father came home I thought that I would rather be hung, drawn, and quartered than wait another second. I told him as he was taking off his coat. "Damn," he said. "Can't you be trusted with anything?"

I rushed upstairs to my room and threw myself sobbing onto the bed. The awful anger in my father's voice made me feel as if I had been cast out into some desolate place, a great plain where I must wander in endless solitude. I would never again go downstairs, I thought.

Even now, when I could understand that my father had

been merely irritated, I felt the pain of that moment. I stood up to poke the fire and put on more coal. It was a quarter to ten. Stephen was going out for an end-of-term drink with Deirdre, and I did not know when he would be home. I turned on the television. There was a programme about whales. The narrator described how the huge mammals nursed their young for over a year. The screen showed a family of humpback whales, mother, father, and child swimming in unison through the blue-grey water. Safe between its enormous parents, the baby rolled from side to side.

A faint smell feathered my nostrils. I looked at the fire, wondering if there had been some rubbish among the coal, but there was no sign of foreign matter. I sat back, thinking that it must be coming from our neighbours. The narrator was discussing violations of the international laws protecting whales: charts appeared, detailing the decline in their population.

The smell was growing stronger, and I wondered if I could have left the oven on. I stood up, walked across the room, and opened the door. The hall was full of dark, churning smoke. Hastily I stepped forward, shutting the living room door behind me. There must be a fire, I thought. I was oddly unsurprised, as if this was what I had been expecting. The smoke seemed to be coming from beneath the closed door of Stephen's and my bedroom. I turned the door handle. There was something pressing against the door; perhaps a book or shoe lay on the floor. I pushed it open. Smoke poured out. Even before I stepped inside, I could feel the heat. The bed was ablaze from end to end, and as the draught came through the open door the flames surged.

For a moment I simply stood there, bathed in heat. There was a noise like a high wind in a forest, a large roaring full of smaller sounds: snappings and creakings. The fire emptied me of everything. I did not think that what I was witnessing was the destruction of my possessions.

Suddenly the paper lampshade on the light above the bed burst into flame. I came to my senses. I backed out of the room, shutting the door behind me to cut down on the draught.

For some reason the smoke was thicker in the hall than in the bedroom, and my eyes smarted so that I could scarcely see the phone. I dialled 999, and on the third ring a woman answered. In phlegmatic tones she asked for the necessary details. Never once did her voice break into urgency. She insisted on checking everything twice, and all the time she was talking I thought only that I must rescue Jenny.

As soon as I hung up, I opened the door of her room. I switched on the light, and rushed towards her bed. There was no one there. In fact it looked as if Jenny had never got into bed; the sheets were drawn tightly up to the top. Then I noticed a bare space on the wall. The poster of the boyish pop star that had been among Jenny's most treasured possessions was gone. I looked around the room, thinking stupidly that she could be there—at her desk, playing on the floor, curled up in a chair. But no, the room was empty, almost uninhabited. Was it possible she could somehow be in our room?

I ran back across the hall, pausing only to put on my winter coat, the thick material of which would offer some protection. I took a deep breath and flung open the bedroom door. Even in my brief absence the blaze had grown hugely. The heat was blinding, the fire a living, raging animal which could not be confined for long.

"Jenny, Jenny," I shouted.

In the midst of all the other sounds I thought I heard a tiny sound, a whimper.

"Jenny," I called again.

But nothing, only the ferocity of the flames, answered me. I began to edge along the wall. It was hot to the touch. I had to be quick. The open door increased the flames, but I was afraid to close it; I needed to know that I could escape. I held my breath as I groped my way around the room. The farther I got from the door, the hotter it was and the more afraid I became that I would be trapped, or overcome by smoke. My hair crinkled. I kept my eyes on the floor but saw nothing. When I reached the far corner without finding her, I turned. The journey back around the room seemed infinitely long. My lungs felt as if a steel band were being slowly tightened around them.

Back in the hall I drew breath. I looked into the bathroom, then ran to the dining room, the kitchen. Nothing, no one. In the kitchen I wondered briefly about Tobias and then dismissed the thought. He could take care of himself.

As I ran back through the house I heard the noise of sirens. I burst out of the front door just as the fire engine drove up. A fireman climbed down from the back. I ran towards him. "There's a little girl. I can't find her," I cried.

"Don't worry, miss. We'll have this out in no time."

I turned back towards the house, and a figure stepped out from beside the front door. "Celia," she said, "here I am."

I enfolded her in my arms as if she were the only living being for miles around. She reached up and kissed my cheek.

"Stand back," said one of the firemen, as he took a hose into the house. Jenny and I separated. The team of firemen ran in and out of the house, manhandling the hoses and other equipment, then they all disappeared inside. I turned to Jenny and was about to ask if she was all right, when her appearance stopped me. She was neatly dressed, with coat, gloves, and outdoor shoes. On the ground beside her were two large carrier bags. From one of them a white tube protruded.

I was staring at the poster when a voice behind me said, "Celia, you're safe?"

It was Irene. "Yes," I said. "We both got out in time."

"Thank goodness. What's on fire? From out here you couldn't tell that there was anything the matter." Beneath her coat Irene was wearing pyjamas and slippers. At the sight of her, I almost burst into tears. I explained that the fire had started in the bedroom and as far as I knew was confined to there.

"That's an odd place for a fire to start—usually it's the kitchen. Of course you'll come and stay the night with us."

I thanked her, and she offered to take Jenny back to her house. Jenny, however, refused to leave. "I want to see what happens," she said. "I want to be here when Daddy gets home."

In a few minutes, the firemen had the blaze under control, and within a quarter of an hour it was totally extinguished. I stepped forward and, climbing over the hoses, made my way inside. The hall was severely blackened, but when I opened the living room door it was like another world. Save for the smell, there was no sign of the conflagration. The television was still on; in the grate the fire still glowed. Jenny's room too was unmarked. I was approaching the bedroom, when the fireman whom I had first accosted came out.

"Excuse me, miss," he said. "Did you have a pet?"

"A cat, and a rabbit."

"I'm afraid the cat was trapped in the bedroom."

I pushed my way past him. There lying on a piece of canvas was the body of Tobias. I remembered the resistance when I had first opened the door. He must have been pressing himself against the door even then, in the hope of escape. And the second time, that pitiful cry, but I had been thinking only of Jenny. Twice it must have seemed that I was on the point of rescuing him, and then I shut the door in his face.

On one side his body was deeply scorched, the hair turned from ginger and gold into a blackened stubble, but the other, presumably that which he had pressed to the door, was unscathed. From the right angle he looked as if merely sleeping. I began to cry, and Jenny, who had followed me, burst into loud tears.

We were standing thus when Stephen appeared. He flung

his arms around us. He squeezed me to him so hard that I thought my ribs might crack, and with his other arm he held his daughter.

"Thank God," he said.

The firemen were rolling up the hoses. Stephen disengaged himself and went over to one of the men, who was directing events in the hall. "Is it safe to leave the house overnight?" he asked.

"Safe as houses," the man said, grinning. "We've covered everything with foam. It would take a miracle to get a fire going now."

"Well, that's a relief," said Stephen. "Have you any idea how it started?"

The man stepped back. "Steady with that," he called. "You'd better ask the chief." He pointed through the open front door.

I followed Stephen outside. The chief was standing beside the garden gate, writing something in a notebook. We went over to him. Stephen introduced himself as the owner of the house and repeated his question. While he spoke I noticed that Jenny had retreated out into the street and was lurking in the shadow of the hedge, inconspicuously in earshot.

The man looked down at his notebook. In a business-like voice he said, "According to my men, there were distinct traces of paraffin in the bed."

It was as if he had held a match to my emotions; with his words, all my rage and grief exploded. A few strides carried me to Jenny's hiding place. I seized her by the shoulders. "You killed Tobias!" I screamed. "You bastard, you little devil!"

Words I had never uttered before poured from my mouth. Dimly I heard Stephen telling me to stop. I felt his hand on my shoulder. I shook him off.

"You set the fire, you killed Tobias. If you'd been lucky,

you might have killed me too. That's what you want, to have me dead. Then I won't be in your way anymore."

Something hit me on the cheek, so hard that I let go of Jenny and reeled back. I leaned against the gate post, cradling my head in my hands. Stephen had slapped me. He turned his back to me and bent over his daughter. "Are you all right?" I heard him ask. "You mustn't mind Celia; she's very upset. She doesn't mean what she says."

While I stood watching, with my hand to my cheek, he took Jenny over to Irene. He said something to the two of them and Irene nodded. Only then did he turn back to me. As I saw his expression, my vision narrowed. All I could see was the gate post. And then nothing.

When I came round, I was lying on the ground in the arms of Irene. She held me close and warm. "You fainted," she said quietly. "Keep your head down."

When I felt well enough to walk, Irene and Stephen led me down the street. Irene put me to bed with a hot-water bottle and a cup of Ovaltine. I sank into sleep as swiftly as I had fallen to the ground.

CHAPTER 28

The sound of voices in the corridor outside my room woke me. It was still dark, but there was a crack of light beneath the door, and I puzzled out from the dial of the clock on the bedside table that it was eight o'clock. "Don't you think you should stay at home today?" the man's voice said. Then the girl's: "No, I have to go to school. We're rehearsing the concert." "Okay, but let me give you a note for Miss Nisbet."

The sounds receded as Stephen and Jenny moved away down the corridor. I rolled over and buried my face in the pillow. Immediately the smell of the fire filled my nostrils. It must have rubbed off my hair during the night. I felt again the heat of the flames scorching my skin and, much worse, the thick smoke which had poured into me, blanketing my lungs, so that I had seen death waiting, ready to seize me if I should for an instant stumble or falter. My palms grew slippery with sweat. The flames danced more brightly. I saw a small figure silhouetted against them, fanning them to greater heights. And then I saw her waiting in the garden, fully dressed, with her carrier bags; she had wanted me to know beyond a shadow of a doubt.

I reached for the bedside light. In the soft glow the walls and furnishings of the unfamiliar room took shape around me. My panic receded. There was a dressing gown on the end of my bed. I put it on and went to see what was happening in the rest of the house.

Everyone had left save Stephen, whom I found sitting at the

330

kitchen table, scribbling on a piece of paper. He stood up as I came in. "How are you feeling?" he asked. "Can I bring you breakfast in bed? Irene left a tray ready."

"I thought I might have a bath if there's enough hot water."

"There's plenty. Let me turn it on for you." He hurried eagerly from the room. There came the sound of the water gushing into the tub. So, I thought, even now all manner of things could be well if I would only agree to be an invalid; then my actions and accusations could be explained as symptoms. He returned carrying a large red bath towel, which he handed to me. "Would you like a boiled egg?" he asked.

"All right," I said, "but not in bed."

The bathroom was dense with steam, and there was a smell of perfume in the air. As I lowered myself into the water, I saw that it had a greenish tinge; Stephen must have added bath salts. On the rack was a loofah and soap; I began to use both vigorously. I was intent on cleanliness. I leaned forward, washing carefully between my toes. The nails were slightly long, and I wished that I had a pair of scissors. I worked steadily up my body. If I had had a razor I would have shaved my legs, perhaps even under my arms. I washed my face and the back of my neck. When I had scrubbed myself pink and tingling from top to toe, I relaxed. I lay back and let my head slip down. The water lapped my forehead and my cheeks. I gazed wide-eyed up into the steam, listening to the sounds of my body roaring in my ears.

At last the falling temperature drove me out. I wrapped the towel around me and stood at the basin to wash my hair. I shampooed it twice, then claimed another towel to use as a turban. Only when I was back in the bedroom did it dawn on me that I had no choice but to put on the clothes I had worn the night before, which reeked of smoke. In fact, I thought, as I buttoned my shirt, I now owned almost nothing besides the clothes I stood up in.

Stephen was bustling around the kitchen. "It'll be ready in a minute," he said.

He had laid a place for me. I sat down, and looked around, thinking how pleasant it was to have a kitchen large enough to eat in. Irene had a notice board next to the fridge, as I had had in my flat in London. Classical music was playing on the radio.

In rapid succession, Stephen brought an egg, toast, and coffee to the table. He sat down opposite me. "How are you?" he said again.

"Tired." I sliced the top off my egg and peered in. "I ache all over, even the backs of my knees. And my chest hurts. When I blow my nose, my handkerchief is black."

"Maybe you should see a doctor. You seem to be in much worse shape than Jenny. She insisted on going to school."

I could taste my anger, a queer, metallic taste flooding my mouth. I drank some coffee and swallowed hard. Then I said that I didn't think a doctor was necessary; after all Irene had taken care of me.

"Well, you must promise to say at once if you start to feel poorly. I rang your office to tell them that you probably wouldn't be in for the rest of the week."

It had not even crossed my mind that on a normal day I would by this time be at work. I could scarcely believe that only yesterday I had sat at my desk, poring over pages, and that presumably I would do so again in the near future. I bit down on a piece of toast and began to chew, counting the number of times, while I waited for Stephen to ask what had happened the night before.

He hitched his chair closer to the table and looked at me earnestly. "Celia, I'm so glad you're all right. Coming home last night and seeing the fire engine outside the house was the worst experience of my life. I thought that you and Jenny were dead, and I thought I would die. I really understood what it means to have your heart stop. And the fact that while all this was happening I was out at the pub made it even worse."

I clenched my jaw to keep from plunging into speech. Last night when I had turned on Jenny a barrier had fallen, and now there seemed nothing to keep me from saying whatever I chose. All the constraints—fear, diplomacy, politeness, self-control—had been burned out of me. Only the desire to see what Stephen would say next kept me silent.

"I wouldn't have cared if the house had been burned to the ground, as long as the two of you were safe," he said. He cleared his throat, and I observed that behind his spectacles his eyes were watery. Perhaps he expected a response, but after a moment he went on. "I feel really badly that you're the one who's bearing the brunt of this. I mean, of course I had a few things in the bedroom, but nothing compared to you. When I glanced into the hall cupboard last night everything looked fine."

With difficulty I ate a mouthful of egg; it seemed to have a smoky taste.

"Anyway," said Stephen, "not to worry. You'll be able to get most of it back on the insurance. While you were in the bath, I telephoned our agent. He suggested that we collect the claim form, to speed things up."

"That sounds like a good idea." Tension rose inside me, like the mercury of a thermometer dipped in boiling oil; I was rushing towards my fate. Such a form would necessarily require the answering of certain questions. In spite of Stephen's protests, I said that I would come too to the insurance company; I could not sit idle.

It was a perfect winter's day, bright and mild, and as we drove along the cobbled streets and through the Georgian squares, the city unrolled around us with particular splendour. The grey stone buildings stood firm against the blue sky. For some reason the words "Earth hath not anything to show more fair" came into my mind. I found myself repeating them silently over and over, like a talisman. They had been written of another city in another century, but they reminded me that there was a world untouched by fire and madness. Stephen prattled away about arrangements and cleaning up.

When we reached the insurance company's office, he double-parked and ran in. He emerged after a couple of minutes with a single sheet of paper, which he handed to me. I examined the form. It was printed in red. Both sides were filled with questions, for most of which a mere single line was allocated for the answer. Vagueness and long-windedness were discouraged. Only for number two was a sizeable amount of space provided: "Describe fully what happened, circumstances under which damage discovered and by whom." And then came question three: "Do you know or suspect who was responsible? E.g., Thief, Carrier, Workman, Motorist, etc. If so, give name and address."

We drew up outside the house. For a moment neither of us moved; we sat in silence, gazing at what had been our home. Except for the fact that the curtains in Jenny's room and the living room were still drawn in broad daylight, everything looked the same. There were even two pints of milk on the doorstep. No passer-by could have guessed what lay within those walls. The only signs of the previous night's events were the broken branches on a couple of the rose bushes.

As soon as we stepped inside, however, disaster was manifest. The smell of the fire was raw and sharp. We both began to cough. Stephen propped the front door open with a telephone directory.

"You know, it really isn't that bad," he said cheerfully, looking around the hall. "I mean apart from our bedroom. Perhaps I should start by getting everything out of there."

"No. We must fill out the form first." I did not know what I would do if Stephen refused.

He smiled affably and nodded. "You're right; that is a good idea. Then we'll know what to do about repairs and estimates."

I sat down at the dining room table. After a few minutes of fussing around getting papers, putting on the gas fire, opening the window, Stephen joined me.

"Maybe while I'm answering the general questions you could start to make a list of everything you've lost," he said. He handed me a pen and paper. "Don't forget to put down the full replacement value."

He began to write briskly, filling out the details of name, address, and policy number. I thought about the insuperable task he had set me. I bent over the blank page and wrote: "1 blue dress, 1 blue suit, 1 pair of black trousers."

At number two he paused briefly, then his pen moved across the page. I could not contain myself. "What are you saying?" I demanded.

" 'A fire broke out in the back bedroom,' " read Stephen. " 'It was discovered by Celia Gilchrist, who immediately called the fire department. The firemen promptly extinguished the blaze.' It sounds like one of Jenny's compositions."

"How will you answer number three: who was responsible?"

" 'Not applicable. Faulty wiring. Question mark.' " He stared intently at the form and continued to write.

"What about what the fireman said last night?"

He hesitated as if he were reviewing various possibilities, perhaps even wondering if he could get away with asking what I was referring to. "Oh, that," he said at last. "I don't see how they can tell anything after they've dumped on all that water and chemicals; besides, there's no point in confusing the insurance company." There was a belligerent edge to his voice. He was frowning as he resumed his task.

I stretched out my hand to cover the form. "Listen," I said.

"I'll tell you what happened. I was watching television. I smelled something odd and came out into the hall. Smoke was coming from under our bedroom door, and when I opened it, there were huge, bright flames. I retreated into the hall, and as soon as I had telephoned the fire brigade, I rushed into Jenny's room. Her bed had not been slept in. I ran all round the house, then I went back into our bedroom. I thought I was going to die, but I went back because I was afraid she was in there and had passed out from the smoke. I couldn't find her. I came out of the room just as the firemen arrived, and I ran to tell them that Jenny was missing.

"Then I turned round and she was standing fully dressed beside the front door, with two carrier bags of her most treasured possessions at her feet.

"I didn't see her pour the paraffin onto our bed, I didn't see her strike the match, but I know she did those things as surely as if I had stood in the room and watched her. She'd been planning the fire for days. It was a thoroughly premeditated act. She waited until she was certain the fire had caught, and then, while I was risking my life looking for her, she scarpered out into the garden with her precious poster."

Stephen's face was stretched and tightened into unfamiliar outlines. Near his mouth a nerve was twitching. His eyes darkened. "Celia, stop. You don't understand the seriousness of what you're saying. I appreciate that you had a terrifying experience. You did something heroic, and it must have been an anticlimax to discover that it wasn't necessary."

"I understand exactly how serious it is," I said. "If Jenny weren't a minor she'd be under arrest. I can even understand how hard it is for you to accept that your daughter is capable of committing arson, but what I don't understand is how else you can explain the evidence. You heard the fireman say that the fire had been started with paraffin. You saw with your own eyes that Jenny was fully dressed and that she had rescued all her favorite things. Earlier in the evening she had even insisted on hiding your Christmas present in the tool shed because she said it would be safer. Tell me how you explain all that."

"You're forgetting something crucial," said Stephen. "Neither of you had the slightest motivation to start the fire. Just because Jenny could have done it doesn't mean that she did. You could have done it, just as easily."

I stood up so quickly that I knocked over my chair. I grabbed Stephen's arm and led him from the room, across the hall, and opened the bedroom door. The blue walls were entirely blackened. Most of the wooden furniture was gone; a few rags hung from the curtain rail. Our bed was like a funeral pyre, little more than a crumbling heap of ashes. In the middle someone had spread a small tarpaulin on which lay Tobias.

I do not know what I had meant to say, but at the sight of his golden body, words fled. A gale of passion swept over me, and I could barely keep my feet. For months I had been travelling through a country increasingly barren and inhospitable, and now, at the end of my journey, I found myself standing at nightfall, alone on a narrow promontory overlooking the sea, and nowhere in the darkening landscape was there any sign of life or comfort. The sobs that shook me grew until the sounds that issued from my lips were more animal than human. I thought that grief would shatter me.

All that short afternoon, while the bright beauty of the day faded, I sat in Irene's kitchen, working on my list. I had decided to wash my clothes, and was wearing once more my borrowed nightdress and dressing gown. There was something reassuring about being dressed in nightclothes in the middle of the afternoon; if I was going to be treated like an invalid, I might as well behave like one. I was scribbling away with a vengeance. Except for a few jackets that I kept in the hall cupboard, I had lost all my clothes and jewellery and books and papers. I tried to visualise each drawer and check through it garment by garment. Tomorrow I would go to various shops to get the exact prices. I had no idea if the insurance company would honour such a claim, but I wanted the list to be as lengthy and accurate as possible; I wanted to bear witness to every iota of my loss.

The front door opened and closed. I drew my dressing gown tight around me and got ready to say something welcoming to Charlotte, who I knew arrived home before either of her parents. A small, dark head peered cautiously round the kitchen door. Jenny scanned the room and, when she had ascertained that I was alone, came in, closing the door behind her.

"Where's Stephen?" I asked.

"He's at the house."

I returned to my list. "Blue pullover," I wrote. "Yellow pullover."

Jenny edged closer until she was standing beside me. "Celia," she said. "I've got something for you."

At last I raised my eyes from the page. She reached into her pocket and held out her hand. Cradled in her small pink palm lay my amber earrings.

I picked them up, one in each hand, and held them to the light. The amber trembled and grew translucent. Within the two tiny microcosms I could see a corner of the table, a chair, the clock on the wall.

If I had been asked to name my most treasured possessions, what I would save in case of fire or flood, I do not know if the earrings would have come to mind; Aunt Marigold had died when I was sixteen, and I did not often think of her. But now, as I stared into the golden drops, they seemed precious beyond price. Some small part of all that I had taken for lost had been recovered. I felt Jenny watching me, and I turned from the earrings to meet her gaze. Steadily we looked into each others' eyes. I saw the flickering darkness of the iris, the black of the pupil, almost indistinguishable. We looked at each other not with anger nor hatred but with the weary intimacy of old enemies. It was as if Jenny knew me better than I knew myself.